Magic of WYLDEFEN

CONSTANCY

TILLY WALLACE

ISBN: 978-1-7385845-9-8

Cover design by Karen Dimmick / ArcaneCovers.com

Editing and proofreading by the team at Kat's Literary Services

To be the first to hear about Tilly's new releases and exclusive offers, sign up at:

https://www.tillywallace.com/newsletter

PART I

1807

1

Eadred Manor, Wyldefen, rural England

Moire Tobin might only have walked this earth for eighteen years, but she knew two things with a certainty that resided deep in her bones. One was that she would only ever love Oliver Hartford, the man who had captured her heart two years previously when they both reached for the same book in a market. Moire had been shyly delighted to find that the handsome, young naval officer shared her fascination with the subject of the book—dragons.

The other truth was that no matter how long she lived, she would never overcome her fear of heights.

Standing in the moonlight that spilt over the floor of her room, Moire leaned out her window and glanced down. Night lengthened the distance. The ground seemed as far away as if she peered over the side of a vessel in the middle of the ocean and tried to find the bottom of the sea. Ivy tendrils clung to the outer stone and beckoned, promising freedom and the sweet embrace of her love.

If she dared.

Moire drew a breath. When she thought about it rationally, it wasn't so much heights that bothered her, but rather the sudden stop at the end. Although it seemed odd to fear the ground. Then she remembered who was waiting for her...Oliver. A brave and caring soul. He had joined the Navy as a young lad of twelve in order to seek a better life and had worked his way through the ranks.

Borrowing strength from the thought of seeing him, Moire hitched up the edge of her dark-blue woollen gown to make it easier to climb. Then she clambered out to sit on the ledge.

"It is no different from climbing a tree." A tree that seemed impossibly tall in the dark, and there might be sharp teeth waiting to tear her apart at its base.

Grabbing a thick branch of the ancient ivy, she began her descent. Her heart pounded with fear of either falling or being discovered by her family. Her father would be furious if her actions reflected badly on him. One careful foot at a time and keeping her gaze on the rough stone wall, she descended the old scrambling plant. When her boots sank into the lush grass, relief flowed up her wobbly legs.

From nearby came a low warble, and the noise reassured her.

"It's all right, Faustus, it's only me," she crooned back.

A shape detached from the shadows and approached. Larger than a horse, it walked with an odd side-to-side gait. Moire's escape had roused the old wyvern. Virtually blind in daylight hours, the nocturnal creature guarded their slumber and the estate. He must have scented her on the night air and come to investigate.

When Moire stretched out her hand, the beast rubbed against her palm in greeting. Wyverns were the ugly and misshapen cousins of majestic dragons. Tied to a five-mile radius from the point of their hatching, they were used as watchdogs by those who could afford the price of an egg.

Eight years ago, loneliness and loss had drawn Moire and Faustus close together. Since that day, they had found companionship in each other. Her family declared the wyvern hideous and treated the lonely creature abominably. Moire knew the ugliest exterior could hide the gentlest of hearts. And the opposite could also be true—beauty could hide a rotten core.

"I am going to Caliban's barrow. Oliver is waiting," she whispered to her guardian.

While he could speak in monosyllabic snatches, wyverns were more adept at communicating through pictures and emotions. That was, if a person was open to receiving such messages. Faustus crooned his understanding and fell into step beside her. Possessing only two hind legs, he used the claws at the juncture of his bent wings like front paws. His scales absorbed the moonlight, and he moved like a shadow. Only his eyes glowed an eerie silver, seeing everything as clear as day.

Together, they walked in silence through the overgrown gardens. Their once pristine beauty now a wild, untamed chaos. At the edge of the forest, Faustus nudged her hand and dropped to his belly. He would wait for her to return and escort her safely home through the dark. Moire scratched his head, using her nails to reach the spots between the hard ridges above his eyes.

Slipping between two oaks, she followed a path etched into the earth by numerous types of feet over the decades. Dappled moonlight illuminated her way. The soft burble of the river that ran through the forest called to her. At last, the path opened into a clearing dominated by a large mound. The barrow, with its surface covered in moss and wildflowers, was a solemn reminder of the magical world she lived in. Caliban, the noble dragon who had raised her family to the highest level of peerage in the land, had lain down and died on the spot. The earth had reclaimed his form, just as the lower ranks of nobility had reclaimed her family.

"Oliver?" Moire called.

"Here," his voice came from beside the barrow.

His tall and lean form emerged from the dark as though a tree had come to life. The sight of him wrapped in moonlight and shadows made her heart swell with love.

"You came," he whispered, his tone a soothing lullaby to her racing heart.

Moire ran to him, wrapping her arms around his waist and resting her cheek against the rough wool of his jacket. Inhaling, she caught the scent of horses and fresh hay. When on shore leave, Oliver stayed with his cousin and helped with the never-ending chores of tending animals and crops.

She drank in the comfort of his presence. "If anyone knew I was here with you, I would be completely ruined."

"You could never be ruined in my eyes." He placed one finger under her chin and tilted her face to claim a kiss.

"I cannot stay long. Father kept me up past midnight, insisting I write to London for wallpaper samples as though their urgent acquisition was of the greatest importance." She had protested, saying she would do it in the morning, but Sir George had grown angry at the idea of waiting a few hours longer.

"I cherish whatever time we have." Fingers entwined, he drew her down to where he had spread a blanket. They sat with their backs against the barrow, the water at their feet, and a canvas of stars above them.

"Sometimes, I dream of having a little farm somewhere. Not too far away, though, so that Faustus can be with me." Moire traced patterns on his palm.

Oliver squeezed her hand. "I imagine a day when laughter washes over Caliban's barrow, and you are free of your family's demands."

An ache shot through her. "They mean well. But since Mother died..." Her words trailed away, remembering that dreadful time eight years ago. "Father relies on me, since I am the practical one. Augusta and Katherine are both destined for grand matches to bring honour to our family."

"You are too charitable, Moire. They treat you as horribly as they do poor Faustus, and you know it." A stern tone entered Oliver's voice. His anger was on her behalf and that of the neglected wyvern.

"They are my family." Her voice broke on the word. *Family.* Each letter heavy with expectation.

"One day, *I* shall be your family." He raised her hand and brushed a kiss across her knuckles.

"It's foolish to dream of being free, to live as I want."

The dictates of society and her family were large stones in a basket she was forced to carry and could never set down.

"Don't say that. Dreams give us hope. Without hope to light our way, what do we have?" Oliver pulled her closer into his embrace.

They sat for hours, sharing their dreams, when a brilliant flash darted across the sky. At first, Moire thought it was a shooting star. Then she gasped as it drew near.

"Look!"

Dancing high above them was a rare sight...a lunar dragon. With wings outstretched, it ducked and dived as it chased retreating moonbeams. Silver scales glimmered like liquid mercury. The majestic creature was said to be a symbol of hope and change.

"It's an omen that our dreams will come true," she whispered.

"A sign that our love is written in the stars." Oliver's voice was full of wonder at the sight.

The silver glow of the lunar dragon cast a spell upon them, filling Moire's soul with a sense of warmth and certainty. She leaned into Oliver's side. Snatches of a dream flitted through her mind, of a future lit by love and blessed by the lunar dragon.

As the winged creature disappeared behind a cloud, Moire rose to her feet. The sky would soon lighten with dawn, and she had to return to her bed.

"Wait, Moire." Oliver stood and took her hands in his. "You are my guiding star. My beacon in the stormiest sea."

The sincerity in his voice made her breath catch. Her cheeks flushed with colour as his words washed over her like a gentle tide.

"Before you go, I would ask one question of you," Oliver said in a serious tone.

"Anything." She couldn't imagine what he wanted to ask.

He reached into his pocket and retrieved something small. Then Oliver got down on one knee, holding up a simple yet elegant ring—an oval moonstone set in a filigree swirl of silver, mimicking the iridescence of the lunar dragon.

"Moire Tobin, would you do me the extraordinary honour of becoming my wife? If you could bear marriage to a humble lieutenant in the Navy." He made light of his position, but determination glinted in his sea-grey eyes. Being only landed gentry, he rallied against a world that would keep him down. The Navy offered him the chance to alter the circumstances of his birth.

Tears gathered at the corners of Moire's eyes. Her heart so full, she feared it might burst. The moonstone glowed with a soft, ethereal light as though it absorbed the magic of the moment. Love flowed through her limbs. They both fought against the place assigned to them. Her father only ever looked upwards and didn't notice who he trod on beneath his raised nose. "Yes. A thousand times, yes. If you could tolerate marriage to a woman who would rather curl up in a library with a book than glide across a ballroom."

"An easy bargain to make." His lips quirked in humour as he slid the ring onto her left hand. Standing, he claimed her lips to seal their promise.

"Forever, my star of the sea," Oliver murmured into her hair, his voice filled with a fierce love that shivered down Moire's spine.

"Forever," Moire echoed, her heart brimming with hope. Whatever challenges lay ahead, their love would remain steadfast.

"Tomorrow...or today, I should say, I will call upon your father and officially request your hand in marriage." Oliver walked her back through the forest to where Faustus waited.

The wyvern emitted a low whine at the approaching dawn. The streaks in the sky already intolerable to his sensitive eyes.

"Until then." Moire let go of Oliver's hand and ran back to the house so that the wyvern could retreat to his burrow and shield himself from the rising sunlight.

At the house, she took his face in her hands and rubbed his scales with her thumbs. "Sleep well, dear Faustus."

Inside, the staff were already up, setting fires and going about their morning tasks. Removing her boots, Moire crept through the house in her stockings and slipped back into her room. The dim light from the guttering candle cast an eerie shadow upon the walls. As though the dark hand of fate reached for her in warning, but she paid it no heed.

She undressed hurriedly, throwing her clothes over a chair and donning a nightgown. Climbing into bed, she snuggled under the chilled blankets and rubbed the glowing moonstone on her finger.

As sleep gathered her close, Moire's thoughts drifted towards the life she yearned for—a life free from the suffocating control of her father. She imagined a cottage by the river. Ivy-covered walls basking in the golden glow of the setting sun. A garden overflowing with fragrant blooms, where bees hummed their gentle songs as they flitted from petal to petal. At night, Faustus would keep a wary eye on sleeping children.

In her dream world, her days were spent exploring the forests with Oliver, stealing kisses beneath the dappled shade of ancient oaks. Their laughter as unrestrained and joyful as the lark's song. In the evenings, they would retire to their cosy home, the fire crackling merrily as they read and shared what they had learned.

"It's foolish to dream," she had said earlier that night.

"Dreams give us hope," Oliver had replied.

Moire submerged herself in the fantasy. Her heart clung to the hope that one day, perhaps, it could become true. She rubbed the moonstone. They were engaged, and there was little, surely, that her family could do about it.

LATER THAT MORNING, the sun streamed through the gauzy curtains and cast a warm glow over Moire's bedroom. The scent of freshly cut flowers wafted from the vase on her dresser, their delicate petals glistening with early morning dew. As she lay in bed, her thoughts were consumed by the events of the previous night. She could still feel the weight of Oliver's arms around her and the heat of his breath against her ear as he whispered vows of eternal love.

A soft knock on the door was accompanied by the low voice of Lucy, the maid. "Tea, Miss Moire."

Moire sighed. Pulling herself from her reverie, she slid out of bed, her bare feet dropping to the cool wooden floor. Today would bring challenges, questions to be answered, and judgements to be faced. But she held tight to her love for Oliver and the memory of the lunar dragon dancing among the stars.

"Thank you, Lucy." Moire opened the door just wide enough to accept the tray laden with steaming tea and buttered toast.

"Did you sleep well, Miss?" Lucy's eyes held a curious glint. Had she placed the flowers on the dresser in the early hours and noticed Moire was missing from her bed?

"Quite all right, thank you," Moire assured her as she closed the door.

She carried the tray to the window seat, where she could watch the neglected gardens come to life with the caress of the morning sun. She ate her toast and sipped tea in the blissful silence. Her father and sisters wouldn't rise until mid-morning, and Moire cherished the unspoiled, quiet hours. Finishing her tea, she dressed in a sage-green, striped gown. Then she swept her long, dark hair into a simple twist and pinned it off her neck.

The moonstone flashed a brilliant purple as a shaft of light caught it. A knot of anxiety twisted in her stomach. She needed her father's approval to marry. Moire slipped the ring from her left hand and slid it onto her right, promising that by day's end, the ring would be back on the correct finger.

Leaving her bedroom, Moire's hours were filled with running the household. The clock on the mantel gently chimed eleven as the other members of the household roused, and their late mother's friend, Lady Beaumont, arrived for tea with Sir George.

As Moire ensured the instructions for refreshments

were relayed to the kitchen, she noticed an advancing figure on horseback out the window. Oliver. Rubbing damp palms against her gown, she hurried to greet him in the entranceway.

"Lieutenant Hartford," her voice trembled. With the servants watching, there could be no embrace or fierce kiss. Instead, she extended her hands, and Oliver clasped them in his.

"Courage," he murmured. His stormy gaze searched her face.

"My father is taking tea in the drawing room." Moire gestured for him to follow her to the partially open door, where they would face the amassed troops in the battle for their love.

Within the elegant parlour, her father sat in the wing-back chair before the window. The seat was angled so the soft light fell on his ageing features in a most flattering manner. Her older sister, Augusta, sat beside Lady Beaumont on the settee. Katherine, the youngest of the family, reclined on a chaise with one hand held to her forehead while Lucy fussed over her. It appeared Katherine had awoken with one of her migraines.

"Father, Lieutenant Hartford seeks a moment of your time," Moire said, clasping her hands before her to stop the tremble in her fingers.

Oliver strode forwards and removed his hat, tucking it under his arm. The light glinted on his brown hair and turned the tips a burnished gold. "Sir George, I have come to ask for your permission to wed Moire."

Sir George narrowed his gaze, and then he chuckled. "Surely you jest?"

Moire's heart surged up her throat.

"I could not be more serious, Sir, if a French frigate were bearing down upon me." Oliver stood proudly before Sir George.

Lady Beaumont rose from her seat and approached Moire. "Why, this is a charming and romantic notion. But you must know, dearest, that it simply isn't possible. Everyone knows of the financial *difficulties* of the Hartfords, which severely limits the lieutenant's ability to provide for you. Apart from the fact that Augusta must wed first, there is the matter of your youth, Moire. Sir George will expect you to wait a few more years before making such a momentous decision."

Moire swallowed to moisten her mouth. "I am a woman of simple needs and do not require a fortune to live. Oliver is a good man, and our love is strong enough to weather any challenges that we will face."

"Of course, dear," Lady Beaumont demurred, and she patted Moire's arm. "But a young woman must acquiesce to the opinions of her family. They only want what is best for you."

Moire's heart stuttered as she faced her father, who crooked one finger under his chin and surveyed them with a stern expression. Oliver tensed his jaw, his shoulders squared. The sun filtering through the drawing-room windows cast a warm glow that belied the cool tension within.

"Father." Moire seized a moment of bravery, and her voice was surprisingly steady despite her inner turmoil. "I understand your concerns, but I assure you that Oliver is truly worthy of our family. He is brave and honourable."

"Moire, our little mouse," Sir George said, his voice tinged with impatience. "It is not solely a matter of character. Lieutenant Hartford is of no breeding, no fortune, and no consequence. I cannot seriously consider this offer when it is so far beneath me."

"Sir George," Oliver interjected, his voice firm. "I may not have been born into privilege, but I am determined to prove myself and elevate my status. I will do whatever it takes to be worthy of your daughter's hand."

"Can you acquire a title?" Sir George's top lip curled in a sneer.

Moire's eyes burned, and she cast her gaze downwards to blink away tears. Beside her, Oliver's hands tightened into fists.

"Father, please," Moire pleaded, her voice wavering. "Do not allow rank and wealth to stand in the way of our love. I believe in Oliver, and I know he is capable of great things."

"Love is a silly, worthless sentiment. My answer is no." Sir George picked up the newspaper and angled it towards the light.

Turmoil erupted inside Moire as she was trapped between her love for Oliver and her duty to her family. "Father..."

"No!" Sir George snapped, and red flushed over his face. "I will not entertain this ridiculous idea. You have quite given me an upset stomach."

"Sir George, I vow to make a name for myself and earn your approval. I will not rest until I have done so." Oliver's voice was laced with hurt.

Sir George snorted like a disgruntled horse and refused

to respond. He feigned great interest in an article, even though Moire knew he could not read the words without his spectacles.

With a curt nod to her family, Oliver turned on his heel and strode from the room.

Moire's world crumbled, but she found a thread of resolve. They would fight to be together. Sir George won this sortie but not the battle. She rushed after Oliver, her skirts swishing around her ankles. "Oliver, wait!"

He was already out of the house and in the driveway when she reached him. His body was tight as he put his foot in the stirrup. The horse snorted in agitation at its rider's turmoil.

"I swear to you, Moire, I will find a way to elevate my status and be worthy of you." Oliver ground his jaw.

"Please don't confuse my father's words with my feelings. It is I who strives to be worthy of you," she whispered.

Their eyes locked. The air was charged between them and carried unspoken words of devotion. Then, with a swift kick, Oliver spurred his horse onwards.

Moire was left standing on the gravel path, her hand raised in a futile attempt to reach out to him as he cantered away. Unable to face her family, Moire hid in the one place they never ventured—Faustus's burrow. Nestled in the cool and damp earth, she curled up next to the wyvern's leathery hide and cried out her heartbreak. Only as twilight dropped over the countryside did she emerge to change for dinner and wash dried tears from her face.

As she took her seat at the table, the tension in the air was thick enough to cut with a knife. Only the clink of silverware on porcelain filled the silence. Sir George, his face a study in disdain, turned to his middle daughter. The cat had not yet tired of toying with the mouse.

"Lieutenant Hartford is an ambitious man, and one must admire his determination to rise above his station." Sir George's voice dripped with sarcasm that fell like droplets of pea consume from his spoon. "I know sailors are not very bright. Does he perhaps think you come with a title and a dowry?"

"Father, please," Moire pleaded, her appetite gone.

"To think of a nobody sailor, hoping to marry into a family such as ours?" Sir George continued, ignoring her plea. "It's almost laughable."

"And who are we anymore? You might pretend, Father, but when Caliban died, so did our status among the Draco Legion. With no dragon bonded to our bloodline, we are not as noble as you claim. You are a mere baronet and no peer." Moire's hands tightened on her cutlery.

Augusta gasped. Never had Moire hurled such an insult across the table. Katherine seemed indifferent, focused on the soup that dribbled back into her bowl.

Sir George turned a thunderous gaze on Moire. "We are an old and noble family, and you will not mention that treacherous...*wyrm,* again. Do you understand?" His tone was clipped with rage. "When you are older, you will understand the importance of making sensible matches for the sake of your family's future. Augusta, with all her beauty, is bound to catch the eye of a duke. Imagine the scandal if you married so far beneath us."

Anger simmered beneath Moire's skin. Her father would never accept Oliver unless he achieved something truly extraordinary. Torn between her love for him and her loyalty to her family, she retreated into silence.

"Very well," she whispered at last, her voice barely audible as she stared at her bowl. "I will try to understand and exercise patience."

"Good girl," Sir George replied in a patronising manner before turning his attention back to his meal.

In her heart, Moire carved the lines of Oliver's face as his vows of love echoed in her ears and let it fuel her resistance.

2

———————

FOUR DAYS LATER, Moire still hid from the barbs of her family. Curled up in her bedroom window seat with an open book in her lap, she watched twilight paint the sky in a delicate medley of pinks and purples. A rustle of the ivy tugged at her troubled thoughts. Peering over the window ledge (but keeping her hands firmly wrapped around the stone for balance), Faustus sat below. The wyvern had one wing up like an umbrella to shield his sensitive eyes from the last rays of light. He flicked his tail back and forth.

"I'll be right down, Faustus," she called. Grabbing her shawl, she hurried through the house and outside. She cast a quick eye over the wyvern, concerned he might be unwell that he ventured out before full dark. "What is it, my friend?"

The wyvern huddled in the house's shadow. "Follow," the creature rasped in a low tone.

He led her through the rose garden, where leggy perennials sagged over the top of hedges long overdue a clip. Through a hole in a yew hedge, they approached a

19

tunnelled walkway made from pleached fruit trees on the sides, while a wisteria rambled over the top.

Faustus stopped at the entrance and gestured with his head. Stepping into the dim tunnel, Moire found a familiar figure with a lantern at his feet.

"Oliver!" Moire rushed forwards. "It is just as well that you sent Faustus. Father would not receive you at the house."

"He cannot keep me away." He drew her into his embrace.

Taking slow breaths, Moire let the thrum of his heart wash away some of her pain at her family's harsh words. "You were so angry when you rode off, I worried you wouldn't return."

"I needed time to think. I'll not allow your father to dictate our happiness." He stroked her hair and soothed the turmoil raging inside her.

"But how can we convince them? Father will not be swayed by mere words." Moire had spent days trying to think of an argument that would convince her father to give his blessing. A hard task when Sir George only respected two things—position and wealth. A third could be added to that list, although not relevant to their plight— beauty.

"We show him. I admit I spent two evenings drowning my sorrows in the pub. But while there, I heard whispers of something that would provide the opportunity to elevate my bloodline and earn us Sir George's respect," Oliver spoke in a resolute tone.

"What is this plan?" Curiosity and hope sprang up inside her.

"There are rumours of a boxing match with a rare prize...a dragon egg." He cupped her face, his gaze intent.

Her breath left her body with a soft whoosh. "A dragon egg? But that is impossible. They are so rare and valuable. People would pay a fortune for one so they could join the Draco Legion." Her mind whirled at the implications. When Caliban died and returned to the earth, her father was stripped of his Drac prefix and reverted to his ancestral title of baronet attached to their estate. Although ten years later, Sir George still lived in denial about the plummet of their status.

"Apparently, this egg was salvaged from a shipwreck. It had been bound for Scotland when the vessel was dashed upon the rocks crossing the Irish Sea." He caressed his knuckles down her cheek.

"The Irish Sea? Then what is it doing here, in Wylde-fen?" The egg had headed south instead of north.

His hands settled on her waist. "Those who retrieved it realised its value and spirited it away before the owner came searching for it. However, there is doubt over whether it is still alive after being immersed in the cold water. Some say it is dead, and its only value is as a curiosity. Others doubt its authenticity."

"What does that mean?" Doubts crept into her mind at hearing the tale.

"They say the egg does not look like any dragon egg and that a wyvern laid it. But I am certain it is from a dragon. This is a sign, Moire. It must be." He searched her gaze, seeking reassurance that she agreed with him.

Moire tried to recollect what she had read of dragon eggs. So few were ever found, and those that were discovered were jealously guarded until they hatched—so others did not steal them. A bright shaft of hope lit her soul. "If others doubt what it is, that means fewer men will fight to win it." The enormity of what he intended to do sank into her. The prospect equally thrilled and terrified her. But Oliver possessed the courage and tenacity to succeed. "If anyone can do this, it is you. And I will stand by you every step of the way."

"You cannot go, Moire. It is an illegal match. Apart from the risk of arrest if we are caught, it will be a bloody scene and no place for a gently bred woman." He took her by the shoulders.

Moire huffed. "You cannot expect me to sit and do needlework while you fight for our future. I will be there to support you and cheer every blow you rain upon your opponents."

"Does your family have any idea that your serene exterior hides a dragon's heart?" He lowered his head to kiss her.

Moire surrendered herself to the pleasure that coursed through her limbs, his kiss more heated than a summer sun. All too soon, he pulled back and showered smaller kisses on her neck.

"Winning the match is merely an obstacle we must overcome," she sighed.

Oliver chuckled. "Perhaps one day, you can write our tale about what true love can achieve."

"And how a lunar dragon blessed us with a stolen egg." She recalled the incredible sight of the luminous dragon dancing among the stars.

Moire stood on her toes to kiss Oliver again while her heart soared as high as a dragon playing among the stars.

———

THREE NIGHTS later the moon cast a soft glow as Moire, draped in a dark-grey woollen cloak, tiptoed down the creaking staircase. She paused for a moment, listening to the soft exhales of the slumbering house. Her family were blissfully unaware of her daring escape. Outside, she crept across the grass until a familiar figure detached from the shadows.

"Faustus," she whispered.

The wyvern approached, his leathery wings rustling like the pages of an old book. The creature's silver eyes whirled as he sat before her.

"Can you take me to the fight, please?" Oliver had instructed her where to find the barn. The wyvern was the quickest way to reach the location, if she could stomach the trip.

"Yes." He dipped his body, an invitation for her to climb on board.

As she placed a hand on his shoulder, fear turned her body to stone. She couldn't. The wyvern would fly far higher than her bedroom window. Her breath came in gasps, and her muscles trembled at the thought of leaving the ground far behind. Or more accurately, of returning to it with a *thump.*

"Safe," Faustus whispered. Turning, he nuzzled her and imagined them flying over the midnight landscape.

The picture projected into her mind was wrapped in a solemn promise that he would never let her fall.

Moire laid both hands on the wyvern's warm side and steadied her breathing. If she didn't brave the short flight, she wouldn't be able to stand by Oliver as he fought for the egg. If he could face physical opponents, she could face her mental one—heights.

Before the tenuous strand of bravery snapped, Moire climbed onto the wyvern's back. Given his size, it was not unlike riding a winged horse bareback. She sat in front of his wings and when he raised them, they secured her position.

"Take me to him," she squeaked as fear stole her voice.

Faustus leapt, and Moire bit her tongue to stop the scream that surged up her throat. She refused to look and buried her face in his warm scales, her fingers locked around his neck. After what seemed like only a few minutes, Faustus landed in a field of wheat.

Moire slid from his back, her knees buckling as though made of jelly, and she leaned against Faustus to let her muscles solidify once more. At the edge of the field stood a barn, light escaping from chinks between the boards. "Thank you, Faustus, for taking good care of me."

"Wait," he rasped and leaned into her touch. The loyal creature would hide in the wheat until the fight was done.

Moire set off, tremors of excitement now replacing fear. By the end of the night, Oliver might be in possession of a dragon egg. At the barn doors, others made their way into the illicit event.

"Out of the way," came a gruff voice accompanied by the scent of stale ale.

Moire froze as a group of drunken men passed her. She clutched her cloak tightly, praying that she wouldn't be the only woman in attendance. It wasn't as if she could have asked one of her sisters to accompany her. Then high-pitched laughter came from inside, and she let out an exhale. There were other women present.

A burly man leaned against the door. "Ticket," he said in a gruff voice.

Moire extracted the crumpled piece of paper from her pocket. Oliver had given it to Faustus. As a competitor, he could give her a free pass to the evening.

The doorman stared at it and then waved her through. Inside, they had made a ring in the middle of the large barn. Men crammed around the edge of the roped-off area. Women were dotted among the crowd like splashes of colour on a drab canvas. Younger lads sat up in the cross-beams and supports, where they peered down like bats. The organisers had stacked crates to create raised seating for those in the back.

Moire didn't want to be squeezed in between the unwashed bodies in the front rows. Nor would she be able to see from further back. Instead, she climbed onto an upended keg that was slightly higher than a chair, but not so high as to trigger her anxiety. The spot provided an excellent view of the ring across heads, and since it stood next to a solid post, she could lean on it for balance.

The air was thick with the stench of sweat and ale. Lively chatter swelled as a short and squat man walked into the middle of the ring and held up his hands. The chatter settled to a murmur. "We all know what we're here for, you lot! Last man standing gets his hands on a dragon egg and his chance to be a toff!"

The crowd roared and stomped their feet. The noise was a visceral thing that tumbled through Moire's body and made her clutch the beam.

"Introducing our first fighter," shouted the announcer, his voice booming across the crowd. "The Beast from the East, feared by all who face him in the ring!"

A deep rumble of excitement rippled through the throng as a mountain of a man lumbered into the makeshift arena. His broad shoulders and barrel chest were covered in a tapestry of scars. Fighters were drawn by lot, and the first few matches were over in less than a minute each. When the Beast's opponent hit the dirt floor, he was dragged away like a fallen tree branch.

The next figure to step between the ropes made Moire's jaw fall open, and her heart missed a beat.

Oliver was stripped to the waist. Muscles clearly defined beneath his skin as he flexed his arms. His hands were bound with cloth.

"Ready for the next bout? We have here the Sailor, joining us while on a bit of shore leave," bellowed the announcer. The crowd screamed with anticipation.

Oliver surveyed the audience, his gaze picking out Moire. He nodded at her, and her heart swelled with pride and worry in equal measure. As he prepared to face the Beast, she sent up a silent prayer to whatever gods might be listening, begging them to keep him safe.

The Beast's eyes held a feral glint, and his lips curled into a snarl. "Let's make this quick, pretty boy," the behemoth growled, cracking his knuckles ominously.

"The Beast will make quick work of the Sailor," a man near Moire chortled.

"The Sailor is stronger than he looks, and he's fast," Moire retorted.

"Ha! We'll see about that," the man scoffed, and he raised his mug to her in a mocking toast.

"Begin!" yelled the announcer. Then he ran for the rope and dived underneath as the Beast launched himself at Oliver.

Each blow exchanged between the opponents echoed through the room, a cacophony of grunts and gasps punctuating the deafening cheers from the crowd. Moire's heart clenched with each hit that landed on Oliver. She gripped the post so tight that her knuckles turned white. She refused to let her fear show. Instead, she raised her chin. Her eyes never left her beloved's face, even as she winced when one blow split his brow open, and blood dribbled down his temple.

"Show him what you're made of!" she yelled out, her voice surprisingly strong amidst the din.

Oliver glanced at her, his chest heaving with effort. Their connection was an anchor, tethering them together in the storm they faced.

"I've fought fiercer squalls at sea!" Oliver taunted. He dodged a wild swing from his opponent, agile as a cat playing with its prey. His nimbleness contrasted with the brute force of the other man, whose face glistened with perspiration. The sound of fists colliding with muscle reverberated through the room, interspersed by the excited cries of the spectators.

As she watched, the tide of the battle turned in Oliver's

favour. His agility and determination gave him the upper hand against the lumbering brute. Each strike he landed brought them one step closer to their dreams, and Moire marvelled at the strength and resilience he displayed.

"Victory is within your grasp," she whispered into the ether, willing her words to reach his ears.

With a surge of determination, Oliver feinted left before launching a devastating right hook that connected squarely with his opponent's temple. The burly man staggered, momentarily dazed, as the crowd erupted in a mixture of cheers and curses.

"Go on!" Moire shouted, her voice joining the fray. "You have him now!"

Oliver grinned, sweat beading on his brow as he pressed his advantage. He danced around his opponent, peppering him with quick jabs that seemed to land with unerring accuracy. The burly man snarled and lunged, but Oliver sidestepped the attack with ease.

"Merely a sailor, they said," Oliver yelled. "We'll see who's laughing when I claim my prize."

With one final, powerful blow Oliver sent the burly man crashing to the ground. The crowd roared with excitement as he stood, panting and triumphant, over his fallen opponent. Moire allowed herself a moment of satisfaction as two men were needed to drag away the Beast.

Then her gaze turned to the fresh competitors, all waiting their turn to step into the ring. The competition was not over yet. Oliver walked a dangerous road to win the dragon egg. Her faith faltered a little.

"You can do it, Oliver." Her words were lost in the din of cheering spectators.

There was no time to celebrate and no moment of respite. The next challenger stepped into the ring. Twice more, Oliver battled and defeated his opponent. Holding his position in the ring and his claim to the dragon egg. Blood ran down both sides of his face and trickled over his chest, mingling with sweat and painting his torso red.

Moire's nails dug into the post at her side when, finally, the last combatant of the evening stepped through the ropes —a lean, fox-faced man whose every movement seemed to be calculated for maximum efficiency. His dark eyes flicked over the crowd, settling briefly on Moire before flicking back to Oliver.

"The Fox versus the Sailor!" the announcer called.

"How good of you to save the last dance for me," the cunning fighter said, his voice smooth and polished like a well-worn sword.

"I must warn you, I've been known to step on my partner's toes," Oliver replied, his voice steady despite the fatigue that slowed his movements.

A ripple of laughter spread through the crowd, and Moire couldn't help but smile at her beloved's wit. But her amusement was short-lived. The small fighter was not to be underestimated. As the last to fight, he had not faced anyone else.

Oliver's body tensed, preparing for the onslaught. Once the match began, the Fox darted forwards like a striking snake, his fists flying at Oliver with alarming speed and from every angle. Oliver parried and dodged, but the wily fighter was relentless, forcing him back step by step.

Moire watched in awe as Oliver, while clearly fatigued

from all the previous bouts, deflected most of the Fox's blows. The smack of fists colliding echoed through the air.

"Stay strong, my sailor," Moire urged. "You can do this. I know you can."

But even as she said the words, doubt gnawed at her. The slippery fighter proved a formidable opponent. Oliver's exhaustion became more apparent with each passing moment. Moire winced at each blow that landed. Pain lanced through her as though she were the one under attack.

"Enough," she commanded and pushed back her doubts. "He will not fail."

Climbing down from the keg, Moire pushed her way through the frantic crowd, using her elbows to make room when rotund bellies refused to move. At last, she was right at the front and close enough to grasp the rope.

Her gaze never wavered from the man she loved, watching as he refused to back down in the face of adversity. With every ounce of strength she possessed, she willed him to victory and turned her thoughts into a beacon of hope in the darkness.

"Is that all you've got, sailor boy?" The Fox taunted with a mocking grin. "I expected more from His Majesty's Navy."

Oliver staggered backwards. Sweat and blood had turned his naked torso into a landscape of pain. The wiry fighter advanced, a wicked gleam in his eyes that sent shivers down Moire's spine. Weariness was etched into every line of Oliver's body. His punches grew sluggish and strained.

"Show him what you're made of, Sailor!" Moire called

out, making her voice heard above the din of the raucous crowd.

Oliver's gaze lighted on her for a moment, and then he focused on his opponent, his fists raised in anticipation. The two men circled each other, each waiting for the other to provide a weakness they could exploit. It was a deadly dance—one wrong step, and the consequences could be disastrous.

"Women make you weak, Sailor," the Fox sneered, his voice dripping with contempt as he gestured to Moire with his head.

"No. She makes me stronger," Oliver replied.

"I love you!" Moire yelled as loud as she could to an answering cheer from the men around her.

At the sound of her words, something remarkable happened. A spark ignited in Oliver as though he drew from a hidden wellspring of strength. For an instant, his eyes flared silver like the lunar dragon. Then he straightened his posture and raised his fists once more.

"Come on, then!" he bellowed at his opponent, defiance lacing every syllable. "Show me what you've got!" Like a coiled spring being released, Oliver lunged forward, his fists a blur as they rained down upon his adversary.

As Oliver pressed forward, Moire's heartbeat synced with each strike, skipping with every near miss. She willed what strength she had to him.

Oliver sidestepped a lunge and followed through with a swift uppercut that landed squarely on the other man's jaw. The Fox staggered back, dazed. Oliver didn't give him an opportunity to recover. He pressed forward, delivering a series of powerful blows that left his opponent reeling and gasping for breath.

"Finish him off!" Moire yelled, then she slapped a hand over her mouth, never expecting to hear such words bellowed from her lungs.

And finish him, Oliver did. With a final, thunderous blow, the Sailor sent the smaller fighter crashing to the ground, unconscious. For a moment, the entire room held its breath. Then the crowd erupted into cheers so loud that they reverberated through Moire's bones. Her eyes brimmed with tears—made of pride, relief, and love—as she watched Oliver stand victorious in the ring.

"Bravo!" cried one man.

"Jolly good show, old chap!" another called, raising a mug in salute.

"Never thought anyone would defeat Darius Blackwood," the man beside her muttered, and Moire tucked the name of the Fox away in her memory.

"To our winner, the Sailor, goes the prize!" The announcer returned to the ring, holding a crate in both hands. A rounded top peeked out of the straw.

He handed it to Oliver, who took the container and stared at the contents. His chest heaved with exhaustion. Bruises formed beneath the sweat and blood. One knee buckled and without thinking, Moire darted forwards and under the ropes.

She wrapped her arms around his waist to lend him her strength.

"You did it," she said, unable to think of what else to say.

"For us." He gazed at her from one eye, as the other had swollen shut. But that one eye blazed with triumph.

Her body ached in sympathy at the toll the brutal fights had taken on him. It would be impossible for her to love him any more, for all that he had willingly endured to secure their future.

"You were magnificent." Her voice was thick with emotion. "Now, let's get you out of here so I can tend to your wounds."

Letting him lean on her shoulders, they left the ring and headed for an open side door. People congratulated him as they passed. Outside, cool, fresh air washed over Moire's skin as they walked a little distance to a well.

"Sit," Moire instructed.

Gingerly, Oliver lowered himself onto the stone edge and placed the crate at his feet.

"Is it dragon or wyvern?" Oliver asked her. Only now did doubt creep into his one good eye.

"I need to tend to you first. We can dream of what the egg contains later." Grabbing the rope, she raised the bucket from the cool depths below. From the satchel she had slung over her shoulder and under her cloak, she pulled out a cloth and salves. By the light of the moon, Moire washed the blood, sweat, and dirt from his body and then dabbed the soothing balm onto cuts and bruises.

The gash above his brow worried her. "This is deep and should be stitched. I fear it will scar."

He winced at her touch but did not protest. "Let it leave a scar, as a reminder of the night I battled for a dragon. Moire," his voice broke on her name. Reaching out, he took the cloth from her hand and dropped it back into the bucket. "I couldn't have done this without you."

"Nor I without you. I rode Faustus even though heights terrify me, but I refused to let you battle alone," she confessed. Although the idea of facing the return trip home made her blood run cold.

"We have both faced demons tonight and emerged victorious." Oliver placed a kiss on the centre of her palm.

"Together, we will face whatever our future holds." She glanced at the crate and a tendril of worry wormed through her. The egg seemed particularly small and the wrong colour to be a dragon.

"Even if it brings us a dragon?" he asked, the hint of a smile playing at the corners of his bruised and split lips.

Moire swallowed. Oliver did not doubt what slept and grew inside the egg, so neither should she.

"Especially if we have a dragon," she agreed, her own lips curving into a playful grin. They stood on the cusp of an extraordinary adventure, and she couldn't wait for it to unfold.

3

After a heart-pounding night and returning to her bed in the wee small hours of the morning, Moire overslept. Or she did until the moment a shaft of bright sun lit the inside of her eyelids a flaming red. She groaned and held one hand to her head.

"Are you sick, Miss? I was ever so worried to find you weren't up and about," Lucy said as she finished opening the curtains.

When she cracked one eye open, Moire found the maid at the side of her bed with a tinge of worry pulling her features tight.

"A little late summer cold is all, and I did not sleep so well." Moire sat up and rubbed her temples. She could still hear the screams of the crowd hammering inside her skull, and her stomach lurched as she remembered riding on the back of Faustus, skimming farmland and rooftops. A fall from such a height would have been fatal.

"If you are sure that is all." Lucy said no more, but she arched one eyebrow.

Not for the first time, Moire wondered if the maid had cracked open her door during the night and discovered her mistress gone from her room. But she refused to ask. If she blithely ignored the maid's hints and comments, she didn't have to confess where she went at night.

Other moments from the previous night dripped into her tired brain. Oliver stripped to the waist, sweat glistening on defined muscles as he fought for a way to sway her father's opinion. The fierce determination he displayed to defeat each opponent. She had promised him she would learn all she could about dragon hatchlings. There was much to do.

"I will be down shortly. If you could arrange for tea and toast in the morning room, please." Flinging aside the blankets, Moire lowered her feet to the ground and wriggled her toes at having something substantial underneath her.

"Of course, Miss. Sir George is up already and asking why his wallpaper samples have not arrived yet," Lucy said as she slowly walked back to the door.

"Please tell Father I will be down directly." Was it Moire's imagination, or did the maid stop and inspect the boots sitting by the dresser? At least she had not stepped in any mud, but there might be traces of straw from the barn.

Once alone, Moire stripped out of her nightgown and scrubbed at her exposed skin with a cloth and cold water to revitalise her senses. Then she dressed in her favourite sage-green, striped gown and laced up a pair of short boots. As soon as she could, she would escape to the forest. Oliver had agreed to meet her at the barrow so they could examine the egg in daylight.

It took three hours before Moire managed to escape her

family. As luck had it, a rider delivered the heavy parcel of wallpaper samples and allowed her to slip away. When she last saw Sir George and Augusta, they were engrossed in holding up squares with the intention of spending a ruinous amount of money on needless decoration.

Grabbing a shawl, Moire wrapped it around her torso and then rushed from the house. She trod the familiar path and soon reached Caliban's barrow. Placing one hand on the mossy covering, she murmured a greeting to the dragon who had slipped from their realm decades earlier than he should have. Some had whispered the he gave up on life in the disappointment at the vainglorious creature her father had become.

While she waited for Oliver, Moire weeded the barrow, pulling out dandelions and thistles that had erupted from the soft earth like whiskers. Soon came the snort of a horse and the thud of hooves. Oliver dismounted in the glade and tied the horse's reins to a nearby tree.

Moire swallowed a gasp. In the dappled light, his face looked worse. Bruises had turned from red to purple, and his swollen-shut eye was ringed by a bluish black. A bandage was wound around his forehead, the crepe visible under the band of his hat.

"Oh, Oliver." She rushed to him and reached out a hand but didn't touch the gash above his eyebrow where a single drop of dried blood stained the fabric. "What a price you paid for success."

He took her hands and kissed her palms. "My body will heal, and every blow was worth it, for it secured our future." He removed the strap of a canvas duffle bag hung over his shoulder.

Sitting on the grass, Oliver loosened the drawstring of the bag and tugged down the canvas. In size, the egg was approximately sixteen inches tall and perhaps ten inches in circumference at its widest point. Doubt was a cold thread winding through her. The egg was far too small to contain a dragon, wasn't it? Nor was it a drake egg. The wingless relatives of dragons hatched from eggs with a distinctive armoured pattern to the shell. They were mossy, earthy tones and resembled green pinecones. That meant it was most likely a wyvern egg.

She knelt beside Oliver and examined the object. At first glance, it appeared a dull grey. Only on close inspection did she notice the tiny silver veins lacing the surface like the finest marble.

"It's beautiful," she said, tracing a vein. Whether it contained a dragon or a wyvern, the creature would be loved.

"Is it a dragon egg, Moire, and not a wyvern? I need admission to the Draco Legion, not a guard dog. That's if the thing is even alive in there." Worry pulled at Oliver's one good eye.

She couldn't lie to him. "I don't know. Dragons are so rare, and I have never seen an egg in person." Moire reached out, her fingers trembling as they brushed against the smooth surface of the egg. A gentle warmth radiated from it, tingling her fingertips and travelling up her arm. She gasped and pulled her hand back as though burned. "It is certainly alive, though. Have no concern about that. Can you not feel it?"

Oliver placed his hand on the shell next to hers. "No. I feel nothing."

"Perhaps it is because of my family's tie to Caliban. There could be some sort of residual affinity for dragons in my blood. Either way, this is good news." Moire tried to lift Oliver's worries and keep their dream alive.

At length, he nodded and flashed a swift smile. "I choose to believe so. But that brings me to my next concern." His expression darkened, and he glanced around, as though expecting to find an eavesdropper. "This is a valuable item, and there are those who would seek to steal it. Last night, the Fox vowed it would be his and that he had a buyer for it."

"Darius Blackwood," Moire breathed the name of the cunning fighter. "I cannot imagine any dragon wanting to bond with such a man."

Oliver clenched his jaw. "Is that the man? I have heard his name before. He dwells in the underbelly of the criminal world. A dragon brings power, influence, and wealth."

"Or destruction," Moire added in a quiet tone. She had read the tales of the devastation that a full-grown dragon could wreak upon the world in the wrong hands.

"I will take precautions. No criminal will steal the creature from us. We must protect it, Moire, no matter what." Oliver stared at the egg.

A shiver ran down Moire's spine. The growing animal had experienced such a fraught journey already, and it was still in its shell. Stolen from under its mother and placed on a ship only to be wrecked and flung into a cold ocean. Then fought over, and now covetous eyes would seek to snatch it to sell to the highest bidder. A chill wind whispered around Caliban's barrow and swirled around the shell.

Moire tugged the canvas bag back over the marbled

surface, to keep the egg warm and to ward off the icy hands of fate. "You must find a safe place to hide it. They take ten years to hatch, and we have no way of knowing how long this one has been in the shell. We could have months or years to wait."

"Ten years?" Oliver repeated, surprise etched on his battered face.

"We need to find a secure place where the egg will be kept warm and undisturbed while the creature inside grows." She struggled to think of such a place. Oliver could hardly carry it around with him at all times, and what happened when he returned to his ship? Could he stash it in his sea chest and hope no one looked inside?

"I shall think upon that. I don't doubt that Blackwood will try to find it, and I cannot afford to lead him to a hiding place." Oliver drew the cord of the duffle bag closed.

Moire resolved to be of use. "I shall learn all I can about dragon eggs and hatchlings from what books we have. If only father would allow me to source more."

Oliver took her hand in his. "Your keen mind is but one of the many reasons why I love you."

Moire blushed at the praise. "I shall begin my studies as soon as I return," she declared, her thoughts already turning to the few dusty tomes on the subject in the family library.

"Be careful, Moire. And might I suggest we do not tell Sir George just yet," Oliver cautioned, his voice low and filled with concern.

She recalled her father's angry words when she had, uncharacteristically, spoken out over dinner about the death of Caliban. Never had she kept such a secret from her family, but Oliver was right. They could wait until they knew more, then reveal the existence of the dragon egg. There was a slim chance Sir George might hear local talk of the fight and how a sailor won, but he didn't normally pay any heed to such gossip unless a peer was involved.

She laid her hand over the top of his. "I will guard this secret until the time is right. For the sake of the innocent creature that lies within—and for you."

Oliver cradled the bundle in his arms, his expression a mixture of determination and concern. "I will find a safe place to hide it, Moire. I promise."

"Take care of both of you," Moire whispered.

Oliver dropped the strap over his head and secured the bag at his side, then he wrapped his arms around Moire to kiss her goodbye. Long after he had mounted his horse and disappeared between the trees, she stood with her fingers touching her lips.

With her thoughts spiralling in many directions, Moire returned to the house to focus on the most immediate task. Researching the differences between types of draconian eggs. No sooner had she stepped inside the tiled entranceway than Sir George's voice bellowed from the drawing room.

"Moire! Is that you? Where have you been, girl? I cannot find my favourite cravat, and I need it for tonight."

Moire drew a deep breath to muster her patience and stepped into the doorway. "I do not know, Father. Perhaps it is in your dressing room?"

"Impossible! I have searched high and low. You will find it for me. I am to dine tonight in Wyldefen with an old school chum, and I simply must look my best." His tone left no room for argument as he waved a wallpaper square of gold and red stripes.

Sighing, Moire abandoned her plans for research and instead began a search for her father's elusive cravat. Thankfully, it was not that difficult. It only took her a solid hour, and getting down on her hands and knees, to find the length of pale-blue silk fallen down the back of a set of drawers. It would need a careful wash and starch before it could be worn.

She carried the fabric with her to the drawing room, only to hear several voices within. Visitors had arrived while she'd been searching. Stopping at one of the many mirrors lining the walls, she smoothed strands of hair back into place and tried to wipe the worst of the dust from her gown.

Entering the parlour, she found Lady Beaumont on the settee next to Augusta. Across from them sat their neighbour, Mrs Radcliffe. The older woman chatted while her son, Samuel, stared at a painting of Sir George with two spaniels at his feet. One held a pheasant in its jaws.

Moire bobbed a curtsey to their guests.

"Ah, Moire, there you are!" Lady Beaumont chirped, her eyes glittering with mischief. "I encountered the Radcliffes on my way here. Samuel was taking his mother for a ride to enjoy the sunshine, and I said they simply had to accompany me on my visit. I seem to recollect you two are acquainted, are you not?"

"We saw each other often growing up, yes." Moire wound the cravat around her hand.

"You used to beat us all at tree climbing, as I recollect," Samuel chuckled.

"Ah. Moire. Where is tea?" Sir George looked at her with a scowl.

"I found your cravat, Father, and shall call for tea immediately." Keeping sharp words to herself, Moire walked back to the doorway and summoned a maid. She passed over the cravat for cleaning and requested a tea tray, scones, and savouries.

Not knowing what to do with herself, she joined Samuel at the painting.

"I say, I didn't know Sir George kept gun-dogs." He gestured to the brown and white spaniels.

"He doesn't. He merely asked for them to be painted in to make him look more sporting," Moire murmured.

Samuel frowned. The Radcliffes had been their neighbours for years. As a child, she used to play with Samuel whenever their paths crossed. The young boy always had at least one dog at his side. He had grown into a good-natured man, although with little time for anything outside of his dogs and horses. She didn't see his sister as often anymore as she had been sent off to a private school to instil all the attributes expected of a noble wife.

Moire perched on a chair and served tea when it arrived. Samuel tried to hook his thick fingers through the delicate handle of his teacup and then abandoned the effort and held it between his hands instead. Her father and Lady Beaumont took every opportunity to show their superior social skills and knowledge of current affairs. Moire did her best to offer Samuel a gentle smile of encouragement. He no more wanted to be trapped in the drawing room than she did.

"Do you go to London much, Mr Radcliffe?" Augusta asked with a wink to Lady Beaumont.

"Good heavens, no." He set his cup down so hard it rattled on the saucer. "Terrible hunting there."

"That rather depends on the prey one pursues," Lady Beaumont murmured over the rim of her cup.

"Are there many rabbits about this year?" Moire asked.

That was all the opening Samuel needed. He launched into a one-sided conversation about the local rabbit population, the best methods to catch them, and his favourite rabbit pie recipe.

"Samuel keeps our larder well stocked with game." Mrs Radcliffe beamed at her son.

The afternoon dragged, and for once, Moire was glad when her father lost interest in their guests. He stood and declared he had to begin preparations for his evening in town, and the Radcliffes were bustled out the front door.

Lady Beaumont pulled Moire to one side. "I understand the Radcliffes are quite comfortable in their living, and everyone expects the title of viscount to settle on Mr Radcliffe's shoulders, should his uncle die without male issue. He would be a most excellent match for a member of this family."

Moire rubbed the moonstone on her finger. "Indeed, he would be a catch for some lucky young lady. My affections are, of course, already taken. As is my hand. Lieutenant Hartford and I only await Father's approval to make our engagement official."

Lady Beaumont rested a gloved hand on Moire's arm. "My dear, Sir George will never agree to the young lieutenant. Far better to take the eminently suitable match before you, than pursue heartbreak."

"If you'll excuse me, I had better see if Father's cravat has been cleaned." Excusing herself, Moire hurried through the house and darted up the stairs to her room. When the door latched behind her, she leaned against it, taking deep, steadying breaths. She could never marry Samuel, even though he was kind. Her heart belonged to Oliver.

Dinner that night was a quiet affair with Sir George away. Katherine stayed in her room with a tray, claiming she had either the Black Death or a sniffle. Only morning would reveal which. Augusta glared at Moire across the table, and their conversation was stilted. For sisters, they had only been fleetingly close when they shared a nursery. Augusta favoured their father in both appearance and temperament. Moire took after their mother. Their differences had created an uncrossable divide between them.

Afterwards, Moire curled up at the window of her bedroom and stared out. Stars twinkled overhead like tiny beacons of hope. Her fingers twisted the moonstone ring, its cool surface soothing her troubled thoughts. As she scanned the night sky, she longed for another glimpse of the elusive lunar dragon.

An hour after her father's raucous return, and once she felt the household was asleep, she slipped from her room and padded down to the library. Lighting a candle, she held it in one hand, running her other along the spines of dusty volumes.

"Dragons and wyverns," she murmured. "There must be something here."

She inspected row after row of titles and found nothing. Odd. How could a family blessed with a dragon not acquire a multitude of books to learn more about their majestic guardian? Moire scanned the shelves until her eyes fell upon a single, dusty volume that seemed quite out of place among the meticulously arranged books on politics and history.

She pulled it free, her fingers tracing over the embossed title. *Dragons & Wyverns: A Natural History.*

As she flipped through the pages, revealing intricate illustrations and detailed descriptions, she noted several passages underlined and annotated by an unknown hand. Frustrated at the lack of books on the topic, Moire wondered if there was hidden knowledge about dragonkind somewhere in their ancestral home. Not just dragons and wyverns, but their wingless cousins, drakes, and the small and beautiful piptere.

Taking advantage of the rare opportunity, like a ghost, she intended to flit into the one place she was usually forbidden unless summoned. Shielding the candle with one hand, she tiptoed down the dark hallway. The door to her father's study creaked open. Her father never locked it, relying on strict rules to ensure everyone stayed out. Within, moonlight filtered through the heavy curtains and cast an eerie glow upon the room.

Her father's desk was buried under fabric samples, and she shuddered to think of the bill that would arrive once he selected furnishings to match the new wallpaper. There were fewer books in here, but they tended to be rarer volumes displayed behind glass in locked cabinets. Previous Sir Tobins had collected them over the years. One day, her father would realise they had value, and he would probably sell them all to buy new shoes.

As she padded across the lush rugs with the lantern in her hand, the light flashed across the portrait hanging above the fire. A stern man gazed down upon her. Drac Rupert Tobin, the first. The man who had found and hatched a dragon egg and established their bloodline as one of the elite families in England.

In the painting, he stood proudly with one knee bent, his booted foot resting upon the dragon egg. The pose reminded her of a hunter with a slain beast at his feet. Moving closer, she peered at the egg. It came to knee height and was a solid, dark grey, rather like a wet stone.

Is this what Oliver's egg should look like? she wondered with a sharp pang of doubt.

The egg Oliver had won was much smaller, paler, and the surface laced with tiny veins of silver. Worry assailed her. Had Oliver fought so hard for a wyvern egg? Or did a dragon egg grow in size and change colour as it neared its time of hatching? She would need to consult books. The shell might become darker as a method of signalling when the creature was about to emerge.

"Sir Rupert, what secrets did you discover?" she asked the portrait. She imagined the man coming to life, his sharp gaze meeting hers as he shared the mysteries of dragons and their eggs. But those secrets remained locked away, and Moire had a difficult mission to uncover them.

As she repositioned the book she had found under her arm, a rustling outside the door startled her. She pressed herself against a shadowed corner, praying that her father would not discover her trespassing. When the noise abated, and with one last glance at Drac Tobin's enigmatic visage, Moire slipped from the study and hurried back to her room. The precious volume clutched to her chest.

The next day, on her way to the study that had once been her mother's, and with her attention on the book in her hands, Moire turned a corner and nearly collided with her father. Sir George stood tall and imposing, his face etched with lines of disapproval. She quickly hid the dragon book behind her back, but it was too late. The action had caught his keen interest.

"Moire, whatever have you got there?" he demanded, his voice booming through the hall.

Caught off guard, Moire stammered, "I...I was just... Father, it is a book about dragons. I wish to study them and perhaps, one day, become a scholar on the subject." She clutched the book with trembling hands.

"Dragons?" Sir George scoffed. "You mean *wyrms?* Preposterous! No daughter of mine will waste her time on such frivolous pursuits. It's unbecoming of a lady, and reading gives you wrinkles with all that squinting."

"Father, please," Moire implored. Disappointment dripped through her at his disdain for every little thing that brought joy to her life. "Our family has a history with these creatures, and..."

"Enough!" Sir George snapped, snatching the book from her grasp. He glared down at her, his eyes cold and unyielding. "Your place is not in the world of dusty old books and fanciful tales. You have duties to attend to and responsibilities as my daughter."

Moire bowed her head in submission. She knew better

than to argue, though her heart cried out against the injustice of it all. "Yes, Father. What would you have me do?"

"Go talk to Mrs Hatton. I saw a spider web in the corner of my dressing room, and there is an unacceptable amount of dust above the doors. Those maids are slovenly," he ordered, his tone sharp and dismissive.

Moire thought the maids were simply overworked. There were too few of them to keep the house as spick and span as her father demanded.

"Yes, Father." She turned for the kitchens. Outwardly, she did as he asked. Inwardly, she vowed she would not give up so easily. She would find other books about dragons, whether or not her father would let her study them. He could not watch her every minute of every day. She would find a way, even if she read by candlelight in Faustus's burrow deep in the ground.

4

Two days later, and with an idea firmly in mind, Moire trod the dew-drenched grass as the first streaks of dawn bled across the sky. She kept her arms wrapped around her body, her coat barely keeping the chill breeze away from her torso. The world was still hushed and sleepy, allowing her clandestine movements to go unnoticed.

Across the meadow behind the stables and tucked beside a stand of trees was the entrance to Faustus's underground burrow. The guard wyvern would have sought his bed as the sky lightened.

"Faustus?" she called, her voice echoing in the damp chamber. "Are you still awake?"

"Yes. Moire." His raspy voice drifted from the shadows, a hint of surprise in his tone. A slither came as she ventured deeper, faint light from behind allowing her to navigate her way. The burrow angled down and then turned two sharp corners. The twists stopped the bright light of day from disturbing the wyvern's sleep, but it made Moire temporarily blind at the loss of all light.

She paused for a silent moment, letting her eyes adjust to the dark. In a chamber the size of a horse stall, Faustus was curled up on a bed of straw. His leathery wings were tucked against his body, and his triangular head rested on the straw. Silver eyes regarded Moire with curiosity.

"Forgive me for disturbing your sleep," Moire apologised.

"Sit." He puffed at the straw beside him.

She sank to her knees on the soft material and was surprised at the warmth and insulation it provided from the ground. "I wanted to talk to you about dragon and wyvern eggs, and how to tell them apart." She knew the egg didn't belong to a drake. The armour those creatures possessed wrapped around their hard eggs as well.

Faustus tilted his head. "Hard. To. Tell."

He sent images to Moire's mind. A flash of eggs that appeared similar in both size and the subdued colour of their shells.

"Oliver has obtained what he believes is a dragon egg. But some whisper it is from a wyvern. I do not know how to tell the difference and..." She paused as worry surged through her, and then she voiced her darkest concern. "It seems too small to contain a dragon." The size of the egg preyed upon her mind, especially when she considered the size of Caliban, who had spanned over thirty feet from the tip of his nose to his tail.

Faustus curled his tail around his body until he could settle his head upon it as he pondered her words. "One. Dragon. Have seen."

Of course. Faustus had been a newly hatched wyvern

when Sir Tobin hatched Caliban a hundred and fifty years ago. "Do you remember what Caliban's egg looked like?"

He closed his eyes and hummed. The image he pushed gently into her mind seemed similar to what the painter had captured in her father's study. An egg of a polished greyish brown. Much like a stone lifted from the river.

"Do wyvern eggs look the same?" Moire asked, her brow furrowed with worry.

"Yes. No. Dragon. Bigger."

Given dragons were substantially larger than wyverns, Moire expected them to have much larger eggs. Her tendril of worry turned into a thick rope.

"Thank you, Faustus, for sharing what you know." She scratched his head, and the wyvern closed his eyes and crooned in contentment at the attention.

When Caliban had sickened and reached his end, Moire, her mother, and Faustus had kept vigil beside the dragon. Despite the approach of winter, they had sat out under the stars with him. Moire had been kept warm by the wyvern curled around her. Her mother had cradled Caliban's head in her lap and sung lullabies to ease his passing into the next realm.

Then, less than a week later, her mother succumbed to the chill she had caught that night. Moire and Faustus had comforted each other, for they had each lost the one person who understood them. Sir George, rather than wrapping his bereft children in love, instead blamed Caliban for the loss of his social standing, which bereaved him more than the loss of his wife.

"Old. Nest," Faustus rasped.

"There's an old nest?" Moire repeated. He showed her

a burrow, similar to his. But with a cluster of eggs nestled among the straw and bedding material.

"Yes."

"Really?" Moire's eyes widened in surprise and a flicker of hope ignited within her. If she could see actual wyvern eggs, she would know how similar or dissimilar they were to Oliver's egg. "Could you take me there?"

"Steep. High," the wyvern crooned.

Bother. She had assumed the nest would be hidden in a hole deep in the ground. Her heart clenched at the idea of climbing a mountain to reach the summit and the abandoned nest.

"The things we do for knowledge," she whispered. If she wanted to learn more about the eggs, she had to be brave. There wasn't any other recourse. "I shall return at twilight, if you would be so good as to take me there. Now, I shall leave you to sleep."

Moire padded back out of the burrow and into the pale light of early morning. As she crossed the meadow, a rider with dogs milling around the horse's feet trotted free of the forest.

"Good morning, Miss Moire!" the rider haled her.

The dogs barked and bounded towards her but skidded to a stop a foot away. No doubt they smelt the wyvern on her clothing and kept a careful distance from the dangerous odour. They sat and waited for the rider to catch up.

"Good morning, Mr Radcliffe. Has your morning hunt been successful?" She shaded her eyes to stare up at him.

"Oh, yes. A good brace of pheasant for supper." He patted the dead birds strung together, dangling from one side of his saddle. Then he slung his leg over the pommel and dismounted. "I was heading towards your house to see you. I found a piptere egg, and since it is quite a pretty thing, I thought that perhaps you might like it. Some ladies blow out the contents and use the shells as decoration."

He reached into the saddlebag and pulled forth an egg larger than what a goose would lay and passed it to her.

"I did not know there were amphiptere in our forest." While their scientific name was *amphiptere*, most people referred to them as *piptere*, which was less of a mouthful.

The smallest of the dragon species, the little creatures were about the size of a large chicken and came in a dizzying array of colours and forms. Some had scales, some feathers, and others a combination of the two. They were popular pets among ladies of society, usually kept in cages or on chains to stop them from flying away as they could be capricious.

"Oh, yes. Two nested over the eastern side of the forest. I think that big wind a few days ago blew this out of the tree. The silly things can't get it back up, nor can I climb that high. The shell is pretty, is it not?" He rapped on it with one finger.

Moire cradled it in her hands, and the same gentle warmth and thrum emitted from the egg as she had felt from Oliver's. The surface was a deep navy, shot through with a grey swirl. "Why, this egg is still alive, Mr Radcliffe. It would fetch a fair price if you were to sell it, or gift it to someone special."

He caught her gaze. "Alive? Well, in that case you must keep it, Miss Moire. I have no need for such a thing. Ruth is at school and cannot have a pet. Nor do I imagine Mother would want it flying through the house. I can hear the maids screeching already, and that would set the dogs off." He grinned and wrapped her fingers around it.

"It is a most generous gift and one I will treasure. Thank you." Her mind raced at the idea of hatching such a creature for herself. Apart from being a dragon companion for both her and Faustus, there would be much to learn that could assist Oliver with his egg in the years to come.

Mr Radcliffe grinned and seemed genuinely pleased at her response. "I see pipteres occasionally when I'm out hunting, but they are skittish things and disappear as soon as I fire my gun. I don't see much point to them as pets myself, but I suppose they are nice to look at. Do you know much about them?"

"Not as much as I would like to know. I am quite determined to learn all that I can about dragonkind." She cradled the egg to her chest while she tugged the scarf from around her neck and wrapped it around the shell.

"You want to study them? I was never one for books myself. I much prefer to be out with the hounds. But you might be interested in my family's library. There's many a dusty old book in there about dragons and such. I remember as a boy looking at them and being terribly disappointed that they weren't adventurous tales of things being burned to a crisp."

"Oh, Mr Radcliffe. Your words are most wonderful to me. How I'd love to see those books." Moire tucked the fabric-wrapped bundle into a pocket.

Mr Radcliffe put his foot in the stirrup and climbed back into the saddle. "You are more than welcome any time, Miss Moire. I'm sure Mother would be as delighted to have your company as would I. We both miss Ruth and the light she brought to the house. Do come for tea, perhaps? Then Mother can show you the books."

Moire was buoyed by the early morning encounter. Mr Radcliffe had given her two rare things. A piptere egg and the chance to hatch the popular pet for herself, and, even more enticing, the lure of numerous books on dragons.

Once inside the house, Moire raced up to her bedroom and deposited the scarf and its precious cargo on her bed. Shrugging off her coat, she surveyed the room for something to turn into a nest. The egg would need to be kept warm until it hatched. The empty basket on top of the dresser would be perfect. Then she found a spare shawl of a soft, grey wool and wound it around the inside of the basket.

Finally, she nestled the dark-blue egg in the very centre and teased the warm material around its edges. As she stood holding the basket, Lucy knocked on the door and entered.

"What do you have there, Miss?" She approached with the tea tray, but her attention was on the basket.

"I encountered Mr Radcliffe on my early morning walk. He found this egg in the forest and gifted it to me."

"That's the oddest-looking goose egg I've ever seen. Did he paint it for you?" The maid had a speculative gleam in her eyes as she set the tray down on the small table by the window.

"No. It's a piptere egg. Those are the little dragons who are about the size of a chicken." Moire left the basket by her bed. There it would be warmed by the sun coming through the window, and she would be nearby if it hatched at night.

The maid's eyes widened. "Oh, Miss. I thought they

only had them in London. What if it scratches someone's eyes out?"

"I have not heard of them being particularly violent. But let us see if the egg hatches first, and then we will worry about any troubling habits it develops." Never having been to London, Moire had not encountered a noble with a piptere attached to a golden leash. Since piptere eggs hatched much quicker than dragon eggs, she would need to learn more about them in a hurry.

With the egg doing egg things in the morning sun, Moire settled in her study downstairs. She laboured over the account books and invoices, a task that her father should have undertaken, or Augusta as the oldest daughter. But Sir George didn't want his most beautiful child to develop a squint from peering at all the columns of numbers.

Having navigated another day with her family, Moire awaited twilight. Then she hurried from the house and towards the wyvern's burrow. Her thoughts flitted between the generous gift from Samuel Radcliffe and the daunting task that lay ahead.

"Faustus?" Moire called as she approached the entrance to his subterranean home. "Are you ready?"

The grey-scaled wyvern emerged, his eyes gleaming in the dark. "Yes. Moire."

Her heart pounded against her ribs, and fear moistened her palms. "I am ready whenever you are."

"Heights. Dangerous," Faustus crooned the words, each laced with concern.

She was trying not to think about that and wished he hadn't reminded her. She had managed, *twice* now, to cling to the wyvern's back and temporarily subdue her fear. For Oliver and their dream, she would attempt it once more. Or twice more, since she probably couldn't walk back from wherever Faustus took her. "I trust you, my friend. And I shall not look down."

Denying that she ever left the ground eased her anxiety. With her eyes closed and her face buried in Faustus's hide, she could pretend he loped across the meadow like a horse.

The wyvern huffed and moved away from his burrow. Then he dipped one wing to enable Moire to climb onto his back and settle herself before his wings.

"Ready." Her mouth was so dry that her tongue stuck to her palate. Crouching low, she wrapped her arms around the wyvern's neck and screwed her eyes shut.

Her stomach lurched as Faustus leapt into the air. His wings beat a steady rhythm as Moire clung on for dear life. To distract herself from thoughts of tumbling from his side, she wondered what she would find in the Radcliffe library.

"Soon." Faustus called out after a while.

Her hands were chilled from the rush of cold air, and the wind tugged her hair free of its pins. By the time they landed, her dark hair tumbled around her face and there were knots in the ends. Sliding from his side, Moire kept one arm on the wyvern to steady her weak knees. She was relieved that in the dark, she couldn't make out how high they were.

"There." Faustus pointed to the darkened top of the hill, and then he began to slowly climb a treacherous path between the rocks.

Loose stones skittered beneath their feet, threatening to

send them tumbling back down. Moire's breath hitched in her throat as they navigated the narrow trail, but every step brought her closer to answers.

"Here." Faustus stopped by a rise of rocks. A dark crack revealed the hidden entrance to the long-abandoned wyvern nest.

Moire had tucked the end of a candle into her pocket along with a tinderbox. "I will need to light the candle, Faustus, and do not want to hurt your eyes."

"Wait." The wyvern slithered away from her and into the tunnel. When he sent her a mental image of him with a wing curled over his head, she took out the candle and the tinderbox and struck the wick.

Shielding the small light with one hand, she crept into the cave. At the very end of the narrow tunnel, in a chamber similar to Faustus's home, the unknown wyvern had made her nest and laid a clutch of eggs. Five of them sat nestled among leaves, straw, and bits of scavenged material. Up close, the intricate patterns and colours on the eggs were astonishing. Moire knelt beside the nest.

"Oh." Her hand slid over what seemed to be cool stone. With a fingertip, she traced the delicate swirls and lines etched into the stone-like surface. There was no thrum of life or warmth from these eggs. The lives inside were forever encased in stone and would not soar across the fields. "What happened to them?"

Faustus heaved a sad sigh. He spoke no words but showed her a terribly hard winter with snow to a depth she had not seen before. The wyvern who laid the eggs had sickened and died. Snow crept into the cave and surrounded the eggs, freezing the creatures inside.

"How sad. If they had hatched, you would have had many friends." Some grand estates had up to half a dozen wyverns patrolling the grounds at night. Then during the day, they all slept in the same burrow for warmth and companionship.

Moire's brow furrowed as she studied the eggs more closely. A sudden realisation washed over her, and the wonder she'd felt only moments ago was replaced by cold dread. "Faustus. These markings. They're similar to the ones on Oliver's egg."

Similar, but not the same. The markings on Oliver's eggs were like delicate veins in marble. These were thicker, like hand-painted swirls. Still, the possibility that Oliver had battled so hard for a wyvern egg made a sob worm its way through her torso. A wyvern did not bring with it a rise to the peerage, to make him acceptable to Sir George. It might improve their fortunes a little, as it could be sold to a local estate.

Wyvern or dragon, it made no difference to her. "I will learn all I can. Whatever hatches, we will be prepared."

Moire cast one last glance around at the mausoleum-like cave of the lost wyverns. Then she blew out the candle. Resting one hand on Faustus's side, the creature guided her back out of the tunnel and into the brisk night air.

Two days later, Moire had escaped to the garden. While she did not possess a green thumb, she was determined to wrest some sort of control back into the grounds that her mother had so loved. There was the additional benefit of her family not wishing to dirty their hands or brush against *foliage*, so she was left to her own thoughts in the pale sunlight.

She grabbed hold of a dandelion when the urgent pound of hooves made her glance up. A rider galloped towards the house. The low sun glinted off the brass buttons on the deep blue and white uniform. Oliver.

Moire abandoned the weeding to hurry along the paths, wiping dirt from her hands onto her apron as she went. "Oliver!" she called out. Joy and dread mixed inside her. What could have brought him here at a gallop?

He halted the horse on hearing her voice and leapt to the ground. The bruises and swelling on his face were finally retreating. "Moire. I've been recalled to my vessel. Another skirmish has broken out with France, and we leave within three days."

"No." One hand went to her chest. While she knew many an Englishman went off to war against Napoleon, until this moment, the cold reality had not wrapped around her heart. "When will I see you again?"

He took her hands, his stormy gaze searching her face. "Months, possibly a year. French and Spanish forces have invaded Portugal, our ally, and there is an outbreak of war on the peninsular. Our Navy is needed to transport troops, including six dragons and their riders."

Sir George appeared on the doorstep, his face pinched with disapproval. "What is the lieutenant doing here?"

"Oliver has been recalled to his ship, Father. He has come to say goodbye." Moire didn't turn, her attention fixed on Oliver. She memorised every line of his face to store away for their long separation.

"Well, see him off, then. You are needed inside to discuss the week's menus." Sir George waved a hand and retreated inside, leaving a footman to stand guard on the step.

"I will write, as often as I can, even if you cannot reply." A letter seemed such a trifling thing to offer when he would risk his life battling the enemy.

"I will treasure every word you can spare me. But there is something I must ask of you, Moire." He tugged her towards his horse.

"Anything," she said.

"I entrust you with this." He untied the familiar duffle bag from the rear of his saddle and handed it to her.

The egg.

"Keep it safe, Moire," Oliver urged. His hands covered hers and the sun-warmed canvas. "Whatever this may be, it could be our key to a better life after the war. I entrust you with all that I am."

"Oliver…" Moire's voice faltered as she clutched the bundle to her chest, her pulse quickening. How could she express her love, her loyalty, and her determination with mere words? Swallowing, she nodded. "I will guard it with my life…until you return to claim it."

"And you, Moire. After the war, I will claim you both and take you from here." He leaned down and placed a tender kiss on her lips. A kiss full of longing and tinged with regret at their parting. Then he brushed a hand along her cheek before turning back to his horse.

"Godspeed, Oliver," she murmured as he climbed back onto the horse and galloped away.

She clutched the bundle to her chest until horse and

rider had disappeared around the curve of the drive. Only then did she consider the safest place for the egg. If her father caught wind of it, he'd sell it off to the highest bidder. Or if he had the patience, steal it for himself to raise their family back to the Draco Legion.

There was only one place, one creature, she could trust to help her keep it safe. Faustus.

Moire hurried around the house and across the field to the stand of trees. With each step, she prayed her family didn't look out the window and wonder what she was doing. The wyvern would be fast asleep. Early afternoon was equivalent to the middle of the night for him.

"Faustus." She paused at the entrance to his lair. It wouldn't do to disturb a slumbering wyvern. He could lash out in befuddlement before he realised it was her. "I'm coming in, Faustus."

With one hand on the cool earth to find her way, she stepped into the downward sloping tunnel. As she approached the second bend that opened into his chamber, and where the light would disappear completely, Moire called out again.

"Moire?" came a sleepy reply at last.

"Yes, dear friend. I am sorry to disturb your sleep, but I need your help, and it is most urgent." With one hand outstretched so she didn't bump into him, she took careful steps across the chamber.

Faustus nudged her hand with his head and Moire dropped to her knees in the straw beside him.

"Egg," he rasped.

"Yes. Oliver has entrusted it to me, but I cannot leave it in the house where it might be discovered by my family. Do you think you could hide it in your bedding?" She placed the duffle on the straw and tugged at the string holding the bag shut, freeing the egg from the canvas.

Faustus hummed and shuffled around in his nest. "Here," he said at length. He projected to Moire an image of what he had done. By scratching at the bedding, he had created a deep impression.

She rolled the egg towards him, and using his clawed wing tips, Faustus gently guided the egg into the space for it. Then he covered it back up.

"Thank you, Faustus." Gratitude warmed her that the egg now nested in a protective haven. As she rose, she brushed her hand along the wyvern's scales in thanks, then she left him to return to sleep.

As she hurried back to the house before her family noticed her absence, her thumb rubbed the moonstone ring, and she prayed for Oliver's safe return. A trickle of excitement replaced fear. The egg was safe with Faustus, and she had her own mission—to learn all she could about dragonkind. Not to mention a piptere to hatch.

At dinner time, she found Lady Beaumont had once more joined their family. As Moire took her place at the table, she kept her whirlwind of thoughts hidden behind a mask of politeness.

"Ah, the little mouse finally emerges from its hole," her father boomed, raising his glass as if in a toast. "We are celebrating that the troublesome naval lieutenant is gone, and we shan't have any more of his nonsense."

Moire wrapped her hands around her cutlery and imagined them weapons to defeat Sir George's words. "We are at war, Father. How can you celebrate sending so many fine young men off to do battle against Napoleon, when many will not return? Do you find joy that mothers will lose their sons? Wives never see their husbands again? Children left mourning their fathers?"

Silence fell across the table. Then Katherine moaned. "Why must you talk of death, Moire? You know it stalks me constantly. Tomorrow I shall be bedridden by my impending demise."

"I am merely saying it is in poor taste to celebrate this war, when so many will perish." Moire couldn't meet her father's harsh gaze.

"Poor taste? You would lecture *me* on taste?" Sir George dropped his wineglass to the table, and the crystal pinged like an alarm as it bounced against a spoon.

"Naturally, Moire is upset at the lieutenant being called away, Sir George. She is young, and this is her first infatuation. She needs a more soothing activity to take her mind off things. Did I hear that Mr Radcliffe invited you to see their library?" Lady Beaumont smiled at Moire across the table.

Moire was grateful for her intervention. "Yes. He did. I shall visit tomorrow if that is permissible? The distraction would be most welcome."

"Very well. But there will be no more talk of war and sailors." Sir George ensured he had the final word on the topic.

Or the final word spoken out loud.

5

Since death had not claimed Katherine overnight, she insisted on accompanying her older sister. Golden sunlight bathed the rolling fields as the two trudged towards Gormsby Hall, the grand estate of the Radcliffes. The air was warm with the scent of blooming wildflowers, yet it did little to improve Katherine's spirits, which had waned before they reached the edges of their estate.

"Must we really walk *all* the way?" Katherine complained for the umpteenth time, her cheeks flushed a deep pink from the exertion. "Why didn't you ask Father for the carriage?"

Moire hadn't asked for the carriage for two reasons. Firstly, she preferred to spare herself the humiliation of refusal and secondly, she enjoyed the walk. Quiet time in their lush surroundings soothed her soul.

But not today with her youngest sibling's incessant complaints.

"The walk will put a most becoming rosy blush to your complexion." Moire attempted to lift her sister's mood. She knew that Katherine, more accustomed to luxuries and leisure, found such treks tiresome. But Moire was determined not to let her sister's grumblings dampen her own excitement about visiting the Radcliffe family.

Even though they had been neighbours for years, Moire had never seen the Radcliffe library. As they crested a hill, Gormsby Hall came into view. The sight of the stately manor house nestled amongst manicured gardens and fountains wrought a miraculous recovery over Katherine. She revived instantly. Her eyes widened with undisguised delight as she took in the elegant lines of the building, and the tall windows reflecting the afternoon light.

"Oh, my. I had quite forgotten how grand it is," Katherine exclaimed, a smile breaking across her face.

As they walked up the sweeping driveway, the front door opened and Mrs Radcliffe bustled out, looking marvellous in a bright blue gown.

"Hello! Welcome, Miss Moire, Miss Katherine." The mistress of the house greeted them warmly, her charming smile erasing any remaining traces of Katherine's earlier irritability.

"I must thank Mr Radcliffe for inviting us, Mrs Radcliffe," Moire replied, grateful for the opportunity to explore their library.

"Oh, Samuel is off somewhere with his dogs, but he will be back for afternoon tea. I have been too long without the company of delightful young ladies. Although Ruth will be home with us for Christmas. Come in, come in." Mrs Radcliffe led them inside the manor.

"Could we see something of the house, please, before Moire settles in with dusty old books?" Katherine asked.

Mrs Radcliffe beamed. "Oh, yes! I do love showing people around." For the next hour, they walked the wide halls and peered into rooms. Gormsby Hall even had a ballroom, the chandeliers hiding behind their covers.

Moire marvelled at the opulent surroundings. The walls were adorned with rich tapestries depicting scenes of dragons and knights while the polished floors gleamed. She wondered how many maids were needed to scrub them all. At length, they stopped before double-panelled doors.

"We have reached the final stop on our tour. Allow me to show you our library." Mrs Radcliffe winked as if she had somehow divined Moire's scholarly tendencies or, more likely, been told of them by her son. With a dramatic flourish, she grabbed the brass handles and flung the doors open.

Moire stood on the threshold, struck by the sheer scale of the room. It was as if she were welcomed into a temple dedicated to knowledge. Carved wooden columns supported the high ceiling. A magnificent fresco depicting dragons soaring amongst the clouds adorned the dome overhead, casting a soft, ethereal light over the entire room. Plush armchairs and chaises invited quiet contemplation, while an elegant globe stood sentinel by the fireplace. And books. Everywhere she looked were books. Walls lined with shelves reached up towards the painted dragons.

She crept towards a shelf on her tiptoes, scared to make a noise and break the enchantment the library cast over her. One glance, and she was captured by the extensive collection of books on dragons. She scanned the titles, each one whispering tantalising secrets about the mysterious creatures that so captivated her imagination. She could hardly contain her excitement at the prospect of delving into the tomes and uncovering the knowledge they held about dragons, drakes, wyverns, and their little piptere cousins.

"Please, feel free to peruse our collection," Mrs Radcliffe offered kindly. "I shall have afternoon tea served at four. Until then, I shall leave you both to explore as you wish."

"Thank you, Mrs Radcliffe," Moire said in an awe-tinged tone.

Katherine wandered off to examine the various trinkets and baubles scattered throughout the room. She had no interest in the books, only the pretty objects sitting among them.

Moire gazed at spines, her vision drinking in titles while she wondered how on earth she would pick one to begin her studies. If she possessed such a library, she would place the rarest books beyond the reach of the casual visitor. She stared at the upper levels and swallowed. Dare she?

Gathering her courage, Moire gripped the library ladder and hoisted herself up onto its lowest rung. She had always found heights disconcerting, and now as she ascended, her pulse stuttered with trepidation. Thoughts of what marvellous texts she might find propelled her ever upwards, determination outstripping her fear.

"Moire, you really shouldn't climb so high!" Katherine called from below, where she reclined on a plush blue chaise lounge. She had draped herself across it like a pampered queen, idly fanning herself as she issued imaginary commands to invisible servants. "Fetch me some tea, won't you? And make sure it's not too hot!"

"I am being careful, Katherine." Moire kept one hand

gripped on the ladder. Her sister would be most inconvenienced if she fell. Once sure of her balance, she reached for a particularly enticing volume with a wide spine. The leather-bound book was embossed with gold lettering: *A Compendium of Dragon Lore*. Her fingers brushed against its spine, and she held her breath as she pulled it from the shelf.

"Ah, success!" she murmured, clutching the precious tome to her chest. Her earlier fear was forgotten in her eagerness to delve into the pages of the book.

"Are you satisfied now?" Katherine asked as Moire settled into an armchair opposite her. "You look like a dragon that has found hidden treasure."

"I believe I have," Moire replied, scanning the contents of the ancient manuscript. As she read, she became lost in the world of dragons. The various species, habitats, and behaviours were all meticulously detailed within the fat compendium.

The hours passed, but Moire hardly noticed the passage of time, so engrossed was she in the secrets revealed to her.

"Good afternoon, ladies!" Samuel Radcliffe's voice broke through Moire's reverie. She looked up, startled to discover the young man standing in the doorway, a bouquet of wildflowers clutched in his hands. Katherine blinked and sat up, her sleepy gaze indicating that she had slumbered while Moire studied.

"Mr Radcliffe, I must thank you for your kind invitation to your family library. I have found many wondrous books. I scarcely knew where to start." Moire closed the book and caressed the cover.

"This room is hardly used, so you are most welcome to it. I came back through the fields with the dogs and thought these flowers might brighten your day, Miss Moire." He extended the bouquet towards her.

"Thank you, Mr Radcliffe." Moire stood and took the posy, a mix of late-blooming flowers and pretty seed heads. She inhaled the sweet scent of the blossoms. The wild-flowers seemed such a simple yet thoughtful gesture. One that carried an unspoken question.

"Since it's getting late, I thought I might offer to take you both home in our carriage after some tea," Mr Radcliffe said.

"That would be most welcome, thank you, Mr Radcliffe. Why, I thought I might expire on the walk here, and the very idea of returning in the dark terrifies me," Katherine said in a breathy voice as she rose gracefully from her chaise.

"I am delighted to do something chivalrous for you, Miss Katherine." Mr Radcliffe offered his arm to Katherine while Moire clutched the flowers and the book.

After a refreshing cup of tea and a scone, they climbed into the Radcliffe family carriage. The wheels rumbled along the dirt road, carrying the little group back towards the Tobin home. An early twilight cast shadows across the meadows.

After several long moments of silence, Katherine leaned forward, eyes alight with curiosity. "Mr Radcliffe, exactly how rich is your family, if I may ask?" Her voice was both playful and probing.

"Katherine!" Moire hissed at her sister's audacity, her cheeks heated with embarrassment. She glanced apologetically at Mr Radcliffe and hoped he would not take offence at such a forward question.

To her relief, Mr Radcliffe chuckled, his eyes crinkling with genuine amusement. "Well, Miss Katherine, you are like my best gun dog and go straight for the target! To be truthful, I do not know the exact extent of our wealth. I leave all that to Father. I have enough to buy a fine horse when I so desire."

"Surely you must have some idea?" Katherine pressed, undeterred by his self-confessed ignorance.

Mr Radcliffe's laughter subsided as he contemplated his response. "No idea, I'm afraid. I believe there are more important things in life than tallying one's fortune."

If the Radcliffes were more frequent visitors to the Tobin home, they would have learned that Sir George did not hold such an opinion. Wealth would vie for first place with preening in front of a mirror.

Moire was grateful for Mr Radcliffe's kind-hearted nature despite her sister's intrusive questions.

"I must thank you again, Mr Radcliffe, for both the ride home and for access to your extensive family library," Moire said when the horses halted before their house.

As they stepped down from the carriage, Moire spied her older sister Augusta, watching them from an upstairs window. No doubt she would report to their father that Mr Radcliffe saw them home. That would add fuel to his determination to see his middle daughter married to a man who would one day, when both his uncle and father passed, have a title settle on his shoulders.

"Perhaps next time you could ride over? There are some lovely hills to canter along, if I could be so bold as to accompany you?" He had an open and hopeful expression in his brown eyes, and Moire didn't have the heart to refuse.

"That does sound lovely." Moire waved and followed her sister inside, who immediately demanded that the maids draw her a bath after her exhausting day.

Later that night, in the sanctuary of her bedchamber, Moire sat engrossed in the ancient tome she had borrowed from the Radcliffe library. The piptere egg lay nestled in its basket on her bedside table. A faint crack, like a twig being stepped on, made her look up from the book. She glanced around the room, wondering what could have made the noise. Then her breath caught in her throat as she spotted a hairline fracture along the mottled egg's surface. A clear sign it might soon hatch.

Dragons took ten years to hatch, but the much smaller piptere took less than ten weeks. As a matter of priority, she should learn more about the small creatures that were much sought after by nobles. She flicked through pages in the book until she came to the section about the amphiptere, with detailed illustrations and descriptions of the tiny dragon species.

"Small but fiercely intelligent," she whispered, tracing a finger along the image of a fully grown piptere. "Pipteres are loyal to their chosen companion, and some have likened their behaviour to cats. They seem insolent to those they deem beneath their notice."

They sounded like small creatures with big opinions of themselves. Moire smiled at the thought of having a piptere of her own, a tiny member of the dragon family that would expand her knowledge.

Two days later, a soft tapping roused Moire from her afternoon reading. Her gaze darted to the egg on her bedside table. A tiny black beak wedged itself in the crack that had ruptured days earlier. She rushed over and cradled the basket in her arms, taking it back to the window seat and watched, fascinated, as the piptere fought to emerge from its egg.

Piece by piece, bits of shell fell away to reveal an indigo head. It arched its neck and chirruped before struggling against the remaining egg. Moire thought it safe to help, since the creature was obviously alive and keen to greet the world.

With care, she prised away more shell until the piptere was free. About the size of a newborn chick, its body was slick from the contents of its embryonic sack. From what she had read, it would need to dry out before she could see if it had scales or feathers. Wings flapped weakly as it learned how its body worked.

"Welcome to the world, little one," Moire whispered, entranced by the dark-blue hide flecked with silver and grey swirls. The newborn gazed at her with intelligent silver eyes as if it understood her words.

Lucy entered the room, intent on fetching the luncheon tray, but recoiled in fear on seeing the hatchling. "Oh, heavens! A dragon! It'll scratch out our eyes or set fire to the curtains!"

"Calm yourself, Lucy. This little creature will grow no bigger than a chicken. They are common pets among the higher levels of the aristocracy." Although her new companion would never wear a golden chain or be imprisoned in a gilded cage.

"Is it a boy or a girl, then?" Lucy peered over Moire's shoulder.

"I do not know. I believe we have to wait until we are informed about gender and the piptere's preferred name. They are somewhat like dragons in that they are born knowing who they are." How she envied that. Even after eighteen years, Moire didn't know who she was.

The piptere nuzzled against Moire's palm and cooed softly. She smiled at the offer of friendship, feeling an instant bond forming between them.

"Bring that tray over, please, Lucy." Moire gestured to the luncheon tray left on the end of the bed. Fortunately, it included sliced meat, and Moire broke off tiny bits and fed them to her new friend. A suggestion she had gleaned from her studies. She delighted in the way the piptere's long tail twitched with satisfaction.

Between the afternoon sun and a rub with an old scarf, the piptere's hide dried to reveal scales on its sides and legs, with a strip of feathers that ran from the top of its head down along its spine to the base of its tail.

"Now, my friend, do you have a name?" Moire asked as the creature's eyelids grew heavy, its belly distended from the meal.

Clipper. I am male. He didn't speak the words aloud but sent them directly to Moire's mind.

"Clipper. Why, how marvellous that you bear a nautical name. A clipper is a fast vessel. Hello, Clipper. I am pleased to meet you. I am Moire." She tucked the shawl around the little creature, and soon, soft snoring noises came from the basket.

That evening at the family dinner table, Moire could hardly contain her excitement. "I have most marvellous news. This afternoon, my piptere egg hatched."

"Good Lord!" Sir George bellowed, his face turning a deep shade of red. "You bought a wyrm into this house? I'll not have it, Moire!"

Moire steeled her spine. "Mr Radcliffe found the egg and gifted it to me, Father. Remember? It would have been rude to refuse, would it not?"

Sir George drew a deep breath and snorted. "I suppose it is a good sign that he gave you a gift, even if it's one of those hideous creatures."

"Pipteres are highly sought after pets among the *ton*. I believe the queen and all her ladies have them. They are loyal and intelligent." A cold lump settled inside Moire that her father might demand Clipper's removal.

"The queen, you say?" Sir George mused, his interest piqued. He stroked his chin thoughtfully before his eyes landed on Augusta, his eldest daughter. "Very well, Moire, you are to give this creature to your sister. It is a fitting pet for a duchess, since others at court have them. Wouldn't you agree, my dear?"

"Oh, yes. Why, I hear Princess Caroline has one that can do tricks. It is all the rage among the ladies as they compete to see whose chicken is the most clever." Augusta smirked at Moire's crestfallen expression.

Beneath the table, Moire clenched her fists and refused to surrender Clipper.

"Pipteres are not chattels. Nor are they chickens. They

have distinct personalities and bond with a person they trust. It is only fair to Clipper, as a living being, that he is allowed to choose his own companion. Otherwise, he will forever try to escape if he is trapped with a person not of his choice." Moire's throat went dry after she made her speech. Would her father extend to the little creature an opportunity not afforded to her? She twisted the moonstone ring on her finger.

Her father huffed and opened his mouth to protest, but Augusta spoke up. "Very well, it shall choose. Although I am sure it would rather live in a fine house in London with a duchess than with a farmer's wife in some dim cottage. It could be decades before enough relatives die to make Mr Radcliffe a viscount."

Sir George chortled and toasted his eldest daughter. Moire fixed her gaze on her plate. Let them believe she would acquiesce to their plans and wed a farmer instead of a sailor. She would be like a stone. Water might erode her surface, but she would remain steadfast at her core. Nothing could erase her love for Oliver. It was the one constant in her life that never wavered.

The next morning, she fed a hungry Clipper who had already grown a little overnight. Then Moire rubbed his hide with a silken scarf to make his scales shine before she carried him downstairs to the parlour.

"Is that it? I thought it would be more...impressive looking." Augusta peered at the young piptere in Moire's cupped hands.

"Clipper is only a hatchling. He will grow to the size of a small chicken, although with larger wings." Moire stroked his feathered head. The deep blue with silver swirls reminded her of a naval uniform with silver buttons, and her heart ached for Oliver.

"I suppose the maid can tend it until it is of a size to impress my friends and can do tricks. Come here," Augusta said in an imperious voice as she extended one arm.

Moire uncurled her hands so that Clipper sat on her open palms. Unshed tears heated her eyes. Her family would strip everything she loved away from her. "Augusta will make a grand match, Clipper, and she will be much about London society once she weds."

The piptere turned whirling silver eyes to Moire. *London?* He asked her silently.

"Yes. It is the largest city in all of England and where our king and queen live." Moire tried to speak with a light tone to hide her despair at losing her new friend.

"Let's get this over with so I can properly acquaint myself with my new pet." Reaching into her pocket, Augusta extracted a golden chain. Before Moire could object, her sister had looped one end around Clipper's arched neck and clicked it closed. Then she tugged on the leash to urge the creature to fly to her outstretched arm.

"Moire?" Clipper squawked as his young body was wrenched sideways and out of Moire's palms.

"You cannot leash him!" Moire flung out her hands to catch Clipper as his untested wings flapped to balance his body.

Augusta had yanked too hard, and combined with little Clipper's flapping wings, he leapt onto her head. His claws sank into the abundant curls. Augusta shrieked and dropped the leash as she frantically batted at the creature. Her once composed visage contorted in panic. Hairpins scattered on the floor as Clipper's scrambling feet pulled her hair loose.

"Get it off me!" she screamed, flailing about wildly and trying to strike the piptere.

"You need to hold still," Moire whispered soothing words to the upset hatchling and her near-hysterical sister. Eventually, she managed to grab him and cradled him against her chest. She undid the golden chain and let it fall to the carpet, where it pooled around the dislodged hair-pins. Clipper's long tail curled around her wrist, either to reassure himself or ensure that Augusta didn't try to snatch him away again

"What a hideous creature. Look what it has done to my hair!" Augusta tried to sweep her tangled locks back up onto her head. "I never want to see it ever again. Vile thing!" With that, she stormed from the room.

"I am sorry that she hurt you. Never again will I let anyone put a chain around your neck." Moire stroked Clipper's feathered head. Her concern for the little dragon's wellbeing mingled with relief. He was hers, and no one would try to take him away from her again.

SEVERAL WEEKS LATER, as autumn leaves spiralled through the air outside, a letter arrived for Moire. She turned the thick envelope over and recognised Oliver's handwriting. She hurried to the privacy of her bedroom before her father could snatch the missive from her. Only when she pressed her door shut did she break the seal and unfold the pages.

In his small, neat script, Oliver recounted the horrors he had witnessed on his vessel and the mighty dragon, Valiant, who fought alongside them in battle. At the end of his letter, he had added a short poem.

"Though miles apart we may be,

Your love shines bright, like moon on sea.

For you, my heart will ever yearn,

Till once again, to you, I return."

His words renewed the love and hope within Moire. No matter the distance or obstacles that lay between them, their love would endure.

Moire traced each letter with a fingertip as in her mind, she imagined Oliver writing the words. A jagged line was a roll of the ship that made his quill slip. The hurriedly formed sentences, when he was called on deck by the captain and he rushed to finish his letter. She kissed the paper, and then tucked the letter under her pillow. There was an important duty Moire had to undertake before she could undress and join Oliver in her dreams.

"We have a mission, Clipper." She held out her hand to the piptere.

The little creature hopped his way up her arm to her shoulder. His tail curled around her neck, and he batted his head against her cheek to indicate he was ready. Like Faustus, while the piptere could talk, he preferred to communicate directly with her mind. And he had to be in the mood. Like a cat, he generally preferred silence and meaningful stares.

Moire opened the door and peered into the hallway to ensure none of her family were about. Her father would find some meaningless task for her to complete if he spotted her. Augusta would demand to know what she was about, and Katherine would probably insist she write a touching eulogy for when death inevitably claimed her.

With a soft tread, she ventured along the hall and down the stairs. Clipper clung to her shoulder, his tiny claws clutching at the fabric of her shawl. Moire slipped through the almost silent kitchens, the maids busy washing and drying the last of the dishes used for their supper.

Outside in the cool air, she drew a breath and listened to the night. Faustus would be roaming the grounds, sniffing out anyone who shouldn't be prowling around the property in the dark. While the wyvern protected the world beyond his burrow, Moire would reassure herself about the safety of something within his home.

6

Moire held a finger to her lips and indicated to her little companion that they were to remain silent, as he liked to chirp and croon as though he narrated events. Clipper tilted his head, and his bright eyes reflected the scant moonlight filtering through the clouds.

She walked across the yard and around the side of the stables. The grass of the meadow was damp and clung to the hem of her dress so that the fabric hung heavier behind her like an anchor. At the entrance to the burrow, she placed a hand on the cool earth.

"Faustus?" While he wouldn't be inside, it seemed polite to call his name before intruding on his home.

When there was no answering reply, she ventured into the earth. Keeping one hand on the side of the tunnel, she followed the curves to the chamber below. Only then did she reach into her pocket for the nub of candle and tinder box. Striking a flame, she lit the wick and held it well away from the flammable hay of the wyvern's bed.

Watching where she placed each foot, Moire made her

way to the back of the nest. There, against the rounded side of the wall, she knelt and dug into the bedding. She uncovered the curve of the egg and placed a hand flat on its surface. Warmth and a faint tingle rippled over her skin.

"Sleep well, my friend, and grow into a magnificent dragon," she murmured as she stroked the shell.

Relief loosened her shoulders. The dream that she and Oliver held for the future remained safe. Moire covered the egg with hay and blew out the candle. Using touch to guide her, she followed the smoothed earth back along the tunnel.

As she prepared for bed and then snuggled under the blankets, she imagined a life where Oliver was admitted to the Draco Legion. At last, her father would have to look up to the naval officer and would give his consent for them to wed.

THE NEXT MORNING, Moire stood at the parlour window, mentally reviewing her list of tasks for the day, when Samuel Radcliffe rode up the driveway. She waited as he dismounted his horse and stomped mud from his boots by the front door before his frame filled the parlour doorway.

"Miss Moire, I wondered if you might be free to ride with me this morning?" he asked, struggling to meet her gaze, his hands clasped nervously behind his back.

"A ride?" Sir George entered the room. "Of course you must, Moire. Take that horrid creature with you. Augusta is quite terrified of it after it savaged her. You are lucky she wasn't scarred for life."

"Clipper did no such thing, Father. He was merely frightened," Moire defended her new friend.

"What savage beast is this? Do I need to fetch my gun?" Mr Radcliffe glanced from Moire to her father.

"Oh, no. The piptere egg you gave me hatched. The little fellow is called Clipper." When Moire left her room that morning, the hatchling had been snoring quietly in his basket nest.

"I would like to see him, if I may?" Mr Radcliffe asked.

"Of course. I shall ask him to accompany us when I go to change and have a groom ready my horse." Moire excused herself, first passing on the message that she required a horse saddled. She quickly changed into her riding habit, which was made of a robust, light wool. Clipper perched on her shoulder and curled his tail around her neck. The feathered tuft on the end nestled against the base of her throat as though she wore a pendant.

Outside, the silver swirls on his feathers and hide shimmered in the sun. The horse snorted at the piptere, and Clipper curled himself tighter around Moire's neck.

"He is a handsome-looking fellow," Mr Radcliffe said as he settled in the saddle.

Clipper trilled against Moire's ears. Apparently, he enjoyed being complimented.

As they rode through the fields, Clipper became bold and darted from Moire's shoulder to swoop and dive around them. She delighted in his antics, the sun flashing along his stripe of feathers.

"Your kind act has brought great joy into my life," she said.

"Ah, well," Mr Radcliffe stammered, fumbling with the

reins. "I just thought...you know, that you might enjoy having such a unique thing."

"Indeed, I do," Moire replied, smiling as Clipper performed a loop-de-loop before returning to her shoulder.

"I must say, Miss Moire, that I do rather...enjoy your company," Mr Radcliffe garbled the words and then fell silent.

"And I, yours. I consider you a dear friend." Moire chose her words carefully, not wanting to offend.

"A friend?" He pulled his horse to a halt.

"Yes. Sadly, you could never be anything more than that to me, as my heart belongs to another." Moire gentled her tone, not wanting to hurt someone who had given her such a marvellous gift as Clipper.

"Oh. Umm...I see," Mr Radcliffe replied, his gaze suddenly distant.

The rest of the ride passed in awkward silence, both lost in their own thoughts.

Back at the house, Mr Radcliffe touched the brim of his hat and then cantered away. Moire shut herself in the study while Clipper slept in a patch of sunlight on the windowsill. On top of the large account book sat a hurriedly dashed note from her father, advising that Lady Beaumont would join them for luncheon and to ensure the menu was to her standards.

"Oh, dear," Moire murmured as she read the rest of the note. Her father wished for his friend's opinion on which wallpaper to purchase. "Augusta had better marry a duke soon." Once her older sister made the much-anticipated *match of the season*, her father could spend his new son-in-law's fortune instead of their dwindling one.

Although, how exactly Augusta would attract the attention of the titled and wealthy suitor from the Wyldefen countryside had never been made clear to Moire. Was it perhaps like the fairytales, and one would happen upon the beautiful young woman after his horse threw a shoe in the neighbouring meadow? As the tales went, the beautiful maiden would offer their home as a place for the handsome noble to wait while a farrier was summoned, and the two would fall instantly in love and be engaged before the end of the day.

Moire blew out a sigh but couldn't proclaim the idea ridiculous. Her own love story started when she touched Oliver's hand as they both reached for the same book. They spent hours discussing that book on dragons before the lateness of the hour summoned her home. She had walked as though clouds cushioned her every step, her heart alight with love for the handsome and thoughtful young man.

Her gaze settled on Clipper, curled up on a shawl on the sill. The little creature grew larger every day and was now comparable to a bantam. From the book she read, he was nearly at his full size.

She had much in her life to be grateful for. "I wish both my sisters will find the same sort of love I share with Oliver."

Once the accounts were done and the menu sorted, Moire and Clipper ventured out into the garden. She appreciated the wild beauty of the overgrown beds, that soothed her mind and offered her a peaceful sanctuary. It also served as a playground for Clipper.

The piptere stretched his wings and soared across the leggy shrubs towards an old, broken fountain. The once-elegant structure was now covered in moss and ivy. He used the claws on the tips of his wings to clamber up the moss-covered stones. Each day, he grew stronger, his body more agile and powerful. Moire couldn't wait to show Oliver the smallest member of dragonkind and share her observations about the creature's growth and development.

As Clipper splashed playfully in the murky fountain water, Moire daydreamed about what creature might hatch from Oliver's hard-won egg. Her mind worried over issues of size. Could a dragon as large as Caliban grow from such a humble origin? If the painting was accurate, her family's deceased dragon had hatched from an egg about half as big again.

Faustus and other wyverns were much smaller, and from what she saw at the old abandoned nest, their eggs were not too dissimilar to the one now resting in the burrow. But Clipper had emerged from an egg the same size as one laid by a goose and had grown many times bigger than the shell that once encased him.

She tried to set aside such worries. Patience was required, as the egg could have years yet to incubate, although a wyvern would hatch in as little as one year. She sat on an old stone bench and watched Clipper bathe in the crumbling fountain basin. As a child, she had delighted in waving her hands through the clear water that spouted from the central piece while her mother sat with a book.

Lost in thought, Moire barely noticed the soft crunch of approaching footsteps. Lady Beaumont, clad in a rich-blue riding habit, appeared in the ragged hole cut through the yew hedge.

"Why, here you are, Moire. How your mother loved

this spot." She brushed a hand over a straggly rose years overdue a prune, with bright-red rose hips ready for autumn. She took a seat next to Moire and watched the piptere finish his ablutions.

"Good afternoon, Lady Beaumont. I was remembering how mother used to sit here and read while I played in the fountain." Perhaps over winter, she could learn how to tend to the roses, and next spring, the sheltered garden might once more be full of the scent from their sweet blooms.

"She was a gifted gardener, and her touch is much missed," Lady Beaumont said.

By more than just the roses, Moire thought. Her family suffered a fate similar to that of the garden without her mother's nurturing hand. Her father was like a climbing ivy spurting rampant growth in the wrong direction and reaching for what he shouldn't. Augusta, a rose of rare beauty subject to infestations of mites. Katherine was the tender perennial who languished in the wrong conditions. What would Moire be, she wondered? A sapling, perhaps, being strangled by the ivy.

For a long minute, both women were lost in silent reflection. Lady Beaumont reached out and took Moire's hand. "I worry for you, Moire. You seem to be retreating from your family more each day."

"I assure you, Lady Beaumont, I have not gone anywhere. I have a scholarly interest in dragons. Since Mr Radcliffe gave me such a generous gift, I have been trying to learn all I can about pipteres." She gestured to the creature who had flown to a sun-warmed stone to preen his scales and feathers. He spread his wings wide to peck at them with his beak. Moire wished she could fly away like the little piptere and leave her troubles behind.

"Your father worries that this interest might be inappropriate for a young woman, and it is to the detriment of your duties." Her voice carried a worried inflection, but there was a glint in her eyes that made Moire guard her inner thoughts.

"I am ever mindful of my family's needs. I do not put reading a book above what they require." Nor would she ever have the chance. It seemed her waking hours were as busy as any housekeeper for a much larger household.

"I understand it is not books that concern Sir George, although he does not wish to see you require spectacles. There is some worry about the amount of time you spend underground in the wyvern burrow." A brief apologetic smile flashed over her face as though Sir George had sent her to demand to know the reasons behind Moire's movements outside the house.

Moire considered her words carefully. Lady Beaumont might be an old friend of the family, but nothing would pull the secret from her about what was hidden in the wyvern nest. "Faustus is old and alone since Caliban died. I try to find a little time to spend with him after I have finished my other chores."

"It speaks much of your nature that you care for such a malformed creature." Lady Beaumont let go of Moire's hand and smoothed a wrinkle in the wool of her habit. "While I could never replace your dear mother, I have done my best to ease her absence by providing what maternal advice I can. I hope you know, Moire, that you can talk to me about anything that might be praying upon your mind."

A cold finger of warning stroked down Moire's spine, but she kept an open expression on her face to conceal the secrets she hid. "Of course. Your counsel is much appreciated."

But not always welcome, she added silently. Nor would she be persuaded from the course of action she had set. Despite what her mother's friend said about Oliver being an unsuitable husband, she would stay steadfast in her commitment to him.

Lady Beaumont patted her knee. "Well, you know I am always here, my dear. Since we are in a conspiratorial mood, I shall entertain you with an intriguing snippet of gossip I heard."

"Oh?" Moire made the syllable noncommittal while she wondered what gossip had found its way to the noblewoman.

"I have a footman in my employ who has something of a penchant for attending rather disreputable events." Lady Beaumont winked as she said the word *disreputable*, as though Moire was supposed to discern exactly what she meant.

"I cannot fathom what sort of event that might be," Moire said, feigning disinterest as she plucked at a stray thread on her dress.

"Why, it was an illegal boxing match!" Lady Beaumont said. "Held some weeks ago. The prize in this competition, however, was not the usual purse of gold. No, these men fought for something far more unusual and rare. It was rumoured that the organiser had procured a stolen dragon egg."

Moire glanced at Lady Beaumont as dread settled in

her chest. She prided herself on maintaining her demeanour and, by clasping her hands together, she stopped the tremble in her limbs. "Dragon eggs are incredibly rare. Such a theft would be reported in the newspapers. Surely it was an exaggeration by whoever sought to attract numbers to their event?"

Lady Beaumont waved a dismissive hand in the air. "Dragon, drake, wyvern…they all look the same, do they not?"

"From what books I have borrowed from the Radcliffes, I understand there are subtle differences." Moire kept her gaze fixed on Clipper. The piptere stopped cleaning his scales and sat with his head at an angle as he, too, listened to the story.

"Apparently," Lady Beaumont continued, savouring each word as if it were a delicate morsel, "a combatant known only as the Sailor emerged victorious and was awarded this egg. A fascinating tale, is it not?" She regarded Moire with a curious expression, judging the younger woman's reaction.

Moire's mind raced. Thoughts tumbled over one another in a desperate attempt to make sense of Lady Beaumont's words. Was it possible that she knew about the egg? If so, how much did she actually know, and what were her intentions?

When Moire did not answer, Lady Beaumont continued. "I think it sounds like something out of a novel. A mysterious ordinary sailor in possession of what might be a dragon egg. Imagine the implications."

"Indeed," Moire murmured, fighting to keep her voice steady. Her mind was consumed by the image of Oliver stripped to the waist and covered in blood and sweat as he fought not just for the egg, but to secure a future for them. Her hands were clammy despite the first bite of autumn chill to the light breeze that swirled around the enclosed garden room.

"Of course, one can't believe everything one hears. Particularly from one's servants." Lady Beaumont plucked a spent flower from a nearby bush and twirled it between her fingers. "Rumours are like weeds—they seed in the most unexpected places and spread with alarming speed."

"I imagine if this mysterious figure was a sailor, he would have returned to his vessel and gone off to fight Napoleon, taking his prize with him." Moire dug her fingers into the fabric of her gown to maintain her calm façade.

"Do you think so? In my tale, I imagine him having a sweetheart whom he entrusts with his prize until he returns from war." Lady Beaumont's gaze fixed on Moire like a fox that spots a trapped rabbit.

"As you say, a fanciful tale. You should commend your footman for his imagination. Perhaps he should put it to paper and submit it to a magazine?" Moire held out her arm, and Clipper flew to her and clambered up to her shoulder. The piptere's small body lent her valuable strands of strength to weave around herself.

"Of course, these are just rumours and have nothing to do with us." Lady Beaumont smiled, but it didn't reach her eyes. "But as a woman with some experience of the world, if I found myself in conversation with this fictional sweetheart entangled in matters of dragon eggs, I would advise her to submit herself to the wisdom of her family. There are many who would stop at nothing to possess such a prize, and her father would know better what to do with such a valuable object."

"If your heroine is fortunate enough to possess such a kind family, led by a father of intelligence beyond reproach, then I am sure that is exactly what she would do." Or, if her father were the sort to sell the family silver to buy himself a pretty frippery, the heroine would hold tight to her secrets.

"A young woman with no experience of the world should indeed rely upon the guidance of her father. Otherwise, she might throw away any chance of happiness in society. Our world is cruel to those who do not follow its rules." Lady Beaumont threw away the bloom in her hand as though the unknown heroine was likewise discarded for her foolish choices.

Moire searched for a change of topic and leapt on something that had occupied much of her father's attention lately. "Father and Augusta are excited about the forthcoming ball, and I know your advice has been invaluable in sorting the finer details."

The older woman's gaze became lighter. "It is an excellent experience for Augusta. When she marries, she will oversee many such events in London."

"I think it will be a jolly evening." Moire tried to keep her voice light. While not averse to dancing with an agreeable partner, she much preferred to be curled up in a library.

"I have it on good authority that Mr Radcliffe will be in attendance. He is quite the eligible bachelor, wouldn't you agree? And a good match for a gently bred young woman." Lady Beaumont clapped her hands together in delight.

"Mr Radcliffe is a kind gentleman." Moire's heart twisted painfully at the hint of an engagement between herself and Samuel. She would only ever love Oliver, and the thought of being forced into marriage with anyone else was unbearable.

"You are such a modest wee creature, my dear. I suspect that is what Mr Radcliffe admires about you," Lady Beaumont remarked. "The prospect of joining your two families would bring numerous advantages, both socially and financially."

"As you have reminded me in the past, Lady Beaumont, Augusta takes precedence in these matters and must marry first. It would be improper for me to consider matrimony until my oldest sister has had her chance to be a bride. Unless you are implying that Mr Radcliffe intends to propose to Augusta?" It might have been petty of Moire, but she found a quiet satisfaction in throwing the older woman's words from an earlier occasion back at her.

Lady Beaumont's gaze narrowed, and her lips thinned.

"Shall we find Father? He is probably waiting for us to serve luncheon." Moire stood and ended the conversation.

Later that evening, after Lady Beaumont had returned to her estate and the family had a quiet supper, Moire stood out in the yard between the house and the stables. Her thoughts were as numerous and far-flung as the stars in the night sky. A shuffling heralded Faustus joining her. The wyvern lowered his head in greeting, and Moire placed one arm under his jaw and cradled his head as she stroked his eye ridges.

"Strange. Men," he rasped.

Her hand stilled as those two softly spoken words

stirred up a hurricane of worry inside her. "Poachers?" It could simply be men in the nearby forest looking for deer or pheasant. Yet the earlier conversation with Lady Beaumont kept playing over in her head. There was no doubt she meant to warn Moire about the danger she might be in. But did her mother's friend seek to prevent or cause it?

"Possible," he hissed.

"Let us do nothing for now. It might be a coincidence." She let him go to prowl the grounds and silently prayed that it truly was a coincidence. If not, where could she hide the egg that would keep it both warm and beyond the reach of those who would steal it?

THE NEXT MORNING, Moire was still abed when Lucy rapped softly on the door and pushed inside with the tea tray. Worries had plagued her mind all night, and she had tossed and turned. Clipper, who had taken to sleeping between her pillows, had snorted and stormed off during the night to his basket for an undisturbed sleep.

Flinging the blankets from her tired body, she dropped her feet to the rug and wriggled her toes.

"You look tired, Miss." Lucy placed the tray on the dresser while she opened the curtains.

"I was reading far too late and slept too little," she said. A small untruth, but not an unlikely one for her. If a novel caught her attention, she found it hard to blow out her candle and go to sleep. She couldn't admit to the maid she had fretted all night that ruffians would creep onto the estate and steal a priceless object won by her secret betrothed in an illegal fight.

"Sir George says reading causes wrinkles and that he never indulged, which is why he has the skin of a youthful lad," Lucy said in a serious tone.

Moire couldn't help the smile that tugged at her lips. Her father believed such things and oft repeated them to his girls, hoping to save them from the horrors of...*ageing.*

"My fate is sealed, it would seem. I shall be wrinkled and haggard by the time I am twenty." Crossing to the window, she greeted Clipper with a caress under his chin. Then she opened the window so he could stretch his wings before his breakfast.

"I thought you might want to know, Miss, that a man came to the door early this morning, asking after a sailor. Funny fellow, he was, with a sharp face like a rodent. Or a fox." Lucy had her back to Moire as she pulled open a drawer and selected a fresh chemise. Then she tossed it over the screen in the corner so that it was to hand when Moire needed it.

A chill washed over Moire, and she rubbed at her arms to dispel it before reaching for her robe. She would have a cup of tea before dressing. "A sailor?" she repeated.

A face like a fox. The Fox. Darius Blackwood.

"Yes, Miss. I said that if he meant Lieutenant Hartford, that he has gone off to war. He looked disappointed but just turned and walked away. Wasn't that odd, though? Why did he come here and not to the Hartford farm on the other side of the village?" Lucy shook her head as she collected the tray and placed it on the little table by the window.

"Perhaps he was lost. But it was most odd. Thank you,

Lucy," Moire spoke with a faraway tone as she dropped to the chair and the maid left the room. Her mind galloped around the estate, searching for a better hiding spot. Then her gaze rested on the wardrobe. Could the solution be as simple as concealing the egg in the bottom of her armoire? It would be warm among the pile of blankets and shawls. Her father wouldn't go looking in there.

The only problem would be if Augusta or Katherine took it upon themselves to poke around in her room. Not that Augusta would pry if Clipper was in the room waiting to pounce. She wouldn't want to risk marring her beautiful face with another encounter with his claws. Katherine was usually too ill or oblivious to search another's room.

Moire poured tea and leaned on the windowsill, mulling over what to do as she watched Clipper dip and dive over the trees. "Whoever you are, *strange men*, you'll not lay your hands on the egg. Not with Miss Moire, Clipper, and Faustus to guard its slumber," she murmured.

No one would steal Oliver's dream. Not as long as there was breath in her lungs. One day, a dragon would emerge from that shell, and Oliver would claim a place among the highest peers in the realm. She held that vision tight in her mind and heart.

7

———

Protecting the egg dominated Moire's dreams. Unfortunately, the ball hosted by her father dominated her waking moments. Though the event was supposed to be practice for when Augusta made her Grand Match (even in her mind, Moire heard the words capitalised to stress their importance), much of the work fell on Moire's shoulders. Or perhaps Augusta was learning to delegate to servants, in which case she performed admirably, given how many things she insisted Moire had to do.

Moire desperately needed time to make a secret nest in her armoire. A little trial and error convinced her that if she removed the bottom from one drawer, the space provided by two drawers together would be ample for the egg. Then she had only to wedge the drawers with something so they wouldn't open, which would deter any nosy siblings. If she prised free a board from the bottom of the hanging portion of the wardrobe, she could access the hidey-hole beneath.

At least during the daylight hours, the valuable object slumbered safely with Faustus. As twilight fell, worry gnawed at her. The dance was a day away. Her father watched her like a hawk as though he suspected she would flee into the night like Cinderella at the stroke of midnight.

Clipper became agitated at the number of people flowing through the house. Also, Augusta became strident in her demands and reminded the piptere of when she clicked a leash around his neck.

"Secure that creature in your room, or I shall have it shoved into a pot and dropped in the well." Sir George pointed a finger at Clipper after the little dragon tried to hide behind a tapestry to escape Augusta. His clawed wing had snagged a thread, and he became entangled when his struggles pulled it from the wall.

"Yes, Father." Moire gathered the piptere in her arms and unhooked the offending claw. Then she hurried to her room. "You must stay here and out of the way. I shall leave the window open for you so you can come and go."

As dark fell that night, she still hadn't had time to secure a new home for the egg. Risking her father's wrath, Moire hurried from the house to Faustus's burrow just as the wyvern was emerging for the night.

"Please, Faustus, stay in your burrow tonight. I could not bear it if anything happened to the egg." She placed her hands on either side of his face.

"Safe," he rasped and sent her the image of his body curled around it.

"Once this blasted dance is over, we will move it into the house." Although the idea made more worries multiply inside her. If she left it outside, she risked some criminal, like Darius Blackwood, who she was certain was the man who asked about the Sailor, stealing the egg. Inside, she increased the chance that her father would sniff it out and claim it as his own.

While Moire had planned to undertake a spot of amateur woodwork to create a space for the egg in her armoire, instead, she fell onto her bed, exhausted from the demands of the day.

"Tomorrow," she promised herself, the growing dragon, and Oliver.

It was just as well she hadn't been tinkering in her wardrobe that night, as Augusta burst into her room unannounced. Clipper squawked in alarm and burrowed under the pillow.

"The floral arrangements are all wrong! My reputation shall be ruined if they are not moved to where we discussed," her sister berated her in a high-pitched tone that cut through Moire's tired mind.

"I shall remedy the situation in the morning, Augusta," Moire promised sleepily, barely raising her head off the pillow.

"Well, see that you do. This could ruin my chance of securing a duke, you know," Augusta said.

Moire doubted that very much, as there had not been any ducal sightings within a fifty-mile radius of their village.

The next morning, she dragged her body from her bed and donned an old gown and apron for the final tasks before the dance. She cast a look at the armoire.

"Soon," she promised. After the dance, none of her family would emerge before the next afternoon, and she would have ample chance to execute her plan while they slept.

Between moving floral arrangements a mere two inches to preserve her sister's reputation as a hostess, cleaning, overseeing the placement of chairs, organising the refreshment table, and supervising the menu for the evening, Moire didn't know how she would have any energy left to dance.

As it happened, she barely had time to wash and change clothes before the first guests arrived. Not that she was needed to greet anyone. Sir George stood with Augusta at his side as the two took all the compliments for organising the evening.

Moire enjoyed a rare moment of peace as her family was otherwise occupied. She couldn't remember the last time they had used the ballroom. Usually, the windows were shuttered and the chandeliers covered in enormous bags pulled tight at the top to protect the crystals.

Tonight, the room was lit with golden brilliance. Rainbows were cast from the pendants and spun around the room. The parterre floor was polished, and couples performed the steps to a country dance. Mr Radcliffe approached her, tugging his cravat and looking uncomfortable in his formal wear. He bowed.

"Miss Moire, you are looking lovely this evening," he said.

She glanced at her gown of cream muslin with an embroidered hem of green vines. It was at least two seasons old and had once belonged to Augusta. But she and Lucy had adjusted it to fit her form, and it was far finer and prettier than anything else in her wardrobe.

"Thank you, Mr Radcliffe. I hope you and your mother are enjoying the evening." She glanced around to spot Mrs

Radcliffe talking with the other matrons to one side. Mr Radcliffe senior was still in London overseeing some business dealings.

"Um...I was wondering if perhaps you might honour me with a dance?" He shuffled from foot to foot as though practising the steps of the dance.

A cotillion was announced, and she held out her hand to him. "Of course."

Having issued the invitation, Mr Radcliffe struggled for conversational topics, and they danced in silence for the first few moves. Moire asked about his dogs, and he happily told her all about the latest litter of puppies.

"You must come to see them, Miss Moire. They will be fine shooting dogs, every one of them." He beamed as he extolled the virtues of the parents who produced the litter.

For her part, Moire managed to keep a smile on her face, even when her partner trod on her toes. Mr Radcliffe was not the suitor she wished to dance with. She focused on the intricate patterns of the polished floor beneath them. Counting each step in time with the music, she pretended that Oliver was here and it was his strong hand that took hers instead.

Then, as the music swelled to its crescendo, a sudden thought pierced her disquiet—the egg. Was it safe? The light and noise would be painful to the wyvern, and she hoped that he had stayed in his burrow with their precious charge. Worry about the sharp-faced man who asked for the Sailor plagued her thoughts, and a shiver ran down her spine, despite the warmth of the ballroom. It had to be Mr Blackwood. The villain who had vowed the egg would be his. Somehow, he had traced Oliver to Eadred Manor.

"I say, Miss Moire, are you quite all right? You look like my Bessie after she got into a rancid bit of meat," Mr Radcliffe asked as the dance ended, and he escorted her to the side of the room.

Moire remembered Bessie was one of his dogs. "Yes. Just a little too warm."

"Ah, there you are." Sir George cut towards them. His trim figure was clad in an ornately embroidered waistcoat of emerald green and bronze with a matching jacket over the top. Lady Beaumont clung to Sir George's arm. The older woman resplendent in a gown of a similar green that complimented her dark colouring.

"Father, Lady Beaumont," Moire murmured as she wondered at the cost of the new outfit, something her father had kept hidden until tonight.

"Mr Radcliffe and I had a most enlightening conversation earlier this evening." His eyes gleamed with something cold as he spoke, and Moire stilled like a rabbit caught in a snare as the hunter approached. "He asked for your hand in marriage, and naturally, I gave my consent."

"No," Moire whispered. The room became too small and full of far too many people. The laughter of the other dancers faded into a distant murmur.

"Augusta should marry first, of course, but society won't take any note of what you do, and you will be out here in the country." Sir George waved his hand.

Lady Beaumont took Moire's hand. "This is the most wonderful news, is it not?"

Mr Radcliffe grinned, as pleased with himself as if his dog had snatched a pheasant from the air and dropped it at his feet.

Moire's heart plummeted like a stone cast into a dark abyss. The finality of her father's words struck her with the force of a brutal gale, leaving her breathless and reeling. She could hardly bear to look at Mr Radcliffe, the man they all decided would become her husband, regardless of her opinion on the matter.

She rubbed the moonstone ring for strength. "I cannot," she said, daring to meet Mr Radcliffe's warm brown gaze. "I am sorry, Mr Radcliffe. You are a most kind man, and I consider you a dear friend, but I cannot."

Lady Beaumont patted her arm. "You are just a little overwhelmed at the news, Moire, that is all. Why, I fainted when Lord Beaumont proposed to me."

"Please, Father, I beg of you to reconsider," Moire managed to choke out. "I have an understanding with Lieutenant Hartford."

"Do not mention that name in this house," Sir George hissed, and his blue gaze turned thunderous. "You shall become Mr Radcliffe's wife. One day, when his uncle and father die, you will be mistress of Gormsby Hall and a viscountess. No young woman could want more."

"Love, Father. I want love. That means far more than any title or fortune," Moire whispered, her eyes burning with tears.

"Love?" Sir George scoffed, waving his hand dismissively. "That is for penniless poets dying in gutters. What matters in this world is wealth and position. You are most fortunate to be offered both."

Moire shook her head. If her father denied her engagement to Oliver, she would rather die a spinster than be forced into a loveless match. "I am sorry, Mr Radcliffe. You deserve a wife who loves you."

"You will do as you are told!" Sir George huffed.

Moire couldn't breathe in the stifling atmosphere of the room full of people. Words wouldn't form in her too-dry mouth. She shook her head, cast a sorrowful look at Mr Radcliffe...and ran. Rather like Cinderella, after all. She pushed through the crowd to gain the space offered by the entranceway; then she darted through the open doors and out into the night. Her skirts flowed around her like an unfurled sail.

Behind her came the distant command from her father to stop immediately and do as she was told. Feet pounded on the tiles behind her. Someone pursued her. She ran faster before she was dragged back inside and imprisoned for her insolence. Out in the drive, she paused to allow blissful cool air to wash over her heated body. A sob welled up in her throat, but she pushed it down. The world outside was shrouded in darkness, and the faint strains of music from the ballroom blended with the gentle breeze and call of owls and other nocturnal creatures.

Then, a high-pitched screech cut through the air and gooseflesh erupted along her arms.

"Faustus." Moire turned in the direction of the alarmed call.

Movement caught her eye, lit by light spilling from the house. A fleeing shadow was barely visible against the darkened shrubbery. A man hurried from the direction of the stables, something clutched in his arms. Some distance behind him, Faustus screamed in rage and charged. The wyvern beat his wings and hopped into the air, gliding a few paces before dropping to the ground and waddling a few more feet.

Fear clenched Moire's heart. "Stop!" she screamed, then she ploughed after the thief.

"Miss Tobin! It is not safe!" Mr Radcliffe shouted. He had been the one running after her, and he continued after her through the dark.

Moire cursed her dancing shoes as she ran over the gravel of the drive and the uneven ground of the lawn. *Faster*, she urged her body; *I must run faster*. She had to catch the slender shadow. Faustus glided past her. He had sufficient height that his claws snagged the shoulders of the man's coat.

The thief cried out and stumbled. As the man threw out his hands to break his fall, the object he carried tumbled to the ground.

"No!" Moire screamed as a sound like a vase dropping onto tiles exploded in the still night.

In one moment that seemed to last an eternity, Moire was frozen in place as the thief stared at the fallen item. Then time resumed, and he abandoned his prize, shooting towards the forest with Faustus in pursuit. Moire ran to where the egg lay. Moonlight caressed the glistening contents.

"No," she whimpered as she fell to her knees. The egg had shattered on rocks in the grass and cracked open as though a giant cook had rapped it against a bowl. Her hands hovered above the poor creature so cruelly ejected into the world. Small wings were folded back against a half-formed body coated in thick, gelatinous sludge.

Sobs broke from her as she picked up a piece of shell

and cried for the death of the dragon and her dream. Gently, she gathered up the embryo, torn years too soon from its nourishing sack.

"Miss Tobin? Are you hurt?" Mr Radcliffe asked as he joined her.

Curious guests flowed out of the house. Some of the men bore lanterns and held them high to illuminate the scene. Moire barely registered their presence as they encircled her. Her world was consumed by the fragile and dead creature she cradled in her shaking hands.

"What has she done?" someone gasped, and speculative whispers spread through the crowd.

"Is that a baby dragon?" a woman asked in a high-pitched voice.

"It was," Lady Beaumont said. Then, in a clear tone, she announced, "that was rather a dramatic and symbolic breaking of an unwanted engagement, my dear. Intact, that egg could have fetched a handsome purse to benefit your family. Or elevated your beloved father back to his previous rank."

The words filtered through the horror swirling in Moire's mind. Surely she misheard, and Lady Beaumont wasn't suggesting she deliberately smashed the egg to sever her ties to Oliver? "I did not do this! There was a man. He stole it."

"What man?" Sir George hurried towards the group. His lip curled in disgust at the dead creature in Moire's hands. "Whatever have you done, girl?"

"Please, you must believe me," Moire implored, her voice barely audible above the rising chatter of the gathered crowd. "I would never harm any member of dragonkind.

There was a thief. Faustus chased him into the forest. Faustus almost had him, but he tripped and dropped the egg."

But her words fell on deaf ears, drowned out by the growing tide of accusations. She scanned the surrounding faces, searching for any sign of understanding. Hoping to find an ally among them. But she only found cold judgement and betrayal staring back at her.

"Mr Radcliffe, you saw the running man, did you not?" She implored the suitor she had only minutes before rejected.

He stared off at the night-blanketed forest. "Your wyvern has scented the trail. Let us hope he catches the fiend."

But his confirmation of her tale went unheard as rumours flowed around them. What need did the guests have for the truth when the tale they crafted was far more entertaining?

"Imagine destroying such a rare creature," someone said.

"I didn't do it," Moire cried over the bundle. Heedless of the damage to her gown, she cradled it close to her body, hoping for some miracle to stir within the lifeless body.

"Miss Tobin just got engaged to Mr Radcliffe. Perhaps that had something to do with it? Lady Beaumont said something about breaking a previous arrangement," a man speculated.

Desperation clawed at the inside of Moire like a caged animal seeking escape. She dared not glance at the guests, afraid to see them believing the hateful lies being spun around her. "You all heard Faustus raise the alarm. He was chasing the man."

"Where is the hideous old thing, then? Where is this thief you claim he chased?" Sir George asked, casting around the circle of light.

"There are too many lanterns. He cannot emerge, or they will hurt his eyes. You will have to extinguish them before he can reappear." Even to Moire's ears, her words had the hollow ring of excuses.

As the accusations continued to crash against her like tempestuous waves, Moire's heart fractured alongside the shattered pieces of the egg. Isolated and betrayed, she tried to speak up but found her voice smothered beneath the weight of scorn.

FAUSTUS DID NOT RETURN for over an hour, and by then everyone had become bored and returned to the house to continue dancing. The thief had escaped into the night. The wyvern was unable to pursue him past the boundary of his tether.

Even Mr Radcliffe, uncomfortable in the silence as she grieved, slipped away. Although he did send a groundsman to watch over her, having roused the man from his bed. With the servant's help, Moire buried the little creature, who never had the chance to draw breath. She chose a spot in the forest close to Caliban as a suitable place for its eternal rest. She laid the shards of egg alongside it, keeping only a tiny portion, which she tucked inside her bodice.

Faustus mourned alongside her. The groundsman

returned to his bed, reassured that the wyvern would guide her back to the house.

"What happened, Faustus?" the words rasped over her tongue.

Moire flung her arms around his neck and huddled against his warm hide as she cried. How would she ever tell Oliver? He had risked so much, entrusted his future to her, and now...everything was shattered. Her dreams were spun glass that had been destroyed on a cold slate floor.

The wyvern's regret and sorrow washed over her. From what Moire pieced together, her father had insisted the wyvern patrol the grounds and would not let him stay in his burrow like he had the previous night. Unable to tolerate the light coming from the house, he had been forced to hover away from his subterranean home. Too late, he had spotted the man emerging from the earth with the egg in his arms.

When there was nothing more Moire could do, and as dawn hovered on the horizon, she let Faustus return to his burrow to hide from the rising sun and dragged her feet up to her room. Her gown and slippers were ruined. As she stripped them off, she touched the shard to her lips. Then she tucked it into a drawer with her stockings.

Climbing into bed, Moire curled into a ball and wept. Clipper huddled beside her and trilled his own words of mourning.

Thankfully, she didn't have to face her family the next day and stayed in her bed. Lucy brought a tray but said nothing. For two days, Moire managed to avoid her father before being summoned to his study. She stood with her head bowed and her hands clasped before her.

"I am ashamed to call you my daughter," he said as he tossed a letter onto the cluttered surface of his desk. "To think you had a valuable dragon egg in your possession, and you selfishly kept it hidden from me."

His words were no surprise to her. Nor did they matter anymore. The egg was destroyed, and all the hopes and dreams it contained along with it.

"At least this will put an end to your nonsense with that sailor. You will marry Mr Radcliffe in a month's time. The banns will be read this Sunday, and the announcement has already been placed in the newspapers." He rose from his chair and stalked to the fire, looking up at Drac Tobin.

"I will not marry Mr Radcliffe, and you cannot force me," her voice was quiet but laced with steel.

"Would you rather be an old, wrinkled spinster, existing on the charity of your betters?" Sir George huffed.

Moire met his gaze. "Yes."

Her father's jaw fell open. Displaying a rare moment of intelligence and realising no amount of yelling or threats would change her mind, he slammed his mouth shut and waved her away. "Go, and stay out of my sight."

That was an easy command to obey. Moire retreated to her room and agonised for hours over how to break the news to Oliver. She wrote to him of the man asking about the Sailor and her suspicions that it had been Darius Blackwood. Then she told him of the intruders Faustus had detected. She pleaded with Oliver to forgive her for failing to move the egg sooner. No condemnation could be worse than that she heaped upon herself.

She promised to devote herself to studying dragons. If somewhere within such knowledge was the information on how to secure another egg, then she would find it. Their dream was delayed, that was all. The ember still lived and would flare brightly one day.

That week, a rather nasty caricature appeared in the newspaper. It depicted a grinning woman hurling a dragon egg to the ground while others around her cheered. The caption read—*break plates at a wedding, but shatter eggs for an engagement.*

Moire threw the paper onto the fire, where the drawn figure crumpled and burned for its crime.

It was some weeks before the footman delivered a package for her, wrapped in brown paper and sealed with plain wax. The knots in her stomach tightened at her name scrawled across it in familiar handwriting. Oliver.

Heedless of the curious eyes of her family, Moire fled to her room and slammed the door. Then she wedged the chair under the handle to ensure she remained undisturbed. Clipper chirruped from his basket, and his eyes whirled with concern.

Her hands trembled as she untied the string and peeled back the paper. In the centre sat a stack of her letters to Oliver. The topmost one, the most recent, detailing what happened that night and her tearful apology, was unopened.

"Oliver," she breathed his name, even as the first slice of betrayal cut through her.

A folded sheet sat atop her returned mail, along with a clipping from the local newspaper. The horrible cartoon of her smashing the egg to celebrate her engagement as those around her clapped and cheered. She unfolded the paper with trembling fingers. A few words were scrawled down the sheet in a hurried hand.

Trust

Love

Our engagement

The egg

All irrevocably broken

We are no longer bound to one another

Those words spread poison through her veins. A sob hiccupped from her chest. "No," she whispered. Her hand curled in the page. "None of it is true. I explained it all in my letter. Why didn't you read my letter?"

Tears rolled down her face. The last shreds of hope slipped through her grasp like sand between her fingers. Desperation clawed at her insides, threatening to consume her whole. Moire stretched out her hands as though she could cross the ocean that separated them and hold Oliver in front of her while she told him the truth.

But her fingers grasped at nothing but air...then with a sickening lurch, the floor fell away beneath her feet, and Moire plunged into darkness.

PART II

1815

8

Eight years later…

EIGHT YEARS HAD PASSED since Moire's heart shattered into a thousand shards, each one a painful reminder of the dragon egg she had lost and the man whose love had warmed the coldest of days. Like the fading colours of an autumnal landscape, time had dulled the intensity of those memories, but they remained forever etched in the recesses of her heart and mind.

Today, Moire sat in the window seat of her room, watching Clipper dive for insects from his perch on the outside sill. The piptere had grown rapidly to his full size, similar to that of a small chicken. Over the years, the little creature had proven himself a loyal companion. He never strayed far from Moire, even though she refused to place a collar and leash on him.

A scrapbook sat in her lap, the pages full of clippings

cut from the newspapers. Each detailed the daring exploits of Captain Hartford during fierce naval campaigns. A wounded fellow officer had generously offered him the ride on his family's dragon, and the pair became the scourge of the French fleet, wreaking havoc on their vessels.

When his loss ached her heart and became too much to bear, she lost herself in the story he had written. The tale she had gathered in the pages of the scrapbook. With each word, her heartbeat echoed in her ears like distant war drums. Her mind conjured scenes of smoke and fire, bravery and bloodshed. At times, she could almost hear the dragon's roar. Every carefully pasted article bore witness to her unwavering love for the man who had once held her heart in his calloused hands.

Oliver might have spurned her, but Moire's affection remained constant.

"I am immensely proud of you, Oliver," she whispered, tracing the lines of ink with her fingertip and reinforcing them in her memory.

"Eight years," she muttered, closing the album with a gentle sigh as if trying to keep the ghost of her past love locked within its pages. "Eight years, and still, my heart refuses to let go."

After the tragic events of that long-ago night, Moire withdrew further from society. Balls and glittering soirées had never held much appeal, and she chose to actively avoid them when possible. Like a shadow under the emerging sun, she slowly faded from view.

She threw herself into her studies and became a constant visitor at the Radcliffe family's extensive library. Samuel Radcliffe's grandfather had had a keen interest in dragons, probably seeking an egg for his family, and he had collected many of the books that fascinated Moire. Once or twice a year, a battered parcel would arrive at Gormsby Hall, addressed to Mrs Radcliffe, containing a rare book about dragons. Mrs Radcliffe said they were sent by some distant relative touring the continent who remembered their grandfather's interests. Each book was passed to Moire, who treasured the knowledge contained within the old volumes.

Moire believed that if she studied the habits of the rare female dragons, she might be able to predict when one would lay an egg. If she replaced the one the thief had destroyed, Oliver might find it in his heart to forgive her, and she could find peace.

"I am going downstairs, Clipper," she said to the piptere. The little dragon's attention was focused on something on the lawn far below. He would join her when he was ready.

Putting the scrapbook away in a drawer, she drew a steadying breath and left her sanctuary. Trailing one hand on the balustrade, she descended the stairs. Pausing at the bottom, she waited for any bellowed summons from her father, but only the clink of china as a cup was placed back on its saucer came from the parlour. It seemed that, for a rare time, her father was content with his day.

Walking on the balls of her feet, Moire snuck across the tiled entranceway to her study. The window looked out on the driveway. While not the best view, once it had allowed her to spy Oliver riding into the nearby forest to wait for her.

Moire savoured the silence that enveloped her like a

comforting blanket. A heavy tome lay open on her desk. Its dense text offered tantalising clues about the mating habits of dragons. The book was the latest one delivered to Mrs Radcliffe, and while it took patience to read the tight script, it offered marvellous rewards.

She traced the lines of text with a fingertip, her eyes devouring each word with the same fervour with which she had once consumed news of Oliver's exploits. Her thirst for knowledge had grown into an insatiable beast over the years. Each new discovery sent her off on a tangent as she delved into the mysteries of ancient languages, magical lore, and the fascinating world of dragons.

"It's here," she muttered, convinced that the secret lay close to hand.

Scholars the world over had failed to penetrate the mysteries of where and when a dragon laid an egg. Moire was convinced that her unique position gave her an unprecedented viewpoint. She had spent her early years in the shadow of the mighty dragon, Caliban. She had shared grief and loneliness with a wyvern. And now a piptere was her companion. No other scholar had lived so intimately with all three different types of dragons.

As the fire crackled merrily in the grate, it cast shadowy fingers over the spines of leather-bound books Moire had collected. Here, amongst the dusty volumes, her intellect soared while her feet remained firmly on the ground. The passage of time had failed to lessen her fear of heights. Only in the pursuit of information could she climb a library ladder, keeping one hand gripped firmly on the wood while her gaze focused on the book she sought. The young woman who had once climbed on the back of Faustus and soared over meadows under a full moon seemed like a character from a book. Nor could she imagine climbing down the thick ivy from her window to the ground. Moire struggled to believe she had ever done such things.

But then, once, she had possessed such a love that made those risks seem worthwhile.

"Moire? Where are you, girl?" her father's voice called.

"In Mother's study," she replied. It wasn't done to shout, so she raised her voice only enough to be heard in the quiet. Even after sixteen years, the room was still *Mother's* study.

Her father appeared in the doorway with a stack of papers in his hand. "What is this nonsense?" He shook the pages as though he held a fan.

Moire bit her tongue from retorting that it looked like unpaid invoices to her. Instead, she left her desk and approached. Taking the bundle, she glanced at the writing. It was exactly as she suspected. "These are unpaid invoices, Father."

"Well, what has that to do with me?" He puffed out his chest at the sheer effrontery of tradesmen to expect him to pay for the goods he procured.

Moire sorted through the slips. One was from the tailor, who had obviously reached the end of his patience with his fashionable client. Three were from small goods merchants for a range of items, from cufflinks to a tea service.

"These are all items you purchased." Her father spent so prodigiously that it wasn't surprising he would forget about a set of cufflinks, but the tea service was an odd addition. Ah. Moire spotted the name in small print at the bottom of the paper. Augusta ordered it.

"Well, see to it, my girl. You know thinking about numbers gives me terrible wrinkles." Sir George placed one hand on his forehead and strode back across the tiles to the parlour.

A defeated sigh left Moire's chest. The unpaid invoices multiplied. Neither her father nor her older sister had any idea about economising or exercising restraint. At times, she imagined she was responsible for two children let loose in a toy shop.

How long before the bailiffs appeared and repossessed the furnishings? Paintings would be stripped from the walls, and the gilt-edged chamber pot snatched from under Sir George's bed.

The book about dragon habits and anatomy was set aside and replaced with a ledger and its neatly ruled columns. A wicker basket contained the unpaid bills that appeared every day. Moire sorted them by date and then by level of urgency. Some tradesmen were given priority—they had to eat, after all. No coin would go to the tailor until the butcher received his dues.

Not that her father appreciated the headache Moire endured trying to balance where their dwindling funds were applied. He would scream the house down if he couldn't have the latest fashion, even though it meant food on the table.

Her cousin would be woefully disappointed when the inevitable day arrived and he became the new Baron Tobin. The coffers would contain nothing but dust. Henry Tobin would inherit a title and an estate with a leaky roof. Even the family's dragon was no more but bones and earth. Since the demise of Caliban, the heir would be barred from the higher echelons of society and the title of Drac Tobin. Being one of the Draco Legion would have brought him a wealthy bride to make up for the other deficiencies of his inheritance.

Moire wiped a hand across her forehead. Those were all problems for her cousin. Right now, she had more pressing concerns. She studied the worn ledger before her, a frown creasing her brow as she traced a column of numbers with an ink-stained finger. The rapidity at which their financial situation worsened was alarming. She tried to make sense of it all, but each calculation only led to yet another disheartening conclusion.

Sums and accounting consumed her for two hours as she agonised over whom to pay. Each month, a larger deficit loomed over her. Pushing the pen back into its holder, Moire washed her hands over her face. What was she to do?

A gig trotted by the window with Lady Beaumont at the reins. An idea sparked in Moire's mind. If she could convince her mother's friend of its worth, she might mention it to Sir George. If Moire suggested cutting expenses, she would be ignored. The same words from Lady Beaumont's lips might be heeded.

Moire hurried from the study to intercept the visitor before she was announced in the parlour. "Good day, Lady Beaumont."

"Moire. You are looking a little peaky, dear. Are you sleeping?" A worried line formed on Lady Beaumont's pale forehead.

"Yes, although I fear even my dreams are troubled," she said.

"Oh? Whatever is troubling you?" She drew Moire to one side, into the shadow cast by a marble statue of a young woman that greeted visitors to the house.

Part of her believed it was a betrayal to reveal their financial woes, but if she did nothing, they would be publicly thrown out of their home. Deciding to take the somewhat lesser of the two horrible options before her, Moire made her confession. "I fear our position is somewhat strained, and I am at a loss as to how to convince Father of the need to curb his spending."

Lady Beaumont huffed a soft laugh, and she rested a gloved hand on Moire's arm. "Sir George has always had an eye for the finer things in life, like your mother. She was such a beauty in her youth and much admired. But I appreciate your dilemma. Do you think a move to smaller premises might alleviate some of your concerns?"

"Yes. I have already made enquiries as to whether it would be possible to lease Eadred Manor. The monthly payments would go a long way to addressing the situation." Moire had found a willing co-conspirator in her father's lawyer, who also despaired of ever being paid. The two of them had discussed many different arrangements. Moving to a smaller home while earning an income from letting the manor seemed the most tolerable of ideas.

"I believe I can prod Sir George in the required direction. I came here today because a plump morsel of gossip has fallen into my lap." She winked, linked her arm with Moire's, and steered her towards the parlour.

Sir George and Augusta rose as their guest entered the room, and they made their greetings. Katherine had left the family home some seven years previously. She had accepted a marriage proposal from Mr Radcliffe. A course of events that took everyone by surprise—including Samuel Radcliffe.

Moire let go of Lady Beaumont's arm to circle behind the two striped settees set opposite each other. She preferred a chair in the corner, where she could observe without being observed.

"You are like sunshine on a dreary day, Lady Beaumont. The countryside has been particularly boring this season," Sir George grumbled as he sat beside his old friend.

Augusta took the settee opposite and turned to raise an eyebrow at Moire. Taking the unspoken cue, Moire walked to the door to summon a maid. Fresh tea would be required. On the new tea set.

"Well, my friend, I may have just the cure for your ennui. You must come join me in Bath," Lady Beaumont said.

"Bath?" Sir George curled his upper lip. "The streets of Bath are littered with those of no worth, playing out their pretensions of being somebody."

"Really? I find the society quite diverting. This season, the Duke of Silverdale is going to grace the entertainments in his hunt for his duchess. I hear he is determined to be wed at last." Lady Beaumont leaned closer as she delivered her news.

"The Duke of Silverdale?" Augusta spluttered and sat up. "Father! He is the most handsome and wealthy man in all of England."

Sir George sucked in a breath. No doubt imagining the embroidered waistcoats he could buy using the duke's line of credit. "I know, dear girl, finally a suitor worthy of your attention. Of course, we shall relocate, but we do not wish to appear too hasty. You are a diamond, and we shall not make his search too easy for him."

Moire thought they should make all haste, given her sister was now the advanced age of twenty-eight. She would have to compete with fresh-faced debutants ten years younger than her. But it did solve one problem for her. A townhouse in Bath would be much cheaper to run. This was her opportunity to drop in another suggestion.

"Perhaps, Father, while we are in Bath, we could lease out the manor?" she said.

"Rent out our ancestral manor? I think not." Sir George leaned back on the settee and glared at her.

Bother. How to make it sound more appealing? "Having a trusted occupant would ensure the rooms were kept clean and tidy. You wouldn't want thieves making off with the marble statutory."

"Certainly not! I suppose if we could find a suitably grateful tenant, I might consider the idea. Augusta will need a new wardrobe to ensure she shines." The doting father smiled at his favourite child.

"I shall make enquiries." Moire already had. A short list of possible tenants sat on her desk.

Sir George placed a fresh scone on his plate. "Make sure they don't have any children. I'll not have sticky fingers touching my tapestries."

While moving and renting out their home would bring some relief to one problem, it raised another. Moire had never left Eadred Manor. Could she leave the only home she had ever known? And what of Faustus? The idea of the old wyvern left friendless and alone made her falter.

While Moire sat lost in her own thoughts, conversation flowed from the sort of townhouse they would take in Bath to how many times Augusta should make the duke propose before she accepted.

Later that night, Moire stood at the window as Clipper settled in his basket for the night. The flowering roses and ivy that crept over the walls of the estate were a familiar sight. One that she had grown to love over the years, even as time made stonework crumble and weeds grew rampant in garden beds. There was a beauty in the decay of the estate, for it was familiar and loved. A heavy weight settled over her, knowing the view would soon be lost to her.

"Oh Faustus, who will care for you when I am gone?" she whispered to the night. Tears pricked at the corners of her eyes. She wiped them away hastily, unwilling to let herself succumb to despair.

The days that followed were a flurry of activity as the Tobin household prepared for their move to Bath. Or they were busy for Moire, who had to organise everything. The family lawyer, Mr Pickleford, was an industrious little man who found both a townhouse and a tenant who met Sir George's stringent requirements.

"I do not like naval people," Sir George grumbled as he oversaw the packing of his clothing into trunks. "They all look like withered pieces of driftwood. They shout as though a storm is raging and only ever want to talk about boats."

Moire couldn't imagine any sort of person more noble than a naval officer. But she kept that thought to herself.

"The admiral and his wife have no children and will take exceedingly good care of the furnishings. They have expressed how honoured they are to spend some time in such a historic home as Eadred." They were also wealthy enough to pay the lease in advance, and Moire had already paid for three months' residency in the Bath townhouse. There was even enough left over to settle some of their bills at last.

"So they should. The Tobins are an old and honourable family." Sir George snatched up a scarf from an open trunk and held it over his shoulder before the mirror.

Some rooms were closed up, the furniture covered in sheets. Sir George had refused to consider the idea of anyone sleeping in *his* bed and had demanded the door be locked once he departed.

Carrying an open ledger, Moire ticked off what possessions were to be relocated with her father and sister, and which were to be stored in the attic or a locked storeroom. Bags of lavender were tucked in with clothing, the sweet scent filling the air as they worked.

"You will stay here and ensure these...lodgers know what they are not to touch," Sir George said that night over supper. He had dictated quite a list of demands, including a floral offering to be placed beneath the larger of his many portraits. "Then you are to go to your sister at Larkspur Cottage. Katherine has written that she is suffering quite terribly from a head cold. You shall go look after the children while she recovers."

"Don't worry that we will miss you in Bath, Moire. Father and I have received many invitations already. We are much in demand and will barely lay our heads in the little house you found for us." Augusta beamed, but there was a frosty edge to it. For years, her father had spoken of the mythical *grand match* his oldest daughter would make. Now, they had a chance of making it a reality.

"Of course, Father," Moire replied dutifully, swallowing the lump in her throat. The prospect of leaving Faustus behind worried her. It wasn't as if the wyvern could pen her a letter if he required anything.

The next morning, Sir George and Augusta set off for Bath, their carriage loaded down with trunks and bags of every shape and size. Moire stood in the doorway, her hands clasped tightly together, as she watched them depart.

"Goodbye, Father, Augusta," Moire called out as the horses trotted off.

Neither her father nor her sibling bothered to wave goodbye. Their attention was fixed on their destination, not on what they had left behind.

9

For nearly a week, Moire had the house to herself. At first, she crept around, not wanting to disturb the silence. Then she grew bold and even sat on her father's favourite chair in the parlour. Only for a few moments though, before she leapt up, convinced he would be able to tell by the slight impression in the fabric. At night, she swaddled herself in a warm shawl and prowled the grounds with Faustus. Clipper sat on the wyvern's back like a tiny jockey.

"I do not want to leave you, my friend," she said as they walked the weed-infested paths through the former rose garden. Now, it was a nightmare landscape of skeletal shapes where ragged limbs begged the passerby for a prune. "I have lost too many I care about over the years."

At times, she imagined her heart was like a lump of clay, each tragedy carving chunks out of it. A slice taken when she lost her mother. A walnut-sized hole for the loss of the egg. The remainder nearly torn in two when Oliver broke off their engagement. Did the tattered organ have enough left to lose Faustus?

"Not lost. Always...here." Faustus tapped his chest with his wing claw.

He was right, of course. No matter how savage the storm that lashed her heart, those she cherished remained safe deep inside her. There was a puzzle. How did a heart fracture yet still hold secure everyone she loved?

Clipper trilled and flew to her shoulder. The wyvern would lose them both. Perhaps she could leave Clipper so that Faustus had a friend of his own species?

"Moire...return?" Faustus tilted his head and regarded her with silver eyes.

She flung her arms around his neck. "I will find a way, Faustus. Even if I must become a milkmaid on the neighbouring farm so I can sneak over at night." Her movements were at the whim of her father. As though she were a foot soldier during war, he commanded her physical form to go here or there with no regard for her desires.

If she were truly a housekeeper, she could have stayed to supervise the running of the house for the admiral. As the over-looked middle child of Sir George, she didn't even have the stability of employment.

"Faustus, wait. Faustus, guard—" the wyvern broke off whatever he had been about to say and instead raised his head to sniff the air.

Waiting and guarding were what wyverns did. They patrolled the grounds of the estate where they were tethered and raised the alarm if they found any intruders. Moire could only remember Faustus's high-pitched screech sounding twice. Once, when Caliban fell ill. The other was when a thief stole something precious from the wyvern's burrow. Both times, her father had ignored the warning, and Moire bore the full force of the outcome.

As the moon held its spot above them, Moire's limbs grew tired. She guessed the hour had slipped past midnight. Tomorrow, she would greet their tenants, and she needed to ensure the house was immaculate before they arrived. Since her body demanded a few hours' sleep before then, she bid Faustus goodnight.

The next morning, a nervous Moire with an agitated Clipper on her shoulder stood at the entrance of Eadred Manor. Clipper's tail brushed back and forth over the skin of her neck and mirrored the flutter in her heart. She smoothed her skirts and tried to quell the anxiety that gripped her. The new tenants would soon arrive, and she was determined to present a serene façade.

The clop of hooves drew closer as the carriage appeared, the old trees casting dappled light over its side as it passed underneath them. The driver halted his team by the portico.

With a deep breath, Moire mustered her courage and stepped forward.

"Welcome to Eadred Manor. I am Miss Moire Tobin," she said with a warm smile as the older couple alighted from their carriage.

"Ah, Miss Moire. We are honoured to be greeted by a member of the family." Admiral Chellum bowed to her and then turned to help his wife down.

"A great pleasure, Miss Moire. We expected to be greeted by the housekeeper," Mrs Chellum said. She had a kind smile, and grey blended with the dark blonde at her temples.

Moire bit the inside of her mouth. She was the house-keeper...and yet wasn't. For the briefest moment, she considered incurring her father's wrath and offering her services to the Chellums.

"Eadred Manor has no housekeeper, Mrs Chellum. Cook does a fine job of managing the kitchens, and I have always overseen the running of the house." That was as close as she could come to applying for the job.

"Oh." A frown pulled on Mrs Chellum's brow, and she took the arm of her weather-worn husband. "We would not expect a noblewoman to enter our employ. I am sure we could find someone in the village to assist if needed."

Bother. Now, her only hope would be to adopt a disguise and pretend to be a villager, applying for the position of housekeeper. That involved far too much deception for Moire.

"Would you like me to show you the house?" Moire suggested, gesturing towards the stone façade.

"If you would be so kind." Mrs Chellum's grey eyes sparkled with kindness, and Moire felt an instant liking for the older woman, whom she guessed to be somewhere around forty.

Sir George would have been horrified had he met Admiral Chellum, who did indeed resemble a weathered lump of driftwood. He could have been no more than a few years older than his wife, but storms had carved deep lines in his face, and his skin resembled tanned hide, giving him the appearance of being decades older. Intelligent blue eyes sparkled in his round face, and he showed great devotion to his wife. Moire decided she liked them both and was glad she had chosen them as the new tenants.

As they walked through the grand rooms and Moire narrated some of the house's history, she grew more comfortable in the presence of the older couple. The admiral proved to be an amusing storyteller, inserting snippets from his adventures at sea where appropriate. When Moire showed them through to the dining room, the admiral told her of the sailors' table, which was hung from ropes to allow it to sway with the movement of the vessel.

When they viewed the bedchambers and the couple picked which would be theirs, he marvelled at the size of the mattresses after the narrow cots onboard. Then he quipped that there would be no need to secure the chamber pot to stop it from sliding across the floor at night. That prompted a fit of giggles from Mrs Chellum, and Moire suspected the couple shared an amusing memory.

"Shall we tour the grounds? The gardens are long neglected unfortunately. My mother had a keen interest in their maintenance. Since her death many years ago, I have struggled to do more than the most basic of tasks. My gardening skills are sadly lacking by comparison." Moire showed the way back down the grand staircase and out to the gardens.

"Don't be so hard on yourself, Miss Moire. You must have lost your mother at a tender age. You are a great credit to her that you have tried to maintain order in the garden. And you take care of the house. Why, there are many young ladies who cannot do a fraction of that." Mrs Chellum took her arm as they strolled a grassy path.

"Thank you for your kind words, Mrs Chellum." A rush of affection for the Chellums surged over Moire. In their warmth and kindness, she had found a balm for the loneliness that had long plagued her at Eadred Manor. What a shame that she must leave when she finally felt at home.

Clipper flew on ahead of them and disappeared through a hole in the yew hedge. He kept them amused with his antics.

"He's a fine wee chap. We had six dragons who fought on our side. There was a sight, Miss Moire. To see those fierce beasts amid the smoke from dozens of cannons. They rained fire down on the enemy vessels. Their wings were so strong the wind near knocked you off your feet when they flew low over us." The admiral strolled through memories of battle.

"To think you were there! Yet, in the retelling, it seems like a story conjured from a book. Why, the noise of it all must have been deafening." Moire imagined the roar of dragons, the blast of cannons, and the yells of men.

"Some men stuffed cotton wool in their ears, not that it did any good. Dragons bellow so loud, it makes your bones rumble." Admiral Chellum held out his arm, and Clipper alighted on the outstretched limb as though he were a hawk.

"My brother was one of the riders." Pride gleamed in Mrs Chellum's eyes.

Moire stopped, and her mouth opened in a silent *oh*. Then she regained her composure. "Forgive me, Mrs Chellum. I did not know your family was of the Draco Legion." This was too perfect. The questions she had!

"Oh, no!" Mrs Chellum waved her hand through the air. "We are gentry but not noble. No, my brother was most fortunate. A fellow officer was terribly injured and could not ride. His dragon agreed that Oliver could instead. The two of them struck fear into French hearts."

"Oliver?' Moire stuttered over the syllables. The ground dropped away from under her feet, and she swayed.

"Yes. My brother is Captain Oliver Hartford." Mrs Chellum grabbed tight on her arm. "Are you quite all right, Miss Moire? You look as though you might faint."

The admiral took Moire's other arm, and the couple guided her to a bench set near the hedge.

Captain Oliver Hartford.

No wonder she took an instant liking to Mrs Chellum. The same blood flowed through her veins as the only man Moire had ever loved.

"I am simply tired, that is all. There has been much to organise in the last few weeks," she whispered to allay the concerns of the Chellums.

Mrs Chellum huffed as though she did not believe Moire, but she said no more on that topic. "Do you know my brother? He used to spend much time in Wyldefen."

Moire encased her heart in ice, lest she betray herself. "Yes, I believe we may have crossed paths some years ago. If I recollect, the Hartford farm is only a few miles from here?"

A smile broke across Mrs Chellum's face. "Yes, it is. Our cousin lives there, not far from the village. Oliver loved spending his shore leave there. We had hoped a young woman had caught his eye, but apparently, he simply liked the sheep."

Moire swallowed; her throat suddenly dry. Clipper, sensing her anxiety, flew from the admiral's arm to her shoulder. The little piptere wrapped his tail around her neck and caressed her cheek with his face. She raised a hand to scratch under his chin, and his small body vibrated in happiness.

"I read some accounts in the newspapers of your brother's exploits during the war. You must be very proud of him." Moire congratulated herself on maintaining a calm and quiet tone. Internally, a powerful storm whipped up and lashed her organs.

"I admit to some sisterly pride in his achievements. It was an honour that Valiant allowed another on his back. Who could have known that when combined, the two of them would make such a fierce opponent?" Mrs Chellum held one hand to her chest.

The admiral chuffed, "He earned his advance to captain. Never heard such applause from the crew when he was given his bars. He will make a finer admiral than myself, if he chooses to stay with the Navy."

The Oliver that Moire had known loved the ocean. "Is your brother retiring from the Navy?"

"He is thinking about it. War allowed him to amass a fortune, but I think he yearns for a quieter life with an intelligent wife at his side." Mrs Chellum's eyes widened as though she had the most marvellous idea. "Why, you must meet him, Miss Moire. Oliver is going to join us here at Eadred Manor. I am sure you would catch his eye."

Moire nearly choked on the thought. Given the harsh tone in the letter she received eight years ago, she was probably the last person in the world that Captain Oliver Hartford wanted to set eyes on.

But then why would he come to stay at her home? A hopeful voice whispered from the depths of her soul.

Moire recovered her senses as she became accustomed to hearing Oliver's name once more. They continued their stroll about the grounds. As they returned to the house, she gestured to the visible mound across the meadow and nestled beside trees. "That is where Faustus, the estate's wyvern, lives. I do worry about him and would ask you to please extend him every kindness. I shall introduce you once it is dark."

Mrs Chellum patted Moire's arm. "You have a kind heart, Miss Moire. I thought most people ignored the creatures."

"Faustus has always been a friend to me. We comforted each other after Caliban and my mother died. He grows old, and my father never acquired another beast to keep him company as other estates do. If ever you have reason to believe he needs me, please write to me immediately." She worried how the wyvern would fare without her and Clipper. At least at Larkspur Cottage, she would not be too far away. The home of her sister and Samuel Radcliffe was nestled in the grounds of Gormsby Hall.

"Once we are acquainted, I shall do all I can to ensure his needs are met. And of course, I shall write if the situation requires it," Mrs Chellum promised.

That evening, Moire joined the Chellums for her last supper at Eadred Manor. In the morning, she would leave for Larkspur Cottage to tend to her sister and nephews.

The rich aroma of roasted venison and rosemary potatoes wafted through the dining room as Moire took her seat at the table opposite the older couple. The flickering candlelight cast a soft glow upon the fine china and polished silverware, creating an atmosphere of elegance and intimacy.

As they ate, conversation flowed effortlessly between the trio. Admiral Chellum regaled them with tales of his naval adventures—the raging storms and treacherous waters he had faced and the thrill of commanding a fleet into battle. His vivid descriptions enthralled Moire, who listened with rapt attention.

"Ah, but nothing could compare to the sight of dragons during the war," the admiral reminisced, his eyes glinting with excitement. "Many a sailor needed to change his britches after a dragon had swooped from above and soared close to our sails."

"It is truly marvellous what you have seen and done, Admiral," Moire breathed, her imagination conjuring images of these epic clashes between man and beast.

"Indeed. Have you ever witnessed a dragon in flight?" He took a sip of his wine.

"As a child, I recall watching Caliban sweeping through the skies above the estate." It seemed like a dream now, watching the magnificent dragon fly across the forest and meadows.

"How tragic that he was lost to your family," Mrs Chellum murmured sympathetically.

Moire stared at her plate. Would Caliban have lived another hundred years or more if her father had been an adequate companion? He spurned the dragon, and that seemed to sap the will to live from the creature.

"Mother, Faustus, and I sat with Caliban through the night on the eve of his death. Mother sang to ease his passing. As dawn blushed the sky above, Caliban drew his last breath." Tears moistened her eyes, and she blinked them away. "Mother followed him less than a week later."

"Oh, my child, what loss you have suffered! Now I understand why you and Faustus are bound together," Mrs Chellum said.

Moire drew a breath and steadied her emotions, which were a tempest inside her. Loss dominated her life. It seemed the Fates decreed that she would never be loved for long. "I have devoted my life to learning all I can about dragonkind. Perhaps it is my way to make sense of Caliban's death." And she hunted for a clue about how to acquire a dragon egg.

The tone of supper had turned sombre, and they each seemed to retreat into their private thoughts. After the meal, Moire excused herself from the Chellums' pleasant company and hurried from the house. Her heart was heavy with the knowledge that this would be her last evening at Eadred Manor, and she had to find Faustus. The wyvern would be somewhere on the grounds.

"Faustus?" Moire called as she approached the edge of the meadow.

A low growl sounded nearby, and Moire turned as the familiar shape of the wyvern emerged from the shadows, his scaly hide glistening in the moonlight. Relief washed over her as she reached out a hand to stroke his snout. Warm breath rippled over her skin.

"There is something I must do. Will you join me?" she whispered, as though she could not speak in a normal tone in the dark. Nighttime was meant for murmured secrets.

He crooned his reply, and together, woman and wyvern entered the forest. Their footsteps were muffled by the soft carpet of fallen leaves. As they approached Caliban's barrow, the scent of damp earth and night-flowering blooms filled Moire's nostrils and evoked memories of other nights by the river.

She knelt before the barrow and placed her hands on the earth. It seemed warm beneath her palms, as though the buried dragon still breathed. Moire murmured a prayer and turned to lean her back against the moss-covered soil.

The wyvern lay at her side, his ugly head in her lap. Moire scratched his eye ridges as she spoke. "I am sorry that I have to leave, Faustus. I will not be far away. Mrs Chellum has promised to write to me if you ever need me."

"Moire. Family." Faustus huffed. His silver eyes closed, and he hummed under her touch.

"Yes. We are family. That means we will always look out for each other." She stayed in that spot, listening to the burble of water from the river and the hoot of owls until she grew chilled. She hugged Faustus, touched Caliban's barrow one more time, and then returned to the house to introduce the Chellums to the wyvern.

Moire had a troubled night's sleep. A sailor strode through her dreams. His pale gaze damning her before he mounted a dragon and took flight. Moire chased him down long, echoing halls as she pled for the chance to explain what had happened...but he never looked back.

She awoke early. Her few belongings were packed away in a trunk, and the lid closed. Clipper clung to her shoulder, his tail tighter than usual. The piptere was also uneasy at the changes ahead. Downstairs, Moire found the Chellums already up and having breakfast. She paused a little too long on the threshold, her brain unable to fathom having company for the first meal of the day.

"Good morning. I am unaccustomed to company. My father never rose before ten," Moire said as she took her seat.

"I can't sleep past dawn. Too many years of being roused from my bunk early." Admiral Chellum winked.

They chatted amicably over breakfast. Moire relished the sense of camaraderie with the older couple. But as they finished their meal, sadness descended. The time had come for her to take her leave.

"If you will excuse me, I must make sure I have everything." In her study, Moire caressed the spines of her books on dragons. She could only take one, and so chose the latest that she had borrowed from the Radcliffes. When she departed for Bath, she would return it to the library at Gormsby Hall.

Once ready, the groundsman shouldered her trunk and placed it in the back of a little gig.

"Goodbye, Miss Moire. I do hope we shall see you again soon," Mrs Chellum called out.

Moire climbed onto the seat. Clipper moved to nestle in her lap. "I hope so too, Mrs Chellum. And please send word immediately if Faustus needs me!"

Not being made of particularly stoic stuff, Moire couldn't sit with a ramrod back and stare at the road ahead. Instead, she turned to watch the manor grow smaller and smaller as they trotted down the path. When she finally sat the right way in her seat, the surrounding scenery was blurred by tears.

10

Larkspur Cottage was a picturesque home not too far from Gormsby Hall. Mr and Mrs Radcliffe had gifted it to Samuel and Katherine as a wedding present—a kind act that horrified Katherine, who thought they would live in the big house with an army of servants to command. Instead, she had a private, beautiful, and comfortable home surrounded by a lush garden. How terrible of her in-laws to treat her in such a thoughtful manner.

The sun caressed the stone cottage and lit it a pale cream. The garden burst with life, despite Katherine's best efforts to ignore it. Vibrant roses, delicate lilies, and fragrant lavender swayed gently in the breeze, creating an intoxicating perfume that filled the air. Moire took a moment to admire the charming scene before her as she approached the cottage.

It could have been her home if her heart hadn't belonged to another.

The groundsman pulled the horse to a halt, and Moire jumped down while he carried her trunk up the path.

143

The front door burst open, and two young boys raced out to greet her.

"Aunt Moire!" Noah, the oldest at six years of age, yelled excitedly.

"Clipper!" Five-year-old Elijah shouted and startled the piptere.

The faces of the boys were flushed with excitement, and three lively dogs followed close behind, tails wagging enthusiastically at the prospect of new company. Moire couldn't help but smile at the sight of them. The ache in her heart eased a little as she gathered her nephews into her arms.

"Hello, Clipper," Noah said as he turned his wide-eyed stare to the piptere.

Like many children, they were fascinated by dragons. While Gormsby Hall boasted two wyverns, the boys had never seen them up close. The children were tucked up in bed when the wyverns emerged from their burrow to prowl the grounds, and the creatures had retreated by the time the family roused in the morning.

The small dragon basked in the attention, safe with Moire nearby. He emitted a series of melodic chirps as he stretched his wings. Then he hissed at a dog that ventured too close.

"Why don't we leave the dogs out in the garden and take Clipper inside? Dogs make him nervous, and your aunt would dearly love a cup of tea. Do you think you could make me one?" she asked Elijah as she took the boy's hand.

The youngest Radcliffe screwed up his face before

shaking his head. "No. But I know where the tea is kept. It is next to the cocoa in the cupboard."

First, the boys helped her to drag her trunk into the hall. Hopefully, Samuel would carry it up to her room when he returned. She doubted she would find her brother-in-law inside, as even in the most horrendous storms, he preferred to be outside with his hounds and horses.

"Moire? Is that you?" a surprisingly strong voice called from the parlour.

Moire closed her eyes and drew a breath before letting it out with a long exhale. For once in her life, she would like to simply be...Moire. Instead, she had to adopt whatever role those around her had cast her in. Today, it would be nursemaid.

"Yes, Katherine," she called out and waved the boys along to play while she tended to her younger sister.

As she entered the dimly lit parlour, Katherine let out a series of pitiful moans at odds with the previous clarity of her voice. She lay sprawled on a chaise lounge, a damp cloth draped across her forehead.

"Oh, Moire. I am dreadfully ill with this horrid head cold," Katherine spoke in a mere whisper as she feigned helplessness. "I expect it will be the end of me. This morning, Samuel merely kissed my cheek and cruelly abandoned me to my fate!"

"He always returns to you at the end of the day. You know he spends his days in the forest or managing the tenants. But I can see you are suffering most terribly." Moire suppressed the urge to roll her eyes at her sister's theatrics.

Katherine's near-death inducing sniffles developed

after their mother died. Moire suspected it was a way of eliciting some attention from their oblivious father. Then, over the years, it became an excuse for not doing any chores or taking any responsibility for her actions. No one could speak a harsh word to her while she lingered on the threshold of death. Although, one had only to announce a ball or entertainment and Katherine would have the most miraculous recovery. Pregnancy and childbirth had been the first time that she had a genuine complaint. Although Moire was thankful that both her sister and nephews were unscathed by the gruelling process.

"You simply must look after the children and run the house in my stead. I cannot in my current state," Katherine implored, her voice cracking with false distress.

"Of course, I shall," Moire said. Her sense of duty overpowered any resentment she might have felt. She knew all too well that Katherine's self-obsession often led her to neglect her responsibilities to her family, leaving Moire no choice but to step in and restore order.

Once the worst of Katherine's symptoms had been placated with a pot of tea and a plate of biscuits, Moire went in search of her nephews. The boys shared a bedroom upstairs, as far away as possible from their parents. When they had moved into Larkspur Cottage, Katherine had converted a sitting room on the ground floor into her bedroom. Which was more convenient for visitors to her deathbed.

Standing in the doorway to the boys' room, her gaze swept over the disarray of toys and trinkets strewn across the floor. With a determined shake of her head, she rolled up her sleeves and crouched down beside her nephews, who regarded her with wide, expectant eyes. Moire had learned that while children delighted in making a mess, they exhibited no enthusiasm at all for tidying it away. Or not without sufficient incentive.

"Well, lads, you have made a valiant effort here to cover every inch of the floor with toys and clothing. Perhaps Clipper would help us return everything to its rightful place?" she said, mustering as much enthusiasm as she could.

Noah regarded the piptere with a serious expression. "How can he help? He doesn't have any hands."

Moire scratched under Clipper's chin. "But he has claws, and he can fly. He also likes to catch things."

She picked up a tin soldier that had been abandoned beside the hearth and held it out to Elijah. "Why don't you throw this in the air and see what happens?"

Clipper had indicated he would assist, but only if the boys tossed the toys so he could practise snatching things mid-air. The piptere hopped to the back of a nearby chair, so his claws didn't dig into her shoulder when he launched himself.

"Ready, Clipper?" she asked, and the small dragon chirruped his assent.

As the child tossed the toy into the air, Clipper swooped in and caught it in his talons before flying gracefully towards an open cupboard, where he deposited the soldier in a wooden box.

"Your turn, Noah." Moire passed him a cotton pouch filled with marbles.

He flung it clumsily into the air, and once again,

Clipper demonstrated his agility, snatching the bag mid-flight and depositing it in an open drawer.

The game continued, laughter lightening the atmosphere within the cottage as the children delighted in their newfound helper. They soon had the room tidy—although not for very long, Moire suspected. To celebrate a job well done, they headed down to the kitchen, where the cook laid out afternoon tea for them.

As the boys were drinking hot chocolate and shovelling scones into their mouths, the back door swung open to admit a rush of dogs and the figure of Samuel. Moire's brother-in-law clutched a gun and a brace of pheasant.

"Moire!" he exclaimed, genuine warmth lighting up his face as he crossed the threshold. "Katherine said you would be coming to stay. You are a most welcome sight."

"Hello, Samuel. The boys and I have just finished tidying their room and are having a well-deserved after-noon tea." Moire fetched another cup and poured hot chocolate for him.

He swapped the brace of pheasant for the cup and took a long sip. Moire stared at the two birds hanging from a wire and then handed them off to the cook. Moire's house-keeper abilities only went so far, and she couldn't bring herself to pluck and gut anything that so closely resembled Clipper.

"It is always wonderful to have you stay." He finished the drink and then swiped a scone from the plate. The dogs settled before the range, stretching out their damp bodies to dry their fur in the warmth.

"It is no hardship to spend time with such fine young men." She smiled at her nephews, both of whom now sported jam moustaches. A dull ache wrapped around her heart. This could have been her home. Her family. Instead, she had a lonely existence, drifting from one place to another without anyone to offer her a safe harbour to drop anchor.

"The hunting was good today, and I saw signs of wild pigs. I shall bag a few, and there will be plenty of meat to salt for the larder over winter." Samuel sat beside his oldest son.

"Can I come pig hunting with you, Da?" Noah asked with wide eyes.

"When you are taller than a rifle," Samuel said and ruffled Noah's dark hair.

"You appear to have worn the dogs out." Moire glanced at where the canines slept. One snored like an old man dozing in the sun.

"I'd rather wear a dog out hunting than myself on a dance floor." Samuel poured more hot chocolate into his cup.

Samuel had always preferred the company of animals to other people. He was an odd match with Katherine but remained solicitous of his wife and never failed to bring her posies of wildflowers. It caused Moire a little pain that her sister didn't fully appreciate the kind man she had married, but they both seemed content with their lot.

By supper time, Katherine had recovered enough to join the family for the evening meal. Moire suspected she felt left out with the laughter coming from the kitchen. After she put the boys to bed and read them a story, Moire turned in for the night. Events of the day had drained her. Curling up in the little room with its single bed, Clipper burrowed between her pillow and the wall. Soon both woman and piptere were fast asleep.

THE NEXT DAY, Katherine seemed much revived.

"It seems Death will not claim me this time, and I have defeated him once more," she said as she lay sprawled over the settee.

Voices came from the kitchen, and Katherine raised her head and waved a hand at Moire. "Go see who that is, would you?"

"Of course." Moire placed her book on the chair as she rose. She only made it to the door when she encountered a young woman. It was Ruth, Samuel's younger sister. Her pale cheeks were flushed red, and strands of brown hair had pulled loose of her hairstyle and brushed against her face. Ruth had the robust constitution of the Radcliffes, matched with the family kindness.

"Moire! How lovely to see you! Mother will insist on your dining with us while you are here. I came to visit Katherine. Is she horribly sick?" Ruth leaned forward and lowered her tone when she asked about the state of Katherine's health.

"Katherine is much recovered, and I am sure she will be even better for seeing you," Moire said.

"I heard your father has let Eadred Manor. Is it true?" Ruth asked.

"Yes, to Admiral Chellum and his wife. They are a lovely couple, and I think will do much to improve our society in Wyldefen." Moire stood to one side to allow the young woman to enter the parlour. Then she went to the kitchen to prepare a tea tray.

When Moire returned, Ruth sat on the settee next to Katherine, who seemed more animated as she led the conversation. "Oh, to have a ball! Wouldn't that be marvellous? Of course, if I were in residence at Gormsby Hall, I would throw one every week. But from here..." She cast a hand around the modest but charming parlour. "Why, there isn't even room for me to teach the boys the dance steps they need to know as they grow older."

Moire thought there was ample room to teach the boys to dance outside in the expansive fields. If one were so inclined. She placed a bet with herself that by the end of the day, that particular endeavour would be added to all she had to do while staying with her sister.

"I find myself longing for the excitement of London. The balls, the theatres, anything but this endless quiet." Ruth sighed and flicked open her lace fan as if to ward off oppressive boredom. "The countryside is lovely, of course, since it is my family home. But there's only so much one can do with flowers and cows. We should confront Mamma, Katherine, and demand that she at least throws a wonderful soirée if they will not open the ballroom."

"Oh, yes! I am sure your mother will agree to a supper to celebrate the return of my health." Katherine poured tea and didn't even acknowledge that Moire had prepared the tray and carried it in.

Once she had a cup of tea in her hands, Katherine leaned back against the settee. Once again, Moire was forgotten. Rather than creep forward to pour her own drink, she picked up a book and sat by the window.

Katherine nibbled the edge of a crustless sandwich. "That reminds me of something Samuel said yesterday. For all that he spends his days with sheep and dogs, he unearthed a titbit of information that might enliven things around here. One of the tenants said that the war hero, Captain Hartford, will be spending some time in Wyldefen."

"Captain Hartford? You mean the dashing navy officer? I've heard such thrilling tales about him!" Ruth tried to fake swoon against the settee but couldn't while holding the cup of tea.

Moire admired her effort. She wished she could swoon at Oliver's name. Instead, she dug her nails into her palms.

"He rode a dragon to fight the French. Can you imagine how brave he must be? And wealthy from all the vessels they captured according to what I read in the newspapers," Ruth gushed.

Katherine hummed and placed one hand on her temple to show she was thinking. "For some reason, the name Hartford is familiar. It has been bothering me ever since Samuel mentioned it, as though I have heard it before."

Moire's heart constricted within her chest. Would Katherine remember the name of a long-ago suitor of her older sister? Moire never thought she had paid any attention the day Oliver had asked for her hand in marriage.

Ruth set aside her teacup, too excited to drink as she vibrated with energy. "Can you imagine the tales he will have to share with us? His presence will certainly enliven our dull little corner of the countryside. I do hope he is handsome. All fabulously wealthy men are."

"That settles it. We must present a united front to your

mother, Ruth, and demand that a supper be held to honour this hero among us. Where is he staying, anyway?" Katherine glanced around the room, seeking the answer among the furnishings.

"Eadred Manor," Moire answered before she could stop herself.

Katherine laughed. "Don't be silly, Moire. That is our home. What would he be doing there?"

Moire clutched the closed book in her lap, curling her fingers around the edge. "Admiral Chellum and his wife have taken the lease on Eadred Manor while Father and Augusta have moved to Bath. When I showed them the house the other day, Mrs Chellum mentioned that Captain..." Moire's tongue tripped over itself in her mouth, and she couldn't say his name. She drew a breath through her nostrils and tried again. "Mrs Chellum mentioned that the captain is her brother and would be joining them for a while. Any invitation sent to Eadred Manor will reach the captain and the Chellums."

Shouting broke out from elsewhere in the house. Katherine let out a cry and held the back of her hand to her temple. "The children! Why must they be so loud? It has quite brought on one of my headaches. You simply have to go deal with them, Moire."

Dismissed like a nanny, Moire rose and took her leave. The boys were fighting with wooden swords in the kitchen. Elijah stood on the table as he was shorter. But Noah had an army of dogs on his side. Clipper perched on the exposed beam high above and refused to be drawn into taking a side. Until Moire walked in, that is, and the piptere glided down to her shoulder.

"What is all this noise about? Your mother has a headache, and your Aunt Ruth is here." Moire jumped back as Elijah parried with his wooden sword, and Noah thrust forward.

"Elijah took my dragon and will not give it back." Noah raced to the other side of the table, knocking over a chair in the process. Meanwhile one of the dogs tried to jump across the table, its claws scrabbling at the wood.

"I don't have your stupid toy dragon!" Elijah answered and kicked out with a foot at his advancing sibling.

"You could have a real dragon of your own if we find a piptere nest," Moire said as she opened the back door to shoo the dogs out.

"What?" Noah paused and regarded her with a suspicious look.

"Years ago, your father found Clipper's egg not far from here. It had blown out of a nest. I have read that pipteres will return to the same spot to lay their eggs every summer like swallows do. If we found their nest, you could hatch your own little dragon." The noise level in the kitchen fell once all the dogs were outside, and Moire closed the solid wooden door.

Both boys fell silent, weapons were dropped to the floor, and jaws hung open.

"Really?" Elijah asked in a hushed tone.

"We can ask your father at supper time for the exact area in the forest if he remembers. They will return to the same tree year after year, and we have only to find it." Now that the idea occurred to her, she quietly admired her brilliance. The boys would insist on examining every tree in the forest now, allowing Katherine plenty of peace and quiet. There were many lessons she could give the boys about wildlife and plants while they searched. Then they could pour over books to find more information about pipteres.

"But you will need to tidy up and wash your hands if you want me to help you find your own eggs." Moire managed to look stern as she indicated the destruction inflicted upon the kitchen battlefield.

For once, the lads tidied up with few complaints. While the company of her much-loved nephews warmed Moire's heart, it did little to dispel the loneliness that settled heavily over her. How was it that among people, she seemed all the more alone?

THE NEXT DAY turned warm and still. The sort of weather that irritated children and the elderly as they became too hot. Moire worked in the kitchen, helping the cook prepare bread. They had propped the kitchen door open with a stone to catch any breeze. Moire dusted flour on her hands before she kneaded dough at the oak table. A shadow appeared in the doorway moments before Ruth burst into the room. The young woman exuded excitement, and a flutter of curiosity rose in Moire. Then she momentarily forgot the bread she pounded to accompany their evening meal.

"Oh, Moire, I have marvellous news!" Ruth exclaimed, her eyes alight with anticipation. "I convinced my parents to host a dinner at Gormsby Hall. Not only will it be tonight, and you're all invited, but they invited the admiral and Mrs Chellum, who replied that Captain Hartford will be there, too!"

Moire's heart stuttered for a beat at the mention of Oliver. Eight years and the mere mention of his name still affected her. What would his actual presence do? She gave the dough a few good whacks to release her inner turmoil. Then she shaped the loaf and dropped it into a mould to rise by the warmth of the fire.

"That is indeed wonderful news. I'm sure it will be a delightful evening." Her thoughts raced ahead, wondering how she would face the man who occupied so much of her heart and mind.

"I shall tell Katherine!" Ruth called out as she hurried through to the parlour.

Moire stared at her floury fingers and wished they possessed magic to turn back the hands of time and move the dragon egg before it had been stolen. But that was impossible. Looking back and wallowing in regret wouldn't serve any purpose. She had to focus on what lay before her, and currently, that was kneading dough.

As twilight fell later that day, Moire had yet to change her gown. Her role as housekeeper and nanny had turned into that of lady's maid as she helped Katherine dress for the evening. While her sister sat before the mirror, she carefully pinned her hair in a fashionable style. Then she teased tendrils to curl prettily around her ears.

"When I become the viscountess, I shall host such parties every night of the week." Katherine sighed and held a hand mirror to look at herself from a different angle than that in the mirror fixed to the dressing table.

"*If* you become the viscountess. Samuel's uncle has taken a much younger bride, and there is hope he will yet sire an heir." Moire reminded her sister that it was no sure thing that the title would ever settle on Samuel's shoulders.

Katherine let out a sigh, and the small mirror dropped to her lap. "Nobody ever thinks of me."

Moire bit back a retort about how unfair it was of the current viscount to not drop dead before fathering a male offspring to ensure Samuel inherited. "If you were hosting lavish parties every night you would soon be penniless, and you would be washing dishes, not waiting for them to be served." Moire placed a diamond-studded clip amongst the pinned hair.

"Oh, but what fun we would have had until the bailiffs knocked on the door." Katherine turned and took Moire's hands in hers. Her eyes, so like their mother's dark ones, sparkled with delight.

"Yes, what fun you would have." Everybody had fun except for her. While her father entertained, Moire sat in the study, tallying up the invoices. She would have to consult with the admiral, but Moire was convinced her father consumed enough alcohol to satisfy an entire vessel full of sailors.

A shout from outside tugged Moire's attention.

"Whatever is that noise?" Katherine turned her head, trying to identify the source of the cries.

Katherine's bedroom on the ground floor overlooked the garden to the side of the house. Moire peered out the window and made out Samuel in the descending gloom... with Noah in his arms.

"It's Samuel, and he's carrying Noah." Moire rushed from the room to the kitchen.

Samuel carried the child through the back door. Noah's face was etched with pain.

"What happened?" she asked, concern lacing her voice.

"I found it, Aunt Moire. The piptere nest. I only wanted to get a closer look, but I slipped and fell," Noah whimpered, tears welling in his eyes.

"In the parlour, Samuel. We can lay him out and see what he has done." Moire led the way, and then helped Samuel place Noah on the chaise lounge.

"I will fetch the doctor. Do you think it is broken?" Samuel paced as Moire lifted the boy's trouser leg.

"I don't think so." She ran her hands down undamaged skin, relieved that there didn't appear to be any obvious breaks.

"My ankle hurts, Aunt Moire," Noah whispered faintly.

A bruise bloomed across the offending ankle where it had been struck in the fall. The child must have twisted it when he landed. "I think it is a nasty sprain. You won't be running around for a few days, but you should be good as new within a week."

Moire fetched a bandage from the cupboard and bound Noah's ankle. The boy remained courageous throughout, despite his obvious pain. Moire distracted him by asking what he saw. "Are you sure it was a piptere and not a pheasant?"

"Oh, yes. It was silver like the moon and all scales with no feathers at all. That's not any pheasant. I could see the nest. There was another, with a blue head like Clipper, looking over the side." Noah told his story, and Moire admitted it did indeed sound like he had found their nest.

While she was terrified of heights and would never scale a tree herself, Moire understood that the thrill of finding a piptere egg for himself had been too great for the child to resist. "When you are able to walk on this, you will have to show me where it is, and we shall formulate a plan to see if they have any eggs."

A moment of doubt flared inside her breast. How cruel to steal the piptere eggs away from their parents. Perhaps there was another way. If they waited until the eggs hatched, a newly born little dragon might willingly bond with the boy.

Katherine had paced to one side of the parlour as Moire tended to Noah. Now, her voice rose in frustration, her words laced with self-pity. "I suppose you all expect me to miss the party and stay here with Noah. It's simply not fair! Why am I deprived of any fun just because I am the boy's mother?"

Ordinarily, Moire would have pointed out that tending to one's children when they were sick or injured was part of the role of being a mother. But tonight, Moire had her own wounds to tend. One that had been reopened by recent news. If she offered to stay with Noah, she would spare herself the heartache of seeing Oliver again. The thought both relieved and saddened her.

She smiled at her sister. "Of course, you deserve a night of entertainment, Katherine. I am more than willing to stay with Noah, so you might go to the supper."

Without hesitation, Katherine swooped on the offer. "Oh, thank you, Moire! You are the only one in this family who understands my needs." Then she swept from the room, leaving Moire alone with young Noah.

"Well, it is just you, Elijah, and me for supper. How about we eat in here with you and then have a story?" Moire suggested.

The lad wiped the tears from his face and nodded. He had been very brave, and she was sure the ankle hurt like the blazes. Some rousing tale with dragons would be sure to distract him.

After everyone had left for the big house and a rare silence had fallen over the cottage, Moire prepared a nourishing bowl of soup for everyone. Alongside it, they would have fresh bread still warm from the oven. The fragrant steam wafted upwards, carrying the scent of fresh herbs and vegetables as she ladled soup. Like most children, they delighted in playing with their food. So Moire would allow them to tear off hunks of bread and go fishing for vegetables in their bowls.

In the parlour, Moire dragged a small card table close to the chaise. Noah was able to rest his bowl and bread on it. Moire and Elijah sat at the table. The boys enjoyed the odd experience, despite the circumstances. Clipper sat on the back of the chaise and chirped at Noah, which was his cue to fish out a piece of carrot for the piptere, who had an odd preference for the root vegetable.

As the boys ate, Moire retrieved a book from her room. The worn leather cover was embossed with the image of a dragon picked out in a gold outline. Her father would be horrified at her reading at the dinner table, but she was sure normal rules didn't apply when eating at a card table next to an injured child. Picking a story that illustrated the might of dragons, she began to read aloud, immersing the boys in a tale of bravery and adventure.

"Once it was said that many dragons soared over the land," she read, "and magic drifted on the breeze. In a small village in the most magical district of Wyldefen lived a courageous knight named Sir Alaric..."

After the meal, Clipper leapt onto Noah's lap, snuggling close as if he too wanted to hear the story. Noah stroked the little dragon's mane of feathers, and Elijah pouted that the piptere didn't sit on his knee.

As Moire focused on comforting Noah, her confused feelings about Oliver's return receded and were replaced by a sense of responsibility. She found solace in looking after her nephews. While providing companionship and distraction to a small, injured boy would never be reported in the newspapers, it conveyed its own sense of satisfaction.

THE NEXT MORNING, Moire sat at the kitchen table, relishing a quiet cup of tea. Noah had breakfasted in his room, and she had just finished clearing away his dishes. Katherine had not yet stirred, and a rare peace hung over the cottage. A flash of yellow passed the window, and then Ruth appeared in the doorway.

"Oh, Moire, I couldn't wait to see you!" Ruth called out excitedly, her cheeks flushed from the brisk walk. "I have so much to tell you about last night's dinner, since you weren't able to attend!"

Moire rose, found another cup, and then sloshed the pot around to see if enough remained for the guest. "Come in. I shall boil the kettle for more tea."

The young woman removed her gloves and bonnet while Moire refilled the teapot.

Ruth sat across from Moire, grabbed a scone off the

plate, and tore it in two. "First, I must say that Captain Hartford is even more handsome than I could have imagined. Not only that, but he is kind and intelligent! Why, he kept the entire room captivated with tales of his daring exploits."

"I am sure he is more handsome in person than the newspapers made him appear," Moire said as she poured tea and then passed it across to Ruth. Personally, she thought the sketches never quite caught the determined line to his jaw. Or the ways his eyes changed colour like a stormy ocean.

As the young woman chatted on about the captain, Moire listened attentively, her hands clasped tightly in her lap to conceal the tremble.

"But I have yet to tell you the best bit," Ruth said, her eyes sparkling with excitement. "He said he is most determined to find a bride during his stay here. Can you imagine? Someone in Wyldefen might become Mrs Hartford!"

As the other woman speculated about who would have the best chance with the captain, Moire's heart ruptured anew. He would marry...but not her. She didn't think it was possible for a heart to break twice. Perhaps if she drank enough tea, she could drown out the pain.

The light caught the moonstone ring on her right hand, and it glowed a faint purple iridescence. No. She did not have enough tea inside her yet to wash away the ache. Pouring herself another cup, Moire forced a polite smile onto her face. "That does sound rather thrilling. I'm sure whichever lady he chooses will be very fortunate indeed."

Fortunately, Ruth did not require an active participant in the conversation apart from the odd murmur. That left

Moire able to seek refuge in the quiet corners of her mind, counting her breaths as she soothed the storm brewing within her.

If only she could find another dragon egg, perhaps then she could heal her relationship with Oliver. She didn't expect him to change his mind about her, but an offer of friendship would mend the rupture inside her. Then, she might be able to navigate the rest of her life. Alone.

"Did you have much opportunity to speak with the captain?" Moire asked, trying to inject a light tone into the question.

"Of course," Ruth giggled. "I made quite certain of that. If he chooses me, obviously, I will decline his first proposal." She dropped a spoonful of jam on top of her scone. "My friends in London say that a man must propose three times. That is how you know he really loves you. It is the third proposal that a lady accepts."

Moire had accepted the first proposal. Her heart had soared with love, and she couldn't imagine refusing Oliver twice, solely to test his devotion.

As the conversation continued, Moire patched up her wounded heart and kept her expression carefully composed, ensuring that no trace of her turmoil was visible to her companion. She focused on the sensation of the cool breeze that wafted into the kitchen and gently caressed her skin.

She had had her chance and enjoyed a glorious two years basking in the warmth of Oliver's love. Now, like a boat slipping free of its mooring, she needed to let him go. She still loved him, which was why he deserved the chance to find happiness. If Ruth earned his love, she would rejoice for the couple.

When they finished their tea, she bid the young woman farewell. The moment she was out of sight, her façade cracked, and she allowed herself a brief instant of vulnerability. Tears welled up in her eyes, but she hurriedly wiped them away with the back of her hand, unwilling to let her emotions consume her.

"Moire! I am simply dying of thirst. Bring me some tea, please!" Katherine's imperious tone cut through the air, shattering the fragile silence that had descended in the kitchen.

"Coming!" Moire called out.

She focused on brewing fresh tea. Selecting the pretty porcelain tea caddy that contained a more expensive blend of tea that Katherine preferred. She scooped out a spoonful and poured hot water over the delicate tea leaves, watching as they bloomed and unfurled like flowers after a gentle rain. With each slow, methodical action, calm flowed through her.

Restored to her usual even keel, Moire picked up the tray and walked through to the bedroom. She set the tray down on the little table beside the bed. Samuel had already left for the day, doing his rounds of the tenant farms on behalf of his father. Katherine sat up and fussed with the blankets around her.

"Ruth has just been. She said it was a lovely evening." Moire poured the tea and added a drop of milk and the requisite two spoons of sugar before handing the cup over.

"Thank you." Katherine took the cup and blew on the

surface before taking a sip. "Yes, there was much laughter and perhaps a little too much wine."

"I am glad you are recovered from your head cold and able to go out and enjoy yourself." Moire might be able to leave now that Katherine was better. But where could she go? She wanted to return to Faustus, but Eadred Manor was no longer her home with the Chellums in residence.

"I am sure it is only a temporary reprieve. Death shadows my every step." A heavy sigh escaped from Katherine.

"We all hope he is not successful for many decades yet." Moire patted her sister's hand. "I will be upstairs with the children if you require anything else."

Upstairs, Noah sat in a chair before the window. His injured foot was elevated on a footstool. Elijah played on the floor beside him, and Clipper moved soldiers as directed by Noah. Moire watched the scene and suspected the older boy quite liked the role of general with a piptere undertaking troop movements.

"How is the ankle today, Noah? Is there any pain?" she asked as she knelt by his side, brushing a stray lock of light-brown hair from his forehead.

"It is much better today, Aunt Moire. It aches a bit but only hurts when I try to walk on it," Noah replied. He held out a cavalry officer between his thumb and finger for Clipper to catch with his claws.

"I am sure we will have you up and hopping around shortly. Perhaps Clipper will sit on your shoulder, and you can pretend to be a pirate," she suggested.

The piptere showed great patience in entertaining the child, and she sent him a wave of love and gratitude.

Although Moire also suspected it had much to do with the carrot Noah had in his pocket, which he used for treats.

She played with the boys for an hour or two, and when Noah slumped in his chair, she helped both boys to bed for a short nap. Closing the door, she crept across the hall to her room with Clipper. She had a tiny writing table pushed under the window, set in the arched roof of the cottage. Moire sat in the chair and leaned against the wall as she gazed out the window.

Clouds obscured the sun as her thoughts drifted back to her conversation with Ruth. While Oliver had amassed a fortune during the war, he was barred entry to the peerage by the circumstances of his birth. The dragon egg had been his hope of entering the Draco Legion. Moire could still make that dream come true. Her hands itched as though she held the right book before her, one that would unlock the last secret leading her to a nest.

She retrieved the heavy tome she had brought with her, the last one that had been sent to Mrs Radcliffe. Placing it on the desk, she turned to the section of most interest to her. Clipper perched on her shoulder, nuzzling her cheek affectionately. Moire smiled, stroking the tiny dragon's head as he trilled in contentment.

Her fingertip tapped a page. "This is it, Clipper, what I have been searching for. It says here that female dragons are secretive and protective of their eggs. But on rare occasions, if a supplicant gains their favour, a female may gift them an egg. It says men are rarely successful and are often covered in fire for their impertinence." The word *supplicant* stuck in her mind, and she ignored the unfortunate consequences of failure. "If I approach a female with sufficient cause in my heart, she might agree to replace the egg we lost."

What would move a dragon to aid Moire's cause? Or, more importantly, what would move a female dragon when men had tried and failed? She gathered what memories she had of Caliban. What had their dragon valued above everything else? Honesty.

Moire drew a shuddering breath. She knew what she would lay before a female dragon.

A broken heart.

Her desire to make amends and see the person she loved achieve happiness would be her offering.

Now, she had only to locate a female dragon with an egg.

12

THE NEXT DAY, Ruth returned to Larkspur Cottage. Since Katherine had decided for a rare change to sit with Noah, Moire decided to go for a walk with the young woman.

"We could look for the piptere nest Noah found," Moire suggested. She was keen to find it and learn what she could about the habitat the parents chose.

"I shall come along, too. Might bag something for supper," Samuel said as he fetched his rifle and called the dogs to him.

It was a glorious summer's day. A gentle breeze rustled the leaves of the trees, carrying with it the scent of wildflowers. Samuel's dogs bounded playfully around them, their tails wagging with unrestrained joy as they searched for any scent of rabbit or game birds.

Moire walked alongside Samuel, while Ruth walked in front of them. They decided to head towards a particular bit of forest where the river sliced through it, and in the same area that Samuel had found Noah. As they strolled along the river, Moire spotted a familiar figure approaching from the opposite direction.

Time stilled around her. Her heart stopped as she drank in the sight of him.

"Captain Hartford!" Ruth cried out with delight, rushing forward to greet him.

Moire stayed frozen to the spot. The years had sharpened Oliver's features, giving him an air of ruggedness and weathered strength. His light-brown hair was bleached almost blond at the tips sticking out from under his hat. His erect posture exuded vitality and confidence. Her heart constricted as her gaze settled on the beloved face, so long absent from her life.

Moire ached to approach him, yet her limbs refused to move. How many nights had she lain awake these past years, longing to hear his voice once more or feel his touch? How many times had she regretted her decision not to move the dragon's egg before it was discovered by another?

"Good day, Miss Ruth, Mr Radcliffe. I hope I am not intruding on your outing?" Oliver said, his attention fixed on Samuel's sister.

"Of course not. The day is much improved for discovering you on the same path." Ruth played the coquette and smiled with lowered lashes.

"Good to see you, Captain," Samuel called out. "You haven't spotted any pheasant on your walk, have you? They seem to be avoiding me."

Oliver shook his head. "No, but I did not go for a walk to find any prey."

"Do say you will join us, Captain?" Ruth chimed in as she looped her arm through Oliver's.

"I cannot refuse your kind invitation, Miss Radcliffe," Oliver said, his tone gracious.

Moire must have made some small movement, or perhaps it was the flap of Clipper's wings, for Oliver turned and met her gaze. His grey eyes burned into her with shock and recollection. Then a guarded mask fell over his features, and he skimmed over the piptere on her shoulder before turning his attention back to Ruth.

Moire had done it. She had laid eyes on him for the first time in eight long years. Her heart resumed its steady thrum. She maintained her dignity and had not thrown herself at his feet, begging forgiveness for something she had never done.

"Oh, why, where are my manners? This is Samuel's sister-in-law and an old friend, Miss Moire Tobin." Ruth waved a hand at Moire where she stood partly obscured by Samuel's larger figure.

Oliver swallowed and ground his jaw. At length, he muttered, "Miss Moire."

"Good day to you, Captain," she whispered.

Samuel, for once sensing the undercurrents between people, took Moire's arm. "I think the spot where I found Noah was not far from here."

As they continued their walk, Ruth insisted that Oliver hold her hand as she navigated the uneven ground, despite the fact that the obstacles were nothing more than mere sticks and stones. They soon left the open sunshine beside the river for the dappled light under the trees.

Moire held her own counsel. She couldn't think of anything to say that wouldn't expose the sorry state of her heart. The captain was the one who broke off their engagement. His long silence had only proven that his love for her had been a fleeting thing. She would not humiliate herself by pleading for a second chance or a snippet of his affection.

Samuel's favourite gun dog, a sprightly spaniel named Jasper, suddenly darted ahead, barking excitedly at something in the branches of a nearby tree.

"Jasper, what have you found?" Samuel called out.

The group followed the commotion made by the dog. Samuel took his bearings. "I say, it was around here that Noah found the nest."

Moire gazed up at the trees, wondering which one held aloft the piptere nest. Following the direction indicated by the dog, Moire spotted the commotion. A small piptere, its silver scales glinting in the sunlight, was trapped in the tangle of branches and unable to free itself.

"Look, there's a piptere caught up there!" Ruth exclaimed, pointing towards the struggling creature.

"I shall free the poor thing," Oliver offered. He stared at the old beech with limbs extending in a variety of directions and picked a starting position. However, he didn't get far before the creature became highly agitated. Hissing and flapping its wings at the human, until Oliver was forced to drop back to the ground.

"It doesn't appear to want to be rescued," Oliver mused.

"I'll have a go," Samuel said. He grasped hold of a different branch and leveraged himself up. Yet, as he too began to climb, the piptere's distress only intensified.

"Stop! Both of you, please stop! You are only scaring it

further," Moire cried out, concerned for the frightened creature.

"I think Moire is right. Perhaps there is another way to help the thing," Ruth said, her eyes wide with worry.

"Could Clipper tell it to calm down?" Samuel pointed to the blue and silver piptere who watched from a branch close to Moire.

"We could certainly try. I wonder if it might even be one of his parents. Did you not find his egg around here?" Moire held out her arm for Clipper to perch on.

"By Jove, I think you are right. Wouldn't that be a co-incidence," Samuel said.

"Could you help, Clipper?" Moire asked her constant companion. "We shall free them, if only they would stop struggling."

"Clipper? Why did you name him that?" Oliver had a sharp tone to the question as he swung his head to regard Moire.

Moire swallowed to moisten her mouth. "It was not my doing. Dragons, both large and small, are born knowing their name."

The captain made a noise in the back of his throat and then lowered his head to say something to Ruth at his side.

Clipper flew to the tree and chirped at the other crea-ture. Its struggles lessened, and it replied in the same chirps and trills.

"Do you think you could try, Moire? You have a way with such creatures." Samuel called his dogs to heel, and they all dropped to the leaves to watch the proceedings.

She glanced up. The piptere was trapped some eight or nine feet up. She had certainly climbed a similar height on a library ladder. But that was different, and she could cling to a rung while she reached for a book. This was untrustworthy branches and a struggling creature.

Just then, the piptere emitted a pathetic cry, and she knew she had to try. "Very well. I will see what I can do." She stripped off her bonnet, as it would only get in the way or get snagged on twigs. Then she looked for a spot to start.

"I can give you a leg up. It will be just like putting you on a horse," Samuel offered. He laced his fingers and made a platform with his two hands.

Moire placed her boot on his palms and stretched above her head to grab a branch. Then Samuel lifted her upward and allowed her to reach the first branch. Her heart pounded, and she kept her eyes on Clipper and the silver piptere above. Experience had taught her that when she had to leave the ground behind, it was better to focus somewhere else and never look down.

"Clipper, could you help me look for handholds," she whispered to her companion.

He chirruped and hopped down a few branches. He waddled along and then jumped down again. Then he bounced on a particular spot. *Here,* he said in her mind.

Moire reached up and placed her hand next to where the little dragon sat. Then she was able to move her feet along while Clipper found the next spot for her hands.

The blue and silver piptere flitted from one branch to another, guiding her upwards by sitting on her next handhold.

"Take your time, Moire," Samuel called softly from below.

With a deep, steadying breath, Moire reached for

another branch. The rough bark scraped under her finger-tips. She hoisted herself up, focusing on Clipper's bright form as he moved ahead of her.

Close, Clipper encouraged her as they climbed higher.

As Moire grasped the next branch, she inadvertently glanced downwards and instantly regretted it. Her stomach roiled as the ground appeared further away than she'd imagined. She gritted her teeth and continued upward, determined not to let her fear control her.

"Thank you, Clipper," Moire whispered between shaky breaths. Finally, she reached the branch where the piptere was tangled.

"Hello, little one. I will have you free shortly, I promise," Moire said gently while trying to ignore the height at which she now found herself. "Clipper, could you ask them to be still and enquire if there is something I could call them, please?"

Her companion chirruped at what might be either his mother or father. It was impossible to tell the gender from looking at a piptere. Only the creature knew how it identified itself.

Female. Lunette, Clipper told her.

"It is lovely to meet you, Lunette, but I am sorry about the circumstances. Let us see what has you trapped." The silver piptere's wings had stilled. Without the fluttering, it was easier to see that a loose vine was wrapped around the dragon's hind legs. Something metallic glinted among the leaves, but Moire could only tackle one problem at a time.

Gently, she worked the vines loose, but they seemed caught. A lump formed in her throat when she saw the reason. A silver chain extending from one leg was knotted around bits of twig that had then become tangled in the foliage of the tree and the creeper.

"I need to cut Lunette free. Do either of you gentlemen have a pocketknife?" Moire called softly, not wanting to startle Lunette.

"I do," came Oliver's firm reply.

"Could you fetch it, please, Clipper?" Moire scratched her friend's chin and then adjusted herself so she could lean against the trunk of the tree.

Clipper dove, snatched the knife in his claws, and returned it to Moire. She rubbed a finger along the mother-of-pearl inlaid in the handle, still warm from Oliver's touch. Then she opened the blade and hacked at the more stubborn foliage. At last, they came away, and she closed the knife and gave it back to Clipper to carry down.

"Once we are on the ground, I can remove this chain." Moire coaxed Lunette into her arms and then tucked the small creature into the folds of her shawl. The piptere hesitated for a moment and then nestled against her, her tiny body trembling from the ordeal.

"Bravo, Moire!" Samuel called up. "Take your time coming down. We're right here to catch you if you need us."

Moire closed her eyes and found the strength to tackle the descent, made more awkward by the precious cargo she now carried. Her fingers dug into the rough bark of the tree. The return climb was a delicate dance between fear and determination. Fear tried to freeze her mind, but she refused to let it overpower her.

"You are nearly down." Ruth offered her encouragement.

As Moire finally lowered herself to the ground, her

boot caught in an unseen root and her weight tumbled sideways, wrenching her ankle and sending a sharp jolt of pain through her leg. She dropped to the earth and flung out her hands to grab the trunk before she stumbled. Now she knew how Noah had twisted his ankle. The exposed roots were intent on snaring feet.

"Are you all right?" Oliver asked. He must have caught her sudden indrawn breath when her boot became snagged.

"I'm fine. Thank you," she said, determined to hide the stab of pain from the others. She settled more comfortably before uncovering Lunette.

"Oh, isn't it simply divine?" Ruth exclaimed, her eyes alight with excitement as she took a step towards Moire and the piptere. "I must have it! My uncle is a viscount, after all, and such a unique creature would befit my station perfectly. And look, it already has a leash."

Moire's heart sank at Ruth's words, her hands instinctively tightening around the trembling piptere. The idea of this delicate creature being tethered and paraded like an accessory was abhorrent to her.

"Absolutely not," Moire declared, her voice firm and resolute despite the pain in her ankle. "Pipteres are not baubles to be shown off at parties. They all deserve to make a choice of their own free will, like Clipper. He chooses to keep me company because I am kind to him." She gestured to the little dragon perched on the branch above her head.

Ruth's lower lip jutted out in a pout. "But surely there must be some way for me to keep it?"

"She. Her name is Lunette. And if you earned her trust, then she might decide to become your companion,"

Moire explained. "You would need to visit this area daily, bringing food and offering gentle words of friendship."

"It...*she* lets you hold her. It cannot be so difficult." Ruth took a step forward, and Lunette reared up and flapped her wings.

Moire murmured to the little creature and ran her hand soothingly down her spine. "Clipper spoke to Lunette, and she remains quiet so that I might free her. I make no demands on her."

Ruth sighed dramatically. "That all sounds so dreadfully time-consuming. In London, you can purchase such a creature from the specialty stores. Perhaps I will simply buy one next time I am in town."

"Sometimes, the most precious things in life require effort and patience. True connections cannot be forced or bought." Moire glanced up and found Oliver's stormy gaze on her. Feeling a blush creep up her cheeks, she turned her attention to the trembling Lunette. "Now, little one, let us see what caused you such grief."

Free of the vines, Moire could now concentrate on the chain and ankle shackle on the piptere. "Someone once leashed this little one, and she either escaped or was let go, still dragging the chain. She is lucky we found her. She would have starved to death if she had been unable to free herself." Anger roiled inside Moire. Someone had either callously let the piptere out with an anchor trailing behind her or had treated her in such a fashion the little dragon fought to escape her captivity.

"Could she have escaped by accident? There may be a reward offered for her return," Ruth said, her tone more subdued now as she realised the piptere would not be her new pet.

"The shackle has a rivet in it. Otherwise, she would have been able to pick a buckle open. Could I have the knife again, please?" She held out one hand.

"Oh, do be careful with a knife so close to its leg. Someone might wish to have her returned to them," Ruth said.

"I shall leave that decision to Lunette. If she wishes to be returned to whoever placed the shackle on her, we can assist in reuniting them." Even as Moire spoke, the piptere hissed, and her scales rose on her back like a cat with its hackles up. It seemed a reunion was *not* the desired outcome.

Oliver's gaze settled heavily on Moire, and she tried to ignore the fact that she was the centre of attention. Lunette needed her. She braced either side of the buckle with her fingers while she worked the tip of the knife into the metal. "It will soon be off, Lunette, I promise. Then you will truly be free."

At the last instance, the knife slipped, and Moire stilled her hand just as the tip sliced into her finger. She ignored the drop of blood as she tugged the shackle free of Lunette's leg. Moire balled the chain up in her hand. She would dispose of it where there was no risk that another creature might become entangled in it.

"All done. Thank you for your patience in holding still, Lunette." Moire brushed one hand down the warm scales that were like velvet under her palm.

The piptere tested her newfound freedom, stretching her wings and lifting first one leg, then another. She brushed her head against Moire's hand and made a series of chirrups and trills.

She thanks you, Clipper said. *One favour deserves another. She will do something for you.*

"You do not owe me anything," Moire addressed Lunette. But then, an idea swirled in her mind. Was there any possibility that the piptere might know how to approach a female dragon and ask for an egg? She wondered how to even word the question so the little creature understood what she sought.

"There might be something that you could assist with. Could you find me in a few days' time?" First, Moire needed to find the lists of dragons and determine which families had a female bonded to their line.

13

ONCE MOIRE HAD FREED the silver piptere, she placed the little dragon on a low-hanging branch. Lunette stretched out her hind legs, flexing them as though testing for any damage. Then she turned her opalescent eyes towards Moire. A soft chirrup of gratitude escaped the piptere's throat.

"Off you go now," she encouraged, her voice low and soothing.

Lunette extended her slender wings and took flight with a graceful flap. Moire watched as the silver piptere soared through the sky, performing an aerial display that captivated her audience below. The little dragon twisted and turned with mesmerising elegance, her body glinting like a ribbon of moonlight in the sun's warm embrace.

"How marvellous," Moire whispered, her earlier anxieties forgotten as she became lost in the entrancing ballet being performed above her.

As if summoned by the beauty of the spectacle, Clipper leapt from his branch and joined Lunette. The two dragons weaved between one another with remarkable agility, their movements synchronised in perfect harmony. It was a sight that brought joy to Moire's heart. Then an ache took hold of her as it reminded her of a night years ago when a lunar dragon had danced above her head. She stole a glance at Oliver, but he seemed as focused on the aerial display as the others.

Words bubbled up in Moire's chest and then formed a dam in her throat. After eight years, here was Oliver and her chance to ask for forgiveness for her actions. And yet, the tense set to his jaw made her doubt that he would even so much as talk to her. While she accepted blame for not finding a more secure hiding place for the egg, she needed to defend herself against the heinous accusations he had believed about her.

There will be a time, she reassured herself. Somewhere private, where she could air an old injury and seek the calming balm of an apology.

The pipteres' enchanting calls reverberated through the air and made a haunting melody that accompanied their movements. Their bodies entwined like delicate silver and blue silk threads. Clipper glanced down and trilled as he broke away from Lunette and glided down to land on Moire's shoulder. Lunette back-winged above them, called out once more, and then flew away.

"Goodbye, Lunette," Moire whispered as the silver dragon soared higher until her form disappeared among the billowing clouds that had begun to gather on the horizon. A pang of longing shot through her as she watched the dragon vanish from sight. The grace and freedom of their flight were a stark contrast to her own grounded existence (notwithstanding her fear of heights).

"Looks like rain is not far away. Shall we head back to the cottage for a cup of tea?" Samuel said.

The women murmured their agreement.

With a deep breath, Moire turned her gaze towards the road that led to the cottage. She drew her shoulders back and took one step. Her ankle throbbed painfully with each step after her awkward landing after she freed Lunette. Despite the pain, she remained determined to make her way home unassisted, her jaw set in resolute defiance.

"The joys of being human. We hide what we feel, unwilling to expose our true selves to others," she muttered under her breath as Ruth took Oliver's arm and the handsome couple led the way. Samuel fell into step behind them, and Moire limped at the very back, surrounded by the dogs.

As they traversed the uneven terrain, the weight of her thoughts grew heavier. She needed to confront Oliver about his unwarranted assumptions but struggled with how to voice her complaints without appearing like a *hysterical woman*. She dug her nails into her palms, partly to distract her mind from the pain in her ankle and partly to hold back her shout of frustration.

If she had been a man, on seeing Oliver, she would have strode up to him, punched him in his square jaw, and demanded an apology. Instead, as a supposed meek woman, she would need to wait for the right opportunity and use carefully veiled words to even dance near the topic. She let out a sigh. At least she had Clipper.

"I think it would be wonderful, Clipper, if I could soar

through the sky without fear or a care in the world, leaving behind all my earthly troubles and heartaches," she said.

The blue piptere trilled softly in agreement, his head tilted as if contemplating the possibility of such a life for his human friend.

"But the Fates did not gift me with wings, so I must make do with the path set before me." Moire focused her eyes on the road ahead. How much further was it back to Larkspur Cottage?

She concentrated on Oliver's figure with his broad shoulders and tall posture. Her finger stroked over the ring on her right hand. What would her life have looked like, if the egg had remained safe in Faustus's burrow? Would Oliver have kept his promise to return and claim her and the unhatched creature? She would never know. Perhaps the passage of time and events of war would have faded his love. Certainly, he could not have loved her as deeply as she loved him. Otherwise, he would not have so easily cast her as a villain in events and broken off their engagement.

Laughter came from the couple up ahead. The dogs bounding around her barked, and Samuel glanced back. Only then did he realise how far behind Moire had fallen and that she limped with each step.

"I say, Moire, are you quite all right?" He hurried back to her.

Moire managed a weak smile. "I am embarrassed to admit to the same injury as Noah for much the same purpose. I landed awkwardly on my ankle when I climbed out of the tree with Lunette. That beech is a danger to our family. No doubt the pipteres nest there knowing that if anyone dares try to reach their nest, they will suffer a twisted ankle on the descent."

Her brother-in-law huffed in laughter. "At least it is not broken, and I won't have to put you out of your misery like a wounded horse." He patted his gun, but the action did little to reassure her.

Instead, she bit back the comment that her heart suffered a far worse fracture and focused on placing one foot before the other on the rough dirt path. The wind whispered through the trees, rustling leaves like a sympathetic murmur from nature itself.

"It is also the other ankle to Noah. We can lean on each other and have two good legs between us," she managed to jest.

At last, they reached a fork in the road that led back to the cottage. Horse hooves clopped along the beaten earth, and a gig appeared around the bend. The newcomers stopped to chat with Oliver and Ruth, and when Samuel and Moire made their slow way to them, she found it was Admiral Chellum with his wife at his side.

Mrs Chellum smiled at seeing Moire and waved. Then a frown tugged at the corners of her eyes. "Why, Miss Moire, are you all right? You seem to favour one leg."

The others swung around to observe her uneven gait as she reached the gig.

"I'll be fine. I landed a bit heavily after rescuing a piptere stuck in a tree," Moire assured her, ducking her head at the attention.

"Why on earth were you climbing a tree? Surely my brave, dragon-riding brother should have rescued the creature?" Mrs Chellum narrowed her gaze at her younger sibling.

"The captain tried, as did Samuel, but the thing became ever so upset about it, and Moire feared it might injure itself. Then Moire climbed the tree instead. She has a gentle touch with such creatures, and it calmed for her so she could free it." Ruth eagerly gave a quick recount of the events.

"Well, we cannot have such gallant actions causing your injury, Miss Moire. I am sure the admiral will not mind giving you a ride back to Larkspur Cottage." Mrs Chellum laid a hand on her husband's arm.

"Of course not. We must offer our assistance to an injured comrade," Admiral Chellum said.

Ruth stood to one side to allow Moire to move closer to the gig. There was just enough room at the very back for one person, or two children who didn't fidget, to sit. As she stared at the seat, she wondered how on earth she would climb up there as there was nowhere to rest a foot to boost herself up.

"Do live up to your chivalrous reputation, Oliver, and give Miss Moire a hand," Mrs Chellum called out to her brother.

Oliver hesitated for a moment before nodding curtly, his jaw set in a tight line.

As he approached nerves fluttered in the pit of Moire's stomach. She'd longed for his attention ever since his return, yet now that he stood before her, she struggled to meet his gaze. His sea-grey eyes, which were once so warm and inviting, now held an icy detachment that sent shivers down her spine.

His strong hands settled on either side of her waist, and he lifted her as though she were no more than a sack of grain. Moire rested her hands on his forearms and dared a glance at his face while they were so close. She sought any sign of the man she had once loved so dearly. But his expression remained impassive and carved in stone.

As Oliver released her and his arms slid away from under her palms, he turned one hand, and his fingers brushed over the moonstone ring—a symbol of their engagement. The fleeting contact of skin against skin sent a jolt through Moire.

"Thank you, Captain Hartford," she whispered, accepting his assistance with as much grace as her throbbing ankle would allow.

Oliver didn't answer. He strode back to Ruth, and the young woman took his arm, leaving Samuel to his dogs.

"Are you quite comfortable there, Miss Moire?" Mrs Chellum asked, her kind eyes studying Moire's face as if she could read the turmoil within.

"Yes. Thank you," Moire replied, forcing a smile that didn't reach her eyes, but it was an effort worth making for the sake of her generous hosts.

"Off we go then!" Admiral Chellum announced, his voice filled with joy as he took up the reins.

"It is quite fortuitous that we met you today," Mrs Chellum said as the admiral guided the horse along the narrow path.

"Oh?" Moire said, her thoughts flying back through time to happier moments.

The older woman continued. "Since the Radcliffes

were so kind as to invite us to dine with them, I would like to repay their offer."

"I am sure they would be delighted to accept." Their lives were bound by the rules of society and invitations. There was a reciprocity expected in actions and invitations. A supper invitation accepted obliged the other party to offer up something of equal value, according to their station. If both parties were of a similar standing, there might be a picnic, perhaps, in warmer weather, or a luncheon. The rules became trickier when there was an inequality among the parties involved.

"Oh, that is good to hear. But you see, Miss Moire, I would dearly like to host a supper at our residence, but..." Mrs Chellum's voice trailed off.

Moire rested her hand on the side of the gig as she turned to converse with Mrs Chellum. She had an inkling as to what might trouble the other woman if she possessed the same generous heart that Oliver once owned. "But you are worried about causing offence?"

Mrs Chellum rested her gloved hand over Moire's bare one. "Yes, that is what nibbles at my heart. Eadred Manor is your home. I wish to have you dine with us but worry that it would cause you discomfort to be cast in the role of guest."

Moire buried her heartache at leaving her home deep inside her. The fault lay with her father, not the warm couple who took up the lease. There would be time enough to examine all her worries in the long hours between going to bed and sleep claiming her. "Shall we speak plainly, Mrs Chellum?"

"Yes, let us. And please call me Charlotte, for I would like us to become friends." Mrs Chellum let out a gasp as the gig hit a bump, and she bounced on her seat. One hand shot out to grab her husband's sleeve.

Moire suspected the admiral did it deliberately, as he chuckled to himself when his wife grasped his arm tighter to keep her seat. She wrapped both hands around the wood of the seat as she pivoted to face forward. "I would leap at the chance to visit you and the admiral, and I miss Faustus. A supper would give me an opportunity to slip out and see him if that would not offend you." It had been over a week since she left home, and she was worried about the old wyvern.

"Oh, marvellous! If you truly do not mind, I shall write invitations as soon as we return to the manor. It will be lovely to host a jolly party. The house seems rather quiet with just the admiral and me roaming the halls." Mrs Chellum glanced at her husband as she spoke.

"And I would be delighted to call you Charlotte if you would call me Moire," Moire said, offering a tentative gesture of friendship.

Charlotte beamed and nodded.

"Perhaps if you have a moment, you could help me find any naval books in the library. I'm too old to be scurrying up the rigging," Admiral Chellum said.

"I'm not sure how my ankle will feel about ladder climbing, but I can direct Clipper. He is very helpful at retrieving things like books." Moire stroked the piptere, who had settled on the gig once they were underway.

"Young lads are brilliant at climbing ropes. I struggle to remember that I used to be able to do it, too." The admiral launched into a tale of his early days at sea as a cabin boy. One who got frightfully seasick on the calmest ocean.

Moire stared at the man who seemed the epitome of hale and hearty. "A cabin boy who gets seasick? Whatever did you do?"

"Since we had left any sight of land long behind us, I simply had to get on with it. Besides, I desperately wanted to be a sailor because it offered me a chance for advancement. Sometimes, we have to push through pain and discomfort to follow the path we want." He winked at Moire and then continued. "I spent many hours with my head in a bucket or leaning so far over the side I worried I would tumble in. Then, as the days turned into weeks and months, I needed that bucket less and less. These days, I can keep my balance and my stomach during the roughest of storms." Admiral Chellum sat tall and proud in his seat as though he imagined himself standing at the helm of his vessel during a fierce squall.

"And yet..." Charlotte leaned in closer to her husband, "...a quiet ocean and land on the horizon still makes the admiral ill. One could almost think it was the thought of returning to shore that affected his stomach, rather than the action of the waves."

Admiral Chellum burst out laughing. "My dear wife has the measure of me. I'd much prefer to be on the deck of my ship than be a landlubber. But she has convinced me to spend some time in the countryside and to try other pursuits. And so, I indulge her."

Before too long, pretty Larkspur Cottage, with its climbing roses draped over the front portico, appeared along the lane. Admiral Chellum pulled the horse to a halt and then climbed down. He offered a steadying hand to

Moire as she slid off the back seat and gingerly placed a little weight on her foot.

Clipper flew on ahead and sat on the wooden fence that edged the front garden.

"I'll not be long, my love. I shall escort our young friend inside," he called to his wife as he guided Moire along the path.

She leaned heavily on his arm. Physical exhaustion, combined with the mental fatigue of keeping her heart armoured in the presence of Oliver, took a toll on her body and mind.

"Thank you for rescuing me, Admiral Chellum," Moire said as they reached the front door.

"I am delighted to be able to offer my assistance to a woman in distress. We didn't encounter many at sea." He patted her hand.

"I hope you have a gripping tale about pirates to share when I come for dinner," Moire said with a smile.

"Ah! I shall tell you about Iron Annie, the most fearsome *woman* pirate on the seven seas," he replied.

"You will have to convince me she is real." Moire had heard of the famed outlaw, but many dismissed her as either a work of fiction or a male pirate who preferred a more feminine guise.

He winked and leaned in closer. "Oh, Iron Annie is very real. As a young lieutenant, she asked me to marry her, but my heart was already taken by the fair Charlotte."

Moire laughed, and her heart lightened. "That is most definitely a story you will have to tell me."

They said their goodbyes, and Moire limped into the cottage.

"Moire?" Katherine called out from the parlour.

Moire slowly made her way to the parlour door. Katherine sat playing cards with Noah and Elijah. She glanced up at her older sister. "There you are. I thought you had all quite abandoned me."

"We found a silver piptere called Lunette on our walk. It had a chain that had become entangled in vines, and I had to climb a tree to rescue her," Moire spoke to the boys, who hung on her every word.

"Was it where I saw the nest?" Noah asked.

"I believe so. Your father said it looked like where you fell. In another day or two, we shall limp through the forest and see if we can find the nest again." Moire had decided what favour to ask Lunette—would the silver piptere donate an egg for the lad? Then a pair of stormy eyes drifted past her thoughts. Or should she jealously use the favour to try to win a much larger dragon egg?

14

───────

TWO NIGHTS LATER, with her ankle bound and feeling much better, Moire stood before the mirror set into the wardrobe door. Her heart fluttered like a hummingbird trapped within her chest. Her hands trembled as she buttoned the last few pearl buttons on her blue silk gown, specially chosen for the evening at Eadred Manor. She took a deep breath, trying to steady herself. It was not every day that one attended a dinner party as a guest in their own home.

"Are you ready yet, Moire? You are going to make us frightfully late," Katherine called up the stairs.

Moire had taken far longer to dress than her younger sister. A tiny part of her wanted to appear her best because Oliver would be there. Another part of her wished she had a gown the same pattern as the parlour wallpaper so she could disappear. In the end, she chose a gown of a rich blue that complimented Clipper.

The younger sister of their cook had been engaged to sit

193

with the children for the night and ensure they had their bedtime stories. Katherine had refused to be left behind. Eadred Manor had once been her home, too, after all.

"Coming!" Moire grabbed a grey shawl and flung it around her shoulders as she hurried down the stairs.

Samuel and Katherine waited below. Her sister was stunning in a gown of deep red. Samuel was presentable but never fashionable. Not that it mattered, with his kind eyes and warm manner.

"I would be the envy of a duke this evening with two such attractive women on my arms." Samuel held out an arm to each of them.

Katherine giggled, being in a fine mood for once. Then she erased Moire's smile by saying, "No duke would look at a spinster of twenty-six like Moire."

Moire halted, and indignation rose through her. Each day, she reclaimed a little more of her voice, and in a rare move, she spoke up for herself. "Augusta is two years older than me, and she has gone to Bath with Father to snare herself a duke."

"Yes, but Augusta is a great beauty. You, Moire, well... you faded away many years ago." A sad look dropped over Katherine's features, and then she breezed out the door to the waiting gig.

Moire stood with her mouth open. Her newfound strength failed with that last comment.

"Don't take her words to heart, Moire. She does not mean it," Samuel said as he accompanied her outside. "Kate speaks without thinking. If that woman were a dog, she'd be a mighty fine hunter, following her instincts and going in for the kill."

"It's all right, Samuel. I know she has a generous heart, even if she does a fine job concealing it." Moire offered him a weak smile.

She knew what Katherine meant in her rather indifferent manner. When Moire had lost Oliver, the joy had drained from her life and form. The last few weeks had convinced her it was time to emerge from the gloom she wore like a night-coloured cloak. She had much in her life to be grateful for and was determined to pursue her studies about dragonkind. In many ways, she was grateful for Oliver's cool indifference. It might at long last extinguish the love that burned inside her, and she could open her heart to another.

Outside, she climbed up into the gig beside Katherine. Samuel took the reins, and the horse trotted off along the road.

The journey to Eadred Manor seemed both too long and too short. As the familiar façade of her ancestral home came into view, Moire's stomach churned. This was where she had grown up and had once been happy. And now, she would enter it as a guest.

The older Radcliffes had already arrived with Ruth. Their forms visible through the parlour window. Taking a deep breath, Moire stepped down from the gig, her satin slippers touching the gravel with a soft crunch. Twilight had only just tipped into night as she glanced towards the meadow behind the stables and wondered if Faustus still slumbered or if he had roused for his nocturnal prowling.

Inside, Lucy, the maid, hovered to take shawls and coats. As Moire handed over hers, she squeezed the maid's hand.

"Here you all are!" Ruth's high-pitched voice greeted them as they entered the parlour.

Samuel moved to chat with his father and the admiral. His mother stood with Charlotte. Ruth stayed close to Captain Hartford's side as he gazed into the flames of the fire.

Moire forced a polite smile; her heart ached as she struggled to find her footing with the reversal of roles. Not that the Chellums made her feel anything but a most welcome guest.

"It is lovely to see you, Moire." Charlotte took Moire's hands.

She smiled and joined the conversation. Her gaze darted to one side. Ruth looped her arm through Oliver's and laughed at something he said. Each tinkling pearl of laugher was a dagger plunged into her heart, the pain sharp and unyielding.

He has found a suitable wife already, and I must navigate my path through the years ahead, she chided herself.

"Shall we go through to dinner? I am famished. The Tobin family was so kind as to leave their staff, and the cook is a genius. I have never been so well fed in my life," the admiral said as he took his wife's arm.

"That is because we are easy men to impress, Admiral, after years at sea surviving on fish and hard biscuits," Oliver said with laughter in his tone. "Why, any woman could have me for as little as an orange to ward off scurvy."

They joked as they took their seats. The admiral at the head of the table. Charlotte, Moire, and Samuel on one side. Oliver, Ruth, and Katherine were arrayed across from them.

The clink of china and the murmur of conversation filled the opulent dining room. Flickering candlelight cast dancing shadows on the walls and reflected off the polished silverware. Moire focused on the delicate taste of her soup. With each course, she turned more inward and retreated from the conversation, letting Ruth shine as she laughed and chatted.

Talk turned to the war and the exploits the men had witnessed.

"You should have seen the captain on the back of Valiant, striking terror into the enemy sailors. You would have been a credit to the Draco Legion, Hartford. It's a blasted shame you do not have your own dragon." The admiral raised his glass in a toast to Oliver.

Oliver's head turned, and his gaze fixed on Moire. "I once had such a dream, but alas, it was...smashed. Now, I would settle for a bride who coveys her own nobility."

Moire's knuckles turned white as she gripped her cutlery. It wasn't just Oliver's dream that had shattered that night. So had hers. Her throat tightened as she struggled to swallow the lump forming there.

"If you were an army man, you could have signed up for a drake hatchling. I always fancied one for myself. They are fantastic hunters and can run down a deer." Samuel spoke with his fork, and a pea dropped to the table and rolled under the edge of his plate.

A wistful look crossed Oliver's face. "When you have soared among the clouds, it is difficult to image being grounded for life."

Unable to bear the weight of his words any longer, Moire's hurt and anger surged within her like a storm-tossed ocean. She dropped her cutlery on her plate with a clang and pushed back her chair with a sharp scrape. All eyes turned to her.

Charlotte touched her hand. "What is it, Moire?"

"Please, excuse me. I need to check on Faustus. I thought I heard him cry out," she garbled the words, then fled from the dining room, trying to hold back the tears that threatened to spill.

Her footsteps made no noise in her soft-soled slippers as she ran along the dimly lit hallway, the familiar surroundings a cruel reminder of happier times. Gasping for air, she threw open a side door and stepped out into the bracing night. The cold air stung her cheeks and drew some of the heat from her pained heart.

"Faustus? Clipper?" she called out. Almost immediately, a rustling came from the darkness, and the wyvern emerged, his silver eyes like two tiny stars. Then a high-pitched chirp came from Clipper, sitting on the wyvern's head. He had sought out Faustus as soon as they arrived.

"Moire." Faustus nudged his warm snout against her chest and rested his head against her for a long minute. Then he stepped back. "Come."

Together, they walked in silence through the over-grown gardens. Moire's thoughts were a whirlwind of hurt and anger. Eventually, they reached a secluded spot. A hidden alcove where she had once spent countless hours reading and dreaming of a future with Oliver.

The old wyvern sank to the ground, tucking his wings close to her sides as he regarded Moire with a mix of curiosity and concern. His dark scales drank up the moonlight but gave only shadows in return. Only his eyes were visible in the dark. "Sit," his voice was a gentle rumble.

Moire curled up against his scaly hide. "Thank you," she whispered, grateful for the comfort and understanding that only an old friend could provide. She wished she could turn back time and make things right, but such things were beyond her abilities.

Once her heart returned to its steady beat and her thoughts calmed, she spoke. "Oliver...Captain Hartford...he hates me for what happened to the dragon egg. And now... now he courts another woman, and it appears he will marry Ruth Radcliffe."

Eight years ago, he had called their engagement *irrevocably broken*, but an ember of hope had smouldered in her chest. Now, saying the words aloud made the situation all too real. Tears welled up in her eyes, threatening to spill over.

Faustus turned his sinuous neck so his head butted against hers. "You. Not to blame," he rasped. The images he sent to her mind were of that horrible night. A man ran across the lawn with the precious object, only to trip and fall. The egg had smashed on a rock hidden in the grass.

"But I am at fault. I knew men were searching the estate, and I didn't move the egg. It would have been safe if I had hidden it in my room," Moire choked out, her tears finally escaping and tracing cold paths down her cheeks. "But what really hurts is that Oliver never read my explanation or asked me what happened. He just...believed those lies about me. One horrible cartoon and the erroneous banns Father had published were all it took for him to break off our engagement. Did he ever truly love me that he could so easily cast me aside?"

As she voiced the question, her heart clenched in anguish. The possibility that Oliver's love had been nothing more than a fleeting fancy was almost unbearable. She had loved him with every fibre of her being, and to think that it had not been reciprocated made something inside her shrivel up.

"We hurt. Because. We love," Faustus rumbled the words. "Do not. Hate. Faustus."

The last words broke through Moire's pain. She flung her arms around the wyvern's neck. "Why would I ever hate you?"

"Faustus did. Bad thing. Hurt Moire." His eyes closed, and his head rocked from side to side.

"You were no more to blame than I was, dear friend." She pressed her face to his neck. She had asked the wyvern to stay in his burrow that night, but Sir George had ordered him to patrol the grounds.

Faustus warbled an eerie call, and it vibrated through his body. It was such a haunting cry of pain that when it ended on an exhale, it drew some of the anguish from Moire's body. She sat up and wiped her eyes with the heels of her palms.

"What a pair we are. What we both need is to forgive ourselves for old actions and move forward. If I cannot find a dragon egg, I might yet find a wyvern egg, so you would have company." She liked that idea. The Radcliffes had two wyverns. She would ask Samuel if she might have an egg if their female laid any.

Moire remained in the garden with Faustus, allowing the silence to envelop them like a comforting blanket. The soft rustling of leaves overhead and the distant murmurs from within Eadred Manor provided a soothing backdrop for her thoughts. As she gazed at the moonlit flowers swaying gently in the breeze, the weight of her heartache slowly lifted.

"Thank you, Faustus. As always, being with you is a balm for my soul," Moire murmured as she stood.

He puffed a quick breath and rose onto his stubby hind legs. Clipper called goodbye to his friend and flew to Moire's shoulder.

She walked back to the house with a lighter step, buoyed by the knowledge she was never as alone as she thought herself to be. She had friends among dragonkind. As she re-entered Eadred Manor, laughter and conversation floated through the air, emanating from the parlour where the dinner guests had gathered. Moire hesitated at the threshold, her newfound composure threatened by the thought of facing those who had witnessed her earlier flight from the table. No, she couldn't go in there, she decided. Not when re-opened wounds were still so raw.

Instead, she slipped away down the familiar corridors towards the library, seeking solace in the quiet refuge of books and memories of her childhood. The door creaked open, revealing rows of well-worn tomes bathed in the soft glow of the fireplace. A flicker of nostalgia brought a ghost of a smile to her lips as she recalled the countless hours spent within this sanctuary.

Moire crossed the room and selected one of her

favourite volumes, an enchanting tale of dragons and daring, and then settled in a comfortable armchair by the fire. As she opened the book, the scent of aged parchment and ink enveloped her senses, offering a wave of comfort. She lost herself in the story as she navigated through a world of adventure.

"Ah! Miss Moire, here you are," a familiar voice called from the doorway.

She looked up as Admiral Chellum walked towards her with a twinkle of relief in his eyes. "I was hoping I might impose upon you to assist me in locating some sea-faring tales within these shelves."

"Of course, Admiral," Moire said. She set her book aside and rose from her seat. Helping the admiral would be a welcome distraction.

"Ah, but what of your ankle? We cannot risk another injury as you ascend the heights," the admiral noted with concern, observing her wince as she took a step.

"Clipper will assist us." Moire gestured to the piptere perched on the back of the armchair. At the sound of his name, Clipper spread his wings and swooped to land on Moire's outstretched arm. "Would you be so kind, my friend, as to help us find books the admiral will enjoy?" she asked.

The little dragon gave an affirmative chirp and took flight once more, soaring upwards towards the higher shelves. As Clipper flitted gracefully amongst the volumes, Moire provided him with directions based on her intimate knowledge of the library's contents. "Three shelves to your left, Clipper. Ah, yes, that short one there with the gold lettering."

With surprising dexterity, the piptere gripped a book in his claws and glided down towards the admiral. His wings fanned the air as he hovered before the older man, presenting him with the literary treasure.

"Remarkable. Quite remarkable. You truly have a gift with these creatures," Admiral Chellum murmured, accepting the book with an appreciative nod. "Thank you, Clipper."

Moire watched the exchange with pride. Other pipteres were taught to do tricks. Clipper displayed his intelligence in his willingness to assist her without any coercion. She believed that him being free of any leash or cage served to deepen the bond between them.

"You are an exceptional woman, Miss Moire," the admiral spoke with genuine respect. "Not only do you have an extensive knowledge of the books in this library, but I have never seen a piptere stay with a person without being on a leash."

"I believe it is because Clipper has free will, Admiral," Moire replied, her fond gaze on the blue piptere as he darted through the air. "He chooses to be my friend. He isn't compelled by a chain or fear. That makes our bond all the stronger. I have been documenting our relationship over the years and noting my observations. I have the foolish idea of publishing a book on the topic."

The admiral stared at her so long a blush crept up her neck. It was a silly idea.

"Why, that is brilliant!" he exclaimed. "A shame that Caliban died when you were still a minnow. Imagine what you could have taught us all about dragons had he lived longer."

She smiled and turned back to Clipper to cover her stab of pain at the mention of Caliban's name.

With each book that the piptere brought down, the pile of ocean-themed stories grew larger on the library table. Admiral Chellum's eyes were full of good humour as he examined the titles and marvelled at Clipper's agility.

Having finished his task, the little dragon alighted on Moire's shoulder and butted his face against hers. She scratched him under the chin in his favourite spot and murmured her thanks.

The admiral nodded thoughtfully as he watched them. "You know, Miss Moire, I can't help but think that you would make an exceptional wife for Captain Hartford. The two of you could talk for hours about the bond he had with Valiant, and you would understand what he lost when the dragon returned to his family."

Moire's breath caught in her throat, and her heart stuttered at the admiral's words. "Thank you for your kind words, Admiral," she began, striving to keep her voice steady. "However, a man like Captain Hartford with his wealth requires a wife like Ruth, educated in all the attributes expected of a lady and who will grace his table and enhance his standing."

The admiral studied her for a moment, his eyes searching her face as if seeking an unspoken secret. "Perhaps," he conceded eventually, "but I maintain that your knowledge and affinity with dragonkind would make you a valuable partner for a man who rode a dragon, especially one who seeks to elevate himself to the Draco Legion. All Hartford lacks is a dragon egg, and he now has the wealth to buy one, should one come onto the market."

"Well, since you have enough reading material to last you a few weeks, shall we return to the others?" Moire changed the topic. She suspected Samuel, who always gave his dogs one last run before they were shut in their kennels for the night, would be as keen to leave Eadred Manor as she was.

15

———

A FEW DAYS LATER, Moire sat in the parlour, keeping Katherine company. She attempted to concentrate on her needlework, but her thoughts wandered, and she pricked her finger for the third time that hour. Lunette had not returned to repay her favour, not that Moire could decide what assistance she would seek from the piptere.

Samuel burst into the room with Ruth on his heels. His eyes sparkled with excitement. "I have brilliant news. Father intends to buy a seaside property and has asked if we want to journey there and see it!"

Katherine dropped her embroidery and gasped. "Oh! That would be fabulous. Sea air is said to be an excellent tonic for those of delicate constitutions like myself. I have been feeling rather weak these past few days."

"The seaside is supposed to be a wonderful place to aid recovery," Moire agreed. She wondered if it applied to battered hearts as well. It would suit her mood to gaze at a stormy ocean and then watch the water settle to a mirror-like surface as the sun emerged. It would be

206

symbolic of the transformation she sought to bring about in herself.

Samuel grinned, rubbing his hands together in anticipation. "What adventures we shall have by the shore. Magnificent waves crashing against the cliffs and the salty breeze invigorating our spirits. Shall we take the children, Katherine?"

"Good lord, no. You want me to recover, not shred my last surviving nerve. Surely your parents could have them for a few days?" Katherine batted her eyelashes at her husband, and Moire suppressed a smile as he melted before her.

"Of course, my love. I shall ask. I do not think it would be a problem. You know how Mother dotes on the boys, and she worries about your health," Samuel said.

Ruth sat next to Moire, and she glowed with her good mood. "I am coming, too. It will be ever such fun."

"It will be lovely to have your lively company, Ruth. Moire always has her nose in a book," Katherine said.

"Well, that is settled, then. We shall embark on a seaside adventure together. Wyldefen to Slatemooth is some thirty-five miles. It should not take us more than a day to travel there if we leave early in the morning." Samuel began making plans.

Katherine's face fell at the mention of an early start, as did Ruth's. Moire hid her amusement. Both women could sleep on the trip, swayed back to slumber by the movement of the carriage.

Two days after that decision was made, Moire dressed and waited in the entrance hall of the cottage for her sister to emerge. The children had been deposited with their grandparents the night before. The large travelling carriage of the Radcliffes would convey them south.

Samuel had woken early to walk up to Gormsby Hall and would collect both Ruth and the carriage. That would allow his wife longer to get out of bed and get dressed.

"Samuel is here!" Moire called as the carriage stopped outside the cottage. A pile of luggage was already lashed to its roof. A grumbling Katherine emerged from her bedroom and walked down the short path.

"I don't know why we have to start at such a hideous hour," she complained as she climbed inside.

Moire held her silence. It was ten o'clock, and she had been awake for three hours. Clipper refused to join her inside the carriage. Perhaps it looked too similar to a cage for the piptere with all the people inside. Instead, he perched on a corner behind the driver where he could survey the road ahead.

The party wound its way through the rolling countryside as they headed south to Dorset. Moire sat next to Ruth, the two of them on the rear-facing seat, as Katherine would become horribly ill if she had to sit there. She gazed out the window without really seeing anything as she tried to decide what boon to ask of Lunette in exchange for the removal of the chain from the piptere's leg. Her bottom was numb, and the warm, sweaty interior of the carriage became nauseous as the day wore on.

At long last, Ruth called out, "Look! We are nearly there!" She pointed to the distant shoreline where the ocean met the sky.

The others leaned forward, eager to catch their first glimpse of the sea. As they drew closer to the little seaside town of Slatemooth, the rhythmic thrum of crashing waves filled the air, accompanied by the cries of seabirds.

Moire leaned on Ruth's shoulder to peer out the window. "It is beautiful in its fierceness," she murmured as she gazed at the waves pounding the shore.

Despite her fear of heights (or of landing on rocks in this situation), Moire was captivated by the towering cliffs that lined the coast, their jagged edges softened by the golden hues of sunset. They all sighed with relief when the carriage halted, and Samuel helped them down one by one. Moire gazed up at the exterior of a charming inn. Three storeys tall, it had a whitewashed exterior and pretty, vibrant-blue shutters on the windows.

Clipper joined her, the little dragon vibrating with excitement at seeing the ocean for the first time.

"Don't wander too far, Clipper." Moire worried about storms blowing him out to sea or seagulls attacking him.

They settled into their rooms. Ruth had a lovely room with a large window facing the promenade and ocean, as did Samuel and Katherine. Moire had a much smaller room, not that she minded. The little square window was like a picture, framing the ocean view.

They met downstairs and ate a quiet supper, all of them tired from the journey. Afterwards, they played cards in the cheerful common room before the fire. Then they all sought their beds.

THEY WERE a much-refreshed party the next morning. The sea air was already working miracles on Katherine, who was out of bed for breakfast with everyone else. Conversation swirled around the dining room.

"Why, Ruth, I worry how you will endure Slatemooth," Katherine said with a devilish grin over her teacup. "I do not think I have seen you last an entire day without the captain at your side. You two are much in each other's company and make a handsome couple."

Ruth giggled and stabbed a slender spoon into her boiled egg. "They do say absence makes the heart grow fonder. I told Captain Hartford we were spending a few days here, and I would not be at all surprised if he rushes to Dorset with a very particular question on his mind."

Moire's stomach clenched. Ruth expected a proposal from Oliver. He was a man who once he made up his mind about something, was quite determined on that course of action. She sipped her tea, her appetite having quite deserted her.

"A promenade first, I think, so we can take the measure of the other visitors," Katherine suggested.

Ruth giggled with excitement, and they fetched parasols and bonnets for the stroll. Katherine and Ruth strode along together. Moire walked behind with Samuel. They wandered along the bustling promenade that stretched between the shops and houses on one side and the seashore on the other. Ladies and gentlemen traded tales of society gossip and scandal when they met.

Moire stopped on the seawall and watched Clipper dive and play in the waves. Below on the sand was a familiar figure conversing with another man she didn't recognise but who had the noble bearing of a fellow naval officer, despite the cane he leaned upon.

"I say, is that Captain Hartford?" Ruth halted and followed Moire's line of sight.

"Why, I think it is. Who is the other gentleman with him?" Katherine twirled her pale silk parasol and made the tassel fringe dance around her face.

"There is only one way to find out," Ruth said. Then she stepped to the edge of the seawall and waved her arms in the air. "Captain! I say, Captain Hartford!"

Oliver looked up and shielded his eyes with his hand. Then he returned the wave. The two men approached, moving slowly through the sand. The other man was leaning heavily on a cane. The group waited as the men climbed the steep stairs set into the stone wall.

"Miss Ruth, Mrs Radcliffe, how lovely to see you here," Oliver said on reaching them. "Allow me to introduce my friend, Captain James Forbes."

The captain bowed to the women.

Oliver continued, "And this is Mr Samuel Radcliffe, and...and Miss Moire Tobin." He seemed to stumble over her name.

Samuel shook hands with the other captain, and the women murmured their greetings. Then Captain Forbes turned a curious hazel gaze on Moire. "Miss Moire Tobin? I do believe I have heard that name before."

Her stomach plummeted. Did Oliver's friend likewise believe she was some dragon-slaying wretch whose only goal in life was to secure a prosperous marriage? If he did, he must also know she failed at the latter, since Samuel had married her sister.

"Well, gentlemen, we are indeed fortunate to have two

such distinguished war heroes among us," Ruth said as she took Oliver's arm.

"What brings you to Slatemooth, gentlemen? I thought you were still at Eadred Manor, Captain Hartford?" Samuel asked.

"Perhaps the captain had a question he needed to ask me?" Ruth said in a low tone, and she lowered her lashes.

"Oh, that is my doing," Captain Forbes said before Oliver could respond. He rested his weight on his cane. "I wrote to Hartford. I came to bathe in the seawater to see if it would give me some relief from this blasted leg, and Valiant wanted a swim, too."

"Valiant is here?" Moire leapt into the conversation, unable to stop herself when she heard mention of the dragon's name.

Captain Forbes was shorter than Oliver, with dark hair and an olive cast to his skin. He had a brooding charm about him, and warmth simmered in his eyes. "Indeed. He'll be out there somewhere catching fish." He gestured with his chin towards the turbulent ocean.

"There is a dragon...here?" Ruth's voice faded to a breathy whisper, and her eyes were round. She clung tighter to Oliver's arm. "I would be ever so frightened to see one."

Katherine cut her sister-in-law down. "Oh, tosh. We grew up with Caliban, and dragons are not so frightful once you get to know them. Are they, Moire?"

"I believe Caliban was exceptionally tolerant of us as children." Moire chose her words carefully. Their mother often cautioned them against climbing all over the proud dragon, not that it had ever stopped them. It was a wonder

Caliban hadn't flattened the both of them under a massive paw.

"Only as an adult, do I now wonder why our family dragons didn't just stand on us when we were such annoying children." Captain Forbes had laughter in his eyes. "But I don't know the name Caliban. Did he assist the army during the war?"

Moire swallowed. "No. We lost Caliban sixteen years ago."

"Oh. My condolences." Captain Forbes fell silent.

Losing a dragon meant an equally dragon-sized plummet in social standing. Although Moire mourned the physical loss of the dragon. Her father's title of Drac had meant nothing to her.

"I was privileged to ride Valiant during the war after Forbes was injured. You did me a great honour, my friend." There was genuine warmth in Oliver's voice as he thanked his fellow captain.

"A favour well returned through my share of the considerable fortune you and Valiant stole off the French," he replied with a chuckle.

"Will you walk with us, gentlemen?" Katherine grew restless, and she took Samuel's arm to continue their stroll.

"We would be delighted," Captain Forbes answered for himself and his friend.

Oliver walked with Ruth. Moire slowed her pace to match that of Captain Forbes.

"Are you from this area, Captain?" Moire asked as they strolled the edge of the seawall.

"No. The family estate is in Yorkshire. Valiant wanted

to come south as he says the ocean is warmer and Artemis has a cove not far from here," he said.

Despite all she had learned in books over the years, dry words on a page lacked something compared to direct, practical knowledge. "Did Valiant wish to pay a visit to Artemis?" Moire could not remember Caliban making social calls. He had seemed content with Faustus for company. There were not so many dragons that they could pick and choose their friends.

Captain Forbes chuckled. "Yes. Valiant informed me that she had summoned him for reasons that are best left to dragons."

Moire's mind spun. Why would Artemis summon Valiant to visit her? Then a connection snapped into place in her mind, and she halted. A breathy "Oh," escaped her, and her eyes widened in understanding.

"I wonder how long before she lays her eggs. And how many?" Moire mused as they continued on their way.

Captain Forbes looked at her with renewed interest. "You understand such things?"

"I endeavour to learn all I can. The passage of centuries has added little to our collective understanding of the intricacies of dragon relationships. No scholars can agree on how many eggs a dragon lays, as they guard their nests zealously due to eggs being stolen." Moire's breath grew short in her chest. This was the opportunity she sought. Her hands itched for her books to devour anything she could find about Artemis before she attempted to petition the dragon for an egg. "Do you think Artemis's family will sell any eggs she lays?"

"Some will sell an egg to the highest bidder, but only if

the female allows it. Usually, I think they are stolen by enterprising thieves, or the female forgets where she has laid them. I always found it most odd though, that if eggs hatch in the wild, why do we not see more unbonded dragons in England?" Captain Forbes raised an interesting question.

Moire agreed with him. "You are right. I can only recollect a dozen wild dragons who are not associated with a family. Perhaps many eggs do not survive the long time between laying and hatching?" She knew one that didn't. Such a fate might befall dragon eggs over the ten years they were vulnerable in the shell.

They approached the others, who had paused to allow the captain and Moire to catch up. "Family legend tells that my ancestor won his in a game of cards and then kept it by the fire in the parlour. But where it came from before that card game, no one knows."

"In my family, Drac Tobin supposedly stumbled upon his egg while out hunting." How to acquire a dragon egg had dominated Moire's studies for some years. But she had not yet found an answer beyond *luck*.

"This will be Hartford's chance. If anyone deserves an egg, it is him," Captain Forbes said as they re-joined the others.

Yes, Moire silently agreed; *this is Oliver's chance*. And her opportunity to make amends. All she had to do was find Artemis and convince the dragon that her cause was a worthy one.

Just then, a roar came from across the sea. A deep rumble like that of thunder. People who had been promenading turned, expecting to see storm clouds and the accompanying crack of lightning. Instead, a dark shadow dropped from the clouds and soared low over the water.

"Ah. Here comes Valiant now." Captain Forbes pointed with his cane.

Clipper flew from a rooftop and huddled on Moire's shoulder. She reassured the trembling creature. "He will not eat you, I promise."

Shouts of alarm went up, along with cries of "Dragon!" Some people ran indoors, while more streamed out to see the rare sight. Most dragons kept to themselves on family estates, and it wasn't every day one turned up at a seaside resort.

Valiant dropped closer to the water until his hind claws dragged through the waves. When he approached the beach, he sank into the foam and waded ashore. His scales glistened a mossy green that matched the colour of the ocean, and he seemed more a sea creature than an aerial one.

People gathered along the seawall to watch. Faces were alight with fear, awe, and fascination as they gazed upon the magnificent beast. Ruth tightened her grip on Oliver's arm, and Moire wondered if it was genuine fear or an opportunity taken to move even closer to the handsome captain.

Valiant swung his head until he located Captain Forbes, and then he let out a low call. The captain waved to the dragon and then he smiled at their group. "I swear this is his favourite part. Ladies, you might want to put up your parasols."

Moire wondered what he meant. Valiant walked a way up the beach, and then the dragon flopped to his belly. He rocked back and forth and used his wings to flick sand over himself. In doing so, he also showered all the gathered onlookers with sand. People shouted and laughed as wet clumps dropped onto top hats, parasols, and bonnets.

Once he had a fine coating of sand on his body, Valiant rolled again.

"Is he itchy?" Moire asked. "That looks like a way to help his body shed old scales."

Captain Forbes nodded. "Yes. It's much easier than doing it by hand."

"I can remember helping Mother with Caliban. It seemed an endless task to scrub a dragon's hide when he was shedding. I wonder why he did not fly to a beach to use sand as an abrasive like Valiant." Moire had so many questions and appreciated the rare opportunity of having Captain Forbes and Valiant to study.

"Did your father not take him? Either my father or I always accompany Valiant on his seaside trips. I think they do not like to be too far from their bonded family." Affection for the dragon was plain on Captain Forbes's face.

"No. My father and Caliban did not have a happy relationship." She watched Valiant enjoying himself. How sad that her father deprived himself of such a close bond with a magnificent creature. She prized each memory she had of Caliban.

Clipper trilled a question in her ear, wondering if he might copy the actions of the larger dragon.

"Of course, you must try it, Clipper. Although you know I enjoy grooming you when you are itchy. But chose a spot well away from Valiant. We don't want him to inadvertently roll on top of you." She scratched the piptere's head, and then he took flight to find a warm spot to roll in the sand.

"However did you stay on the great beast's back, Captain Hartford?" Ruth asked Oliver.

"For battle, the dragons allow us to fit them with a special harness, and the rider is clipped in so that we cannot fall while fighting. But even without it, there is a spot between the neck ridges that holds a rider somewhat like a saddle." A crowd drew nearer as he spoke. People were amazed to hear from the man whose name had filled many newspaper articles with daring exploits during the war.

"Perhaps once Valiant has rinsed off, Hartford, he might allow you to give the people of Slatemooth a practical demonstration?" Captain Forbes said to his friend.

Shouts of agreement came from the assembled crowd, eager for an impromptu show. Children pushed past the adults to sit along the seawall, legs dangling over the side. They screeched in enjoyment every time Valiant flicked sand into the air.

Oliver chuckled, and the tight lines around his eyes eased. "What say you, Miss Radcliffe? Would you like to see how I climb aboard Valiant and soar through the clouds?"

"Oh, yes. Although I would be ever so afraid you might fall." Her hand tightened on his forearm.

Moire shared Ruth's sentiment. How she longed to see Oliver where he should be—riding on a dragon. But her mind conjured all sorts of horrible scenarios in which he plummeted to the ground before a horrified crowd. Not that her opinion mattered. Nor was it sought.

16

OLIVER SWEPT a bow to the crowd. "Very well, then. If Valiant is agreeable, we shall put on a demonstration of our fighting moves." Then he trotted down the steep steps to the sand.

He approached the basking dragon, who lay on his side with his wings extended to soak up the summer warmth. The grey-green scales of the great creature shimmered like gems plucked from the ocean and reflected the sun's rays.

"Valiant, might I disturb your rest, oh mighty one?" Oliver called out, his voice tinged with both respect and familiarity.

The dragon raised his enormous head, his snout covered in sand, and he regarded the captain with eyes the colour of vibrant emeralds. A low rumble escaped his throat as if he were chuckling at some private joke. Watching the exchange roused Moire's curiosity as to how the dragon accepted someone not from its family line as his rider.

"The people here have heard of your magnificence in battle. Would you mind giving them a demonstration of your ability?" Oliver asked in a light, playful tone.

Valiant responded with a soft snort that created a small sand cloud. Then he rose with surprising grace for such a large creature. Shaking like a dog, a fine spray of sand misted the air. Once clean, he seemed to bow to the captain, extending one leg towards him to offer a steep path to climb.

"Thank you," Oliver said as he reached up to grasp Valiant's sturdy limb. With practised ease, he climbed onto the dragon's back, positioning himself between the hard neck ridges.

Even though Moire had grown up with Caliban and climbed over his massive form as a child, she still held her breath in wonder that the dragon allowed the man to sit atop him. Horses, and occasionally wyverns, also allowed people to ride them. But a dragon was many times larger, far more opinionated, and had the ability to spit flame.

Clipper rubbed his face against Moire's cheek. *Clipper, sit on Moire,* he crooned.

She touched the piptere's chest. They were friends, and she adored the little dragon. That was why she allowed him to perch on her shoulder. Did the massive dragon have a similar relationship with a human as a human had with a piptere? There was a line of thought to consider later. Especially since most pipteres were unwilling when made to sit on a shoulder like some sort of living decoration.

The onlookers were captivated by the spectacle before them. Their faces displayed a mixture of astonishment, delight, and a touch of fear. After all, it was not every day that a battle-hardened dragon took an ocean swim and then a sand bath in front of you.

"Are we ready?" Oliver shouted to the people on the road.

A cheer went up, and the dragon answered with a rumble, flapping his wings in anticipation. The sight left Moire breathless, her chest tightening with equal parts joy and trepidation as she wished for a safe journey for both rider and steed.

With a deafening whoosh, Valiant unfurled his wings and leapt into the air. His immense wingspan cast an all-encompassing shadow over the crowd as he flapped upwards. A hush fell over those gathered as they stared in amazement. The dragon and his rider were now silhouetted against the backdrop of the endless blue sky. Then Valiant turned and dipped to soar above the rooftops of the town.

The sun glinted off Valiant's hide as he banked gracefully up and to the right, completing a sweeping arc as he dropped back towards the ground before surging up again. Oliver never seemed to move or even wobble. His hands gripped the spines in front of him.

Moire's heart leapt into her throat as she watched the pair so high above the ground. She clasped her hands tight to stop a tremble of concern. To think they performed such manoeuvres while far out at sea and with enemy cannons firing at them!

"You still care for him," Captain Forbes murmured from her side.

His comment caught her off guard, but her response

came without hesitation, her eyes never leaving the airborne spectacle.

"I never stopped, Captain Forbes. A woman continues to love long after all hope has faded," she admitted softly.

"A man's love is etched in stone," Captain Forbes said.

A stone that shatters into a thousand pieces when tested, Moire thought. "A stone heart would surely make a sailor sink to the bottom of the ocean if he fell overboard."

The injured captain chuckled.

Moire closed her eyes for a moment, allowing herself to be swept away by the sounds of Valiant's powerful wing-beats and the awed murmurs of the onlookers. What would it be like to soar through the clouds, at one with the dragon, as though you had wings yourself? People would be like ants to Oliver from such a great height. When she had ridden Faustus, the land had been blanketed in night, and she had still pressed her face into his hide as fear clawed at her.

When Moire opened her eyes, Valiant performed a breathtaking loop. The crowd gasped, sure that Oliver might tumble and fall.

"I cannot look!" Ruth called out. "Tell me when it is over." Then she placed a gloved hand over her eyes.

At one point, Valiant flew straight upwards as though he were an arrow shot towards the sun. Then he twisted like a corkscrew as he spiralled back to the ground. People either froze to the spot or scattered as he plummeted lower, sure the dragon would crash into the promenade. Barely a dozen feet from the ground, Valiant levelled out and glided to the sand. Rumbling came from the dragon as he passed overhead, the creature laughing in enjoyment at either the flight or the terror he created among the onlookers.

A chorus of wild applause and cheers erupted from the gathered crowd as Valiant landed and stirred up the sand. Oliver grinned as he slid down the dragon's leg to the ground. His eyes were alight with happiness and exhilaration, something Moire had not seen for many years. Remembering the young, hopeful lieutenant he had been stirred up bittersweet nostalgia and longing within her.

Brave children, egged on by their friends, climbed down the seawall and crept along the sand to be closer to Valiant. Their eyes were wide with curiosity and wonder, but they kept a respectful distance from the majestic beast.

Oliver trotted up the steps, the previous tension now gone from his shoulders, his stride long and languid. Men wanted to shake his hand. Women touched his jacket as he passed by as though they could capture wisps of the clouds against which he had brushed.

He bowed to Ruth, yet his gaze settled on Moire as he said, "What did you ladies think of our little performance?"

Before Moire could respond, Ruth took his arm. "Why, Captain, I feared you would fall to your death before my very eyes!"

Questions arose from the crowd, and Moire retreated a few steps. Captain Forbes stood gazing at the dragon, a look of longing on his face. It could not be easy for him to see another ride his family dragon after an injury left him incapable.

"You made a most generous and gracious offer when you allowed Captain Hartford to ride Valiant after you were injured," Moire said as she joined him away from the throng of people.

"It was Valiant's decision as much as mine. Hartford is a good man and seems more born to it than I." His hand tightened on his cane.

Moire glanced to where Ruth gazed up at Oliver with open adoration. "It is no easy thing to watch another do what we wish we were capable of doing ourselves."

"Despite this glorious sunshine, we are a gloomy pair, are we not?" Captain Forbes jested.

Moire managed a smile. There was something about Captain Forbes that engendered trust. Finding a tendril of bravery within her, she asked a forward question of the captain. "Captain Forbes, might I ask your permission to address Valiant? There is much I would ask him while he is here, if you would allow it?"

Captain Forbes studied her for a moment. "I sense you have the heart of a scholar, much like myself. Very well, I have no objection. But be warned that Valiant might not be in a conversational mood. He is picky about who he talks to."

"Thank you, Captain." She touched his sleeve and before bravery abandoned her, descended the stone steps built into the wall.

At the bottom, her boots left shallow imprints in the sand as she approached the reclining dragon. The sand shifted beneath her feet, reminding her of the fine line between solid ground and the vast unknown that lay beyond. As she drew nearer, she became acutely aware of the dragon's immense size, larger even than Caliban had been. Valiant's sea-green scales glinted like sunlight on water. He lay with his head resting on his front paws, his half-lidded eyes focused on a point out at sea. The soft sound of his breathing accompanied the murmur of waves.

Clipper remained on her shoulder, bravely refusing to leave her despite his own fear. His small body trembled, and his tail tightened around her neck. His loyalty warmed Moire's heart, and she stroked his side with a finger to reassure him.

Some ten feet from Valiant, Moire stopped. She bowed and extended her arms, palms up to show she did not conceal any weapon.

"I am Moire Draca Caliban, and I seek your wisdom, oh mighty Valiant," she said in a clear voice, tinged with reverence. She used the old form of her name, reserved for those of the Draco Legion who were fortunate enough to have a dragon as part of their family.

She held her pose as the dragon studied her. Then he answered with a low voice that reminded her of a lonely wind through trees in winter.

"Caliban is missed," Valiant said.

The comment took her aback. Did dragons know when one of their kind passed to the next realm, or was he told the news by a human? "Yes, he is much mourned."

"How did he pass?" the dragon spoke softly, so their conversation stayed private and didn't boom out to the crowd above them on the promenade.

Moire stood and clasped her hands loosely in front of her stomach. Meeting the dragon's wise, old gaze, she dredged up the painful memory. "Caliban grew ill, but I cannot say what caused it. I sat with him that night, as did our wyvern, Faustus. My mother sang to him to ease his passing. With the first blush of dawn light, Caliban's soul flew from his physical form and joined the stars."

"You honoured our brother. Speak, little one. I sense you have many questions. I shall listen until I grow bored," Valiant rumbled, his voice low and resonant like the shifting tides.

Moire wondered what would happen when he grew bored. Would he extend one foot and squash her in the sand, or would a burst of flame move her along? "Thank you. I have devoted myself to learning all I can about dragonkind."

Moire had so many questions. To those swirling inside her, she added how Valiant had known of Caliban's death, and were they brothers in the sense they had the same mother, or did he mean in a more general sense of dragon-type brotherhood?

Before she could ask her first question, Valiant lifted his head and sniffed the air. "You are not alone."

She placed a hand on Clipper to both shield and reassure him. "No. This is Clipper. He is a piptere and my friend."

"I do not see many of his kind. They all fly away when they see me. Come, little cousin, you are safe with me," Valiant crooned to the terrified piptere.

"I will not let any harm come to you, Clipper." Moire reached up and untangled the piptere's tail from around her neck. She wasn't exactly sure how she would protect Clipper. But she would grab a parasol, prise the dragon's mouth open, and climb inside to rescue him if she had to.

With a quavering trill, Clipper edged along Moire's outstretched arm. Then he hopped onto Valiant's immense leg. Clipper's wings trembled as he met the much larger dragon's gaze. Valiant held still for several long seconds until the little piptere butted his head against his enormous muzzle.

"You do not leash him." Valiant gazed from Moire to Clipper.

"Never! He is my companion, and despite his small size, he has taught me much about dragons." Moire's voice held a trace of bolstered courage borrowed from the little piptere.

Valiant chuffed and blew warm air over Clipper, who trilled and held out his wings to receive the heated blessing. "That is good. It is not right that our kind are kept in cages."

"I would educate those who do, if I could. A willing partner enriches our lives so much more than a bound servant." Moire stood taller as she imagined a world where wealthy ladies were forbidden from latching gold or silver chains around their pets. Instead, they would have to earn the pipteres' companionship. Her dream dissolved as she realised that would never happen. Nobles didn't want their expensive pets displaying a preference for the company of a maid or footman instead.

Valiant huffed again and peered at Moire as though he were taking the measure of her. "This is Caliban's doing. I sense his touch within you."

Moire's vision misted as tears formed. If she carried a small piece of Caliban inside her, then in a way, he did not really leave them. "As a child, he nurtured a fascination for his kind within me. I consider myself blessed to have had what time I did in his presence."

Clipper chirped and hopped along a foreleg as robust

as a tree branch, the piptere becoming more relaxed in the dragon's presence. A thoughtful hum emanated from Valiant's throat as he mulled over her words. His gaze drifted towards Oliver, who had untangled himself from Ruth and stood at a distance conversing with Captain Forbes. For a fleeting instant, Moire wondered if the dragon could sense the complex history between her and the man she still loved.

"Very well. Ask your questions, Moire Draca Caliban, and I shall do my best to answer them," Valiant agreed, his voice tinged with a hint of bemusement.

Moire took a moment to gather her thoughts, not wanting to waste the unimaginable opportunity before her. She dearly wanted to ask Valiant about the nature of his relationship with Artemis. But she could no more ask a dragon that sort of question than she could ask it of a woman who was not an intimate acquaintance. "Valiant, may I ask what it is you like about the ocean? Is it better for you than swimming in freshwater lakes?"

A thoughtful rumble vibrated through Valiant's chest, his eyes momentarily drifting towards the expanse of sea that stretched out before them. Waves greeted the shore with a gentle caress today rather than a hard slap.

"Each body of water holds its own charm," he began, his voice rich and sonorous. "But the ocean...it has a rhythm, a heartbeat that echoes my own. Its vastness reminds me of the endless sky, inviting exploration and adventure. As for freshwater lakes, they have their own serenity, but there is something...bigger about playing amidst the waves."

"Thank you, Valiant." A smile tugged at her lips as she

glanced back at Clipper, who seemed to have found a comfortable spot nestled atop the dragon's head. "Captain Forbes tells me you prefer to use the sand to help shed old scales. I remember as a child working until my arm ached to scrub Caliban. I cannot remember him ever mentioning a journey to the seaside instead."

"Ah, sand is quite useful for scratching those hard-to-reach itches," Valiant rumbled. "Afterwards, I like to dive in the waves. The cool water washes away the last of the sand."

"Salt water is very drying, though." Moire peered closer at a patch where old scales had fallen away to reveal the new underneath. The area appeared dry to her. She reached out a hand and brushed her fingertips over the spot. "You could do with an oil after your sea bath."

Valiant exhaled a long sigh. "Captain Hartford used to have the sailors oil me down regularly. It is one thing about war that I miss."

Moire glanced around. "This is a seaside village. I imagine there will be a plentiful supply of fish oil if you did not mind the odour. I am sure we can organise many willing hands to scrub it in all over."

"Talk of fish is making me hungry. Ocean fish are tastier than their freshwater counterparts," Valiant continued, a hint of mischief glinting in his eyes. "They possess a certain piquancy that I find irresistible."

"It's probably the salt." Moire grinned. When they set out for Slatemooth yesterday, never had she imagined she would have the opportunity to discuss dietary preferences with a dragon.

The dragon's gaze momentarily shifted towards the

horizon, where the azure expanse of water met the sky. "The sea calls to me. It has an untamed wildness that stirs my soul."

"You sound like a philosopher or a born sailor," Moire murmured. Once, Oliver had spoken of the ocean in the same way to her. The sea infected the souls of those who sailed upon her or soared over her.

As Moire continued to speak with Valiant, she noticed Captains Hartford and Forbes watching her intently, their heads bent together in private conversation. Anxiety fluttered inside her, wondering what they might be discussing.

Her gaze then drifted to Ruth, who appeared quite put out that she was no longer the centre of Oliver's attention. The young woman's lips were pressed into a thin line, her delicate features marred by an unmistakable pout. Samuel's younger sister was accustomed to being the focus of every gathering, where her charm captivated all who looked upon her.

Yet here, Ruth was relegated to the background as a magnificent dragon conversed with Moire. It was an unfamiliar—and somewhat thrilling—sensation for Moire, who had spent so much of her life feeling unseen and unheard.

Another, more impertinent, question for Valiant bubbled up inside her. Did she dare hint at another reason Valiant had come to the seaside village? If she didn't ask now, she might never have another opportunity. "I believe that Artemis is not far from here. I wonder if her family might know where to find sufficient quantities of oil to ease the dry patches on your hide?"

A laughter-filled noise rumbled through Valiant.

"Artemis has a fine hide. But she is occupied elsewhere. I will make do with fish oil if the village has barrels to spare."

"I shall find out and organise a team of volunteers to tend to your hide." Moire bowed and held out her arm.

Clipper butted his head against Valiant's eye ridges and then flew back to Moire.

Artemis was occupied elsewhere. What did that mean? Hope surged through Moire. Her suspicion was that it meant the female dragon was laying her eggs.

17

Moire approached the children, who were sheltering in the lee of the seawall. Excited chatter rolled off them as they elbowed each other and gazed at the sunbathing dragon. Jaws dropped as they turned to stare at Clipper perched on her shoulder.

"Who would like to help oil Valiant?" Moire asked.

Various expressions raced across their features, most of them looking confused.

"Oil a dragon?" a young boy repeated, and he pointed at Valiant, in case Moire meant some other dragon or some other type of creature entirely.

"Yes. Valiant has come to the seaside to help loosen old scales. Those underneath need a good oiling to keep them supple and stop them from itching. As you can see, there is rather a lot of dragon, and it takes many hands with brushes to reach everywhere." Moire explained the task before them.

"Yes!" A chorus of eager agreement rose from them, and some children even jumped up and down on the spot.

With so many willing helpers, they would soon have every itchy spot on Valiant's hide attended to. "Excellent. I need the stronger lads to find us a large quantity of fish oil. The rest of you need to fetch brushes with short, stiff bristles like you use to get mud off a horse and soft cloths for sensitive areas. We also need buckets, please."

Four taller lads, who appeared to be around fifteen years old, darted up the steep steps to fetch oil. The younger children scattered to retrieve brushes and rags from various places in the village. Moire wondered how many mothers would assume their children meant the items were required to groom an imaginary dragon, not an actual one.

She waited on the sand, and after ten minutes, a rumbling came from along the road as the boys rolled barrels over the cobbles. The lads worked as a team to lever the heavy load down the steps. Their young muscles strained against the weight, but their faces were lit up with eagerness to participate in the unique experience.

The barrels were stood upright to one side of Valiant as the children ran back waving rags like a gaggle of Morris dancers. Others had metal or wooden buckets crammed with brushes of different sizes. Moire smiled at their enthusiasm. Despite her introverted nature, she enjoyed sharing her passion for dragons with others. The obvious delight of the children made it easier for her to speak in front of so many of them.

"Well done, everyone. Now, the hard work starts. Buckets need to be filled with oil. Brushes and cloths will be dipped into it. Brushes are used on Valiant's body in a strong circular motion. Only use the cloths on the wing membranes and use a gentle stroke as though you were brushing a grumpy cat. Wings are very delicate, and you must be careful not to damage them." Moire took the brush offered to her by a young girl and demonstrated coating the bristles with oil and then scrubbing the dragon's side.

Valiant groaned in pleasure and flattened his body further to make all his itchy spots accessible.

"Remember that despite their size and how tough their hides look, dragons are very sensitive creatures. You must treat Valiant with the utmost respect and care," she called out as children lined up to dip their brush or cloth into the open barrels of oil.

Moire broke them into groups, each with a part of Valiant to attend to. The smallest children were tasked with gently rubbing his outstretched wings. Moire thought there was less chance of them being accidentally injured away from the dragon's massive body and legs.

"Is this right, Miss Moire?" A girl of around twelve approached Valiant and mimicked drawing circles on the patch of hide.

"Yes, that's right." Moire smiled to encourage the children.

"It's just like scrubbing the floor!" another girl called out.

"But the floor doesn't breathe and move!" another girl shrieked in laughter as Valiant heaved a deep sigh and blew a shallow furrow in the sand before him.

"Are you sure he doesn't mind?" a young boy of about five asked with a slight tremor in his voice that portrayed his nervousness.

Moire placed a hand on the boy's shoulder. "He understands we are helping him, and he trusts us. It also feels good to him."

Swapping the brush for a soaked cloth Moire tackled a delicate wing, wiping oil across the surface and then buffing it in as though she polished a piece of silver. The children chatted and laughed as they worked. Valiant lounged contentedly as numerous small hands worked diligently to groom his magnificent scales.

"Be careful around his eyes," she reminded a boy who bravely groomed the dragon's face.

Surrounded by the laughter and chatter of the children, a sense of peace washed through Moire. She had taken command, shared her knowledge, and inspired these young minds. "Marvellous," she sighed.

The bravest among the children climbed atop Valiant's enormous prone form, their small hands clutching brushes soaked in fish oil. With each stroke, the dragon's scales gleamed a little brighter, and the creature rumbled appreciatively, basking in all the attention.

"Mind you don't get any oil in his nostrils," Moire warned the boy brushing Valiant's snout. "We don't want him sneezing fire now, do we?"

The boy cackled in laughter. "No, Miss."

Captains Hartford and Forbes approached and surveyed the children who clambered over Valiant like industrious ants.

"Captains. Have you come to inspect the work of the crew?" Her good mood bolstered her enough to let her smile openly at Oliver.

"Indeed, Miss Moire. I am most impressed by your crew. Why, they are each worth two of my sailors who never tackled the job with such gusto." Captain Forbes grinned at a boy perched atop Valiant, scrubbing at a particular spot at the base of the dragon's neck. Valiant made a noise suspiciously like a hundred cats purring.

Oliver picked up a girl trying to brush Valiant's front leg and placed her on his bent knee. She balanced as though she were on a branch, then set to work.

"He will expect this from now on, Forbes. You had better enlist the local children of your village and train them in the care and maintenance of a dragon," Oliver said to his friend.

"By Jove, you are right there, Hartford. What a splendid idea! Don't forget his tail, lads. It often gets neglected." Captain Forbes gestured to the long whip-like appendage.

The two captains removed their jackets and rolled up their sleeves. Each man took up a brush and set to work. They took a side each, enabling them to supervise the eager children. Moire kept an eye on those buffing Valiant's wing on one side and relied on Clipper to monitor the activity on the other side from her.

The children worked alongside the war heroes. Laughter mingled with words of encouragement and praise.

"Valiant is looking splendid, everyone!" she called out.

Adults gathered along the wall to watch, and one figure broke away to descend the stairs and approach. Ruth took off her gloves and selected something from the pile of brushes and cloths.

"I say, Captain Hartford, permission to become part of the crew?" she called out.

Oliver spoke without looking up from where he worked under the wing joint in a tricky-to-reach place. "Of course, Miss Radcliffe. Many hands make light work."

Ruth grinned at Moire and stepped to where Oliver worked beside the rib cage. The young woman reached out and grasped the edge of Valiant's spread wing. A faint tremble ran through her fingers, but it was impossible to tell whether it was from nervousness or excitement. Then, perhaps driven by a desire to impress Captain Hartford, she swept a dry brush across the membrane with gusto.

"No!" Moire called out, realising too late that the woman brandished a stiff-bristled brush on the wing instead of a cloth.

Valiant roared in indignation at what probably felt like a lash across his skin. He jerked his wing away before it was damaged, scattering the girls standing around the edges, but he caught Ruth square in the chest as he swept it back against his side. The blow flung the woman backwards.

"Miss Radcliffe!" Oliver called out, and he lunged sideways in an attempt to catch her. But he was too late, and the dragon had acted too swiftly in a moment of pain.

The young woman was blasted away and landed with a sickening thud; her body crumpled to the sand. A gasp rippled through the crowd as they watched in horror, and the children cried out and scurried away.

"Ruth!" Moire shouted and rushed to where she lay unmoving.

"Is she dead?" one of the girls cried out.

Moire's chest tightened at the sight of the limp form. Ruth's bonnet had come loose and rested in the sand nearby. The younger woman appeared lifeless as Moire knelt by her side. Only by concentrating did she notice the shallow rise of Ruth's chest. She eased one hand under the fallen woman's head, and when she withdrew it, blood stained her fingers.

"There is a rock here, under the sand," Moire called over her shoulder.

"Valiant did not mean to harm her," Captain Forbes said as he limped around the dragon's side. He patted his agitated companion. Valiant now swished his tail and keened in a low, mournful tone.

"No one blames Valiant, Captain Forbes. It was a horrible accident. Ruth didn't listen to the instructions and used a dry brush on his wing. The dragon merely reacted to the sudden pain he felt." Moire placed her fingers on the young woman's neck. A pulse fluttered under her fingertips. "We need a surgeon. Now."

"There is one not far out of the village. Take Valiant, Hartford. He will be quicker than any horse," Captain Forbes said.

"Yes. I am sorry and will do whatever I can to help," Valiant rumbled as his eyes whirled.

"Go. We shall carry her to the inn," Moire said.

"Very well." Oliver strode to the dragon and jumped up his extended front leg to reach his back. Valiant unfurled his wings and leapt into the sky.

Moire focused on the unconscious woman and the task at hand. She scanned the assembled people and called out. "We need a way to carry her up the stairs and along the road. Does anyone have something we could use to fashion a makeshift stretcher?"

"I have a blanket in my basket," a middle-aged woman

answered. She stepped forward and tugged a blanket from the wicker basket hooked over her arm.

"Thank you," Moire said, accepting the folded bundle with a nod of gratitude. Her fingers brushed against the soft fabric. She shook it out and laid it next to the prone figure. "Now, I need four strong volunteers to carry her."

"I am not much use, I am afraid." Captain Forbes tightened his grip on his walking cane.

She patted his arm. "I need you to wait for Captain Hartford's return. I suspect the doctor has not travelled by dragon before, and you will need to direct them to the inn. You should also inspect Valiant's wing. He may require a soothing balm for the membrane."

Four men stepped forward and offered their help. They gently lifted Ruth from the sand and laid her on the blanket. When they raised her body, a dark patch stained the ground under her head. Under Moire's watchful eye, they stretched the blanket taut between them, creating a stable surface upon which to transport the too-still woman.

"You must keep her body level and support her head," Moire instructed them as they bent to lift Ruth from the sand. With two on either side, they slowly made their way up the steps. Moire hovered behind as two men stretched their end of the blanket up over their heads to ensure she stayed level with her feet as they tackled the steep path. Step by step, they made their way to the top. People gave way as the sad procession continued along the road.

"Mind your footing," Moire called a warning as uneven cobbles threatened to trip up one of the volunteers.

As they neared the inn, a small crowd had gathered, drawn by the sight of the injured lady and the unusual procession. Murmurs of curiosity and concern rippled through the throng. When they reached the building at the end of the promenade where they stayed, Samuel and Katherine rushed out.

"Ruth!" Samuel shouted when he saw his sister.

"She was caught by Valiant's wing and struck her head," Moire quickly explained to the distraught sibling. "Captain Hartford has gone to fetch a doctor."

"We must get her to her room." Samuel reached for his sister but did not touch her. Worry pulled at his eyes.

Katherine clasped one hand to her chest. "I knew that dragon might injure someone. That was why I insisted on staying inside with Samuel and away from any danger. Thankfully, I am perfectly fine."

"Don't be silly, Katherine. We both climbed all over Caliban as children, and he never hurt us," Moire spat out. "It was a horrible accident."

The four men shuffled inside. The high-ceilinged lobby buzzed with hushed voices and anxious whispers as if a swarm of bees had found their way into the chamber. Samuel took the lead to show them the way to Ruth's room.

"We were family to Caliban and grew up with him; that was different. What if this dragon is just saying it was an accident," Katherine muttered.

"Valiant is most apologetic. Ruth grabbed his wing and rubbed too hard with a brush. He cannot be blamed for reacting to something that hurt him." Moire wondered what had got into her sister that she now forgot the careful way Caliban treated them. Family or not, dragons didn't just go around hurting people for no reason.

They reached the top of the stairs, and the men carried Ruth into the room and settled the blanket on the bed.

"Thank you, gentlemen. Your help is most appreciated," Moire said to the stretcher-bearers.

The men nodded and, with hurried glances at the injured woman, took their leave.

Still, Ruth had not roused, and she appeared like Sleeping Beauty—held captive under some curse and unable to open her eyes.

"Will she be all right?" Samuel grabbed hold of Moire's forearm.

She placed her hand over his. "Let us hope so." Her gaze drifted to the large window, praying for Valiant and Oliver to return with the doctor.

Katherine shooed Samuel from the room, then she and Moire gently removed the blanket from under Ruth. Next, they unlaced her boots and, rather like undressing a doll, stripped off her spencer and gown. After loosening her stays, they left the young woman in her chemise. Then they pulled the blankets up to keep her body warm and for modesty's sake when the doctor finally appeared.

At last, a roar came from outside. Moire rushed to the window as gusts of wind from heavy wings batted air against the thick glass. The crowd below parted as Valiant descended and landed outside the inn. Oliver sat astride the creature, a pale-looking man clasped before him like a maiden mounted in front of a knight on his trusty equine. White knuckles gripped a medicine bag, and the doctor swayed as though he might faint. As Valiant settled on the ground, the doctor leaned over and would have fallen but for Oliver snatching hold of his jacket. Then the medical man vomited. Valiant barked in outrage and turned to glare at him.

"Oh, dear. Valiant will need another bath," Moire murmured as both captains were needed to man-handle the doctor to the ground.

Oliver paused and glanced up, and for one heart-stopping moment, he held Moire's gaze. Then he hurried the doctor inside. Footsteps clattered up the wooden stairs, and the cracked door swung open.

The doctor looked an unhealthy colour, and he swayed as though he were on a ship in rough weather, but to his credit, he immediately set about assessing his patient.

"When did this happen?" he asked as he placed his hands under Ruth's skull and felt the injury to her head.

"Less than an hour ago. We moved her from the beach to here but kept her horizontal, and she was not jostled in any way. She does not appear to have any other injury apart from where the back of her head struck a rock," Moire explained what had happened.

The doctor made a noise in the back of his throat as he took her pulse and lifted each eyelid to peer at Ruth's pupils. He shook his head and muttered under his breath. Moire clasped her hands together while they waited to hear the prognosis.

"Well, doctor? Will she recover?" Samuel asked in a pleading tone.

"She has suffered a severe contusion to her head. There is a depression, but the skull does not seem to be fractured. She is fortunate it is her only injury. I have seen men recover from greater blows, so the situation is not hopeless. But it is in the hands of God. No man can know how the brain is affected by such blunt-force trauma. She will either wake from the concussion, or she won't." The doctor delivered his findings.

The group exchanged worried glances. Katherine pulled out a chair and seated herself at her sister-in-law's bedside.

"She will wake. I know it. We shall keep vigil until then." Samuel held out his hand and shook the doctor's one.

The doctor snapped his bag shut. "I'll call in tomorrow and see if she has woken."

"Would you like a ride back to your cottage, Doctor?" Oliver asked.

The medical man blanched and rushed to the door. "No force on this earth could compel me to get back on that infernal beast. Man is not meant to fly! I shall take a horse, as God intended man to travel."

Moire sympathised with the doctor. It had taken an extreme set of circumstances to convince her to climb on the back of a wyvern, and Faustus was much smaller than a dragon.

She glanced at Oliver. Once, she had faced her fear of heights to be at his side as he fought for their future. She drew a shaky breath. So many dreams were shattered by hidden rocks. Men should be employed to remove them from the ground so others had a chance at happiness.

Samuel reached for her hand and squeezed. "She will pull through, Moire. She simply has to. Mother will be devastated."

Oh, gosh. Mr and Mrs Radcliffe had to be told!

Oliver stalked to the window to stare out at the sea.

Captain Forbes had made it up to their floor and stood just inside the door. Deep furrows lined his brow, and guilt simmered in his eyes.

"Perhaps we could leave travelling back to Wyldefen to tell them until tomorrow? Then we might at least have better news to pass on. I am sure Ruth will wake by morning." Moire adjusted the blanket up under Ruth's chin and touched a hand to her cheek. Her skin was cool to the touch.

"Yes. Yes. Excellent idea, Moire." Her brother-in-law stood behind his wife, and both stared at the unconscious woman.

"I shall see about supper for us all. It will be a long night as we keep vigil," Moire said.

There was little any of them could do but wait and pray to whatever deity they believed in for a speedy recovery.

<h1 style="text-align:center">18</h1>

THE FRIENDS and family took it in turns to descend to the dining room in pairs to eat a quiet meal before returning to Ruth's bedside. Two chairs sat on either side of a small table pushed up against the wall. Two more chairs were by the window. Moire sat at the table opposite Captain Forbes. Samuel and Oliver were by the window. Katherine sat on the bed because the chairs were too hard for her delicate bottom.

When twilight dropped, the candles in the lanterns were lit and cast flickering shadows over concerned faces. Ruth still hadn't roused. A sombre atmosphere hung heavy in the air, broken only by the muffled sounds of horses' hooves on cobbles and distant voices outside.

A deck of cards sat on the table between Moire and Captain Forbes. The captain would pull a card at random and then stuff it back into the stack as though he needed some way to keep his hands occupied. The weight of guilt clung to him like the stubble forming on his chin.

"This was not your fault. If anyone is to blame, it is me.

I should have noticed that Ruth had a brush in her hand and not a cloth." Moire dragged a stray card closer to her and turned it over. The four of clubs. Did it mean anything? She heard that those with magic in their veins could discern the future or answer pressing questions based on the card a person chose.

His head snapped up, and tired eyes fixed on her. "Surely you do not blame yourself, Miss Moire? You did Valiant a great service organising the children to oil his scales. I should have thought of it myself. No, you must dissuade yourself of any sense of responsibility here. Valiant is bonded to my family. All responsibility for his actions falls onto our shoulders." He twisted in his chair, leaning against the wall to stretch out his injured leg. "I will not leave you to stew in guilt alone."

An unworthy thought entered Moire's brain. If Ruth had not been trying to impress Oliver, she would not have grabbed Valiant's wing so abruptly or abraded his membrane so hard with the brush. It had been a foolish and silly thing to do to impress a man. But then, Moire had created the opportunity for it to happen.

Captain Forbes gathered all the cards into a neat pile, but he cast glances at the motionless figure under the blankets. "To see a young, vibrant woman struck down so. It…" his voice trailed off, and he closed his eyes to draw a deep breath through his nose. He swallowed hard as if what he saw behind his closed eyes left a bitter taste in his mouth.

"Life is a fragile thing," Moire mused. "One moment we are laughing and dancing, and the next, we find ourselves at the mercy of forces beyond our control."

"Indeed. It is a harsh reminder that we must cherish the

time we have with those we love," Captain Forbes agreed, his voice a sombre echo.

A soft sigh escaped Moire's lips at the truth of his words. She reached out and rested her hand on his. "Captain Forbes, I hope I am wrong, but I suspect events have awoken a painful memory for you."

"My fiancée...she was taken by a fever while I was at sea. They say it came on swift, like a summer storm. She was cold in the ground by the time the letter from her mother reached me. What a fool I was. We were robbed of what time we could have had together. I had wanted to wait to marry her until the war was over." His hand curled into a fist as though he shook it at Death himself, then he released his fingers. Grief clung to him like an unwelcome shadow.

"I'm so sorry," Moire murmured, her heart aching with empathy. "I can't imagine how difficult it must have been for you. No wonder the sight of Ruth pains you so."

He pinched the bridge of his nose and then finally met her gaze. "It is a pain I wouldn't wish upon anyone, Miss Moire. But life carries on, as it always does, and we must learn to do so as well. I only pray that Miss Radcliffe is given the opportunity to carry on with her life." His voice wavered slightly, betraying the rawness of his emotions.

"Loss can be an unbearable burden." Moire's attention drifted to Oliver, who was engaged in quiet conversation with Samuel. All of them bore scars that none could see. "But sometimes, by sharing our grief, we find solace and the strength to continue. I suspect you are more resilient than you imagine, and I hope you find a little peace to ease your soul."

The atmosphere in the room was hushed as they listened to Ruth's shallow and unsteady breaths. Across from Moire, Captain Forbes spoke softly, sharing memories of his deceased fiancée whose life had been snuffed out too soon by the cruel hand of fate.

"Every day feels like a struggle without her," Captain Forbes confessed, his voice barely audible. "But I keep sailing towards the horizon."

"Life can be relentless in its savagery." How well she knew the cruel twist of fate. "But you are young, Captain, and dare I say your heart might know love again one day."

"Ah, to be a woman who can so easily transfer her affection to another." He used a gentle teasing tone, and she took no offence at his words.

"On the contrary, Captain. A woman's love is constant regardless of the fierce storms it must weather. It is men who seem more easily blown from love's true course." She dared a glance at Oliver as she spoke and found his gaze heavy upon her.

They continued their conversation in hushed tones. She liked the quiet captain, and her own shattered heart empathised with his. As they reached the midnight hours, silence enveloped the room. At times, they dozed in awkward positions, propped up by the walls or slumped over the little table. As the first light of dawn filtered through the thick glass window, Moire stretched and relieved an ache in her back from a long night. Clipper had snuggled down on the top of a dresser where Moire had placed her shawl. Now, the little piptere stirred and fluttered down to her lap.

"I shall let you out, Clipper. Perhaps Valiant will be

kind enough to take you fishing for breakfast," Moire whispered to her companion.

She carried the little dragon to the window and pushed it open to allow him to fly free. She breathed in deeply of the salty air and let the fresh breeze stroke her cheek. Then she pulled the window shut as a faint rustle came from the bedsheets. Ruth stirred.

Moire shook Samuel awake as she stepped towards the bed. Katherine was curled up at the end like a cat, fast asleep. A slim shaft of sunlight crept into the room and caressed Ruth's face. Moire held her breath and watched with anxious anticipation as the woman's eyelids fluttered open. She raised a shaky hand to touch her forehead.

"Ruth!" Samuel exclaimed, relief evident in his voice as he rushed to his sister's side and took her hand. "Thank God, you're awake."

The others in the room stirred, including Katherine, who bore the imprint of the blanket on one cheek.

"Wh-where am I?" Ruth asked weakly, her voice a faint whisper as she looked around the room. Confusion clouded her eyes.

Relief flowed through the room at the sound of her voice and chased away the lingering shadows.

"You had a fall and hit your head. We brought you back to the inn." Moire stood at Samuel's side.

Ruth closed her eyes, and her forehead furrowed. "I do not remember."

Mentally, Moire comprised a list of tasks to do now that Ruth was awake. Everyone needed to be fed, bathed after a night spent in their clothes, and rewarded with a few hours of sleep. Then, Mr and Mrs Radcliffe would need to be informed about their daughter's injury and recovery. "The doctor said that is to be expected. You have suffered a terrible concussion and will be abed for a few days yet."

"Rest, Ruth. You are safe with your family and friends. We shall explain everything when you are up to it." Samuel patted her hand.

Ruth made a noise of agreement and then drifted back into a healing sleep.

This is a sign that even in the darkest times, there remains hope, Moire thought.

They were a happier group when they descended for breakfast. The scent of fresh-baked bread wafting through the inn made their stomachs rumble. When they returned to Ruth's room, the mood had lifted, and optimism replaced concern.

Katherine sat at the little table and drank a cup of tea. Moire stood by the window, watching Clipper sunbathe on Valiant's shoulder as the dragon stretched out on the sand. Both Captains Forbes and Hartford had returned to their rooms to bathe and change clothes.

Samuel took the chair opposite his wife. "Kate, you must return to Larkspur Cottage to inform our parents about Ruth's accident."

Katherine chewed the rim of her teacup, and her mouth tightened. "Why must I always be the one sent away?" Frustration tinged her words. "I have experienced more sickness and death than any of us. I am the only one of us so qualified to care for Ruth."

"Think of our boys, Kate. I am sure Mother will want to be here. You cannot leave them with no one to care for them." Samuel took her hand and uncurled her clenched fingers.

"I am thinking of them! What sort of mother would I be, when my thoughts are consumed with worry for Ruth? Why, I would barely even know if my children were in the room with me or not." Katherine dropped the teacup to the table, and she clasped one hand to her chest. "You cannot torture me thus, Samuel. To make me choose between those I love when you know how sensitive I am to the feelings of others."

Moire suspected there would be tears if Katherine did not get her own way. It was odd that she wanted to nurse Ruth back to health, but she probably thought that preferable to wrangling two rambunctious boys. She watched the gentle rise and fall of Ruth's chest and made the decision for her sister.

"I will go and care for the boys at the cottage until you return, Samuel," Moire offered. She did not mind staying with her nephews. Ruth's recovery was paramount, and she would aid that in whatever way she could. Even if that meant leaving the peaceful little seaside town with her task unfinished.

"Yes! Moire should go. She is so much better at juvenile games than I. With my delicate constitution, I am more suited to quiet pursuits and will make an excellent nurse for Ruth." Katherine leapt on Moire's offer and gave her no room to change her mind.

"I will depart after the doctor has been if that is agreeable to you, Samuel?" She would need to use the family carriage for the return trip, and then it could carry back the older Mrs Radcliffe to Slatemooth.

"Of course. I shall write a letter for you to give to Mother." Samuel rose and walked to the sideboard to fetch pen, ink, and paper.

"If I can be spared, I'd like to have a last walk on the beach before I go." Moire checked once more on Ruth to reassure herself the woman slept. Next, she retrieved her shawl from the dresser and shook it out before wrapping it around her body. After excusing herself, she slipped from the room.

Scandalously, she left the building without a bonnet. Let the sea breeze tug at her hair. She had long hours in the carriage to fix her appearance. She nodded to the children who called out to her as she walked along the road that followed the curve of the beach below. Moire breathed in the salty air, letting it fill her lungs and chase away the heaviness that had settled within her chest.

As she approached where Valiant dozed in the warm sand, Clipper must have spotted her. The piptere flew to her shoulder and rubbed his face against her cheek.

"Ruth is awake, and we return to Larkspur Cottage later this morning." Moire kept one hand on the stone wall as she took the worn steps to the beach.

Clipper grunted and headed for one last swim. He didn't like being shut in the carriage.

"At least you can fly free, my friend. I am the one who has to sit for endless hours." She walked along the beach, navigating a path between the dry, loose sand and the wet stuff the retreating tide washed over.

Lost in her thoughts, the rhythmic sound of the waves lapping against the shore provided a soothing backdrop for her introspection. There was a delicate conversation she wished to have with Valiant. She rehearsed what to say in her head so that she wouldn't offend the dragon.

She paused to pick up a smooth, cerulean stone, turning it over in her hands before casting it into the sea. It disappeared with a plop and attracted the attention of a seagull who thought it was a fish ducking back under the surface.

"You need to throw with your hand to the side if you wish to skim a stone," a voice said from behind her.

Moire turned to find a handsome and dapperly dressed man who would have been more at home in a grand parlour than on the beach. He appeared to be in his early thirties. His raven-black hair was like an inkwell spilt upon the canvas of his brow, and merriment sparkled in dark-brown eyes.

"I was never much good at that," Moire stammered in surprise at being addressed. Samuel had tried to teach her when they were children, but she didn't seem to have the knack, even when she was handed the perfect smooth and oval stone.

"I must confess, I only learned the skill in the hope it would impress a young woman," the man said with a slight bow.

"Did it work?" Curiosity pulled Moire a step closer to the stranger.

"Oh, yes. That is how I won my love. By skipping a stone five times across a river. To this day, it remains the most impressive feat I have ever accomplished." He chuckled as he used the toe of his boot to dig in the sand for any loose stones.

Moire couldn't help but stifle a laugh. "I am sure there

is a statue erected to your achievement on the spot where you stood by that river."

"Yes, I quite imagine there is." He winked.

Clipper skimmed across the waves and flew to Moire. She held out her arm, and he landed on her forearm. Long claws dug into the fabric of her sleeve, but not so deeply that he scratched her.

"Did you have a good swim?" she asked the piptere.

He trilled and then peered around her at the stranger. He sent her the image of him drying himself off on Valiant's broad back. "Off you go then. I will join you shortly."

Clipper leapt into the air and flew to his much larger friend. The stranger stared in amazement.

"Is that creature yours? It doesn't have a leash. How do you control it?" he asked.

"Clipper keeps me company because he wishes to, not because he has no other choice." She really needed to write her book on the topic to educate people. Then they would see there was far more to the intelligent little creatures than parlour tricks. "No one tries to put a collar on a dragon. Why is it acceptable to do it to pipteres just because of their smaller size?"

"Well, no, because..." The man waved in the direction of Valiant. He stared at Moire for a long moment. "How remarkable."

Valiant rumbled a greeting to Clipper as the smaller dragon settled on his back. Moire wasn't entirely comfortable with the conversation with the odd man. He did not introduce himself, and she could not demand a name of him. "If you will excuse me, sir, I must attend to Valiant."

The stranger's gaze turned to the dragon. "He is a fearsome beast, is he not? Can you imagine having one dozing by your front door?"

She did not have to imagine. Once, Caliban had slept in the sun right outside Eadred Manor. "Good day to you, sir."

The stranger touched the brim of his top hat and turned to walk back up the beach. Moire hurried to Valiant and Clipper.

"Good morning, Valiant." Moire stopped a respectful distance from the dragon. Clipper could sit on the dragon's head if he wanted as he could fly away if he needed.

"How is the girl?" Valiant rumbled.

"Ruth awoke this morning, and we are hopeful she will fully recover." Moire cast a critical eye over the dragon. They had oiled most of his hide before the unfortunate incident, and it wouldn't take too much effort to finish the job.

"Good. She hurt my wing." Valiant stretched out his right wing. A bright pink scratch ran for some six inches close to one edge.

"Captain Forbes will apply a soothing balm to help it to heal." Thankfully, the stiff brush hadn't torn the membrane, but dragons could be a tad dramatic when injured. Particularly if they thought it marred their appearance.

"You are not silly like the other girl. I much prefer your company." Valiant lowered his head to his paws and stared out at the sea.

"Thank you, Valiant, that is a great compliment. There is something I wished to discuss with you if it would not be too impertinent." This was her last opportunity to talk to the dragon. It could be days or weeks before she could return to Slatemooth, and the dragon would have returned to his estate by then.

The dragon turned a curious eye on her, which she took as permission to continue. Drawing a steadying breath, Moire laid her heart bare to the creature.

19

AFTER MOIRE HAD TOLD her story, tears burned in her eyes, and she wiped them away with the heel of her palm. She bowed her head. "Thank you, Valiant."

The dragon returned the gesture, then he wandered down to the water's edge with Clipper perched on his shoulder like a parrot riding on a pirate. Valiant kept on walking through the waves until he paddled out to sea with Clipper sitting atop his head.

Her conversation with the mighty dragon had exceeded her expectations, and hope swelled in her chest. Finally, she could make amends for an old wrong, and she had found an ally in the brave and battle-hardened creature.

Moire walked to a pile of boulders at the base of the wall and found a flat spot to sit in the sun as she watched Valiant playing in the waves. Clipper took flight and circled about him. The piptere was a flash of blue among the seagulls who feasted on the fish flung skywards by the dragon's wings. If not for the distress it would cause Faustus, how

257

she wished for a home by the ocean. Somewhere that had a cosy spot where she could sit and watch the waves.

That made other thoughts tumble through her mind. A wyvern was tethered to a property, but young hatchlings were often moved or traded before that perimeter snapped into place. If there was a way to release Faustus from his bond to Eadred Manor, would he follow Moire to a new home?

A quiet voice in her head pointed out that she would never have her own home. As a spinster, she lived on the goodwill of her extended family. Housekeeper to her father. Nanny for Katherine. Companion to Augusta.

A boot scuffed on rock, and she turned as Captain Hartford walked along the rocky edge. He halted on seeing her and cast around as though searching for an escape route.

Had fate made him walk her way this morning, giving her an opportunity to open a festering wound? For too long, she had clung to her love for him. After talking to Valiant, she had a way to heal and find some measure of peace with Oliver. While they could never be what they once were, couldn't they at least be...friends?

"Valiant is quite a remarkable fisherman," she called out before he returned the way he had come.

A smile flashed across his face, and he stared out to sea with a look of open longing on his face. His feet stopped moving, and he decided to join her instead of fleeing. "He kept us well fed when we were at sea, and he can dive deep to catch larger fish with his claws."

"Clipper will have a distended belly with the number of fish he is eating out there. He will sleep all the way back to Wyldefen, and for several days after that, I imagine." Her room would smell of fishy burps for weeks. Having been brave and initiated a conversation with Oliver, she dared a little more. "It has been...good to see you again, Oliver."

Good wasn't the right word. She wanted to say *heartbreaking*, or *soul-shattering*, but she wasn't so brave as to expose how much she still loved him. The passage of eight years and so much pain had not dimmed her love. Others would think her silly if they knew how it burned bright inside her. She was a lighthouse that continued to shine long after the ocean had dried up, and no vessel would ever pass by again.

He stood quiet before her, his hands clasped behind his back as though he waited for the admiral to descend to the deck for an inspection. Then he cleared his throat. "I must confess that I only accepted my sister's offer to stay with her because I...I wanted to see that you were happy. I thought to find you with a gaggle of children following you around like geese."

The ache in her heart cracked open a little wider. Happy? Her life certainly contained moments of joy. Watching Clipper hatch. Playing with her nephews. The companionship of Faustus. But true happiness such as that she had when she had basked in his love? No. "I...am content. But why did you think I would have a large number of children around me? Did you think I became a governess or schoolteacher?"

"I...you...that is...you married Mr Radcliffe." He ground his jaw, and a frown pulled his brows down low. He removed his hat and ran one hand through his sun-bleached locks, tugging at the ends. "But I have since learned that you did not."

"No. I did not," was all she could whisper as events flooded back into her mind. The horrible attempt to make her agree to a surprise proposal was what prompted her to flee the house that night. At least Samuel had acted honourably, and refused to go through with it when he realised how completely Oliver possessed her heart.

Oliver drew a deep breath and exhaled with flared nostrils like Valiant. "I heard you talking to Forbes last night. You claimed a woman's love is constant, and it is men who are blown off course. But that is not true. It is women who are affected by fickle winds, while I have remained steady at the helm. You have always been my guiding star, and I would navigate by none other."

Moire's mouth opened and closed as she waded through his nautical metaphors. Never had she wavered in her affection for him in the last ten years. From the moment their hands touched over a book in the village market, he had been her one true love. Eight years of frustration churned inside her, and a storm rattled against her ribs and demanded to be set free. "Need I remind you, Captain, that you broke off our engagement? Not I."

"Did I?" His hand curled into a fist as though he struggled with some internal battle. Oliver spun on his heel and strode away from her, his broad shoulders tight.

Moire could bear it no longer. She deserved answers and an apology. She jumped off the rock and onto the sand. "Did you ever love me?" she shouted at his retreating back.

He halted in his tracks but remained turned away from her.

Emboldened and realising this was her only chance to escape the turmoil pulsing through her veins, Moire continued, "We were much in love for two years. Did you learn nothing during that time about my character? How could you believe a scurrilous newspaper article based on vicious gossip, and find me guilty of the most heinous crime without even reading my letter that explained all?"

He turned in slow motion. His hat was discarded to the sand as he flexed his hands at his sides. An ocean of pain shimmered in his eyes. "My worst fears were confirmed by that article. The egg was broken, and your engagement to another announced. I admit I was a coward and could not open your letter. My love for you is so deep, I could not bear to read your words that you no longer loved me." He drew a shuddering breath and let out his tightly curled fingers. "Do you know how many men on our ship received such letters with every bag of post? Sweethearts who changed their minds, could not wait, and instead chose to marry another. I was angry and in pain. That, I freely admit. To hear your voice tell me it was over would have been salt in an open wound."

"But I wrote no such thing. I explained the events in my letter and begged for your understanding. For your forgiveness." She rasped the words, her throat raw with emotion.

Oliver's eyes widened, and once more, he tortured a lock of hair between his fingers, pulling at it as he relived painful memories. "I...I thought..." He shook his head again. "When my mind calmed some weeks later, I wrote and begged your forgiveness for judging you so quickly while I was struggling from the hurt of it all."

"No." Too many words were assaulting Moire's mind at the same time, and she struggled to make sense of them.

He paced closer to her and gestured out to sea. "Ask Valiant if you do not believe me. It was he who pointed out that any woman who grew up with a dragon would never deliberately shatter an egg."

"No, I mean, I never saw any such letter. After you returned mine unopened and....and said our engagement was irrevocably broken, I took to my room for some weeks. I no longer had any reason to rush to see if there were any letters for me. Anyone could have taken your letter." The storm inside her rolled from side to side, and she clutched her stomach as nausea surged up her throat.

Who in her family could be so cruel? Had it been Sir George, Augusta, or Katherine? She couldn't imagine Katherine doing such a thing. Her younger sister had seemed oblivious to the burgeoning love between Moire and the young lieutenant, and while she could be thoughtless, Katherine would never be so deliberately cruel. Which of her father or older sister had betrayed her trust and so utterly destroyed her life?

Another face shimmered before her. That of Lady Beaumont. Her mother's dear friend had been most vocal in disapproving of Moire's relationship with Oliver. The older woman had tried to persuade her to call off their engagement, but Moire had refused. Could she have spotted Oliver's letter on a visit?

Oliver took another step towards her. "I poured out my love for you. Begged your forgiveness for judging you in haste. I asked for any sign that you still loved me. My only reply was a newspaper cutting detailing your engagement to Mr Radcliffe and saying that the banns had been read. I took that as all the confirmation I needed that my worst fears were true. A few months after that, my cousin wrote and, in his news from Wyldefen, told me that Miss Tobin had married Mr Radcliffe."

Moire breathed in sharp gasps as anguish lanced her anew. The world spun and darkened at the edges as though night threw its inky blanket over her. She swayed on her feet, and only Oliver taking hold of her arms kept her upright. Tears further dimmed her vision. "None of it was true. Father had placed news of the engagement in advance before I had refused Samuel. A few months later, he proposed to Katherine and married her." A low moan rolled over her tongue, and she sank to the nearby rocks with Oliver's assistance.

"Who? Who played such a cruel trick on us and stole all those years we could have had?" Ruptures tore through her heart to think that anyone in her family had kept Oliver's apology from her and sent such a deceptive reply. A single word kept flying through her mind...why? What motive could anyone have to deny her happiness?

His Adam's apple bobbed above his cravat, and he stroked her hair. In a quiet tone he asked, "What happened that night? I have always wondered and would hear it from you now if you could bear it."

They sailed into the eye of the storm together, and the air around them stilled. But it was a temporary peace. Too much had been done to ever be undone. Moire had to make the best use of the small window of opportunity to, at last, forgive herself. "Faustus had scented strange men about the estate the day before. My maid said a man came to the house, looking for the Sailor. A man with a sharp, fox-like face. I worried it was Darius Blackwood, come to steal the egg."

"Blackwood! I thought you would both be safe when he heard I had returned to my vessel." His hand slid down to cradle her face.

"Before I could move the egg, we had the dance that night. I begged Faustus not to prowl the grounds and stay in his burrow. When Father announced I was to marry Samuel, I refused and ran from the house."

Oliver leaned closer to her side and took her hands in his. She drew a quick breath, relishing his touch before continuing her tale.

"Faustus screeched in alarm. His call was so loud that those inside heard it. Samuel followed me outside. In the light cast from the house, a man ran across the lawn, clutching something to his chest. Faustus was close behind him. I yelled out and ran after them both. The man stumbled and dropped..." She couldn't breathe, even after the intervening years, the moment hurt so much. Closing her eyes, she willed her lungs to draw one more breath. "He dropped the egg," she whispered the last word, and a tear rolled down her cheek.

Oliver let go of her hand to wipe the tear away.

"The man ran with Faustus in pursuit. I rushed to the spot, hoping against hope that the shell was hard enough to survive the impact. But it had broken on the stones hidden in the grass." A sob ripped through her as she recalled the creature exposed years too early to the world. Small wings had been tightly pressed to a half-formed body, and it had seemed almost wyvern-like. "By then, people had emerged from the house, drawn by the noise. I was kneeling on the ground beside it, but there was nothing I could do." Her tears flowed freely now. Moire held out her hands as she recalled picking up the foetus and cradling its slippery body in her arms.

"The newspaper article said you had smashed the egg to the ground." He repeated an old untruth. "There was no mention of a thief."

"People prefer ugly gossip to the plain truth." How did you defend yourself against old lies that were so ridiculous and illogical? She fled the house and had no time to fetch the egg to make such a petulant and horrid display. "I had no part in the destruction of the egg, unless you wish to blame me for choosing such a poor hiding place. Of that charge, I plead guilty." She tried to meet his gaze, but he blurred before her.

Oliver remained silent but drew a handkerchief from his pocket. He dabbed at her tears. "Did you really refuse him?"

A pained sob broke from her chest. "Of course! I love only you. Have always loved only you. How could I wed another when I was waiting for you to return and claim both me and the egg?"

He brushed his hand along her face and cupped her cheek. "Radcliffe would have provided you with everything I could not. Wealth. Position. Security."

"I never wanted any of those things. Only you...and our dream." Her voice was a mere whisper. The storm inside her was spent, and she was left exhausted in its wake.

His thumb stroked her cheek. "How you must hate me when that angry letter was the last word you had from me."

Moire reached up and placed her hands around his neck. "I could never hate you. All I wanted was the chance to explain and, one day, make amends."

He closed the distance between them and kissed her. His lips grazed hers with such aching tenderness that more tears escaped her closed lids.

"I am so sorry, Moire. I have been such a fool. When I learned at the dinner party that your sister had married Mr Radcliffe and not you, I didn't know what to do. Then, when I saw you at last...you were like a ghost ship, sailing past me, silent and untouchable. How can you ever forgive me?" he whispered, resting his forehead against hers.

"I forgive you far easier than I forgive myself." Years of pain were washed away by his touch and apology. "I have devoted my life to studying dragonkind in the hope of finding another egg for you. I am fortunate in that the Radcliffes have an extensive library, and they allowed me free access to it."

He blew out a sigh. "I had hoped the books would fuel your study, instead, they must have confused your sister. I understand she does not much read."

"The books?" Realisation slammed into her. "*You* sent them."

He nodded. "I have thought only of you. In every port, I scoured the bookstores for anything on dragons that might aid your scholarly endeavours. I sent them to Mrs Radcliffe at Gormsby Hall, assuming they would reach your hand."

Moire swallowed a laugh. "They did. Indirectly. Mrs Radcliffe, Samuel's mother, thought they were sent by an old and somewhat confused relative. Whenever one arrived, she left it on the desk in the library for me." Could she love him any more? For eight years he had remembered her interest and sent an anonymous book when he found one. Then excitement lit through her. "You do not realise how marvellous they have been. Through my study, I have discovered that there is a rare protocol where a supplicant can make a plea to a dragon for an egg. But you cannot ask for yourself, only for another, and it must be judged a worthy request. Valiant told me that Artemis summoned him here. She has now absented herself from her family's estate to lay her clutch. I am prepared to lay my cause before Artemis in the hope of replacing what you lost."

His eyes widened, and he drew in a breath. "Truly? I now have the funds to buy an egg, but they are rarely offered up for sale. Do you think Artemis would gift you one?"

Moire laced her hands with his. "I have spoken to Valiant, and he will support our cause. He believes you would be an admirable addition to the Draco Legion but had not mentioned it as you cannot ask for yourself."

Hope and love flared in Oliver's eyes, and he kissed her again. Moire wished he would never stop, then a fresh obstacle made her place her hands on his chest and break away. "Ruth will make a wonderful wife for you when you become Drac Hartford."

If you love something, you have to set them free.

That was why Clipper would never wear a leash. And why she had to let Oliver go to live his life. No matter how it would pain her to watch him marry another. New agony tore at her heart, but at least now, an old wound could heal.

Confusion clouded his sea-grey gaze. "Ruth? But I have

merely been kind to her while I tried to find the words to say to you."

"Oh, Oliver. The girl is obviously in love with you. We all believed there to be an understanding between you. She even told us that you followed her to Slatemooth to propose." Moire rubbed the moonstone ring on her right hand. He had once asked her to be his wife. Now, it would be another who walked through life at his side.

He swallowed and picked up her right hand. He brushed a fingertip over the moonstone ring. "You still wear it."

"I have never forgotten that night. I had thought seeing the lunar dragon was a sign that our dream was blessed by the stars. Now, I know it was only a magical moment and was never meant to be," she spoke in a hushed tone as she let go of her dreams. Like scattering ashes over the ocean, every hope and wish she once made merged with sea mist to fade from her view. In doing so, she breathed a little easier despite the pain.

His eyes widened in panic. "What have I done?"

"You must honour the unspoken agreement between you. I could not bear to cause Ruth such pain as I suffered, but I wish you both every happiness. I will seek out Artemis and, with Valiant's support, pray that she will gift me an egg...for you." Moire's voice broke, but no more tears filled her eyes. It seemed she had cried herself dry at last.

Oliver caressed her cheek, and Moire leaned into his touch. It would be the last time they shared such an intimacy.

"I'm sorry," he rasped. "I have been such a fool, and now I have lost everything."

She kissed him once more. A parting kiss filled with the sorrow of what would never be. "Some loves are not fated to be, and at least we are not as doomed as Romeo and Juliet—no one has died. All I ask is that you allow me to witness the egg's hatching and that you find a more secure location for it than a wyvern burrow."

He nodded, his chest heaving, but he said no more.

Untangling her hands from his, Moire rose and walked across the sand with as much dignity as she could muster. She kept her back straight and her eyes forward, unable to glance behind her in case her heart broke anew.

At the top of the stairs, she walked like a sleepwalker back to the inn. Only later did she remember the well-dressed man who touched his hat as she passed. The same man who had spoken to her about skimming stones.

20

THE WIND CHILLED as Moire wandered back to the inn. Cold tendrils tugged at loose strands of her hair and whispered a ghostly caress against her skin. Clipper had flown from Valiant and huddled close. With his tail wrapped around her neck, he pressed his whole body against her and offered what comfort he could. Although she had made peace with Oliver at last, releasing him to marry Ruth was a leaden weight in her chest. But to her, the alternative was unthinkable. How could she have demanded that Oliver break Ruth's heart and cause a friend such torment?

No, better that she bears the sorrow of a love lost. Ruth would bring joy and happiness to Oliver's new life, unburdened by a painful history.

On returning to her room, Moire's fingers trembled as she packed her few belongings into the worn trunk. Her thoughts raced back through the years and remembered every stolen moment, touch, and kiss with Oliver. She traced the edges of the book on dragon lore, made all the more special knowing that over the years Oliver had hunted the tomes out in dark corners around the world.

"Time to lay old memories to rest," she whispered, her voice barely audible.

Clipper trilled from the bed, his eyes whirling with concern. Moire picked up the piptere and placed a kiss on his head.

"There is no reason why the two of us can't have adventures," she said. But the words rang hollow through her. Duty to her family would never allow her to strike out on her own.

With a final glance around the small room, Moire ventured into Ruth's chamber. Relief washed over her as she found her friend sitting up, her face pale but animated as the doctor examined her. Ruth met Moire's gaze with a weak smile that stirred up a strange mix of affection and sorrow.

"Miss Radcliffe is a strong young woman," the doctor declared, folding his stethoscope and tucking it into his coat pocket. "Her prognosis is favourable, though she must remain in bed for at least a week to recover fully from her concussion. Then she must be cautious for some months that she does not overexert herself."

"Thank you, Doctor," Moire said. She approached the bed and took Ruth's hand. "I'm so glad you are on the mend. Valiant is terribly sorry for what happened, although I am sure Captain Forbes has already told you that."

"Indeed," Captain Forbes said from his position by the window. "Valiant wishes to make a formal apology once Miss Radcliffe is well enough to venture outside. He does not wish the young lady to have any ill feelings towards him."

Ruth paled, and her gaze darted between Moire and Captain Forbes. "I am not as brave as you. I am not sure I could approach him without fainting."

"We will not let that happen, I can assure you," Captain Forbes said quietly.

Moire turned to Katherine and Samuel. "I am packed and ready to return to Wyldefen. I am sure your mother will want to hasten to Ruth's bedside, and you should expect her by supper tomorrow night."

Samuel clasped Moire's shoulder in a gesture of brotherly affection. "Thank you, Moire. I do not know what we would do without your loyalty to our family."

Indeed, Moire had so many familial obligations that it left little time for leading her own life. Not that it contained much except her books, Clipper, and Faustus.

"That is what families do. We support each other," she said. But her brain corrected her words. Someone in her family had betrayed her and smashed any chance she had of happiness. She might never have that life, but she would have an explanation if she were brave enough to demand one of them.

Down below, the Radcliffe family carriage waited for her. The driver took her trunk and lashed it to the back. Samuel handed her up as the salty air filled her lungs and seagulls called overhead. Moire committed the scene to memory, for Slatemooth would soon be a distant one.

Clipper settled on the seat beside her, and Moire fussed with her shawl to make a nest for him. After eating far too many fish, he had a rather distended belly and a sleepy look in his eyes. She hoped the fish stayed in his stomach and that the swaying motion of the carriage didn't bring on a bout of travel sickness.

As the carriage began its slow procession along the coastal road, Moire allowed herself one last glance back at the beach. Oliver stood on the seawall. His gaze met hers, and even over the distance, a great sadness rolled off him. She offered a small, bittersweet smile before turning back in her seat to meet the road ahead.

The journey from Slatemooth to Wyldefen stretched out before Moire like the unspooling thread of a tapestry. The landscape gradually shifted as the salt-lashed cliffs and crashing waves gave way to rolling hills and lush meadows flecked with wildflowers.

As the carriage traversed the undulating terrain, Moire reflected on her parting from Oliver and the path that lay ahead. Words of apology had been spoken, and old wounds began to heal. Oliver would always possess a piece of her heart, but now Moire needed to forge her own destiny. Beside her, Clipper burped in his sleep and the sharp tang of fish filled the carriage.

"At least I only have to accommodate the needs and habits of a piptere, and not a husband," she consoled herself. Then she dropped the window to allow the fishy odour to escape.

The day wore on, and night fell. While she never took a step, exhaustion tugged at Moire by the time they turned into the iron gates of Gormsby Hall. The moon cast a pale glow over the house's stonework as the carriage came to a halt. Moire leaned her head against the window, taking in the familiar sight of the stately home.

No lights were on, and the Radcliffes must have all been abed.

The coachman opened the door. Moire scooped up Clipper, still asleep in her shawl, and cradled him to her as she hopped down.

"Thank you," Moire murmured to the coachman. Then she hurried to the front door as the cold of the night wrapped around her.

Grasping the brass knocker, she rapped sharply four times and hoped someone within would hear her. Moire counted her breaths as she waited and had got to thirty when the heavy oak door creaked open, revealing a bleary-eyed servant holding a candle, its flickering light casting shadows on the walls. He blinked in surprise at the sight of Moire and tugged at his dishevelled dressing gown.

"Miss Moire! Why, we were not expecting you at such a late hour," the old butler said as he stepped aside to allow her to enter.

"I have urgent news for Mr and Mrs Radcliffe. Please rouse them immediately," she instructed, her voice steady despite the anxiety churning within her.

"Of course, Miss." The servant nodded, and he shuffled off to do her bidding.

Moire paced the dimly lit parlour, the whispers of her skirts mingling with the ticking of the grandfather clock. She wrung her hands together, trying to formulate the right words to convey Ruth's condition without causing undue alarm. Clipper watched her from atop a nearby bookshelf, his silver eyes reflecting her concern.

Soon, the parlour door opened, and Mr and Mrs

Radcliffe appeared, both clad in their dressing gowns and nightcaps, their faces etched with worry.

"Moire, my dear, whatever has happened? Where are the others?" Mrs Radcliffe enquired, her voice laced with distress.

"Please, sit down," Moire urged, gesturing to the plush armchairs. Once they had settled themselves, she took a deep breath and began. "Ruth has suffered a head injury and concussion. The doctor says she is expected to make a full recovery, but she must remain in bed for at least a week and be slow and cautious about doing too much."

Mrs Radcliffe gasped, her hand flying to her chest. "Oh, my poor girl! How did this happen?"

"An unfortunate accident. She fell and struck her head on a rock in the sand. She is being well cared for by Katherine and Samuel," Moire explained.

"First thing in the morning, I shall leave for Slatemooth," Mrs Radcliffe declared, her maternal concern evident. "I cannot bear to be away from my darling girl. She will need her mother to oversee her recovery until she can be moved back here."

"Moire, you must be exhausted from the journey to bring us this news. You will stay here tonight, won't you?" Mr Radcliffe asked.

"Of course." All Moire wanted to do was fall into a bed and snuggle under a pile of blankets.

Instructions were issued to the butler, and he showed Moire to a room close to where her two young nephews slept. However, sleep proved elusive. She tossed and turned. Every time she closed her eyes, Oliver's sad gaze sailed through her dreams.

Unable to find respite in slumber, Moire rose from the bed and wandered through the dimly lit halls of the great house. Her bare feet made no sound on the plush rugs laid along the hallways. As if guided by some unseen force, she arrived at the Radcliffe library. She hesitated for a moment before easing open the heavy wooden door and stepping inside. The library had always held a special allure for her, with its towering shelves filled with countless volumes on dragons and their mystical world.

By the light of a single flickering candle, Moire explored the shelves, running her fingers along the spines of ancient leather-bound books. Here, amidst the scent of ink and parchment, she found comfort and an escape from the turmoil in her mind.

Lost in the rows of books, Moire stumbled upon a tome she had not noticed before. Diminutive in size, it would easily fit in a gentleman's pocket. Its cover was worn and faded, the title barely discernible. She didn't think it was one sent by Oliver, but it might have arrived at Gormsby Hall in the earlier days before Mrs Radcliffe left them on the desk for her.

"A Field Guide to Dragon Species," she whispered. Intrigued, she took the little book and settled into a nearby armchair.

The text was handwritten, and the drawings were pencil sketches and water colours. It appeared to be a personal journal kept by a gentleman who was an avid dragon scholar. He had drawn any dragon he encountered on his journeys. The tiny book took her on a trip across Europe as the unknown author sought out rare types of dragons. One had a heading but no drawing or details.

Under "Lunar dragon," the rest of the page was blank. The explorer had failed to find a single one in all his travels.

"Ah, there at least is one thing I have witnessed that you have not," Moire murmured as she recalled the night long ago when a lunar dragon had danced among the stars above her and Oliver.

She tucked the book into the pocket of her dressing gown and wandered back to her room.

THE NEXT MORNING, sunlight spilt through the partially open curtains and lit Moire's bed. Clipper chirped and appeared to have slept off his overindulgence in fish. After dressing, Moire hurried downstairs. Mrs Radcliffe was already prepared to depart and embraced her husband under the portico.

Noah and Elijah fidgeted, their cheeks flushed pink from the chill in the air.

"Aunt Moire!" Noah exclaimed on seeing her. "Grandmama says that Aunt Ruth is hurt." Worry lined his young brow.

"Yes, but she will be better soon. Until then, Grandmama will keep her company and watch over her recovery." Moire took each boy's hand.

"Goodbye, Mrs Radcliffe," Moire called out as the older woman placed her book and needlework on the seat of the carriage.

"Safe travels, dearest," Mr Radcliffe said, his voice firm despite the worry for his daughter that was etched on his face.

"Goodbye, Grandmama!" Noah and Elijah chimed in unison, their faces brightening when Mrs Radcliffe leaned down to kiss their foreheads.

"You two behave while I am gone. And mind what your Aunt Moire tells you. She is in charge until your parents return," she admonished lightly, her lips curving into a smile.

"Of course, Grandmama," the boys promised, their eyes wide and solemn.

As the carriage pulled away, Moire watched it disappear down the long drive, her thoughts tangled like the ivy that clung to the stone walls of Gormsby Hall.

"Will you stay here, Moire, or return to the cottage?" Mr Radcliffe asked after the carriage had disappeared from view.

"I think we will return to Larkspur Cottage, Mr Radcliffe. I promised Noah that we would hunt out a piptere nest." She winked at Noah.

"When will Momma and Poppa be home?" Elijah asked, his small voice quavering with uncertainty.

"A few more days. Until then, you will have to make do with Clipper and me." Moire held out her arm as her piptere friend flew down from the open window of her room.

After breakfast, Mr Radcliffe organised a servant to take their luggage to the cottage in a cart. Then Moire and the boys set off on foot. Both Noah and Moire were much recovered from their twisted ankles, and they enjoyed the walk. Clipper flew on ahead, and Moire had asked him to find Lunette if she was in the nearby trees.

They took a path through the forest, where the dappled

sunlight filtered through the trees. Noah and Elijah raced ahead. Their laughter echoed around them, the sound mingling with the rustle of leaves and the distant melody of birdsong.

"The tree is not far from here, Aunt Moire!" Noah called out excitedly as he recognised his surroundings.

"Yes, I think you are right, Noah." Moire slowed and stared at treetops. Somewhere around here, she had climbed a tree to rescue the caught piptere, and she had twisted her ankle on the descent.

As they ventured further into the woods, the shadows lengthened. Then, among the deep green came a flash of silver followed by one of blue.

"Look!" Elijah shouted as he pointed to the foliage.

There, sitting on a branch, were Clipper and Lunette, the little silver piptere.

"Hello, Lunette," Moire said as she extended a hand towards the creature. To her delight, Lunette nuzzled her palm, and warm breath tickled her skin.

"Can they really understand us?" Noah whispered, awestruck.

"Yes. Pipteres are very intelligent, just like dragons. It takes a great deal of effort for them to speak, though, and they prefer to use pictures and words that they send to our minds." Moire explained how she communicated with the creatures.

While travelling from Slatemooth to Wyldefen, Moire had pondered what favour to ask of Lunette. She had decided to see if the female was open to the same sort of petition as dragons.

"Lunette, would you do me the great honour of gifting

Noah an egg so that he might have his own piptere friend?" she asked.

Lunette tilted her head and regarded first Moire and then Noah.

"I will never let anyone place him in a cage, and I will be the best friend a piptere has ever had," Noah promised in a solemn tone.

Lunette chirped and then nodded. Spreading her wings, she asked Moire and the boys to *follow*.

"Shall we?" Moire asked of the boys, who nodded eagerly.

Together, they trailed behind the magnificent creature. Clipper flew beside Lunette, and at times, the pipteres danced around each other. At last, Lunette led them to a particular tree. She flew high into the boughs and chirped to them. Moire's heart sank. Neither she nor Noah could climb that high.

Not egg. I help, Clipper spoke in her mind.

Not an egg? Moire pondered what that might mean.

Clipper was a blue flash among the greenery as he darted from bough to bough and climbed higher until he disappeared from view. Moire wished she could see what was in the nest. Had the eggs hatched by now? It had been some weeks since Noah first spotted it high in the tree.

After several long moments, wings fluttered above. Silver and blue were merged as Lunette and Clipper fluttered to the ground. They each used one wing to stabilise their descent while they cradled something between them.

Lunette chirped, and Clipper took a step back to reveal a hatchling curled by its mother. Red and copper swirled over its body.

"Oh. How marvellous," Noah said as they sat on the ground before it.

Lunette brushed her face against the hatchling, and then she nudged it towards Noah. The young boy held his breath as the piptere took a few wobbly steps in his direction. Then it paused and looked back at its mother, who trilled encouragement.

Noah held out his hands, and the piptere nestled against them. With an awed look on his face, Noah picked the piptere up and cradled it to his chest. He stroked a feathery copper head with a fingertip.

"He says his name is Chalco," Noah whispered in wonder.

"Chalco. That is a marvellous name. I believe it means copper in Greek. Thank you, Lunette, for entrusting Noah to be a companion for Chalco." Moire bowed her head to the piptere. She might be a tiny dragon, but she still possessed the same maternal attachment to her clutch.

Lunette dipped her head in return and sent a wave of gratitude and friendship to Moire.

"I want a big dragon that I can ride," Elijah announced.

Moire laughed. "Perhaps you will, one day." If Artemis gifted her with an egg for Oliver, there was every chance his nephews by marriage would know the joy of a dragon when they were older.

With a soft trill, Lunette took to the sky, her wings stirring the air around them as if bidding them farewell. As Moire turned her attention back to the boys, she smiled. In the precious bundle of copper feathers in Noah's hands, she saw the promise of countless adventures yet to come.

"We should take Chalco back to the cottage. I imagine

he will be hungry. Then, Noah, I will show you how to care for him, and we will make a nest for him to sleep in." She helped the boy to his feet as he kept the piptere held to his jacket and would not let him go.

Elijah ran ahead of them, his arms outspread as he imagined he was a dragon soaring through the sky. These were the moments of contentment that would repair the cracks in her heart. If she sought out such sparks of joy and glued them all together, then one day, she would be whole again.

21

Back at the cottage, Moire asked the cook for any scraps of meat to feed the hungry hatchling. Once he had gobbled enough to round out his tummy, Noah carried him upstairs to his room. Moire fetched an old blanket, and they made him a warm nest. Soon, gentle piptere snores drifted around the room.

Noah displayed a maturity beyond his years as he dedicated himself to learning about pipteres and how to care for the hatchling. He patiently groomed Chalco's feathers with a scrap of silk and fell asleep clutching a book about dragons. Elijah remained firm that he would have an actual dragon to ride when he was older and not a toy like a piptere. Moire suspected a tiny bit of jealousy was behind his words. Whatever drove him to say such things, he also wanted to learn all he could about dragons, and that fuelled his devotion to improving his reading.

Two days later, Moire stood at the parlour window watching Clipper sun himself on a bough of the old oak tree outside the cottage.

"Miss Moire, there is a letter for you," the maid called out from the doorway.

"Thank you." Moire took the letter, her father's handwriting scrawled across the front like the tendrils of an angry vine.

She broke the wax seal, unfolded the parchment, and read the words that dictated yet another change in her life. Sir George summoned her to Bath immediately. Her presence was required to run their new household and to write replies to the many social invitations Augusta received. Moire's new duties would include being a secretary, alongside the role of housekeeper. There was no consultation or request from her father nor any enquiry as to the health of his youngest daughter and grandchildren. The sheet contained only her new orders, delivered with the expectation she would obey at once.

Travelling to Bath would pull her away from the quiet refuge of Larkspur Cottage. Moire had planned to return to Slatemooth and request an audience with Artemis. But she could not deny the bonds of blood, even when it bound her to those who failed to understand her desires. Perhaps once she had smoothed whatever kerfuffle had erupted in the new Bath home, Sir George would allow her a brief visit to Slatemooth to find Artemis.

Another question loomed in her mind. Someone had perpetrated a cruel betrayal on her and Oliver, and Moire would know who. This was her opportunity to confront her family before she sought a dragon egg.

The thought of leaving Noah and Elijah behind, those two bright-eyed boys whom she loved so dearly, tore at Moire's heartstrings. Who would help Noah with Chalco?

She could stay a day or two longer, but Sir George called, and she could not ignore his summons.

At least one concern was settled later that day. As Moire sat outside with the children enjoying the warmth of the afternoon, the Radcliffe carriage rattled along the road and stopped outside of the cottage. Samuel jumped to the ground, waved to them, and then turned to help down Katherine.

"Momma! Poppa!" the boys shouted as they rushed to greet their parents.

Samuel scooped Elijah up into his arms, and Katherine embraced Noah.

"It's good to see you both. How is Ruth?" Moire asked, scanning their faces for any indication of the young woman's recovery.

"She is much improved, and Mother has things in hand," Samuel said as he led the way up the path.

"I found the chairs horribly uncomfortable. Not to mention all those people coming and going made the room cramped, turned the air stale, and gave me a terrible headache," Katherine grumbled.

Moire suspected that with the arrival of the older Mrs Radcliffe, her sister was deprived of her starring role as nurse and had probably been relegated to sitting in a corner.

"Perhaps a bath will help, especially after your long journey?" Moire had some empathy for her sister. A full day in the carriage left one longing for a hot soak to ease tired muscles.

"Oh, yes. You are a dear Moire. I would be lost without

you." Katherine raised one hand to her forehead as they entered the parlour.

"You will have to manage without me; I am sorry. Father has summoned me to Bath. He and Augusta need me there." Moire clasped her hands before her.

"Oh! Typical. Father never thinks of me." Katherine delicately eased herself to the chaise.

Moire bit back a retort. She was a ball tossed back and forth between members of her family. No one thought for a moment that the ball might prefer to choose its direction.

"We shall miss you, as will the boys, Moire." Samuel had taken up a position by the window.

"I have a piptere, and his name is Chalco!" Noah burst out, unable to contain his news any longer.

"Have you? By Jove. You two found the nest, then?" Samuel ruffled his son's hair.

"We did indeed. Your father will help you with Chalco, Noah. It is not so different from raising a puppy. Chalco needs to learn boundaries to his behaviour." As long as the little creature remained free of any leash, Moire didn't think the boy could go wrong by emulating his father's kind approach to his dogs. Certainly, the canines all loved him for it.

"Are we to be home to one of those horrid creatures? I will never rest easy again." Katherine stared at Moire aghast.

"Pipteres are no bother, Katherine. They prefer being outside, and when they are inside, they like to be curled up asleep. Noah and I have established rules already. Chalco is allowed in the kitchen and his bedroom." Moire only hoped the few days she had were enough to ensure the piptere settled easily into the household.

"See, Katherine, the same rules as the dogs. We will manage, Moire. Don't worry about that." Samuel winked, and relief washed over her.

"I shall write to you, Aunt Moire, and tell you all about our adventures and how Chalco grows," Noah declared, his young face set with determination.

Once more, Moire packed her battered trunk. There was no private carriage for her journey to Bath. Her father required the Tobin carriage to convey him and Augusta to their entertainments. Instead, Moire would travel on the public coach. The next day, Samuel drove the gig to take her into the village.

The large coach stood outside the inn as luggage was lashed to the top and rear. Samuel passed up her trunk. The driver pointed to Clipper. "Those things aren't allowed inside. Chickens go up top."

Samuel frowned and looked on the point of arguing, but Moire didn't have the mental strength to battle over where she sat. She rested her hand on Samuel's arm. "We'll be fine up top. Clipper doesn't like the tight confines anyway, and I suspect the air will be fresher with the driver."

"Very well then. Safe travels, Moire." Samuel pecked her cheek in brotherly affection and then steadied her as she climbed up to sit beside the driver.

It was a long and uncomfortable journey. It rained. A lot. While the driver had an oiled great coat, Moire did not. Clipper huddled under her coat, and she curled her body around him as best she could. Nor did the seat have any padding, being only a hard plank of wood.

Despite the descent of night by the time they arrived, Bath bustled with activity. The public carriage dropped Moire some distance from the townhouse her family inhabited on Pulteney Street. Moire paid a boy with a barrow a coin to cart her trunk while she walked beside him, glad of his company in the dark. By the time she reached her new home, she was drenched, sore, and defeated.

When she rang the bell, the maid who flung the door open stared at her as though she were a vagrant begging in the street. Then her gaze slid to Clipper, and her mouth dropped open in a silent O. Moire did not recognise the girl as most of their staff stayed at Eadred with the Chellums.

"I am Miss Moire Tobin. Sir George sent for me," Moire said by way of explanation.

The maid stood aside, and the boy deposited Moire's trunk in the tiled entrance. She hoped her family were out so that she might fall into bed and have a good night's rest to steel herself before encountering them.

"Who is it? Is it the earl?" Augusta's voice called out in a sort of hushed shout from the front room.

When there was no answer, her sister appeared in the doorway, a frown creasing her forehead. "Oh, it's you. You look frightful."

"Hello, Augusta. It rained on the way here, and I got rather wet." Moire plucked her damp skirts away from her chilled skin.

"How did you get wet inside a coach?" The frown deepened. Something she would never do in the presence of Sir George, who would be quick to point out that frowning created wrinkles.

"I had to sit up with the driver. Pipteres are not allowed inside the public coach." A silly rule when Moire thought about it. Clipper was far better behaved than any chicken.

"Then your condition is your own fault. You insisted on keeping that horrid creature. You should have sold it like Father and I suggested." Augusta waved a dismissive hand at Moire.

"I shall remove myself and tidy my appearance if someone would be so good as to show me to my room." Clipper shivered against Moire, and they both needed to warm up.

"The maid can do that. I am waiting for my escort, so you'll not be required tonight. Father has already gone on to meet his acquaintances." Augusta peered at her reflection in a mirror with an ornate gilt edge. She tweaked the placement of an arching ostrich feather in her hair and smoothed down a stray tendril of hair.

Once dismissed, Moire resisted the urge to curtsey. "I shall see you in the morning, Augusta. I do hope you have a lovely evening," she murmured.

The maid, whose name was Bertha, showed Moire up the stairs and past the spacious and light bedrooms on the first floor to the smaller ones on the second. At least she had a room at the rear of the building away from the bustle of the street and with a view over the tiny garden below.

"Thank you, Bertha. Could I trouble you for a jug of hot water, please?" Moire couldn't ask for a bath when water would have to be lugged up four flights of stairs from the kitchens below street level. But she could pour enough in a bowl for a quick wash before climbing into bed. Clipper would be able to bathe in the shallow bowl and warm his bones.

THE NEXT MORNING, sunlight stabbed at Moire's closed eyelids. She had failed to close the curtains the previous night, since it had been dark outside. She groaned and rolled over, wondering what the day would bring. Her muscles had recovered from the journey, at least. First, she opened the window for Clipper to fly out and stretch his wings. Then she dressed in a simple blue and cream striped gown and draped a cream cotton fichu around her neck, before tucking the ends into her bodice.

Descending the stairs, Moire was relieved to find the house quiet as her family slept late after only returning home in the wee hours. She encountered the maid and asked for directions to the dining room and requested a simple breakfast. A butler appeared in the doorway as she finished her toast and coughed discretely into his hand. Staring at the man, Moire wondered what state the accounts would be in. They were supposed to be economising, not taking on more superfluous staff.

"Miss Moire, Miss Tobin asked me to leave a list of tasks for you," he said as he approached with a folded sheet of paper.

"Thank you..." Moire trailed off, since she didn't know the man's name.

"I am Dodd, Miss Moire." He inclined his head.

"Thank you, Dodd." She took the sheet and scanned

her instructions. Most of the tasks seemed to be collecting parcels of various things Augusta had bought the previous day. At least she would get to explore Bath in the sunlight while she visited the various shops and businesses.

"I hope all the purchases have been paid for," Moire muttered under her breath.

After breakfast, she shrugged on a short spencer in a navy blue and tied the ribbons of her bonnet under her chin. As she left the house and walked the short path to the street, Clipper trilled from above and glided down to perch on her shoulder.

Moire stroked his head and down his feathered spine. "Stay close, Clipper. There will be other pipteres about Bath, and I do not want anyone thinking that you are an escaped pet." He snorted and narrowed his eyes at her at being called a *pet*. "I share your sentiments, but others hold to old beliefs and do not realise you are as intelligent as your larger relatives."

Moire enjoyed the bustle of the city and walked slowly to watch the pedestrians and admire the gowns and bonnets worn by the women. Her thoughts drifted back to Larkspur Cottage, and she wondered how Noah was getting on with Chalco.

Once her arms were laden with packages, she turned back towards their townhouse. A strain rippled along her arms as she navigated the cobblestone streets. A parcel balanced on the top of her armload wobbled and then slid to one side. Moire heaved in exasperation. It would be too heavy for Clipper to pick up and deposit back in her arms.

Just then, a man swooped on the paper-wrapped package.

"Thank you, sir," she said as he rose. "Oh, it's you."

Before her stood the stranger she had met on the beach at Slatemooth. His fashionable dress was perfectly in place among the social set of Bath, rather than making him appear over-dressed on a beach.

"Hello. It seems we are destined to meet. Allow me to introduce myself. I am Mr Henry Tobin." He stood tall and elegant, his dark hair tousled by the breeze and his eyes twinkling with amusement as they met hers.

"Tobin? Why, that is my name. I am Miss Moire Tobin." What a coincidence to meet someone who shared her surname. Then the syllables of his name rattled around in her mind until they rang a bell.

"Henry Tobin?" she repeated his name again and studied him with renewed interest.

"Yes. Your cousin, Henry Tobin. It has been many years since I was last at Eadred Manor." He swept her a bow. "Allow me to assist, dear cousin. You should not carry such a load on your own."

A blush rose to her cheeks at his offer, but before she could protest, he had already relieved her of several parcels. Their fingers brushed against one another as the transfer took place, sending an unexpected thrill up her arm.

"Thank you. I am embarrassed that I did not recognise you." She focused instead on the uneven texture of the cobblestones beneath her feet, the distant chatter of townsfolk, and the gentle warmth of the sunlight on her face.

"I am not surprised you do not recall my face. You were only a child of some ten years of age when we last met. I do not mind sharing your load; it is only proper for a gentleman to aid a lady in need." His face wore a disarming smile.

This was not just any gentleman but Sir George's heir. The man who would one day inherit the baronet title and Eadred Manor. The gentleman who had angered her father many years ago, and they were not to speak his name.

"Allow me to escort you home. I had hoped to find Sir George here. I wish to make amends with him. For too long have we been estranged over some silly nonsense." He fell into step beside her.

Moire searched her memory but couldn't recall what they had fallen out over. "It is never too late to heal old wounds. I am sure Father will listen to whatever you have to say. You are, after all, his heir."

Mr Tobin made a noise in the back of his throat. "I see your piptere companion has accompanied you to Bath."

"I would not be without Clipper. He is my dearest friend." Unable to raise a hand due to the few remaining parcels she carried, Moire instead tilted her head to nudge the little dragon. "I am trying to remember the last occasion you came to Eadred."

"It has been sixteen years since I last visited the ancestral manor." He paused on the side of the street and looked both ways before indicating a path through the traffic for them to take.

Sixteen years, why that was when…Caliban died. An itch niggled at the base of her skull. Did the death of their family dragon and the consequential loss of their status among the Draco Legion have something to do with the disagreement between her cousin and father?

"That is a lifetime, is it not?" she said. Her thoughts sat

by the deathly ill dragon as his sides had laboured with his last breaths.

"I think it was fate that we have crossed paths once more. Might I say you have grown into a most agreeable young woman, Miss Moire. You were a slight and reedy child, from what I remember." He laughed, and his eyes crinkled charmingly.

She had been an insubstantial child. Her mother used to tell her to be careful that a strong wind didn't blow her away. That was no longer a problem, as her arms were usually carrying a heavy book or the weight of her worries kept her feet on the ground.

As they walked, Moire wondered if their meeting was indeed fate. Her cousin might provide a welcome distraction from her heartache over Oliver and Ruth and lift her spirits. Certainly, he was a jovial companion. His eyes sparkled with humour, and he laughed often and in a way that lightened the air around them. He also seemed genuinely interested in her thoughts and opinions, particularly as they pertained to dragonkind.

"Do you think all pipteres should be free?" he asked.

"Most definitely. Should they not be allowed to choose their companions, as we do?" On her visit to the stores, Moire had seen three pipteres chained and carried by a maid walking behind a grand lady. Clipper had chirped at the sad creatures and huddled closer to her side.

"But dragons do not choose. They are bonded to the person who is present when they hatch." Mr Tobin pointed out.

"You are quite right, Mr Tobin. Perhaps it is because of their smaller size that pipteres should be free. It is too easy for us to capture them and place them in a cage like a misbehaving chicken. No one would attempt to chain a dragon to a tree or confine one to a barn." Robust conversation rose between them as they argued the rights of pipteres and dragons. Wyverns and drakes were a topic best left for another day. Then they reminisced about the few shared childhood memories they had and exchanged stories of their respective adventures in the intervening years. Mr Tobin regaled her with tales of his travels, painting vivid pictures of distant lands and exotic creatures, while Moire recounted her scholarly studies to learn all she could about dragonkind, particularly about dragon eggs.

"Ah. Are you perhaps trying to restore your father's title of Drac? It was a great loss for the entire family when Caliban died at such a young age." He paused at the bottom of the path to her new home.

Her father? The denial was on the tip of her tongue, but instead, she smiled and nodded rather than tell an untruth. "Do come in, Mr Tobin. It will be a great surprise for my family."

A SLIGHT MOMENT of trepidation made Moire pause at the bottom of the path leading to the townhouse. Inviting her estranged cousin inside would, undoubtedly, cause a scene. Yet she sailed straight into those turbulent waters without giving any regard to the consequences. What had come over her in recent weeks?

Casting her mind back, the change in her began when she learned Oliver had returned to Wyldefen. Like a long-dormant seed, her resolve to stand up for herself had cracked through its tough protective outer shell. No longer would she be blown by the whims of her family. Learning that one of them had cruelly betrayed her and Oliver had severed her familial bond of loyalty. Day by day, she became more determined to navigate her own path, even if it was a rocky and lonely one.

For once in their lives, it was time for her family to face the consequences of their actions.

"Do come inside, Mr Tobin." Moire smiled as the butler swung open the door.

"I shall follow wherever you lead, Miss Moire," Henry replied as he surveyed the opulent surroundings.

As they made their way across the tiles, the sound of animated voices drifted from the parlour. Within, Sir George and Augusta were engaged in a lively debate, poring over a stack of invitations that had arrived for various festivities. They seemed oblivious to Moire's entrance. Their attention was wholly absorbed by the selection laid out on the low table before them as the cards were ordered by their perceived importance.

Ah, a game of whose invitation trumps whose, Moire thought wryly as she placed her parcels on a nearby table with a soft thud. Henry followed suit, depositing the load he carried next to them. She cast a sidelong glance at him, noting the slight tension in his shoulders.

"Father, Augusta, I have returned from my errands," Moire said, her voice barely carrying over their excited chatter as they compared the ornate cards. "And I have brought a guest."

"Indeed?" Sir George replied absentmindedly, not even lifting his gaze from the gilt-edged cards.

"I simply cannot decide, Father. Do we accept Lady Vesper's dance or Lord Cunningham's soirée?" queried Augusta, her delicate fingers fluttering over the invitations like a butterfly trying to decide which flower to alight upon.

"Cunningham is only a viscount, and I've not heard any whispers of the Duke of Silverdale attending his evening. Whereas Lady Vesper is the wife of an earl, and her dance will attract many of the upper echelon." Sir George leaned back on the settee and stared at the ceiling with tented fingers as he considered who would be at each event.

Moire shot a sideways glance at her cousin, who winked as they waited to be acknowledged.

"The dance it is. I shall wear my new spring-green silk for *when* the duke asks me to dance." Augusta sighed and clutched a card with silver swirls to her chest. Her gaze shifted sideways and alighted on Moire, as though she had only just realised there were others in the room. "Oh, you are back. I hope you collected all the more important purchases first."

Moire drew a deep breath and steeled herself for the introduction that would inevitably cause a stir.

Augusta rose gracefully from her chair with the soft swish of silk. Her attention seemed to be on the parcels, but as she drew nearer, her gaze flicked to one side and alighted upon Henry Tobin.

"Why, who is this handsome stranger, Moire?" she asked. Her eyes narrowed as she studied him, the cogs in her mind visibly turning as she tried to place the man with the slightly familiar features before her.

"Augusta, Father, this is Mr Henry Tobin. I encountered our cousin while running my errands. He was most chivalrous and volunteered to help carry all of Augusta's purchases," Moire said, her voice steady despite the frosty atmosphere that dropped over the room. Unspoken tension swirled in the air like a brewing storm.

"Henry Tobin? You impertinent scoundrel, to think that you would be welcomed in this house. I am not dead yet!" Sir George blustered. He laid down an invitation and straightened himself on the settee to glare at their visitor. There was no warmth in his eyes, only a deep suspicion.

"Sir George, Miss Tobin. It is an honour to renew our acquaintance," Henry replied with a polite bow, his own gaze never leaving the elder Tobin's face. An undercurrent of worry threaded through his words.

Augusta's mouth hung open, evidently shocked by Henry's presence. Whilst Sir George merely stared at him with a frigid, unyielding gaze.

"Father, Augusta, Mr Tobin has expressed his desire to —" Moire began but was cut off by Augusta's sharp laughter.

"Desire? What possible desire could there be between us and this...stranger?" she sneered, her disdain dripping from every word.

Moire wondered what tales their father had told his eldest daughter about their cousin, his heir. Had he elaborated on the nature of their disagreement?

Henry remained silent, but his dark eyebrows shot upwards.

"Augusta, please. Mr Tobin wishes to extend an olive branch, to make amends for past misunderstandings," Moire implored in a soft tone.

"An olive branch," Augusta echoed incredulously, her eyes widening in disbelief. She glanced at her father to ensure she followed the correct cues for the situation.

"Amends?" Sir George scoffed and proceeded to inspect his manicured nails.

"Indeed, Sir George. It is my greatest wish to heal the rift between our families." Henry placed his top hat on the table and approached his uncle.

"And what possible reason could you have for this sudden change of heart?" Sir George narrowed his cold eyes even further.

Henry stopped by the settee and placed one hand on the chintz-patterned fabric. "I believe it is time to put aside past grievances created when I was a foolish youth. Let us forge a new path towards understanding and harmony. It is my dearest wish that our families become much more, intimately, entwined," he murmured the last word and glanced at Moire in a way that made a blush rise up her chest and heat her cheeks.

Sir George snorted. "You were an exceptionally foolish youth." His voice remained as frosty as winter air blown off snow.

"Yes, Sir, I was. I ignored the good counsel you gave me at the time. I thought myself in love and, as the old saying goes, marry in haste, repent at leisure. Three years ago, my wife passed. Since we were not blessed with children and my parents both died a long time ago, I realised I was alone in this world and that you are my remaining family." He clasped his hands behind his back and bowed his head at the mention of his wife's passing.

Moire felt a pang of sympathy for the man before her. She could well imagine the anguish of losing someone so dear, especially when one had devoted their life to them. Then she wondered if, yet again, her family sought to interfere in the marital decisions of its members. Thus far, only Samuel had met their stringent requirements. And the Duke of Silverdale. Although that gentleman probably wasn't aware of the fact he was to wed Augusta yet.

"Go on. You were saying how intelligent and valuable

my advice is." Sir George's expression wavered, and the ice cracked ever so slightly. He folded his arms across his chest and appeared both sceptical and curious.

"Since I lost Cecilia, I have sought to right the wrongs of my past. I prostrate myself before you, Sir, as a way of showing that I am sincere in my intentions for a reconciliation." He moved to kneel before his uncle and stretched out his arms with a bowed head as though he laid himself upon an altar.

Sir George huffed but looked satisfied by the penitent position of his nephew. "You speak prettily, but actions mean more than words. Time will tell if your apology is genuine," Sir George replied, his tone still guarded yet tinged with something that resembled cautious acceptance.

"Of course, Sir, I would expect nothing less." Henry rose and bestowed a charming smile upon them.

Augusta left her stack of parcels to return to her father's side. She stood behind him to study her cousin. "He is well made, at least, and handsomely clothed. He will not do us a disservice when the acquaintance becomes known."

A handsome face is forgiven more easily than a plain one, Moire thought.

"I heard mention of attending a dance this evening. Perhaps I might join your party to demonstrate my resolve to become a closer part of this family?" Again, he glanced over his shoulder at Moire.

Did she have something stuck in her hair that he kept looking at her? She raised one hand and touched her dark locks, swept up off her neck. Sometimes, Clipper pulled strands free when he tried to nestle closer to her. Or she might have a stray leaf caught from when she brushed under a low-hanging tree.

"Very well, Mr Tobin," Sir George said finally, his voice strained but resolute. "You may accompany us to the dance this evening. It would only be proper for my heir to be present, after all."

"Thank you, Sir," Henry replied. "I assure you, I shall do my utmost to honour your trust. I hope my lovely cousin, Miss Moire, will do me the honour of a dance?"

Augusta snorted, and Sir George's forehead wrinkled in a rare frown. "Of course not. Moire has duties here. She cannot be gallivanting off to dances."

Moire clasped her hands tightly together to stop a tremble as she stepped forward. The new, *bolder* Moire would make herself heard. "I am a member of this family and do not see any compelling reason why I can't attend a dance."

"Surely the Tobins should present a united front to society?" Henry interjected smoothly, his eyes meeting Moire's with a twinkle of mischief and determination. "Would it not cause unwarranted speculation if Miss Moire was omitted from our party when she is here in Bath? People might gossip as to why you have shut her away in this lovely home. Imagine if rumours swirled that she had the plague or some other sickness."

Moire bit her lip to stop a snort. Augusta would be ostracised if the social set thought she was likewise contaminated with some dreadful illness. Feeling a little puckish, she coughed into her hand and was rewarded by a suppressed chortle from her cousin.

"But...but...Moire attend the dance? Absolutely not! Why, all she has are those dowdy gowns." Augusta's horrified exclamation pierced the air.

Moire flinched as her sister's disdain for her presence in society was made all too clear. If her gowns were dowdy, it was because their father spent all his coin on pretty dresses for Augusta and Moire had to make do with hand-me-downs or what little funds were left over.

"I think we shall allow it on this occasion, Augusta. A lady of such standing as yourself should have a companion." Sir George tapped his chin as he considered his daughters.

Moire swallowed her reply. Apparently, the housekeeper was allowed out after all, in the role of a mousey lady's companion. As the conversation continued around her, Moire caught sight of Henry pulling faces at her from across the room, his playful expression a balm to her wounded pride. She smiled in response, the corners of her lips lifting ever so slightly. It seemed that despite the frosty atmosphere, she had found an unexpected ally in Mr Henry Tobin.

"You are right, Father. I should have someone to hold my shawl and reticule," Augusta mused.

Their voices hummed like bees in a hive, their words stinging and disapproving. They discussed Moire as though she wasn't even in the room. Her cheeks burned with embarrassment, and she fixed her gaze on the intricate pattern of the rug beneath her feet. Her newfound resolve to stand up for herself had exhausted itself already.

"We are in agreement, then. Moire may attend. It's not

as if she will draw attention away from you, Augusta," Sir George chuckled.

"Thank you, Father," Moire murmured. She had only bought one best gown, and it would have to do.

As the tension in the room slowly dissipated, Moire clung to the small victory she had achieved. She would attend the dance, and though her role may be that of a mere companion, it was a chance to rub shoulders with society. And, perhaps more significantly, it was a chance to learn more about Henry Tobin, the man who had shown her unexpected kindness amidst the storm of her family's disapproval.

"Until this evening. Cousins, Sir George." Henry bowed, winked at Moire, and took his leave to prepare for the evening.

A flurry of activity erupted once Henry had left. Both her father and sister demanded a bath to begin the arduous beauty routine necessary to ensure they looked their best when they stepped out the front door that evening.

Moire hurried down to the kitchen and instructed the maids to begin heating water. Then two copper tubs were carried up the stairs and placed in each bedroom. She experienced a moment of longing as she surveyed the airy suite occupied by Augusta. What would it be like to be spoiled and have everything you ever wanted?

It would probably make you a shallow and greedy person, the voice in the back of her mind whispered.

Perhaps. But for once in her life, how she longed for someone to adore her and shower her with all she wanted. Then she chastised herself for falling down a maudlin rabbit hole. Although, to be fair, this standing up for herself thing was new and would take a bit to get accustomed to.

When her resolve was stronger, she would ask who took her letter from Oliver and sent him the newspaper cutting in return.

Since there was no official lady's maid in their household, Moire slipped into the role. After her sister had been bathed, scented, and patted dry, Moire helped Augusta into her undergarments before fetching her new ballgown.

Made of a jewel-coloured emerald silk, the capped sleeves were trimmed with intricate gold embroidery. The rounded neckline was modest yet alluring. A gold ribbon accentuated the empire waist, and Moire tied it in a perfect bow at Augusta's back. The train swished behind, and intricate gold stitching created floral patterns along the hem and bodice.

Moire affixed a diamond necklace around Augusta's slender neck. The piece was a cherished heirloom from their late mother. As a final touch, Moire arranged Augusta's long chestnut waves in an elegant up-do, weaving in glittering hair pins that matched her gown's embroidery.

Moire stood back and took in the full effect, and her heart swelled with sisterly affection. "You look divine. The duke is sure to dance with only you this evening."

"I suppose I shall do." Augusta preened in the mirror. "I hope you do not make us late. You have yet to change."

"I have been somewhat occupied up until now," Moire replied.

When her sister turned back to the mirror, Moire stuck out her tongue. Then she picked up her skirt and ran out the door, undoing her laces as she raced to her room. She had no time for a bath. Her clothing was hastily discarded, and she washed herself with the cold water left in the basin. Next, she found a clean chemise. Valuable time was taken to redo her hair in a simple knot. She teased a few strands from the sides and added a jewelled comb, the one piece of jewellery she had from their mother.

From her wardrobe, Moire took down her one good gown. Made of dark-blue silk, it had embroidery that started around the hem and spiralled up around the skirts, winding around the waistline and finally up over one shoulder, where it dropped back down like a waterfall. Navy was an unusual colour choice for an unmarried woman, but at her age, Moire thought the rules for young women no longer applicable. Besides, she thought the colour suited her darker hair.

Her only problem was doing up the delicate shell buttons on the back of the gown. Clipper offered, but she couldn't risk his claw snagging on the silk.

"You must stay here, Clipper. I do not want to risk you in a ballroom full of people who might want to seize you for themselves." She scratched the piptere under the chin in his favourite spot. "I promise that tomorrow we shall take a walk by the river, and you can look for fish."

Mollified, he padded at his blanket and settled down.

With a shawl thrown over her arm, Moire hurried out the door and down the stairs. Luckily, as she reached the second-floor landing, she encountered the maid.

"Oh, Bertha, could you please button me up? I cannot reach." Moire turned to show the exposed stays and chemise.

"Of course, Miss Moire." The maid's nimble fingers soon had all the fastenings done up. "You look lovely, Miss," she said on finishing.

Moire grinned. She *felt* lovely for a change. "Thank you!" she called out as she rushed down the stairs.

"We are waiting, Moire," Augusta called from below.

"I'm coming!" Moire replied as she reached the last set of stairs. Holding up the edge of her skirt, she made her way down as quickly as she could without tumbling.

Her older sister and father waited in the entranceway. Sir George still cut an imposing figure, even at the age of fifty-five. His clothes were impeccably tailored to show off his trim frame. He took a pinch of snuff from a silver tin and placed it on his hand before snorting it. The little silver snuff tin was snapped shut and placed back in his jacket pocket. Then he wiped his nostrils with a starkly white handkerchief.

"Let us be off. It's one thing to be fashionably late, but we don't want anyone else setting their sights on the duke in our absence." He crooked his arm, and Augusta took it, the two preceding Moire out the door.

Moire fell into step behind them. A good mood bubbled through her. She was wearing her best gown. She felt pretty, and there was even an excellent chance that Henry Tobin would take her hand for at least one dance. What more could a woman ask for?

Oliver's face shimmered before her, but she swatted it away.

"We had our chance, and it was not to be," she reminded the phantom memory.

Her fledging resolve had recovered a little from

bringing her cousin into the house and reminded her that she was forging her own path, not staring down a fork not taken. Moire straightened her back and allowed herself a small measure of excitement at what the evening might bring.

23

After they exited the carriage, Moire trailed a few steps behind as they entered the grand assembly room. She soaked in the atmosphere, pausing at the doorway to survey the crowd, washed in a golden glow from the dazzling chandeliers. Musicians sat upon a raised platform at one end and played a familiar tune that made her tap her toe.

"Isn't it splendid?" Augusta exclaimed.

The room was filled with the murmur of animated conversation punctuated by delicate notes of music. Ladies in exquisite gowns twirled around the dance floor. Silks and satins in pale cream were the background to the occasional splash of bold colour.

"Come now, Augusta. Let us make our presence known." Sir George urged them further into the throng of guests.

Moire stayed close behind but not so close that she risked treading on Augusta's short train.

"Miss Tobin!" A high-pitched voice squealed. A blonde

woman of short stature wearing the palest of green bee-lined for Augusta and took her hands.

"Lady Seymour, what a delight," Augusta cooed to her friend.

"Come, you simply must join us. The duke is some-where here, and we are trying to spot him." Lady Seymour tugged Augusta towards her gaggle of friends.

"My shawl." Augusta dropped the patterned silk over Moire's arm and hung her beaded reticule from her hand. Then she was whisked away to join the group of fashion-able society ladies.

"Ah, there are the chaps, and I spy the Earl of Denton." Sir George strode confidently towards a group of fashion-able gentlemen. As he engaged in their conversation, his laughter and animated gestures exuded the confidence of a man who knew where he belonged. Moire watched him for a moment, wishing she could summon such ease in this sea of strangers.

Her determination to attend had been a bold one at the time. Now, she found herself alone, left to navigate the swirling currents of high society like an untethered boat. She cast a wistful glance towards the now-distant figure of her sister, who effortlessly merged with her noble friends and acquaintances.

Moire's first action was to deposit her sister's shawl and reticule on a chair. She would not spend her evening impersonating a wardrobe. She placed the shawl, with the bag nestled underneath, on a velvet, padded chair pushed up against the wall. Its mates on either side also held a collection of discarded items. Moire removed her soft woollen shawl and added it to the pile.

She hummed along to the music under her breath as she wandered the edge of the room. When she reached one side, where open doors led to the balcony, Moire discovered something that made her heart clench. Three pipteres were each chained to an ornate stand in the corner. One creature had blue and green feathers like a peacock, and it sat slumped with its head hanging low. Of the other two, one had light bronze scales, the other a mix of feathers and scales like Clipper but in hues of green.

"Oh, you poor things," she whispered as she approached.

Outrage surged through her at the sight of the magnificent little dragons so cruelly restrained. She battled a strong urge to free them. Her fingers twitched with the desire to undo the delicate chains that bound the pipteres to their perches. It was wrong that such intelligent creatures were treated as mere ornaments. Their legs shackled, and their spirits stifled. It went against everything Moire believed about the natural world and the importance of living in harmony with it.

But...freeing the creatures would cause trouble and potentially ruin the evening.

She had to do something and find a way to give the pipteres some comfort. The little peacock-coloured piptere worried her the most. The sickly little dragon looked as though it had given up on life.

As Moire neared, it shuffled along its perch away from her. She paused and took slow, even breaths, letting them get used to her presence. Then, she reached out and scratched the green piptere as it seemed the most outgoing of the group. Next, she found the itchy spot on the bronze one. The blue and green piptere watched with a curious gaze.

"Would you like a scratch, too?" Moire asked.

The other two trilled, and the slouched creature tilted its head. Moire reached out, gauging the piptere's reaction as, with the gentlest touch, she stroked its head with a fingertip. All the while, she murmured soothing words to the frightened thing. Soon, it realised she meant no harm and leaned into her touch. The softest purr of contentment rumbled through its jewel-like body.

Opal. Female. The timid creature gently showed Moire how it preferred to be identified.

"Get away from that! It's mine!" a strident voice called.

Opal trembled under Moire's touch, and she didn't have to ask to know the voice belonged to a woman who considered herself the *owner* of the unfortunate creature.

"I was merely stroking her head." Moire stood between the piptere and the advancing woman.

Of middle years, she had the rotund appearance of either too many children or too many sweet treats. Or possibly a combination of both.

The woman scoffed. "Its name is Peaky. And you cannot touch it. It bites."

Moire counted to ten in her head as she did when Noah or Elijah misbehaved and told herself this was a chance to educate the woman. "Pipteres only bite when they are frightened or in defence of themselves. And she told me her name is Opal."

"What nonsense. The things cannot talk." The woman placed her hands on her substantial hips and glared at Moire.

People turned to watch them, and Moire felt the heat of their scrutiny through the silk of her gown. If she made a scene, her father and Augusta would never forgive her.

"Pipteres are highly intelligent, and they do indeed talk. You just have to listen. You are fortunate to have such a lovely companion as Opal." Moire nodded and took her leave before she said more—or berated the woman for her cruel treatment of a creature who obviously lived in fear of the person who held her leash.

As Moire turned away from the tethered pipteres, she focused on the music, the laughter, and the whirl of dancers before her. She promised little Opal that she would do *something* to alleviate her conditions by the end of the evening.

With that silent promise made, Moire continued her exploration of the venue and discovered where the refreshments were laid out. A glass of punch would give her something to do with her hands while she watched the dancers. The centre of the table held a glass bowl large enough to bathe a child and a wriggly one at that. Moire picked up the ladle and filled a glass with ruby-red punch. The drink had a fruity taste and the sharp tang of lemon that revived her senses.

Clutching her glass like a lifeline, Moire resumed her position at the edge of the ballroom, where she could observe the kaleidoscope of colours and faces. The rustle of silk skirts and the soft whisper of delicate satin slippers added to the overall melody. She caught snatches of conversation. An upcoming engagement, a scandalous elopement, the latest fashion trends. It created an odd sensation of being both part of the scene and detached from it.

"Good heavens! Is that Lady Blewitt cavorting with young Lord Fitzwilliam?" a shrill voice exclaimed nearby, causing Moire to turn her head. A group of elderly ladies, resplendent in their finest brocades and jewels, were clustered together. They surveyed the room, their critical gazes missing nothing like a flock of colourful vultures.

"Indeed, my dear," another replied, her tone dripping with disdain. "One wonders how she manages to keep her reputation intact, carrying on with a man young enough to be her son."

"Reputation? Ha! I daresay it has more holes in it than a well-worn piece of lace," the first woman cackled.

"Ah, Miss Moire, I have found you at last," a familiar voice called out, drawing her attention away from the gossiping matrons.

Moire turned as Henry Tobin approached, his darkly handsome features illuminated by the soft glow of the chandeliers. Her heart skipped a beat. Augusta was right. He was exceptionally well-formed.

"Mr Tobin. I was just admiring the spectacle from afar," she replied. "But perhaps there is something to be said for entering the fray?"

"Indeed. One cannot truly experience a ball from the sidelines. Shall we brave the dance floor together?" He extended his hand to her in invitation, his eyes gleaming with mirth.

"I think I can be so bold with you as my partner." Moire set down her empty glass and accepted his offered arm.

The musicians played a tune that Moire knew the steps to, and they were soon laughing as they joined the other dancers. Every time they circled the floor and came near the corner with the perches, Moire's attention was drawn to the pipteres.

"Is everything all right, Miss Moire? You seem rather distracted?" Henry asked as they sought out a glass of punch after a particularly vigorous country dance.

"I am sorry, Mr Tobin. The plight of those pipteres bothers me. One in particular seems to have an...unkind... companion." She struggled to criticise a woman whose name she didn't even know. But one look at the forlorn Opal had tugged at her heart.

"Do you wish to set them all free?" Henry whispered in a conspiratorial tone.

"Do not tease. If only I could. But father would never forgive me if I created such a scene." How her hands itched to undo the collars and let the chains drop to the ground.

He fell silent for a few strides. "What if you could free one? Would that suffice?"

Moire halted and stared at him. "You would be a conspirator in such a thing? But it would break the tentative peace with Father before you had even established it."

He cast his gaze downwards. "Some things are more important than the good regard of Sir George."

She didn't know what to say and hugging him would be considered highly inappropriate. Instead, she stood a little taller. "The blue and green one. I fear she is ill-treated."

Henry tapped the side of his nose and placed her hand in the crook of his elbow. Then he leaned his head closer to hers. "Later this evening, I shall manufacture a distraction that will give you sufficient time to unchain her."

Moire swallowed a giggle. He would help her, and one

piptere would fly free. What words could adequately express the gratitude surging through her? "Thank you."

The music softened and hinted that the next dance would be the scandalous waltz. Many places refused to allow the dance, which required the man to hold his partner close for the entirety of the movement. Although some balls were allowing it to be danced just the once.

Moire's gaze drifted across the ballroom and alighted on her sister, surrounded by her acquaintances. They were like a flower border in a garden, each bloom beautiful in its own way. A murmur of excited whispers rippled through the crowd as the Duke of Silverdale approached, his regal bearing drawing all eyes towards him.

While not an overly tall man, he moved like one used to commanding everyone's attention. He stopped before Augusta.

"Miss Tobin, would you do me the honour of dancing the waltz with me?" the duke asked in a voice that carried easily over the hum of conversation.

Augusta's cheeks flushed a delicate pink, but she composed herself quickly, curtsying gracefully before accepting his outstretched hand.

"Of course, Your Grace. How magnanimous of you to ask," she replied, her tone sweet and demure, like honeyed tea sipped from a fine china cup.

As they joined the other dancers, a knot of ladies gathered nearby, their fans fluttering faster than hummingbird wings as they exchanged knowing glances and whispered gossip. Moire didn't need to stand close to know what they said. Fortune smiled on Augusta that she was singled out by the most eligible bachelor in all of England, and one waltz might change her life forever.

The musicians played, and at first, only Augusta and the duke spun around on the floor. Then, one by one, other brave couples joined them.

"Your sister appears to have made quite the impression upon the duke," Henry observed, his lips quirking into a wry smile as he watched the couple glide effortlessly across the polished parquet floor.

"Do not be deceived. This is the culmination of a plan as well orchestrated as any made by Nelson or Wellington." For years, Moire had listened to her father and sister discuss how Augusta was destined to be a duchess and the best way to elicit a proposal. At least someone's dream was a step closer to becoming real.

"I wish her the best of luck in her campaign for his heart. Shall we join them or adjourn to the supper room to discuss our battle strategy?" He waggled his dark eyebrows.

For a moment, Moire didn't understand his reference, and her heart stuttered that he might mean they discuss a similar type of proposal. Then her senses returned to her, and she realised he meant freeing the piptere. "Oh, yes. Let us find a free table now while everyone is watching the duke and Augusta."

In the supper room, they found a table and selected from the range of dishes on offer.

"You're very knowledgeable about dragons, Miss Moire. Where did you learn such things?" Henry asked as they took their seats.

"I am grateful for all I learned with Caliban. A young girl could have no better teacher than a patient dragon."

Her gaze misted as she remembered her youth, peppering the mighty dragon with questions as she climbed over his back. Odd, when she thought of it now. As a child, she had no fear of heights and often lamented that Caliban would not take her flying with him.

"I met him only the once. As a lad, your father introduced me to him as the most likely heir. It must have been a great shock to you all when he passed. And at such a young age for a dragon, too." He spoke in a low, comforting tone as he shared her pain.

Moire swallowed her bite of fish sautéed in a lemon sauce. "Yes. He should have reached at least three hundred years old. Some illness came over him. I think that is partly why I have studied them, to learn what snatched his life prematurely."

Conversation flowed easily between them, interspersed with laughter and shared smiles. Henry was an attentive and charming companion. To her delight, he appeared to share her interest in dragons and asked her many questions about them.

After they finished their supper and Moire had sipped a cup of hot chocolate, Henry leaned across the table. "The evening draws to a close. Shall we return to the ballroom and implement our plot to free the prisoner?"

The supper room had filled after Augusta's dance with the duke, and there would only be a few more dances before the evening concluded. Now was their chance. Glancing around the room, Moire spotted the horrid woman who *owned* Opal. She was at a large table, laughing with her friends. Good. She would not notice the creature being freed.

"Yes. Let us seize this opportunity." Moire rose and left the room with Henry at her side.

"You get into position, and I shall create a diversion." He winked as they split apart.

Moire circled the room until she stood close to where the pipteres were chained. Henry moved to the other side of the room. When she was in position, his gait changed to a swaying lurch as though he were intoxicated.

"Where did she go?" he all but shouted. "Have you seen my wife?" He tackled another gentleman and nearly dropped to his knees. The other gent caught him under the elbow.

People turned to stare at the drunken display. As Henry lurched from one gentleman to another, demanding to know the whereabouts of his wife, Moire crept closer to the perches. She crooned to Opal as she approached, and the little creature trilled in response.

"Be still, little one," she whispered soothingly. Thankfully, the leg shackle wasn't riveted but rather had a sort of clasp. Her fingers worked deftly at the silver mechanism. With a soft click, the metal cuff fell away and with it, the chain. Moire draped the chain over the perch, the open cuff dangling over the side.

"You are free, Opal. May you find happiness beyond this room." Moire gestured to the nearby open door.

Opal's sea-green gaze met Moire's in silent gratitude. Then the piptere took flight. She darted through the open doors and disappeared into the night sky. Moire murmured an apology to the other pipteres for not freeing them. All of them being gone would be too coincidental and result in awkward questions. But there would be other opportunities.

She hurried away from the corner before anyone noticed her. Picking up her shawl and Augusta's, Moire was seated in the chair, waiting, when her family finally noticed her.

"Did you see your cousin making a drunken spectacle of himself? He had to be hauled away by two footmen," Sir George said as they left the ballroom and waited for their carriage.

"Perhaps he imbibed too much to overcome his nerves? Besides, I doubt anyone will talk of it. Not when everyone is gossiping about Augusta and the Duke of Silverdale. I heard two matrons say they expected an announcement by the end of the month," Moire said.

Augusta turned to her with a wide-eyed stare. "Did they really? Oh, Father, to think all our work will soon come to fruition."

"Quite. I always said you were destined for great things," Sir George replied, patting his daughter's gloved hand.

Moire trailed behind. Once again. But this time, she didn't mind. Augusta had finally captured the attention of the duke, and Moire had not only freed a miserable piptere from the bonds of servitude, but she enjoyed her evening with a charming companion.

At long last, she was on a path to contentment, and nothing could deflate her good mood.

24

OVER THE NEXT FEW DAYS, when she wasn't rushing around to satisfy Augusta's needs, which was literally a full-time position now that she had attracted the attention of the duke, Moire enjoyed the company of Henry. Often, her cousin helped her on mad dashes across Bath to purchase a specific sort of perfumed water Augusta heard the duke favoured. Or to buy new gloves in the exact shade of buff the duke preferred. Or innumerable other tasks that a lady's maid would undertake.

Today, Augusta had hurried from the house to meet the duke at the Pump House, where they would sample the water. Moire had a blessed stretch of time all to herself. Particularly since she intended to ignore the list of chores Augusta had left tucked under her plate at breakfast time.

Day by day, Moire inhabited her true self more, and her rebellious streak grew. Although it was not quite strong enough yet to confront her family about treating her as unpaid help, or the letter someone hid from her.

Today, the sun cast a warm glow on the honey-coloured stone buildings as Moire and Henry navigated the busy streets of Bath. The air was alive with laughter, music, and the clatter of carriage wheels against cobblestones—the city's vibrant social scene was in full swing. Moire glanced up at the elegant façades, admiring the beauty of her surroundings, and her gaze lingered on the intricate iron-work that adorned the balconies above. Not that she would ever stand on one of the little platforms.

"Do you think dragons can swim?" Henry asked as they approached the river.

"Oh, yes. In fact, they are quite remarkable fishers. I understand they provide sailors with plenty of fish when they accompany a vessel out to sea." She recalled the day she stood on the beach and watched Valiant swimming among the waves.

"It saddens me that Caliban died so young. I know some would think my regret is because I will never be Drac Tobin now that our family has tumbled from the Legion back to the ranks of a mere baronet. But I am sorry that I never got to know him," Henry said as they crossed the road to walk the lime chip path winding along the riverbank.

"I wish I had appreciated my childhood with him more at the time. It is only after the passage of all these years that I have realised how much I could have asked him about the habits and rites of dragonkind." Moire clung to a treasure no one could ever take away from her—her memories of those years with the patient dragon.

"I find it odd that dragons do not have some sort of succession such as we do. Your father's title will one day settle on my shoulders, but there was no hatchling to replace Caliban. Or did he not father any offspring?" Henry paused to watch two ducks trying to paddle upstream.

Clipper, who had accompanied them but preferred to flit above their heads, dived into the water with a splash. Then he rolled onto his back and used his wings to float with the motion of the current.

"I think it might be because dragons have such long lifespans. Some can reach five hundred years old. Which I suspect is also why there are so few dragon eggs. They have little need to replace their population and keep their numbers to what the land can support. If dragons were as numerous as sheep, they would have to eat us to survive," Moire said.

Henry stared at her. "Sometimes, cousin, I cannot tell if you jest or not."

Moire had pondered the low numbers of dragons and decided it was the natural order of things that a family would eventually drop from the Draco Legion. Theirs was not the first, nor would they be the last, to be demoted when they lost their dragon. The war saw three dragons die in battle against the French and their families were stripped of their rank and privilege in return for the sacrifices that were made.

"Despite the work of scholars over the centuries, there is still little known about the breeding of dragons. They are remarkably private about matters of reproduction, and anyone impertinent to ask such questions does not survive to hear the answer." Moire laughed as Clipper disappeared beneath the water and reappeared with a tiny fish in his jaws.

"To add to the mystery, no one knows when or where a dragon lays her clutch," Henry said as they continued their stroll.

"That lack of knowledge is not restricted to dragons. So-called learned men also know woefully little about the female of our own species." That was one piece of wisdom her mother had imparted to her. If she ever found herself with child, she was to seek out an old wise woman experienced in the delivery of babes and to avoid the modern doctors with their heavy reliance on bleeding to cure every ailment.

Henry barked in laughter, and his eyes sparkled. "Well said, Miss Moire, well said. Do you think you might use your feminine intelligence to ferret out the secrets of dragons of your sex?"

His questions danced close to the edge of what she had gleaned from old books and then augmented by conversing with Clipper, Lunette, and Valiant. Knowledge that she intended to use when she approached Artemis.

"Sadly, I am not acquainted with any female dragons who can engage in such an intimate conversation. I would very much like to pen a book about pipteres, though." Moire changed the topic to the smallest member of dragonkind as Clipper emerged from the water and rained droplets onto the path as he flew to her arm.

"You have a remarkable way with these creatures. I have never seen one respond to commands without being leashed." Henry reached out and scratched Clipper's head.

Moire kept her arm outstretched so the damp creature didn't drip on her skirt. "A gentle approach based on trust and understanding yields far greater results than a forceful method ever could."

As they continued their stroll, Moire explained her various training techniques and behavioural observations of pipteres, which all adhered to her guiding principles of humane treatment and trust.

———

LATER THAT WEEK, Moire sat alone at the breakfast table. Her sister and father had not returned from a soirée until well after midnight. One which, thankfully, Moire had not been invited to. Her sister mentioned the lady throwing the event was most put out that her piptere had escaped during some previous event. Apparently, the gossip was that the creature had been stolen by another jealous lady and the owner intended to track down the thief and have her arrested. Moire hoped Opal had flown far away from Bath and would thrive free of the cruel owner.

A stack of letters and invitations was piled high on the sideboard. Moire flicked through them as Noah had promised to write to her once a week about his progress with Calcho. One letter had the familiar neat script of Katherine. Her sister must have addressed it for her son. Moire took the letter to the table and poured a cup of hot chocolate to accompany her crumpet.

Once she had buttered her crumpet and dolloped a spoonful of marmalade on it, Moire slit the seal on the letter and unfolded it. Another sheet with Noah's boyish scrawl on it was enclosed. Katherine had included a quick note to say that Ruth's recovery continued.

We were all delighted when Ruth announced her engagement to her captain. I believe a woman should marry young. I do not understand why some cling to spinsterhood...

The words blurred before Moire's eyes as her heart clenched in her chest. The letter fell from her fingers and saved her from reading the rest of Katherine's tirade against those who remained unwed. Oliver had done the honourable thing, as she knew he would, and followed through with his proposal to Ruth. The news was not unexpected, but seeing it laid out starkly in black ink still hurt.

"It is a sign, Clipper," she whispered to the piptere who sat on the windowsill, watching pedestrians in the street. "It is long overdue for me to let go of the past."

The future was not as gloomy and dire as she once thought it might be. Her cousin had provided a bright spot in her life and was the only blood member of her family to encourage her studies of dragonkind. The Radcliffes did, but they were Katherine's family. Moire blinked away the moisture in her eyes and took a bite of crumpet, which she washed down with a mouthful of hot chocolate. Once fortified, she picked up Noah's letter. Her nephew's obvious delight in his piptere companion warmed her heart.

Today, Augusta sent Moire to hand deliver acceptances to certain events. Apparently, she didn't entrust the job to the local lad who usually ran such chores. Not that Moire minded. It was a gorgeous day with a light breeze that lifted her worries.

Once again, as she rounded a bend, she encountered Henry. He touched the brim of his top hat, crooked his arm for her, and fell into step at her side. They strolled along the bustling Royal Crescent, where the lively chatter of excited visitors mingled with the rhythmic clop of horses' hooves.

"The buildings here are so lovely." Moire admired the harmonious curve of the buildings, their pale stone gleaming in the morning light. "It is no wonder that Bath is said to be the epitome of grace and beauty."

"Yet even such splendour fades in your presence, dear cousin." Henry's eyes were lit up with appreciation.

"You are a shameless flatterer," she laughed, giving him a playful nudge. "But I admit I have much enjoyed your company these last few weeks."

"My friendship will always be extended to you," he replied soberly, his amiable expression turning serious. "And I hope we have many more such opportunities to discuss dragons over the years to come."

"Oh, so do I! No one else in my family cares to talk about piptere training methods or dragon behaviour." Like a plant long deprived of sunlight and water, she soaked up every moment of such conversations with her cousin.

"My favourite so far has been our lengthy debate on the proper technique for grooming a dragon's scales." The grin returned to his face.

That comment made her footsteps falter. For it was grooming Valiant that led to Ruth's accident...and then her engagement after weeks of slow recovery. Had Oliver sat at her bedside, reading aloud and feeding her peeled grapes? Shaking off such thoughts, they walked further into town. Occasionally, Moire checked an address so she could deliver one of the cards in her basket. Now that Augusta's name was linked to that of the duke, their townhouse experienced a flood of invitations. Every one was scrutinised by

Sir George, and its merits were weighed before a response was issued.

After Moire delivered the last card and her basket was empty, except for an old shawl that Clipper liked to curl up in, they found themselves in a quieter corner of Bath, where bustling streets gave way to serene parks. The rustle of leaves and the gentle chirp of birdsong accompanied their leisurely stroll, providing the perfect backdrop for their conversation.

"From my observations of Clipper, I believe pipteres possess an extraordinary capacity for empathy," Moire said, her eyes bright with enthusiasm as they discussed her favourite topic. "Because the bond between Clipper and I is based on friendship, I think he can sense my emotions."

"Why, that is quite remarkable. Do you think it applies to dragons as well? Did Caliban have such a connection to your father?" Henry asked as they waited for a smart curricle to pass before they crossed the road to the park.

Moire thought that any such link between the two was probably what poisoned their dragon. Before she could consider how to answer Henry's question, a flash of iridescent colour caught her eye. Her heart leapt with joy and surprise when she recognised the peacock-coloured piptere gracefully soaring through the sky—Opal.

"Look, Henry! It's Opal," she called in excitement and tugged on his sleeve. The dazzling hues of Opal's feathers shimmered like the precious gem she was named after as she played among the trees.

"Is it really the freed prisoner?" Henry stared up, trying to fix on the quick-moving creature.

Moire set down the basket that contained a dozing

Clipper and stretched out her arm. Opal swooped down and landed gracefully. The piptere climbed up Moire's arm to nuzzle against her face. The once sad and dull creature appeared much improved.

"Hello, Opal." Moire examined the piptere as she caressed under the little dragon's chin. Opal leaned into the touch and trilled low and slow like a purr.

Opal. Content. The piptere sent the message to Moire.

"I am glad to hear it. If you ever need anything, seek me out or find Clipper." At the mention of his name, the blue and silver piptere awoke and clambered out of the basket.

"Extraordinary. Quite extraordinary," Henry breathed, his eyes wide with wonder.

Moire stroked Opal's plumage and continued her examination. Thankfully, there was no sign of any injury or long-term damage from the neglect. No longer did the piptere slump; her posture was now erect, and she did not cower in fear. The dull glaze had gone from her eyes, and they whirled a clear green.

Clipper chirped and flew to a low-hanging branch. With one last caress against Moire's cheek, Opal fluttered over to join him. The two pipteres engaged in an animated conversation with lots of trills and chirrups. Then they took flight, circling each other as they spiralled up into the sky. Their iridescent feathers and scales shimmered in the sunlight as they performed an elegant aerial dance. Each swoop and glide was perfectly synchronised as if the pipteres were connected by an invisible thread.

"They dance like partners long familiar with one another," Moire said, her voice barely more than a whisper, afraid to break the magical spell the display cast.

As Moire watched, something shifted deep inside her. A purpose took root. The gift of Clipper from Samuel all those years ago had lit a passion inside her for the little creatures. Watching the mesmerising spectacle of their aerial acrobats fanned that passion hotter and into a conviction that she needed to share her knowledge with others. A world of possibilities unfolded before her like a map, guiding her towards a new path she was eager to explore.

"I want to become a teacher," she burst out. "To show the world that there is a better way to bond with pipteres. One built on trust, respect, and empathy."

Henry remained silent at her side. The dance ended, and Clipper returned to Moire. Opal soared higher, a spark of green and blue against the sky, until she disappeared from sight. Clipper perched on Moire's shoulder and rubbed his face against hers as he chatted excitedly about the pretty female.

"What is he saying?" Henry peered at the piptere.

"That Opal is his friend. Clipper told her of the forests of Wyldefen and about the other pipteres who live there. They are free in the forests of Wyldefen as men are not allowed to trap them to sell as pets or take their eggs. She has promised to visit us." She scratched Clipper's head and sent him waves of gratitude for helping the other piptere.

Henry shook his head, wonder alight in his eyes. "You have pipteres flocking to you. What could you do with dragons? Why, I believe you could even convince a female to hand over an egg if you asked one, dear Moire."

Moire stared at him, and her breath caught in her throat. His words skirted so close to her plan. But he couldn't possibly know. Could he? Then she laughed to break the tight silence that had formed. "There is a magnitude of difference between making friends with a sad piptere in need of a friend and a bonded female dragon capable of torching you alive for your impertinence."

Clipper fluttered down to the basket and padded at the shawl in the bottom. Once he was settled for the return walk, Moire picked up the basket and slid her arm through the handle.

"You know, this reminds me of an old rumour I heard a few years ago. Something about a dragon egg being found at Eadred Manor, but some misfortune befell it." The humour dropped from Henry's gaze and was replaced by something cooler...and calculating.

Worry rippled down Moire's spine at the turn in the conversation. She enjoyed his company, but now a suspicion took up resident in her that *his* interest hinged on her knowledge of dragonkind. Did he only strike up an acquaintance because of what he thought she could do...lay her hands on a dragon egg?

Mentally, she waved an admonishing finger at herself. What did she really know about her charming cousin? He had appeared on the beach at Slatemooth and attached himself to her like a shadow. All the while, he directed almost every conversation to dragons as though he tested the extent of her abilities.

"The reports were misinformed. It was an old wyvern egg that a thief found in Faustus's burrow, left over from many decades ago when a pair of wyverns lived at Eadred." That was the story she had constructed for her father, who had never once ventured into the home of the guard wyvern. Aided by the foetus being too partially formed to confirm which subspecies it belonged to. Moire's inspiration for the tale had been the fossilised nest Faustus had once shown her.

Henry huffed and blinked, which restored the usual humour to his dark eyes. "Indeed? I am sure there was a rumour of a dragon egg being in the area at the time. But the years play many tricks on my memory, and I am probably confusing the locations."

With great effort, Moire kept her expression serene and unruffled. "A dragon egg somewhere in Wyldefen? That sounds like a story from a fairy tale and would be an extraordinarily rare occurrence. It has been at least fifty years since there was a new dragon hatchling. I shall consult my books as to where exactly the last egg was found."

Henry offered his arm once more, and this time a sliver of reluctance made her pause before accepting. Taking heed of the internal warning, and not wanting him to realise anything was amiss, she offered a shy smile and tucked her hand into the crook of his elbow.

"I understand there is to be a grand musical event tonight being held by your neighbour from Wyldefen, Lady Beaumont. Is it true the duke will be in attendance?" Henry said as they headed back to Pulteney Street.

"Yes. Augusta can hardly sleep with the excitement of it all." They chatted of inconsequential things, who would be singing and other guests attending. The change to a lighter topic gave Moire time to calm her turbulent thoughts.

When they reached her family's townhouse, she bid farewell to Henry at the bottom of the path.

"I hope to see you this evening," he said and bowed over her hand.

"Until then," Moire replied and carried the basket with Clipper up the path.

One thought raced through her mind as she closed the door behind her—who was Henry Tobin, and why was he so interested in dragon eggs?

25

THAT EVENING, Moire stood before the small mirror propped up on the dresser in her bedroom, carefully scrutinising her reflection as she adjusted the sea-foam green silk gown that hugged her slender frame. As she moved, the fabric shifted in hue and darkened, just as the ocean did with the tug of currents. The gown had originally been purchased for Augusta, who tried it on once and declared it *too plain*. Moire gratefully accepted the item from her sister and then twirled gleefully in her room with it.

Tonight, she accompanied Augusta and her father to a musical recital being hosted by their dear friend, Lady Beaumont. The wealthy and elite of society in Bath had been invited to hear a famous songbird who was briefly visiting the town.

Moire stroked Clipper's head and dropped a kiss to the very top. "Have a good evening, my friend. I will leave the window open a fraction for you." The evening chill would invade her room, but it was a small price to pay to allow the piptere to come and go as he pleased.

Grabbing up a shawl made of a delicate wool that complemented her gown, she hurried from her room. Down the two flights of stairs, she rushed to wait in the entrance for her family. They would walk to the event since Lady Beaumont resided with her son, the earl, only a short distance away.

Augusta appeared not far behind Moire, her cheeks flushed with excitement. "*He* will be there tonight. Lady Beaumont said he specifically asked if I would be attending."

He referred to the Duke of Silverdale. Augusta's budding romance appeared to be gaining speed, somewhat like a snowball rolling down a hill. Moire only hoped her sister wasn't flattened when it tumbled over her.

Moire only half-listened to Augusta's excited chatter, her mind considering other things. Like would their cousin Henry be in attendance, and what were his intentions? His questions about that horrible night eight years ago and dragon eggs made a tingle of alarm race over her skin.

As they stepped outside into the crisp evening air, Moire glanced up. The moon hung full in a cloudless night, and stars were scattered like diamonds on velvet. On such nights, she always scanned the skies for a lunar dragon, but she had never seen another one. Her studies said that none lived anywhere in England or Europe and that the rare type of dragon was only found in the most remote regions of Russia and China. Had the one she and Oliver saw been lost?

Or had it been searching for its stolen egg?

Pushing the thought aside, she hurried after her family. It was a gentle ten-minute stroll to the lavish property owned by the earl. A garden of clipped greenery framed the pedestrian pathway to the front door. Carriages took the driveway, which curved around the green space. Mature trees enclosed and sheltered the garden, making a quiet sanctuary between street and house.

"Oh, do you think he is here already?" Augusta peered into one of the windows as they approached.

"Remember, Augusta, you do not want to appear too keen. One does not yank in the line on the first bite of the fish. You must ensure it has a good bite on the bait," Sir George said.

Moire stared at her father. It was a surprisingly accurate analogy. "I didn't know you were a fisherman, Father?"

Sir George shuddered. "Your grandfather enjoyed outdoor pursuits and inflicted them upon me. As a boy, I spent many an hour shivering and drenched by the river."

They entered the lavish home, and Moire stopped to stare at the opulent surroundings. Marble statues stood at the compass points in the entrance and regarded the visitors with cool, eternal gazes. They followed the other guests across the patterned tiles to a set of double doors flung open. Within, an enormous drawing room had been turned into a private theatre. Chairs were lined up in neat rows, with a centre aisle left clear.

At the front and to one side sat a pianoforte with a sombre-looking man waiting at the keys. Behind him, two more men clutched their instruments, one with a violin and the other a flute. Footmen in black livery circulated among the guests and offered glasses of champagne before everyone took their seats. The room was abuzz with anticipation, punctuated by the occasional burst of laughter or spirited conversation. Moire scanned the crowd. Lady Beaumont had drawn together the cream of society.

The hostess, resplendent in a deep-wine gown and diamonds about her throat, detached herself from a small circle of laughing people and approached.

"Sir George!" She took his hands and kissed his cheek. Then she greeted Augusta and Moire. "You both look enchanting. I am sure this will prove a most magical evening."

"Is he here?' Augusta leaned close and whispered, perhaps a little too loudly, as those closest to them turned around.

"Not yet, dear. But do not fear. Silverdale likes to keep others waiting, not be the one waiting. He will appear moments before the performance starts. You mark my words." Lady Beaumont patted Augusta's arm.

"Let us make sure there is a vacant seat beside you, Augusta, right at the front." Sir George pointed to where he believed was the optimal position for their fishing expedition. "There won't be room for you, Moire."

As her sister chatted politely to her new friends, Lady Beaumont took Moire's hand and clasped it to her. "It is wonderful, is it not, to see Augusta so happy?"

"Yes. I think everyone deserves a chance to find happiness." Moire hoped that once her sister was favourably settled, she would be allowed to follow her own dream. However unorthodox it might be.

"But she will not be the only one to find happiness on this stay in Bath," Lady Beaumont said in a soft tone so they were not overheard.

"I imagine many proposals are made due to the magic

cast by this town." It was, after all, simply another venue for the never-ceasing marriage market.

Lady Beaumont laughed. "Come, Moire, you cannot be so naïve. Your cousin has been paying court to you these last few weeks, and it is obvious you are smitten with him."

"Smitten?" Moire's throat went dry, and she regretted her decision not to take a glass of champagne. Yes, if she were honest with herself, she had been smitten by her handsome and charming cousin. What lonely and heart-broken woman wouldn't be swayed by such ardent atten-tion when they needed it most?

But now...her emotions cooled as she considered exactly *why* he paid court to her and not Augusta. "There appears to be some confusion, Lady Beaumont. I have been polite, and, yes, I have enjoyed Henry's company. But there is no more to it than that."

"Oh, but a little birdie tells me that discussions have already taken place. It is a lovely ending to your story. You will stay at Eadred Manor, and your mother would delight in knowing you will one day be its mistress, just as she was." Lady Beaumont smiled, and a trace of sadness for her lost friend glistened in her eyes.

The musicians played a soft prelude, signalling that the performance was about to commence.

"We shall discuss it later. I do hope you will allow me to assist with preparations for the happy day." Lady Beaumont stroked Moire's cheek and then hurried to find her seat amid the rustle of silk and satin. As her family took the best chairs in the front row, Moire moved nearer to the back. With her thoughts and emotions in turmoil, she sought a little privacy to allow her mind to settle rather than being crammed elbow to knee with everyone else.

A woman appeared in a doorway and with a slow, measured pace, walked to the centre position. Tall and robust, she wore a gown of pale cream covered in glittering embroidery. An ostrich plume jutted from her hair. At the same moment, a heavy tread walked down the aisle. The Duke of Silverdale.

He strode to the front, inclined his head ever so slightly at the singer, and then dropped into the vacant chair next to Augusta. Just as Sir George had planned. Moire let out a sigh of relief. It boded well for a favourable outcome for her sister. If her father were busy with the wedding of the season, he would have scant time to contemplate any nuptials of Moire's.

The first haunting notes of the singer's voice soared through the air and filled the room with a melody both ethereal and enchanting. Heads turned in rapt attention as her song wove its spell around the captivated audience. Her lilting voice seemed to tug at the heartstrings of those present, evoking a myriad of emotions that shimmered on the faces of the guests.

"Breathtaking," the woman in front of Moire murmured, and she clutched her hand to her chest.

The man beside her leaned in close and whispered, "Mesmerising."

Moire couldn't tear her gaze from the entrancing figure at the front of the room. Yet even as she allowed herself to be swept up in the beauty of the performance, other emotions gnawed at the edges of her consciousness, threatening to tear apart her enjoyment of the evening.

As the singer's words swelled into a crescendo, Moire reflected on the path that lay before her. Any happiness she once dreamed of finding with a handsome naval officer eight years ago would now be bestowed on another. If she put aside her suspicions about Henry's motive, there was some merit to such a match. She could remain at Eadred Manor and would always be near Faustus. Using the knowledge gleaned from the books Oliver had sent to Gormsby Hall over the years, Moire could find a wyvern nest to gift Faustus with companions in his twilight years.

The more she thought about it, perhaps her reservations about Henry were simply nerves at letting go of an old fantasy she had constructed. She had frequently admonished herself to find a new dream, and this could be it. Marriage to Henry. Life as mistress of Eadred Manor. Writing her book on piptere training methods and conducting talks and classes throughout England.

So why, when she conjured that future in her mind, did it not seem quite...right?

The music continued, each note weaving a tapestry of emotion that mirrored Moire's inner turmoil. She was torn in different directions as old dreams simmered and dissolved, but new ones struggled to emerge as though they were trapped in deep, sticky mud.

The singer's final notes reverberated through the chamber, and tears glistened in the eyes of some of the audience —a testament to the powerful performance.

"Bravo!" people called and rose to their feet to applaud.

As the singer refreshed herself for the next set, guests mingled. A circle formed with the duke and Augusta at its centre. Moire smiled at her sister, who thrived on the attention. While they had become estranged over the years, sisterly affection still dwelt within her. However, she found it increasingly difficult to focus on the pleasantries of the evening as her thoughts splintered in different directions.

"Moire, you look ghastly. Did you eat something that didn't agree with you?" Sir George observed on his way past her to fetch more champagne.

"I fear I might have, Father. If you'd excuse me, I shall go outside for some fresh air and see if it settles my stomach," Moire said.

"It would be better if you went home and laid down. We don't want Augusta's evening marred by you being sick in a potted plant." He arched one brow and tsked under his breath at the disaster such behaviour would cause.

"Yes. You are right. Please pass my apologies to Augusta and Lady Beaumont." Moire nodded to her father and left the room.

In the marble tiled entrance, she wrapped her shawl around her shoulders and stepped out into the night, crossing the drive to the semi-circle of garden. The contrast between the crowded house and the quiet of the trees was as stark as the difference between day and night. Where the former had been filled with noise and chaos, the latter offered tranquillity that seemed almost otherworldly. The cool breeze soothed her frayed nerves, and for the first time that evening, Moire could finally think clearly.

Following the path, she found a bench tucked beneath a spreading elm sheltered by camellias on either side. She sat and leaned her head against the bark of the tree as she gazed up at the stars through the foliage. She closed her eyes and drank in the quiet. Her thoughts stilled and her breathing slowed as she considered what to do about the impending proposal from her cousin.

The tendril of warning that wrapped itself around her heart suggested caution. Yes, she would keep her guard up and her wits about her. The path ahead might be treacherous, but that didn't mean she couldn't navigate a safe course through it. A good captain could guide his ship through shallow and rocky waters by staying alert.

That would be her—alert as she ventured into unchartered waters.

A walking cane tapped on the cobbles not far from where she sat and drew Moire's attention. She peered through the trees as a familiar figure approached the patch of forest—Henry. Smartly dressed in his evening attire, he fixed on the large house with its brightly lit windows and faint strains of music wafting from the open door.

Lady Beaumont had probably invited him so she could observe them together. Her mother's friend should really learn to hold her tongue. Every time she had quietly advised Moire of an impending engagement, she had fled the house and it ended in disaster. At least this time she was already outside and could disabuse Henry of any such ideas before they were given voice between them.

As Moire gathered her courage to confront her cousin, rapid footsteps approached Henry. Her heart clenched. Was it a robber about to attack the well-dressed gentleman?

"Tobin!" a soft masculine voice called out.

Henry halted and leaned on his cane as he waited for the stranger to catch up. "You should not be here. You are supposed to be in Wyldefen."

"You were taking too long. I had to ensure you were

still on task. Otherwise, a man might think you had scarpered and broken our agreement," the stranger said in a low tone with an almost sibilant hiss to it.

His words raised gooseflesh along Moire's arms and itched at a memory deep in her mind. She had heard that voice before...but where?

"I will pay what I owe you, Blackwood, you know that. It has simply taken a little longer than I thought. Rather like trying to get a neglected cat to eat out of your hand, I have had to dangle a few treats to get my cousin to trust me," Henry said.

Moire slapped a hand over her mouth to stop a startled gasp. They were talking about *her*! Not only that, but the name Blackwood lit a memory that flared into life. Darius Blackwood. The Fox. The wiry fighter Oliver had beaten to win the egg. The man she long suspected had come to their kitchen door asking for the *Sailor*, and the man who stumbled and dropped the egg while fleeing from Faustus.

A sudden gust of wind rustled the leaves overhead, momentarily drowning out their voices. She needed to get closer without being seen. Rising, she crept from tree to tree, moving like a ghost flitting through a cemetery.

"I have waited eight long years, but my buyer is running out of patience." Blackwood moved to stand in the shadows, his back to the garden sheltering Moire.

"Their patience will soon be rewarded. I'm not going to rush and marry the timid little mouse without knowing if she can provide what you seek. I am to repay the debt only, and it is not large enough to be saddled with her for life." Her cousin barked a high-pitched laugh as though an absurd thought had occurred to him.

"*Can* she do it?" Blackwood's voice dropped lower, and Moire had to strain to catch his quiet words.

Henry tapped his walking cane against the iron railing that fronted the house as he considered the question. "Yes. I have listened to her prattle on about dragons for weeks, but I finally learned enough to know it is within our grasp. It confirms what I overheard at Slatemooth."

Prattle on? Moire couldn't decide what offended her more. That Henry thought marriage to her so unbearable, that he never had any genuine interest in her, or that he found dragons a boring topic of conversation. She decided the comment about dragons hurt more, for they meant the world to her.

An icy chill ran down her spine as she considered the implications of the conversation. Henry had heard her talking to Oliver that day on the beach when she said there was a way to petition Artemis for an egg. Perhaps that meeting had been accidental, or had Henry followed her deliberately? Prodded to do so, perhaps, by his debt to the criminal. One which would be repaid when she presented him with a dragon egg.

Well, he should prepare for disappointment. Henry Tobin would *never* hear anything else about the topic from her lips.

"Get it done. I want that thing in my hands by the end of the week," Blackwood growled. "Otherwise, I will find other ways to collect on my debt." Then he turned and stalked away, disappearing among the shadows.

Henry sighed and ran a hand through his hair. "Here I come, little cousin. To dazzle you and sweep you off your feet," he muttered with his gaze fixed on the house.

Moire froze. What would she do if he strolled through the dense trees? He might spot her among the shrubbery. She dug her nails into the bark, ready to shuffle around the trunk to keep it between her and Henry. Thankfully, he followed the drive where no branches would snag at his clothing.

Once Henry disappeared into the house, Moire darted out of the garden to the street and set a course for her home. Only then did she wonder if Blackwood watched the house, waiting for Henry to emerge victorious in sweeping the *little mouse* off her feet. Just in case he stood guard, she didn't stop or dare to glance over her shoulder until she reached the safety of the townhouse.

26

———

After a restless night, Moire awoke with a start as the first shafts of early morning light pierced the thick glass of the window. Her heart raced from the troubled dreams that had plagued her sleep, and echoes of Henry's deceitful words lingered in her mind. With a sigh, she pushed herself up and swung her legs over the side of the bed while rubbing at weary eyes.

"Good morning, Clipper. I hope you slept better than me," she murmured.

The little silver and blue piptere had raised his head from his nest in the basket when she stirred. Now, he fluttered over to the bed. Sensing her distress, he hopped up her arm to nuzzle against her cheek in comfort.

"I need to decide what to do. Let's go find some peace by the river." The lower reaches of the Avon River flowed through Bath, and there was a serenity in watching the ripples of water that she much needed.

She dressed hurriedly in a robust and plain gown made of light wool in a mossy green. Then she grabbed a shawl and crept from the house without either bonnet or gloves. At such an early hour, she wouldn't encounter anyone of consequence, and she could pass for a servant hurrying on some task for her household.

As she stepped outside, the cool morning air kissed her cheeks. The town was just beginning to stir, the gentle hum of activity slowly building with the rise of the sun. Together, she and Clipper made their way along the road towards the river.

She picked a spot not far from Pulteney Bridge and sat on the dew-kissed grass. Clipper hesitated only a moment before diving into the water. His playful antics brought a smile to her lips as he splashed about, chasing after a group of ducks that quacked indignantly at his intrusion. The sight of Clipper fully enjoying the moment without any worries lightened her troubled heart.

"They think you are an odd sort of duck, Clipper!" Moire called out.

Laughter bubbled in her chest as the piptere darted among the ducks and attempted to emulate their grace as they wove through the water, barely creating a ripple. Clipper's wings sent droplets of water flying through the air. The ducks, no longer irritated or startled by the little dragon's presence, accepted him as one of their own and paddled alongside him.

As Moire watched her companion play, the peacefulness of the river was a balm to her worries. As she pondered Henry's conniving intentions, it deepened her sense of betrayal and entrapment. If she were to marry him, it would be nothing more than a loveless union forged from deception and ulterior motives.

He wanted a dragon egg. Not her. And certainly not her *prattle* about dragons.

And yet...no matter how deep his lies cut, she kept picking at the wound. If she married him, she could stay at her beloved Eadred Manor and be near Faustus. What sacrifices was she prepared to make for that?

"Could I trap myself in such a marriage, where my heart would never find its companion?" she whispered to the babbling water.

Clipper finished his watery antics and flew to her side. He shook his wings dry before he nuzzled her hand. Concern was etched into his reptilian features.

Moire should be happy, he said. *Faustus understands. Does not want you sad.*

The tiny dragon's affection reignited her desire to study dragonkind and continue to unlock their mysteries. Then she remembered the story Admiral Chellum told of when he first went to sea as a young lad and suffered horrible seasickness. When she asked how he overcame it, he said he had to. That sometimes, you had to push through to follow the path you wanted. That was the decision Moire would make, to push through towards the future *she* wanted.

"Thank you, Clipper. I must be true to myself, however daunting that may be," Moire declared in a firm voice. "As much as I long for love and family, I would rather remain a spinster who followed her dreams than be ensnared in a cold marriage."

Saying the words aloud breathed life into her new dream, and it surged through Moire to fill all her hollow spots. Once Augusta was married and Katherine's children were older, Moire pictured herself as a teacher, sharing her knowledge of dragonkind with eager minds. It was a daring dream and an unusual one for a woman, but it filled her with purpose.

And Clipper, the piptere reminded her as he inserted himself into her vision.

"Quite right. Together, we will find our way in the world. Free of the shackles others would impose on us." With those words, she realised how similar she was to Opal and the other pipteres—chained to unfeeling masters. Her breaking free of her family was symbolic of the freedom she fought to give all of them. Human and dragonkind alike.

The piptere trilled softly in agreement. They sat together in silence as the sun rose higher and dried off the last bit of damp clinging to Clipper, and the day edged from dawn into morning.

"Time to go back. We have much to do." When she rose, Moire stood taller. Determination laced her spine with steel.

She stretched out her arm, and Clipper flew to it, then hopped up to her shoulder. His tufted tail curled around her neck. As she made her way back along the road to the townhouse, a familiar voice called her name.

"Moire?"

Startled, she turned to find Captain Hartford standing in the road with a flush to his face as though he had run to catch her. His eyes crinkled in concern.

She wanted to call out his name, but he was no longer her Oliver. "Captain Hartford. This is unexpected."

"I was coming to find you." He carried his top hat in his hands, his fingers curled into the brim.

"Is Ruth recovering well?" She had letters from Katherine, but they contained scant detail on how the young woman fared after the terrible head injury and were full of her sister's concern about an odd freckle on her arm.

"Yes. Since returning to Gormsby Hall, she has made quite a remarkable recovery. Although she is somewhat altered with its passing." His forehead furrowed as he chose his words.

"Altered? In what way?" Moire had heard stories of people changing after a blow to the head.

"The only word I can think of to describe it is calmer. And a little more thoughtful about her actions." His lips quirked in a quick smile.

That didn't seem a terrible outcome. Ruth had been flighty and impulsive, like many young people. Traits that had contributed to her actions that horrible day. Drawing a breath, Moire found the strength to say, "I wanted to offer my congratulations. Are you in Bath because of the forthcoming wedding?"

Oliver's frown deepened. "No. I came to find you."

Moire's strength was rapidly draining. She loved him still. Blast it! It seemed to be an eternal flame inside her that simply refused to be extinguished, no matter how much she doused it. "Well, I appreciate you coming here to tell me yourself. But there was no need. Katherine had already written to inform me of Ruth's engagement to...to... her captain." The words were dry in her mouth.

Moire's heart raced, and her palms were clammy as she tried to hide her feelings of despair. She turned away, ready to flee back to the safety of her home and wallow in her misery, when his warm fingers curled gently around her wrist.

"Moire," he rasped her name. "I'll not have yet another misunderstanding drive us apart ever again. Your congratulations are directed at the wrong person."

She stared at him, confusion mingling with hope in her chest. "What do you mean?"

"Miss Radcliffe is to marry Captain Forbes," Oliver explained as his thumb gently stroked the back of her hand.

That didn't make sense. Everyone knew Ruth was infatuated with Oliver, and he had been about to propose. Moire dropped her gaze to the toes of her boots as she tried to make sense of it all.

"We both followed Miss Radcliffe to Wyldefen. Forbes has a rare patience. He sat and read to her every day at Gormsby Hall while I tended to Valiant. Did you know he writes his own poetry? And it transpires that Miss Radcliffe has a beautiful singing voice. She began creating melodies to accompany his prose." Here, he paused to shake his head in wonder. "To observe them was to witness the rare alchemy of two kindred souls finding one another. As we did years ago." He dropped his hat to the ground. Keeping hold of her wrist, he caressed her cheek with his now free hand. "Forbes became a houseguest of the Radcliffes so that he might visit her daily. It did not take long before he offered marriage and was accepted. Much to the delight of everyone."

Moire closed her eyes as tears prickled at the corners. This was too marvellous to believe. She must have fallen asleep by the river, and she dreamed of his touch.

"You are free?" she barely managed to ask, each syllable squeezed from a throat tight with expectation.

"No. I was never free. For my heart has always been yours." Raising her hand, he removed the moonstone ring from her finger and held it before her. "Would you still have a weary sailor who longs to find a place to call home and put down roots?"

A hiccup surged through her and emerged as a strangled gasp. She covered her mouth, not believing that after so many years and heartache, they had found their way back to each other. She swallowed her tears and straightened her spine. "That is most unfortunate, Captain Hartford. Because I intend to pull up my roots and travel England and then further afield in my quest to educate people about pipteres and their unique intelligence. It is my mission to see them freed from the chains that bind them."

He laughed, a short burst of happiness and surprise. Then he, too, donned a serious expression. "If you would allow, I have a little experience in navigating further afield and wish to apply for the position of guide on your expeditions. In fact, I had been considering leaving the Navy to start my own shipping company. Perhaps I could offer you the use of my new vessel?"

She couldn't hold back her love or excitement any longer. "I once said yes, a thousand times yes. My answer has never changed. My reply and my love have always been constant despite the storms we have weathered." Moire held out her left hand, and Oliver slipped the modest ring onto her finger.

"Thank God," he breathed. "I could not bear the thought of the vast empty ocean before me without you by my side."

Then he kissed her most passionately. The two of them saying with their lips all the things that words could not. Clipper, by this point, had grown bored and fluttered to a lamppost, where he preened his tail as he waited.

After a very thorough kiss that left Moire more breathless than running after her nephews, Oliver rested his forehead against hers. "With that matter sorted, there is a pressing issue. Charlotte sent me to find you. Faustus has become agitated and cries your name, and they are unable to calm him. She thought it best I seek your advice immediately."

Alarm flared through Moire. Her thoughts turned to the wyvern she considered a part of her family. "He must be sick. I need to pack my things and will leave for Eadred Manor at once." Her mind raced to the books she had read and those that detailed sicknesses that assailed dragons.

"I have a carriage. I will fetch it and meet you at the townhouse," he said.

"Thank you. I will be ready within the hour." That gave her time to race back, change her damp gown, and pack her trunk.

After another heated kiss, they parted ways. Moire hurried along the road, Clipper flitting above her. Her mind churned with worry for Faustus. Was it an age-related illness, or had he injured himself while prowling the estate at night?

When she reached the townhouse, Moire trotted up

the stairs and hastily changed. Then she gathered her belongings and shoved them in the trunk. She made one last glance around the room and checked under the bed to ensure she had everything before summoning two footmen to lug the trunk down the stairs.

Moire picked up Clipper's basket, which contained the shawl he used as a blanket, and a book for her. She followed the footmen, wincing at the thud of the luggage against each step. Would it wake her family? She had dashed off a note to her father and intended to leave it on the side table at the entrance.

But it would appear Sir George was already awake, no doubt planning the next move in Augusta's campaign to win the duke. He emerged from the parlour, wrapped in a bright-blue velvet banyan, his features schooled into a bland expression as he pointed to the luggage. "Throwing out old clothes?"

"I have received word that Faustus is ill. I am leaving at once to tend to him." She tugged on her gloves as she stood at the bottom of the stairs.

The footmen carried the trunk to the door, placing it on the tiles to await further instruction.

"Don't be silly. You cannot simply abandon your family for that...creature," Sir George spat out.

Moire wondered what Faustus or Caliban had ever done to her father that he so vehemently disliked dragonkind. Or was it as simple as they didn't bend to his will? That was why he refused to have a cat in the house—they could not be ordered about.

Moire gripped the handle of the basket tight and kept

her tone even. "I am not abandoning anyone. You and Augusta have a full social calendar here, and I doubt you will even miss me."

Sir George took a step closer, his shoulders stiff. He huffed as he tried to control his temper. If he flew into a rage, he risked breaking the capillaries in his face and it would never do to have a ruddy-red complexion. "Your duty is here, with us. You always were a selfish child, thinking only of yourself."

"Selfish?" That word made indignation swell inside her. "For *years*, I have served this family as secretary, house-keeper, nanny, and now lady's maid. All the while, I have endured your utter disregard for my feelings. Now, when I choose to tend to one who genuinely cares for me and who himself has given this family decades of loyal service, I am suddenly 'selfish'?"

Her accusation hung in the air as her father stared back at her. Shock was etched on his face that she had stood up to him.

Soft footsteps trod the stairs as Augusta joined them. "What is all this racket?" She wore a pale-pink silk banyan, and her long hair was still curled in its protective overnight rags.

Before Sir George could muster up a smart reply, someone rapped on the brass knocker. One of the footmen swung open the door to the figure of Oliver. He glanced at the players frozen upon the stage and raised one eyebrow at Moire in an unspoken question about whether she required assistance.

"Could you load my trunk, please, Captain Hartford? I

will be out directly." Moire nodded at him to indicate she would finish things here before she joined him.

Eager for an escape from the tension in the house, the two footmen each grabbed an end of the luggage and headed out the door.

"Moire believes she is leaving us to tend the loathsome wyrm back at Eadred," Sir George said to Augusta, complete with rolled eyes.

Augusta scoffed. "Nonsense. She cannot leave. I have a promenade this afternoon with the duke and then a supper with my friends. I will require her assistance to dress and prepare for both. And I have a mountain of correspondence that she must reply to."

Moire glanced down at Clipper, who curled into a small ball in the basket. His eyes whirled silver with concern as he stared back at her, but he stayed put and didn't flee outside like the much larger footmen.

It will be all right. She brushed her reassurance over him.

"If you walk out that door, my girl, you will be severed from this family. We will deny any connection with you, and you will no longer have our support." A low, steely tone entered her father's voice.

"I rather think, Father, that I will fare far better without your support than you will without mine." Years of neglect and oversight flowed through her limbs. She loved her family, but did that mean she had to sacrifice her life for them? "You have taken everything from me—all my dreams and hopes—and turned me into nothing more than a servant. But still, it is not enough. I suspect even if you drained me to a mere wraith who silently wandered the halls, you would still demand more of me." Moire's voice became a sad whisper. They took and took and yet were never satisfied.

Sir George's face contorted with anger, but before he could respond, Moire pressed on, feeling a fire ignite within her that had been smouldering for years.

"Before I leave, I would know which of you took Oliver's letter to me eight years ago and sent him a false report of my engagement to Samuel?" She glanced from her father to her sister.

The room seemed to hold its breath as her question hung heavy in the air. Words were storm clouds waiting to burst. Sir George frowned. But it was Augusta who looked away, unable to meet her sister's gaze as her cheeks flushed with guilt.

"Augusta." Moire's heart sank in her chest. She had suspected, but to see the confirmation was a dagger through her soul. "Why Augusta? Once, we were as close as two sisters could be. Then, after Mother died, we drifted apart." Moire took a step towards her sister.

Augusta shook her head. "I am to marry a duke. That sailor was far beneath us in every conceivable way. Position, wealth, and breeding. Such a match would have been disastrous and could have ruined my prospects."

No. Self-serving as it was, that reason didn't sit right. "Title and fortune aside, Captain Hartford is from a good family. Marrying him would never have impacted any proposal you might have received. Tell me, Augusta, how did your cruel actions eight years ago advance your prospects? For it would appear that we are both still unwed."

For all her life, Augusta was told she would marry a duke. Her sister was older than her by two years, and yet Moire couldn't recollect any possible romances over the years...Oh! Now she understood.

"He who covets, destroys what he cannot have," Moire whispered.

"Whatever are you talking about?" Augusta waved one hand while the other clutched the newel post.

"You have never loved or been loved. That was why you drove Oliver and me apart." It was equivalent to a jealous child snatching a toy off another just to toss it behind a dresser. Before her sister could deny the accusation, Moire carried on. "Your efforts were for nothing. Captain Hartford and I are to be married."

At that, her father rallied. "Don't be ridiculous. You will never marry that sailor! I have forbidden it."

"Then it is fortunate I will be severed from this family once I leave this house. I do not seek, nor do I require your approval. I love you both and wish you every happiness, but I cannot continue to exist solely for your benefit. I must live my own life and follow my own path." Moire picked up the basket with Clipper and walked to the door.

"You are not to leave this house! You have been warned, Moire. Step out that door, and you can never return! You will be dead to us!" Sir George roared, risking a rare apoplexy.

Moire kept her back straight and never turned. She walked straight out the door and to the waiting carriage. Oliver stood beside it and held out a hand to help her up. She placed the basket on the backwards-facing seat, and Clipper climbed out. Oliver tapped on the roof, and the carriage moved off. Only then, with the family townhouse fading in the distance, did Moire collapse into Oliver's arms.

She wept as she left behind the only life she had ever known. But one where she never truly belonged.

27

THE CARRIAGE TRUNDLED along the roads as Moire exhausted her tears. In a way, she mourned the family she never had. One where her mother lived, and she kept a close relationship with Augusta. For all that Katherine might appear oblivious to the world around her, Moire never doubted that her sister loved her family and had a kind heart. Nor did she treat Moire any differently than she did everyone else.

At times, Clipper asked for the window to be dropped so he could fly alongside them for a while. Or he would dart off into the meadows and then return to snooze for a little longer. As the miles passed, Moire told Oliver of her final confrontation with her family, the realisation that Augusta had taken his letter years ago and driven the wedge between them, and her father's declaration that she was cast out.

"We will build our own family. You, me, Clipper, and whatever other assorted creatures we collect along the way," Oliver said, and he kissed the top of her head.

Moire reclined in his arms, her feet up on the seat as she stared out the window. "I wish there was a way for Faustus to join us. It might sound silly, but I do not want to live too far from him; it will be hard enough when I travel around England and overseas. Do you mind terribly that we must find a place in Wyldefen as our permanent home?"

"Of course not. I have always admired your bond with Faustus, and it doesn't matter to me where we make our home. The important thing is that it will be *ours*." Oliver had his long legs stretched out, and his boots were up on the opposite seat. Somehow, he seemed comfortable in the cramped and swaying carriage, which probably reminded him of being onboard a ship.

Then, she turned the conversation to her duplicitous cousin and his criminal associate. "While in Bath, I spent much time in the company of my cousin, Mr Henry Tobin. I met him at Slatemooth, too, although at the time I did not recognise him. That day, when I told you about petitioning Artemis for an egg, he was standing on the seawall, and..." She needed a moment to collect herself before telling Oliver of what she overheard.

"And?" Oliver prompted.

There would be no secrets between her and Oliver. Moire would tell him everything. "He heard us. He paid attention to me in Bath solely to earn my trust and, so he believed, my affection. Last night, after leaving a recital, I was hidden in the garden when he approached the house. Another man ran up to him. A man we both know from the past. Darius Blackwood."

Oliver sucked in a breath, and his feet fell to the floor with a thump. "He's after another egg."

"Yes. It transpires my cousin owes some sort of debt to Mr Blackwood. They plan for Henry to sweet-talk me into getting an egg from Artemis for him. Which he will promptly deliver to Mr Blackwood for his buyer." Moire tried to fathom how the man could waste years plotting ways to steal or otherwise acquire an egg to sell. If he had applied himself to study like Moire had, he might have learned other ways to legitimately acquire one.

"Are you in danger?" Oliver turned her on the seat so he could search her face. Worry pulled his brows low on his forehead.

"I have foiled their plan by fleeing our townhouse. Which I also did eight years ago, as I suspect it was Mr Blackwood who stole the egg from Faustus's burrow." It was odd how running away from things created pivotal moments in her life.

Hours trundled by, and the colours of early evening spread across the sky—soft pinks and lilacs that deepened into blues and purples as day made way for night. The air became cooler, carrying with it scents of distant wood smoke. Clipper settled back in the basket, his tufted tail covering his eyes like a mask.

Oliver dozed at times, propped up in the corner with his arms crossed. As a seasoned war veteran, he possessed the ability to snatch sleep wherever he could while remaining ready to spring into action if the alarm went up. As he snoozed, Moire studied his features at her leisure. Time and the sea had weathered him and roughened away the freshness of youth. But it left him all the more hand-some for it.

Her heart fluttered, and she hid a grin behind her hand. The dreams of the girl she had been at eighteen had turned into the reality of the woman she was at twenty-six. She had ventured beyond a point of no return when she turned her back on her family. But instead of fear, excitement took root inside her as she imagined what adventures she would have with the man soon to be her husband.

Finally, the carriage passed between the gateposts that marked the entrance to Eadred Manor.

"Oliver, we are here." She didn't need to shake him awake. His eyes opened immediately.

Night had fallen, and the moon sat alone in the sky without any clouds to play with. The ivy-clad walls of the manor were bathed in a ghostly silver. The carriage came to a halt as the silence outside was shattered by a terrible screech, echoing through the night like a banshee's wail.

"Faustus!" Moire fumbled the latch in her hurry to get out.

Clipper gave his own high-pitched cry as he climbed out of the basket and took flight through the open door.

When she stepped down onto the gravel of the drive-way, Moire tugged her shawl tighter around her shoulders. But it was the horrible call of Faustus that made her shiver, not the chill air.

"Oliver! Miss Moire!" called Charlotte as she rushed out of the manor to greet them. "I am so glad you found her, Oliver."

"I think you can call me Moire, since we are to be sisters soon," Moire said as Charlotte hugged her brother.

"Truly?" She glanced between them.

"Yes. After eight years of considering my offer, Moire has agreed to be my wife." Oliver raised Moire's hand to kiss her knuckles.

Charlotte emitted a quiet *eep* of joy, and Moire was enfolded in her embrace. "Marvellous. I always longed for a sister instead of this fellow. But I never knew you two were so well acquainted, and I cannot believe my brother kept this from me. I will hear your tale in detail, but only after you have tended to Faustus. He does not appear to be injured, and I can only imagine it is some sickness. I have tried everything, Moire, but nothing seems to soothe him."

"Faustus! I am here!" Moire called out. Then she turned to the little piptere, who perched on the roof of the carriage. "Help me find him, Clipper."

Clipper launched himself into the sky, and he soared across the lawn as Faustus's cries grew fainter, yet more urgent.

Moire took hold of Oliver's hand. "We must find him. Something terrible must be wrong."

They hurried across the lawn, following the darting figure of Clipper and drawn by the fading wails of the wyvern. The moon illuminated their path and guided them towards the edge of the forest.

"Faustus!" Moire called out again.

"Moire!" came his answering rasp at long last.

Moire and Oliver exchanged a brief look before plunging into the darkness, following Clipper. Not too far into the forest, they found Faustus huddled by a beech tree. The old wyvern made a high-pitched keening noise.

"Faustus!" Moire ran to him and flung her arms around his long neck. "I am here, old friend."

"Moire. Not. Hate. Faustus," he warbled.

"Of course not. I love you, Faustus. I could never hate you," Moire assured him as she knelt beside the distressed wyvern. She reached out to stroke his scaled head, trying to offer some comfort. Was that the source of his agitation— her long absence? It had been many weeks since she last saw him, with first her stay with Katherine and then at Bath. He might think she had left because she no longer cared for him.

"Faustus. Bad," he wailed. When the wyvern dared to look at her, his eyes whirled with alarm.

Oliver sat on his heels beside her, his hands flat on his thighs. "Moire has never said a bad thing about you, Faustus. You are much loved."

"Forgive. Faustus. Follow. Faustus. Urgent." With a groan, he climbed to his hind legs and, using his clawed wing tips for balance, Faustus walked deeper into the forest.

They stayed close enough behind him to see the swish of his tail as he ambled along the overgrown path. Clipper darted from tree to tree, keeping apace in the foliage. Moonlight filtered through the canopy overhead, casting a ghostly glow on the moss-covered trunks of trees and ferns that nestled beneath their shelter.

Moire knew where they were going, Caliban's barrow. Whatever confession Faustus needed to make, he wanted to do it beside his old friend. They reached the clearing by the river. In the heart of the glade sat Caliban's funeral barrow. A sombre and sacred place that held great significance for Moire and Faustus.

Caliban had died curled on his side. His back to the trees and his feet and head towards the water. When the earth reclaimed him, the barrow was created in the same semi-circular shape. Faustus approached what was once Caliban's belly and lowered himself to the ground. Clipper settled on the top of the mound and watched from beside a patch of wildflowers.

"Faustus. Sorry," he keened. He washed Moire in sorrow, regret, and love.

"What did you do, Faustus?" She tried to make sense of it, but his mind was agitated and the images he sent her were a jumble. Memories were mixed up with feelings. Then one flared brighter. The night a thief stole the egg. Faustus in pursuit. The thief stumbling and dropping the precious object.

"Oh, Faustus. That wasn't your fault." She rested her hands on his side. For Oliver's benefit, who did not share the bond with the wyvern, she said, "Faustus blames himself for Mr Blackwood stealing the egg and breaking it."

Faustus looked between the two humans, his eyes shimmering with tears. It seemed as if the weight of the world rested on his scaly shoulders, and Moire felt her own anxiety increase in response. What had driven him to such despair now, after so many years?

The wyvern crawled closer to the barrow. Using the claws on the tips of his wings, he transcribed a square into the flower and moss-covered grass that lay between two ribs of Caliban. Then he peeled the grass back to expose the dense, dark earth beneath. He began to dig, sods of earth piling up beside him as he tunnelled with great care. When he reached the point where his entire head, neck, and shoulders disappeared into the barrow, he withdrew and began to keen again.

"Faustus. Kept. Safe. Sorry. For hurt." He infused each word with such pain and grief that Moire could have forgiven him anything.

"I'll look." Oliver crouched down and peered into the tunnel. The shadows swallowed him from view.

Moire held her breath. What was inside Caliban's barrow? Surely no more than dirt, tree roots, and bones?

Scuffling preceded Oliver backing out of the tunnel. His body hunched over something. When he turned, he cradled a large...egg.

Moire let out a gasp. The egg had a polished grey surface like a wet stone and was crisscrossed with delicate sea-green veins. It was...

The egg.

"It's hatching. There is a crack." Oliver traced a jagged line that raced over the surface.

"You took it?" Moire sat back on her heels. Stunned. Fierce emotions surged through her, and her throat constricted.

All the heartache of shattered dreams.

The misunderstanding with Oliver and a broken engagement.

Years of torment and trying to make amends.

All that time, Faustus knew the egg was concealed inside Caliban.

Moire couldn't speak. Her heart pounded, and blood thrummed in her ears. She bent over her knees until her forehead touched the damp earth as she drew quick, shallow gulps of air.

Oliver's hand rubbed her back in a gentle, circular motion. "Breathe, Moire, just breathe. Long and slow."

She laid her hands on the ground, and her fingers curled into the dirt. All those years lost, and for what?

Faustus started an eerie keening punctuated with words. "Moire. Hate. Faustus."

Oliver kept up his steadying touch on her back. "The past cannot be changed, Moire, and even if it could, we are exactly where we were always meant to be." He spoke in a low tone. "We are here together. We have the egg. Throughout all these years, Faustus has kept it safe from those who would have stolen it. Blackwood would never have stopped once he knew it was here."

The tempest blew through her, or perhaps it was Oliver's soothing presence. As much as it had caused her grief and suffering, Faustus had done his duty. He had guarded something immeasurably precious in the only way he could. By making everyone think it was gone.

No wonder he was in such a state of agitation. She looked at Faustus, his weary eyes betraying the burden he had carried alone for so long. The wyvern had hidden the egg not out of malice or greed but rather to protect it from those who would do it harm. He carried the guilt of what had happened. Now, with the dragon egg about to hatch—and it must contain a dragon, for it took so long to incubate—Faustus had to urgently call her back from Bath in the only way he could.

Sitting up, she wiped her eyes and then got to her feet to walk to Faustus. She glanced at the dragon egg nestled on the soft grass. It could wait a few more minutes. After all, it had waited eight years.

Moire knelt by Faustus and wrapped her arms around his neck. "Thank you, Faustus, for all that you have done. Your clever idea worked and kept the egg safe. If you need my forgiveness, then you have it with all my heart. We are family. Sometimes, out of love, families might hurt one another. But because we love each other, we forgive." Then she placed a kiss on his scaly face.

The keening stopped, and his eyes whirled silver. "Forgive. Faustus?"

"Yes. I think I understand why you didn't tell me. If I had known it was here, I would have been compelled to check on it. And I would have written and told Oliver. My words and actions would have alerted others that it was still here. Eight years is a long time to keep a secret. You did much better than I would have." She stroked his face.

Some wounds would heal. Like this one. The wyvern did what he thought was best for Moire and Oliver. Other wounds would take decades to scab over. Like Augusta's treacherous actions in sending a false report to Oliver and causing the rift between them. That was driven by her sister's self-interest and jealousy, not love.

Moire joined Oliver by the egg. Sure enough, a fine fissure ran along its surface, widening ever so slightly with each passing moment. Her breath caught in her throat as she realised what was happening. The creature within was preparing to make its entrance into the world.

Clipper fluttered down and sat on the grass beside them as, in the quiet of the night, a faint tapping came from within the egg. The fissure expanded in a starburst pattern as the occupant struggled to break free. Then, with a pop, a chunk of shell fell to the ground, revealing luminescent scales smeared with albumen.

As the shell continued to splinter, Moire struggled to contain her excitement. To witness a hatching! If only she had paper and a pencil. Every moment would need to be recorded later for her book.

More pieces fell away, and Oliver took each one and made a pile to one side. With a thud, the last large piece fell away to reveal a hatchling who was much larger than Moire had expected from the size of the egg. The little creature had been curled tight inside, taking up every inch of space. Only now could it unfurl its body.

"We need a cloth to rub the amniotic fluid from its scales." Moire removed her shawl from about her shoulders. Going to the river, she wet half and balled it up. Then she began wiping the dragon clean. It was indeed a dragon, and not a wyvern who had taken an abnormally long time to hatch. This creature had four legs.

The hatchling mewled as it struggled to stretch new wings. Clipper chirped in response.

"Let me help, little one." Moire wiped each wing free of the sticky fluid with the damp half of her shawl and then used the dry half to dab away the water.

"Hello there, little one," Oliver said softly, reaching out a tentative hand. The dragon stretched its neck to nuzzle against his fingers, a sigh of contentment escaping its tiny form.

"You are a beauty," Moire breathed, tears of happiness pricking at the corners of her eyes.

It was paler than any dragon she had ever seen. The

scales were a cream colour—not a boring shade of cream, but the glistening beauty of a pearl. Under the moonlight, the dragon glowed.

"Faustus, what kind of dragon is this?" she asked, half-suspecting the answer but needing the wyvern to confirm it before she believed it.

"Lunar. Rare. Wise. Kind. Graceful," he rasped as he crouched low and extended his head to sniff at the newcomer.

Moire recalled the night long ago in the same spot when a lunar dragon had danced in the sky above them. Had it been a sign of things to come or a mother dragon looking for a stolen egg?

"Our new friend has qualities to match yours, my love," Oliver teased. He reached over and cupped Moire's face, pulling her to him for a gentle kiss.

When they broke apart, happiness surged through Moire. "Congratulations, Drac Hartford, your line is blessed with a lunar dragon." She used his new title. With the arrival of the hatchling, he was elevated to the Draco Legion and afforded a title equivalent to a duke.

His eyes widened as only now did the importance of the moment hit him. "*Our* line is blessed."

Moire couldn't help but laugh through tears as joy and awe bubbled through her. Her father and Augusta had schemed for years to secure a fortune and title for her older sister. Now Moire had both, due to the constancy of her love and devotion to her family.

"Your name, little one. What shall we call you?" Moire asked as the hatchling rubbed its face against her hand.

"Constance. I am she. I am yours, Moire," came a surprising, melodic voice.

"We are honoured to meet you, Constance." Moire bit her lip to stop more tears from spilling at the intensely personal meaning behind the name. "But you cannot be mine because then you would belong to my father." Such was the way of their world; dragons were attached to a male line, not a female one.

Oliver reached out and took her hand. "We belong with Constance, and she belongs with us. You will soon be a Hartford."

Yes. They all belonged to one another. Could there be a more perfect moment than this?

28

"Hungry," Constance announced, to the accompaniment of a gurgle from her stomach.

Oliver and Moire laughed. They had rushed to find Faustus, and none of them had anything hidden in their pockets to feed a hatchling.

"Let's get you back to the manor and see what we can find in the kitchen for you." Oliver scooped the dragon up.

Clipper fluttered down and perched on Moire's shoulder, his whirling gaze fixed on the hatchling.

As they walked back to the house, they didn't need a lantern to light their way with Constance. The lunar dragon radiated a soft luminescence as though Oliver cradled the moon in his arms. When they crossed the lawn, Charlotte stood in the doorway with the admiral at her side.

Several lanterns were laid out around the step as though they organised a search party.

"Light. Hurt," Faustus whined.

Moire rested one hand on his lowered head. "You

should go and rest, Faustus. We will care for Constance, and you can see her tomorrow night. I will come see you in your burrow as soon as I can."

Faustus rubbed against Moire's palm and then made his way back to his underground home.

Charlotte hurried along the drive, the admiral not far behind. "I was ever so worried! Thank goodness Faustus seems more settled now, but..." She halted and stared at the creature her brother carried with a mixture of disbelief and wonder.

"I say, I thought you held a lantern, but is that a dragon?" The admiral peered at the creature.

"Yes, it is. I would like you both to meet Constance. Constance, this is my sister, Charlotte and her husband, Admiral Chellum." Oliver made the introductions as though they met at the edges of a dance floor.

Charlotte's hands went to her mouth.

"I shall have to salute you now, Drac Hartford." Admiral Chellum chuffed with laughter and slapped Oliver on the shoulder.

"Faustus's agitation was because Constance was about to hatch, and I wasn't here." Moire gently stroked the dragon's head. Even in the low light, her delicate scales were opalescent, seeming to shift colour from milky white to soft greys, the mossiest of greens, and palest blues.

"Extraordinary...and so beautiful." Charlotte reached out a tentative hand to touch the hatchling's side. Which resulted in a loud gurgling noise.

Oliver chuckled. "And she is so hungry. Constance requires feeding."

Oliver carried the baby dragon to the kitchen, the cook

having been roused by the commotion. Thankfully, she was a sensible woman and used to dragonkind, as she had been with the family since long before Caliban died. Without so much as a raised eyebrow, she fetched a bowl of meat offcuts for the hungry creatures as Clipper also required dinner.

While Oliver fed Constance and Moire ensured Clipper did not miss out, they told their tale from when they first met in the market ten years ago to the boxing match with its rare prize, and the cruel twist of fate that resulted in their prolonged separation.

After a meal that left her small stomach distended, Constance emitted a very unladylike burp and announced she was tired and that she would sleep with *her* Moire. Oliver carried the dozy dragonet up to Moire's room, where she carefully arranged a nest of blankets for Constance before the fire to ensure the dragon was warm and comfortable. Clipper snuggled in next to his new dragon friend.

They all murmured their goodnights, and Oliver brushed his hand against Moire's as she closed the door. While they had been in the forest with Faustus and Constance, Moire's trunk had been deposited in her room, the bed made up, and the fire lit. Her eyes drooped from sheer exhaustion as she undressed, leaving her clothes in an untidy pile to deal with in the morning, and then tugged on a clean nightgown.

Soft snores came from the hatchling, now fast asleep in her makeshift nest, alongside a slight trill from the slumbering Clipper.

Moire slipped under the blankets of her bed. Her body craved rest. The events of the last few days had taken their toll on her, both physically and emotionally. Within moments, she succumbed to a deep and dreamless sleep. For what need had she of dreams now when they had become real?

THE FIRST LIGHT of dawn crept into the room and woke Moire. Excitement had replaced exhaustion, and she couldn't sleep when there was so much to do. Sitting up in bed, she gazed at the bundle before the now cold fire. Constance lay curled around Clipper, keeping the smaller piptere warm, and his head was a blue patch against her pale side.

Moire dropped her feet to the floor, and the dragons stirred. Clipper called out as he stretched and then flitted to the windowsill to preen in the morning light. Constance shook herself and then stood on wobbly legs.

"Good morning, Constance and Clipper. I will assume you both require breakfast," Moire said as she rose.

"Yes. I am very hungry," Constance said as she stepped out of the nest of blankets and sat on the rug.

Moire padded across the cool wooden floorboards and knelt before Constance. She stroked the dragon's head to reassure herself the creature was actually in her room and it hadn't all been a dream.

"Clipper will keep you company while I fetch a bowl of meat from the kitchen." Then she sat back and studied the dragon. Had she grown overnight? A few of her pearl-like scales seemed dull. "I will also find some oil. Your scales will need lots of attention as you grow."

Moire slipped into her favourite green brocade dressing gown and tied the sash snugly around her waist. In bare feet, she left her room and padded along the hall, following the familiar path to the kitchen. As she approached, the scent of freshly baked bread and coffee wafted through the air. Cook would be up early to ensure everyone was nourished.

Oliver sat at the worn oak table, a mug clutched between his hands. He smiled at seeing her. "I couldn't sleep and thought Constance might wake you early to be fed. Cook is slicing beef for her."

"Her rumbling stomach works as efficiently as a rooster crowing to wake you early. Although in truth, I am too excited to sleep and had to check she really was there...in my room." Moire rested one hand on his shoulder.

Oliver put down his coffee and drew her into his arms. Their lips met in a tender kiss. Only when the cook emerged from the larder did they jump apart.

"I have the beef. Does she need vegetables with it?" Cook held up a bowl containing the sliced meat.

"We should offer a few." Moire searched her memory for details of dragon dietary requirements. While mostly meat eaters, they did require some vegetable matter for their digestive system.

Moire found a tray and placed the bowl on it while the cook rustled up an accompanying dish of carrots and beans.

"Where would you like to make our home?" Oliver asked as he retrieved a carrot from a bucket.

Our home. Those words made love flow through her limbs. "Somewhere as close to Faustus as possible."

"There is an estate not far from here that I have been

considering. It's close enough to Eadred Manor so that you may still regularly visit Faustus, but it would provide us with the privacy and freedom we need to live our lives as we choose, away from your family."

"Family," Moire repeated, savouring the word as it danced upon her tongue. She had turned her back on hers when she walked out of the Bath townhouse. Her father declared she was no longer a Tobin and dead to them. That suited her just fine. Being a Hartford meant having a family that welcomed her with open arms.

"Our family...you, me, Constance, and Clipper. And perhaps, one day, others." His words carried the weight of a promise.

Moire hummed, and mischief bubbled inside her. "We have a dragon, a piptere, and a wyvern, even if Faustus cannot leave here. I assume you mean I can add a pack of drakes to our family? For that is the only thing I am now lacking." The wingless dragons were difficult for her to study due to their close bonds with each other and their riders. Not to mention that they were all enlisted in the army. So far, anyone in authority had declined to answer any letter she had sent asking questions about drakes.

While Cook had her back turned, Oliver wrapped his arms around her and whispered by her ear, "I can see, *Draca Hartford*, that I shall have my hands full with you."

She didn't know which bit of that sentence thrilled her more. Hearing her new soon-to-be title on his lips or the idea of his hands all over her. If she thought too much on the latter, her knees wobbled. She turned in his embrace for one more lingering kiss. Their future lay before them like an open book. Each page was blank and waiting for them to write their own story, and Moire couldn't wait to pen their adventures.

"There is much to be done. You must write to the Draco Legion to notify them of Constance's hatching. And you must find a home for her...for *us*. She cannot stay here, or my father might try to lay claim to her." A thousand things spun through Moire's mind.

"When Constance is presented to the Legion, I would have you beside me as my wife, Moire." Oliver kept hold of her hand.

There was another matter to add to the things they must do. Organise a wedding at short notice.

"I would suggest that if you are content to look after matters that relate to dragonkind, perhaps we could enlist Charlotte to ensure we are wed as soon as possible? I can vouch for my sister's skills in getting things done. She would have made a formidable captain." Oliver read Moire's mind and lifted one worry from her.

She let out a sigh. "Yes. That would be lovely. Speaking of all matters dragon-related, Constance's scales are a little dull this morning, and she has grown overnight. She will need to be oiled, otherwise she will get terribly itchy." Moire searched in the cupboards for oil and brushes.

Soon, they had everything they needed piled up on the tray. Moire glanced at the back door. "Would you mind feeding Constance without me? I am worried about Faustus, and I want to check on him. I would rather not leave it until dark."

"Of course. Take as long as you need with Faustus. I am sure I can cope with oiling scales. While she is little, the job won't give me a sore arm like tending to Valiant." He kissed her cheek and picked up the tray.

Moire paused on the doorstep, looking out to the stables and the meadow beyond. She had descended the stairs in her dressing gown and barefoot. Should she return to her room for shoes? No, she decided, it would be nice to feel the warm earth under her toes, and she'd not be long.

She hurried across the yard and around the side of the stables. The ground was damp and not too stony beneath her toes when she followed the path worn by Faustus over the decades. The entrance to his burrow was hidden among the tangled roots of an ancient oak tree at the edge of the forest. As she approached, the earthy scent filled her nostrils, mingling with the faint aroma of hay from the nearby stables.

"Faustus?" she called softly as she entered so as not to startle the wyvern.

She received no response, only the echo of her own words reverberating through the darkness of the under-ground passageway. With one hand on the side of the tunnel, she began to descend into the earth, picking her steps carefully lest she stand on a stone.

"Faustus, I just want to see if you are all right," she said, but again there was no answering warble.

The dim light that filtered through the entrance was gradually replaced by a more pervasive darkness as Moire walked deeper into the burrow. Her breaths grew shallow, and she strained for any sound from her wyvern friend.

Before she could call again, a high-pitched cry and frantic scrambling came from his nesting chamber.

"Faustus! What is happening?" Moire hurried around

the second corner. Normally, she would be plunged into pitch dark at this point, yet a light glowed from the end of the tunnel.

The commotion and cries grew louder. Her mind raced with what might have befallen Faustus. Did wyverns have nightmares? But that didn't explain the light. It might be one of the staff refreshing his bedding straw.

She turned the corner, bracing herself for whatever awaited in the nest, only to be confronted by a sudden, blinding flash that seared her retinas and disorientated her senses. Instinctively, she threw up an arm to shield her eyes, gasping as her vision swam with dancing spots of colour. The light piercing her skull became a blow that rattled her bones. The world tilted beneath her, and as her knees crumpled, she thought she saw men standing over the prone wyvern.

* * *

Moire moaned and tried to touch her aching head, only to find her hands wouldn't move. The air was stuffy and hot in her lungs. Blinking away the cobwebs of confusion, she discovered her hands were bound tightly together, and she was lying on the floor of a covered cart. The rough jostling of the vehicle, as it travelled along an uneven road, sent sharp pains shooting through her limbs, but she fought the urge to cry out in discomfort.

Something large and warm was pressed behind her in the confined space. A slumbering cow?

"Moire," rasped Faustus.

"Faustus, what happened?" she whispered, her voice as hoarse as the wyvern's.

At her back, Faustus trembled, his distress palpable even without words.

"Men. Blind. Faustus." Vocalising failed him, so instead, he sent a series of images to her mind. Two men had entered his nest while he was asleep and blinded him by lighting lanterns around him. Then one bludgeoned him until he was dazed. That was when Moire had called out, and the men laid a trap, hitting her in the head as she entered the chamber.

She wriggled and managed to roll over to face him. Chains were wrapped around his form, and a sack had been placed over his head. "How did they get you into a cart?"

A chilling picture formed in her mind. A man stood over her unconscious body, holding a knife. The threat to her was obvious and sufficient to buy compliance from the wyvern, who climbed into the cart that had been hidden among the trees and allowed himself to be restrained to save her.

Since his burrow was over by the trees and some distance from the house, no one would have noticed the activity. Particularly at such an early hour. How long would it be before Oliver and Clipper noticed that she hadn't returned? Oliver had told her to take as long as she needed with Faustus. It might be an hour or more before he went in search of her.

"We must escape, Faustus." She twisted her hands to see if the rope would come loose.

She didn't have to ask who had done this to them. A

chill down her spine said there were only two men who would do such a thing. Her cousin and the Fox. What a predicament. Apart from being bound in a cart heading away from the estate, she was barefoot and only wearing a nightgown and robe.

As they jostled along, the canvas at the front was tugged up, and a grinning face appeared.

"Ah, you are awake, cousin. That was dashed impolite of you to run off just as I was about to propose. But here we are now, and we have been reunited," he said in a cheery tone as though they were chatting at a picnic.

"I left because I knew exactly what your horrid plan was. You never liked me and found my blathering about dragons boring." Moire huffed. Imagine finding dragons boring!

"Excellent. That saves me time having to explain the plan. This also means I don't have to marry you." He made a choking noise in the back of his throat as if he were gagging on something. "Why don't you use this time to rehearse what you will say to Artemis? We don't want to disappoint Mr Blackwood, now do we?"

Never would she hand a dragon egg to that man. She set her features in a hard expression and then turned her face to Faustus.

Her cousin laughed. "You will obtain an egg from her, cousin," Henry said in a chilling tone. "Because if you fail to do so, I'm afraid this poor old wyvern here will pay the price. Do I make myself clear?"

"Abundantly," she said through gritted teeth, anger flaring hot within her. How dare he threaten Faustus?

"Good," Henry said, satisfied with her response. He

dropped the canvas back down, plunging them once more into darkness.

"We will find a way out of this, I promise," Moire whispered. There were a few hurdles to them both escaping. Her bound hands. The chains. Her lack of shoes. And the little fact that the sun had risen, and daylight burned the wyvern's sensitive eyes.

Faustus's only response was a pained moan that made Moire's heart clench. As the cart continued to bump along the rough road, his distress grew more pronounced. That was when she realised they must be venturing past the five-mile boundary from Eadred Manor. With each agonising inch they took beyond the wyvern's tether, his connection to their home stretched to breaking point.

"Moire...it hurts," Faustus whimpered, his mental voice strained and weak.

Moire banged on the sides of the cart. "You have to stop! Wyverns can't go past the five-mile point!" she yelled, hoping they would hear her and stop the cart.

The canvas lifted once more on Henry's smug face. "Consider this an experiment. What happens to a wyvern after the five-mile mark? We will soon find out." Then he dropped the covering again.

While never one to give in to violence, Moire experienced a strong urge to punch Henry Tobin in the nose. Tears stung her eyes as helplessness washed over her. What could she do in their current circumstances to ease the pain ripping through her friend?

She started talking, letting her ideas tumble forth. "Wyverns are tethered to their home. Some say that happens where they are hatched. But that isn't always true, as often wyverns are sold as hatchlings and moved to other places. That made me think that it might be the concept of home that binds a wyvern. That is what creates the place where they belong."

A moan came from her friend, and Moire mentally scrambled to continue her line of thought. "People are similar. Eadred Manor is no longer my home, Faustus. I have severed my tie with my father, so I must find a new place to call my home."

"Eadred. Not. Home?" Faustus whimpered.

"Not anymore. You are my family, Faustus, along with Clipper, Constance, and Oliver. We will all make a new home. It will still be in Wyldefen, but somewhere else." She wiped away a tear and continued to talk, sharing memories to show how much he meant to her. She started with her earliest memory of him. The evening when, as a three-year-old child, her mother allowed her to stay up late to meet the wyvern.

As Blackwood pushed the horses along the road at a near gallop, they must have reached the point where the wyvern's mental tether snapped. Faustus let out a heart-wrenching cry that pierced Moire. Then his body convulsed with agony.

"Moire. Home," Faustus said on a long exhale as his body slumped. He lay immobile, and his chest stilled.

"Faustus," Moire cried as she leaned against his side. "I'm sorry."

29

Moire's wrists ached from the tight bindings, but that pain paled in comparison to the ice-cold fear for Faustus that settled in her heart. She pressed her cheek to his flank, praying she would sense any movement, inhale of breath, or beat of his heart. The cart continued to jolt along the rough terrain. Every creak and groan from the timbers reverberated through her.

Faustus remained unnaturally still and silent.

"Faustus. Please. Don't leave me," she whispered. Her tears moistened his slate grey scales.

A minute passed with no response. Then another. The silence stretched into an eternity. Just as despair threatened to engulf Moire completely, she heard it. A ragged breath. Then the faint pulse against her skin.

"Thank goodness," she breathed, relief washing over her in a warm wave.

He was alive, if barely so.

"You can do this, Faustus. I shall devote a special chapter in my book to you and how your tether snapped,

386

and you were freed." She brushed her roped-together hands along his hide as she spoke, composing the paragraphs to detail his terrible ordeal and how he emerged out the other side.

As the minutes lengthened into hours, the wyvern's breathing grew steadier. At long last, he drew a deep sigh and spoke in a faint rasp. "Pain. Gone. Moire. Home."

"I am glad it no longer hurts." She pondered his last two words and what they might mean. "Faustus, do you mean I am your home now?"

"For. Now," he wheezed.

How extraordinary and sad at the same time. Faustus was free of one leash, but another still bound him. They had much to learn about how the tether worked. All the books and scholars said it was based upon a physical location. But Moire was now the wyvern's home anchor point.

"I am honoured to be your home. You always reside in my heart." She leaned closer to him.

With a soft rustle of scales, Faustus turned to nuzzle her from under the sack. His warmth was a welcome comfort in the shadowy confines of the cart. He said no words, but he sent her waves of gratitude and loyalty.

Over the course of their terrible journey, Moire dozed in snatches of exhaustion. When she woke, she wondered if Oliver searched for her. He would know something had happened, for surely there would be marks of the cart around Faustus's burrow that hinted at their fate. Besides, women didn't usually run away barefoot and in their dressing gowns when they had a dragon hatchling and a loving fiancé waiting for them in the house. Not to mention

Clipper, her constant companion. She would never abandon him.

Clipper! The thought struck her that he might have seen something from her windowsill. Even now, he might be flying along the road on their trail to mark the way for Oliver. Unless he hadn't noticed due to consuming his breakfast alongside Constance, and the household had no idea where she had gone.

The cart jolted to a stop, and Moire and Faustus slid against the wooden slats. She winced as her flung-out hands scraped painfully across the rough surface, bringing the sting of a splinter in her finger.

"Do you smell that, Miss Moire Tobin? The hint of salt in the air. Can you guess where you are?" Darius Blackwood called out in a sing-song tone as footsteps moved around the cart.

The canvas covering was thrown back, and Moire screwed up her eyes against the sudden light after so many hours trapped in the dark. She was glad the sack remained over Faustus's head to protect his sensitive vision. When she opened her eyes, it was to a breathtaking view of the ocean—wild and tempestuous. The sky overhead was a turbulent mass of foreboding clouds, while waves crashed against the jagged cliffs with a thunderous roar.

"Let me assist you, cousin." Henry grabbed her elbow and steadied her as she hopped down from the cart. "We don't want you taking any unexpected tumbles before you fetch what we want."

She took his offered assistance rather than fall from the cart with her hands still tied. Dizziness flowed over her when she stared at the cliff edge. Vertigo crept over her as she gazed out at the frothy waters churning far below. Her body ached, and bruises formed from being tossed around in the cart like a sack of potatoes. Her parched throat rasped with each shallow breath, and her mouth was as dry as if it were lined with sandpaper.

"We need water, please," she croaked.

Henry and Blackwood exchanged glances before the latter reached under the cart's seat and pulled out a canteen. He unscrewed the cap and handed it to Moire. Her hands trembled as she drank greedily, the cool liquid bringing some relief to her cracked lips and desiccated throat.

"Faustus will need some, too. But you must be careful not to uncover his eyes." She held the canteen out to Henry.

He stared at it as though she had lost her mind. "The wyvern?"

"That is the only Faustus here." She jiggled the canteen. "I will do it if you untie me."

Blackwood huffed. "It's not like she can run off. She's barefoot and wearing a nightgown."

He took the canteen from her hands, pulled out a knife from a sheath strapped to his arm, and sliced through the rope.

Moire rubbed her wrists, the skin was chaffed and torn by the rough fibres. Taking the canteen back, she climbed into the cart and approached the wyvern. "Faustus, I have some water. I will pull the sack away from your mouth, but it is still daylight, and I don't want to harm your eyes."

She tugged at the rough hessian from around Faustus's snout but kept it bunched up over his sensitive eyes.

"Twilight. Soon," the wyvern croaked.

"Yes. It appears we have travelled all day." She placed the lip of the canteen to his mouth and then tilted it.

The wyvern eagerly drank the cool liquid, gulping it down in large, noisy swallows.

When she had emptied the container, Moire climbed back out of the cart. "There is another pressing issue." She pulled a face at her cousin and hoped he could interpret her needs.

He frowned, and then his eyes widened as she jiggled up and down. He gestured to the cart. "Use the other side. We'll stay on this side, and don't even think of running off."

She could argue, but what was the point? With a curt nod, she hurried around the side and squatted by the bulk of a wheel. That relieved some of the anxiety that curled inside her.

"Why are we here?" she asked when she straightened and returned to the men. Artemis lived in Dorset, but they weren't at any grand estate. There didn't seem to be any dwelling of any kind within sight.

"Artemis has her lair in a cave set into these cliffs. There is a very narrow path down to it." Blackwood used the knife still clasped in his hand to point to a section of rocky grass that looked the same as all the rest.

She vaguely recalled Valiant mentioning a cove that Artemis liked to use. It must be down below. Moire closed her eyes for a moment, drawing in deep breaths and trying to still the trembling in her limbs. Fear churned like the turbulent ocean, and she couldn't let it overwhelm her.

"We don't want to hurt either of you. All we want is the egg," Henry said, his tone stern but not unkind.

Moire's attention drifted back to Faustus, still bound in chains and immobile in the cart. She couldn't afford to fail and would do whatever it took to protect those she loved.

Blackwood took hold of her upper arm and walked her closer to the edge.

The wind whistled as it whipped around Moire, and the sea below crashed against the jagged rocks. She couldn't help but shiver, despite her attempts to focus on what had to be done.

"You can only reach Artemis's cave via that path. Unless you can fly," Blackwood explained, pointing towards the edge of the cliff. His fingertip traced the narrow, treacherous trail snaking down the rocky outcropping.

The sight of it sent a jolt of sheer terror through Moire. Her stomach lurched at the thought of traversing such a dangerous path. Even a mountain goat would find it difficult.

"Y-you cannot possibly expect me to walk down there," she stammered. The very notion was utterly preposterous.

Blackwood merely raised an eyebrow, his cold gaze locked onto hers. "I'm not asking you to do it. I'm telling you."

Moire's heart clenched, and she gasped for air. She couldn't let them harm Faustus, but the fear that gripped her seemed insurmountable, suffocating her like a vice.

"Panic on that path, and you'll tumble into the ocean," Blackwood said. His eyes were dark and unyielding. "Fail or refuse, and there will be consequences." He mimed drawing the knife across his throat and pointed to Faustus.

She couldn't bear the thought of the wyvern being hurt

because of her shortcomings or her inability to face her fears. With a quiet sob, Moire sunk to her knees, the world spinning around her. "Please, don't hurt him," she whispered.

Once, she had faced her fear and climbed onto the back of Faustus to fly to a boxing match, where she had watched Oliver beat the Fox to win the egg. She could face her fear again, especially if it meant she found a way to defeat the Fox in doing so. That idea poured steel into her spine.

She might be terrified, but fear would not control her. Standing as tall as she could, she took a step closer to the edge of the cliff. "I'll do it."

Henry escorted Moire to the cliff's edge, his hand firm on her arm as though to hold her together. The roaring of the wind and waves below clawed at her senses, filling her with a sense of vertigo even before they approached the perilous path that awaited her.

Her heart thudded in her chest. Each beat screamed its rejection of the dizzying height. For once, she didn't worry about smacking into the ground. Instead, she would be met by the cold, wet embrace of an angry sea. Moire clenched her teeth so tightly she thought they might shatter under the pressure, but she held her head high.

She took a moment to stare at the narrow, treacherous path that snaked down towards the ocean. It was barely more than a ledge, the jagged rocks jutting out like the spine of some ancient, malevolent beast. Her breath hitched, and her legs wobbled beneath her, threatening to betray her.

"Keep your eyes on the path, not the drop," Henry said and gave her a push.

"Easy for you to say," she muttered under her breath but took his advice nonetheless. With each step, she focused on the ground beneath her feet and the cliff face beside her and refused to let the churning expanse of water enter her line of sight.

The wind tugged at her hair and the edges of her robe as if eager to tear her from the precarious perch. Trembling, Moire placed a hand on the rough rock face to steady herself, and her fingers found purchase in the uneven surface. She curled her fingers into cracks and grooves, hoping it would be enough to hold her if she lost her footing.

"Faustus needs me. I cannot fail. Besides, I had intended to petition Artemis anyway, just not under these circumstances." She encouraged herself with each step. Though her heart raced with terror and her body ached for solid ground, Moire persisted. Each step along the treacherous path took her closer to Artemis.

At last, the dark mouth of the cave loomed up ahead. Moire focused on the shadow, and finally, she stepped onto the floor of the cave and left the perilous cliff path behind her. The gloom that enveloped her was as thick as a London fog—suffocating and oppressive. A faint whisper of salty air clung to her hair and robe, but the chill inside the cavern seemed far colder than anything she had faced outside.

Moire took a minute to compose herself. Sadly, there was little she could do about her appearance. She re-tied her dressing gown and smoothed her tangled hair off her forehead. As she did so, her fingers grazed over a bump. No doubt from Mr Blackwood when he struck her.

Her eyes adjusted to the dim light, and she discovered it was illuminated by the soft blue glow of bioluminescent fungi. She stood in a cave that was the approximate size of a ballroom. Shapes moved within the deeper shadows.

"Artemis," Moire called out in a strong tone. Dragons disliked hesitancy or nervousness, both of which meant weakness. "I am Moire Draca Caliban, and I seek an audience with your esteemed self."

"Caliban? It has been many years since he passed," a deep, resonant voice reverberated off the walls of the cave.

"Caliban is much missed. I will carry my memories of him until my end." Which might not be that far away, given her current circumstances and the horrifying path she had to traverse to get back to Faustus.

"You may approach Moire Draca Caliban," Artemis said.

Moire walked further into the cavern. A shape loomed above her and formed into the female dragon. From her books, Moire had learned that Artemis was a slate grey that appeared silver in some lights. Her scales absorbed what little light came through the cave entrance and made her somewhat easier to see in the dark. Although she didn't have the glowing opalescence of Constance.

This female was as large as Valiant, who was easily the largest dragon Moire had ever seen. Artemis sat curled upon a nest that appeared to have been made from tree trunks lined with shredded blankets. Her eyes were a pale gold and glowed like two lanterns in her massive head.

Moire curtseyed and then stood, clasping her hands before her. "Wise Artemis, I stand before you a penitent..."

"Are you barefoot?" Artemis interrupted Moire's practised speech.

"Umm...yes." Moire glanced down even though the soles of her feet were *painfully* aware they did not have the protection of shoes.

"And you are not even dressed. Is being barefoot and in some form of night attire supposed to sway me with your act of humility?" The dragon didn't sound impressed if that had been Moire's ploy.

"No. When I walked outside of my house this morning, I had only thought to be a little while, then I intended to go back into the house to dress. And put on my boots." This audience with Artemis wasn't going how Moire had rehearsed it in her head.

Artemis huffed, and her breath stirred up eddies of dust from the cave floor. "How odd. Was this a spur-of-the-moment decision?"

"You might say that." Certainly, being struck over the head, kidnapped, and torn away from those she loved hadn't entered into her plans for the day.

"Continue." A wing flicked in her direction before settling back against the dragon's side.

"I petition you today on behalf of Captain Oliver Hartford. A noble and honourable man. During the war, he was permitted by the most brave Valiant to replace his rider, the injured Captain Forbes. Together, they were a formidable pair and won many victories for England," Moire said.

"Ah. Valiant has mentioned this Hartford. In fact, he would go on all day about him if I didn't tell him to shut up. He said you might seek an egg on his behalf." The weight of the dragon's golden gaze made Moire feel both exposed and vulnerable.

"If you judge my request to be a worthy one, it would be a great honour to bestow an egg upon Captain Hartford." The books Moire read held scant knowledge about how to ask a dragon for an egg. Most lords stole them, won them in games of chance, or stumbled upon them in the woods like the first Drac Tobin. The lack of information was probably because the females flamed those who approached for the impertinence of asking.

"Let's come back to your shoes. Or lack of them. Why are you barefoot if you didn't intend to intrude on my privacy today?" Artemis leaned forward over her crossed forelegs and narrowed her eyes at Moire.

Moire had had enough. All she had wanted to do today was ensure Faustus slept, tend to Constance, kiss Oliver, play with Clipper, and possibly plan a hurried wedding with Charlotte. Tears of frustration stung her eyes, but she refused to cry.

Using a claw, Artemis tugged a blanket free and held it out to Moire. "Why don't you sit down and tell me the truth?"

"Thank you." Taking the woollen blanket, Moire folded it until she had a nice, thick wedge and then placed it on the ground before sitting. She drew her knees to her chest and wrapped her arms around them. "I had intended to petition you for an egg on behalf of Captain Hartford, who I believe to be most worthy. But then the other egg hatched, and she is the most exquisite lunar dragon called Constance."

"You have a lunar dragonet?" Surprise and wonder dripped from every word.

Love swelled in Moire's heart as she thought of Constance. "Yes. She said she is mine, and I am hers. But that cannot be. Only men are admitted to the Draco Legion."

Artemis let out a snort. "Males. Always think they know best. Lunar dragons bond with female lines."

"I have not read of that in any of my books." Lunar dragons were exceptionally rare. None had been seen in England or Europe for centuries. They were only found in the most remote regions of China and Russia.

"Were the books written by men?" Artemis asked in a tone as sharp as a whip.

"Well...yes." That was an easy question to answer. Moire had only found one book written by a woman, and it had been so remarkable it had stuck in her mind.

Artemis laughed. Something Moire didn't know dragons could do. "You are worried she cannot be yours because your father will take her from you. To replace Caliban."

"Yes." That one syllable contained all of Moire's fears about Constance's future.

"But that's not why you're here, is it Moire Draca Constance?" Artemis used Moire's new name, referencing the dragon bonded to her new family.

"No. I'm here because two horrible men whacked me on the head, bundled me into a cart, and threatened to kill Faustus—he's our guard wyvern—if I don't get them one of your eggs. They are waiting on the cliff above." She curled her hands into fists.

The dragon tilted her head, curiosity blazing in her eyes. "You care for a wyvern?"

"Of course I do. He is my oldest and dearest friend. I am also blessed to have the company of a piptere called Clipper, who flies free. In fact, I am writing a book about pipteres and advocating for them all to be set free. They should not be chained like dogs or caged like parrots." Indignation spiralled free as Moire thought of the sad pipteres attached to perches at the ball in Bath. At least she had freed one, and she would let loose more every time she had the opportunity.

Silence fell within the cavern, broken only by the faint drip of water echoing through the darkness. Finally, Artemis spoke, her voice like the crackle of embers in a dying fire. "You are most devoted to dragonkind. Good. I have a proposal for you. One that may resolve your predicaments—both current and future."

Moire moved to kneel on the blanket. "I would be most grateful for your assistance, Artemis, if it ensures the safety of those I love. Never would I willingly give an egg, from any type of dragon, to such men as those who hold Faustus above us."

Artemis leaned closer, her breath warm and tinged with the scent of smouldering embers. "Then listen well, Moire Draca Constance. Should you accept my plan, you will need to be braver than you have ever been. To succeed, I demand that you face your fears and plunge into them."

Moire nodded, and then Artemis unveiled her idea.

30

Moire's feet were frozen to the floor of the cavern. Possibly *actually* frozen as opposed to just metaphorically as her bare feet were frigid with cold. Fear clenched her heart.

"I can't," she rasped, her head shaking in denial.

"Yes, you can. You have come further than anyone else. You have loved deeply and navigated your life with loyalty and devotion to dragons and family. If you want to free Faustus and stop these foul men, you know what must be done," Artemis rumbled as she rose to her feet and shook like a wet dog, shaking out kinks and stiff muscles after her time curled in her nest.

Still unable to move, Moire's brain was busy trying to figure out which path before her was the least terrifying. The narrow and dangerous path carved into the cliff, or climbing onto Artemis? Both had a high likelihood of seeing her tumble to the ocean below. Only one came with the promise of being caught before she slammed into the water.

The dragon's scales shimmered in the low light like

polished silver. She stretched one leg forward, her claws gleaming like polished obsidian.

"Come," Artemis said.

"Do you promise to catch me if I fall?" she asked, trying to keep the tremor from her voice.

"You will receive all the tender care of one of my hatchlings," the dragon replied.

That didn't reassure Moire. Dragons rarely raised their offspring as their eggs were either destroyed by natural events, stolen, lost (ten years was a long time to remember where you put something), or sold by their bonded families.

As she approached the outstretched limb, her hands were slick with perspiration, and she forced herself to remember her love for her dragons and Oliver. She did this for them. To make a safe place for her new family to flourish.

"I can do this," she said, taking a deep breath to steady her nerves. One cautious step at a time, she ascended the rough scales and sinewy muscles of Artemis's leg. Her fingers gripped the hardened ridges. With each movement, fear threatened to overwhelm her, but she pushed it aside, focusing on the rhythmic rise and fall of the dragon's breath under her.

"Keep your eyes on me. I am your earth now," Artemis instructed, her voice a soothing balm amidst Moire's tumultuous thoughts.

"You are my earth," she repeated as she took her place between Artemis's shoulder ridges, finding grooves for her legs and feet and a natural place to sit. Before her, the short neck spines crossed one another and formed a handle to hold on to. The dragon was large enough to fool her brain into thinking she was on the ground. Solid, massive...no different to sitting atop Caliban's barrow.

That thought prompted another. As a young girl, she used to climb up onto Caliban's back and beg the dragon to take her flying. The idea had exhilarated young Moire. Then fear had taken hold of her after her mother died, and she learned how fragile life could be.

Moire settled herself on the dragon's back, her gaze drawn to the twilight-streaked sky beyond the cave entrance, beckoning like a beautiful and deadly abyss. With a surge of determination, she tightened her grip on one of Artemis's spines and whispered her readiness.

The great dragon moved forward. Each step towards the cave entrance made tremors shudder through Moire's body. Her heart pounded so loud it seemed to echo around the chamber.

"Remember that you are stronger and braver than you ever imagined," Artemis spoke in a soothing, low tone.

"Stronger. Braver," Moire repeated the words and tried to stop her teeth from rattling with fear.

As they reached the precipice, the wind whipped against her face and carried the salty tang of the sea below. Moire screwed her eyes shut tight, not wanting to witness the vast expanse as they leapt into the void.

"Here we go!" Artemis called out, her tone rich with excitement.

The sturdy rock beneath them vanished, replaced by the sensation of plummeting through the air. Moire screamed. Her knuckles whitened as she clung to the spines and dug her knees in to stay anchored to the dragon's back. Her stomach surged, and she would have been sick if not for the tight grip fear had on her throat.

The sickening dread levelled out as the dragon made strong and steady beats with her wings. Lifting them higher into the air.

"Open your eyes," Artemis called, her voice swirling back to Moire with a rush of wind.

Moire shook her head. She didn't need to look to know how perilously high they were!

"Open your eyes. Trust me," Artemis insisted.

Biting back a sob of pure fear, Moire did as instructed and cracked her eyes open. She gasped at the world laid out beneath her. The ocean stretched out in an endless patchwork of greens, blues, and stormy grey sprinkled with diamonds from the last caress of the setting sun.

Moire dragged her gaze back to the horizon and the neck and head in front of her and away from the swirling ocean below.

"Tell me it isn't what you always imagined as a child asking Caliban to take you flying," Artemis said.

The dragon's words triggered long ago memories. Moire's fear of heights had taken hold when she had lost the one person in the world who had told her she could fly. Without her mother, she became grounded. Then her family added the weight of their expectations that pressed her deeper into the earth.

"I can fly," she whispered. "And it is as magnificent as I ever dreamed it would be."

The night she had flown on Faustus, the wyvern had skimmed low over the fields, and Moire kept her eyes shut the entire time. Riding Artemis was...incredible. Her fear had not vanished entirely. The knot of worry still sat in her stomach, waiting to become an anchor dragging her below the surface. But terror was now tempered by the exhilaration of flight and the trust she placed in her newfound ally.

"Good. Now, you will not be afraid when you fly on Constance," the dragon said, a hint of pride audible in her tone. "Lunar dragons may be smaller than other dragons, but they are fast and very agile."

Artemis had given Moire a precious gift—belief in herself. Over time, it would erode the long-held fear.

"Thank you, Artemis. Now let's free Faustus and deal with those treacherous men." Moire bent low over the dragon's neck and dared a look to the side. They had travelled some distance from the cliffs in what seemed only a few short flaps of enormous wings.

The dragon flew in a gentle arc and returned to the land. The two figures above the dark cave entrance were lit by the last strands of fading light. Artemis angled her wings, guiding their descent towards Henry and Blackwood, who looked up at the approaching dragon with poorly concealed fright. Both men stepped back to the side of the cart as though the flimsy wooden vehicle would offer them protection if needed.

Artemis's legs bent as she absorbed the impact of landing. Her claws splayed on the rocky ground. Then she extended her front leg to ease Moire's passage to the ground. She tried to maintain an air of confidence, despite her trembling legs. Her gaze met the two men, who seemed uncertain whether to flee or stand their ground.

"Gentlemen, my petition to Artemis has been successful. There is only one remaining condition to be satisfied,"

Moire greeted them coolly, even as her blood thrummed in her ears. Neither acting nor deception came easily to her.

"What condition?" Blackwood eyed the dragon suspiciously, but greed glinted in his eyes.

Meanwhile, Henry edged around the side of the cart as though he intended to climb into the back and pull the canvas over him to hide.

Moire clasped her hands before her and said the words given to her by Artemis in the cavern. "According to dragon law, the female will only give the egg to the chosen person. It is not handled by the supplicant. Since I have successfully pleaded your case, *Captain Hartford*, Artemis will now take you to where the egg is hidden."

She placed some faith in the criminal being clever, as successful ones usually were, and that he would play along with the little charade.

"Yes. Of course," Blackwood said, standing taller as he stepped forward.

Artemis's golden gaze never left his face, scrutinising him like a cat watches a mouse. Would she play with him or roast him?

The dragon snorted as though an unpleasant odour tickled her nose, and a plume of smoke curled from her nostrils. Both men flinched. Henry ducked lower behind the cart as though he expected her to shoot a fiery ball at him.

"Before I take you to the egg, Captain, why is that wyvern chained?" the dragon rumbled.

"It's dangerous, that's why. We were tasked with... dealing with it." Blackwood glanced over his shoulder at

Faustus, the sinuous form straining against the chains that bound him.

Moire dug her nails into her palms. Oliver would never refer to Faustus, or any type of dragon, as *it*. He shared her respect for them, deepened by his time with Valiant.

"I am more than capable of dealing with such problems. Unchain him, and I shall solve that dilemma on our way to the egg," Artemis said.

"Very well. Come along, Tobin, you heard the dragon; unchain the wretched beast." Blackwood leaned into his new role as captain and delegated tasks to Henry, who was still hiding behind the cart.

The two men unlocked the chains holding the wyvern to the wooden boards. Henry's hands trembled as he fumbled with the heavy links.

"Careful now, Tobin. It wouldn't do if you lost a finger now, would it?" Blackwood cautioned, a hint of mockery lacing his words.

"Yes, *Captain*," Henry muttered under his breath, casting a scowl at Blackwood before returning his attention to the task at hand.

When the men finished, they jumped to the ground. The sack remained in place over the wyvern's eyes as the fading light hadn't quite surrendered to night yet.

"Thank you, Artemis," Moire whispered. Relief eased some of the tension in her muscles. At least Faustus could move around now.

"Come, Captain, I shall take you to your prize." Artemis lowered herself to allow Blackwood easier access to her back.

Moire held her breath as Blackwood, still pretending to

be Oliver, climbed onto Artemis's back. His skin drained a ghostly pale, and his movements were awkward and stilted as he struggled to find where to sit. She wondered if, like her, he suffered from a fear of heights.

With a powerful downstroke of her wings, Artemis lifted off the ground and hovered just above the cliffside.

"Bloody hell!" Blackwood yelled as he clung to a spine.

"Really, Captain, you act as though you have never ridden a dragon before. This should all be mundane to you after your months of fighting from atop Valiant," Artemis replied, her tone cool and measured. "Now, let us deal with your little problem." She stretched out a front limb and gently grasped Faustus around his middle, lifting him clear off the ground.

With one backwards glance and a wink, Artemis plunged down the cliff, leaving nothing but a whisper of wind in her wake.

Please, let this work, Moire prayed silently, her gaze fixed on the point where they had vanished.

Moments later, Artemis reappeared, her claws empty and her great wings carrying her out towards the sea. This part of their plan had involved her plucking up Faustus and depositing him in her cavern, where he could shelter until night fell.

As the dragon flew out to sea in the last of the fading light, she was like a silver star shooting across the water. Moire let out an awestruck breath. Artemis was magnificent. The dragon climbed higher and higher, her enormous wings carrying her effortlessly through the sky.

While Moire had a vague idea of what the dragon had planned, the knowledge that Blackwood was a criminal who had brought his fate upon himself didn't ease the tight knot in her stomach.

"Where are they going?" Henry said from beside her. He peered out to sea, Artemis and her rider disappearing into the shadows.

As they watched, Artemis banked sharply to the left, and then a tiny figure plummeted towards the water below like a stone tossed into a well.

Moire gasped, her hand flying to her mouth. "Oh, dear Lord!"

Had it been an accident or deliberate? Artemis said she would give Blackwood a chance to explain, not...this.

"That dragon just murdered Blackwood!" Henry cried out, his eyes wide with horror.

Moire stared at the spot where the man known as the Fox had disappeared beneath the waves. It wasn't supposed to end like this. She hadn't wanted anyone dead, only for justice to be served.

She turned to face Henry. "You might want to leave before Artemis returns. And don't ever think to harm me or any member of my family, human or dragon, ever again."

Henry held up his hands and backed away from her. "You can keep your dragons. I'm glad Caliban died. I want nothing more to do with them." Then he paused, and his worry was replaced by a grin. "Although I should thank that one, as I am now freed of my debts."

Moire's mouth opened, but she had no words. Her cousin had just watched a man fall into the sea, and he was glad because it had wiped his slate clean.

Henry scrambled up onto the cart and picked up the reins. He smacked them against the horses' rumps, and the equines, which hadn't even lifted their heads despite a dragon being nearby, now took off at a canter along the dirt road.

Moire sank to the grass. Closing her eyes, she took a deep breath. She and Faustus were free, and never again would Darius Blackwood try to harm those she loved.

"Did we do the right thing?" she asked the sea breeze.

A low rumble answered from the depths of the cave below. Wings beat, these ones smaller and more bat-like as Faustus rose with the moon and landed beside her.

"Moire. Free," he rasped.

Moire climbed to her feet and flung her arms around the wyvern's neck. "We are both free. It is rather a long walk back to Wyldefen, though."

Laughter shook the wyvern's body, and he sent an image to Moire of the two of them. Moire bent over his neck but with her arms outstretched, embracing the freedom of flight.

"Yes, I suppose we should fly." Over time, who knew, she might come to look forward to the idea without the hard clench from deep inside her?

Then came a shuddering roar like a blast of thunder. Moire jumped, thinking a storm about to erupt. A flash of blue that couldn't possibly be lightning shot past her. And it trilled.

"Clipper!"

The piptere landed on her arm, hopped to her shoulder, and wrapped his wings around her face as he nuzzled against her cheek. She stroked him and murmured her reassurance that she was all right. If Clipper was here, that could only mean...

Wings beat the air, and a shadow dropped over them, but not the one she expected. This dragon had scales of a watery green colour.

"Moire!" Oliver shouted as he slid down Valiant's outstretched front leg.

The warmth of Oliver's arms enveloped her as he pulled her into a fierce embrace. Clipper squawked out of the way and fluttered to sit on Faustus. The scent of leather and sweat filled her nostrils as Oliver kissed her and held her tight.

"Are you unhurt?" he said, his voice thick with emotion as he scanned her for any injury.

"I am bruised from our ordeal, cold, hungry, and my feet hurt. But neither Faustus nor I sustained any permanent injury. We don't have to worry about either Henry Tobin or Darius Blackwood again, either. Artemis has seen to that," she reassured him. "She also made me face my fear of heights so that I would be unafraid when Constance was big enough to carry me."

Valiant snorted. "Typical female. She did not wait for me to deal with the problem."

Moire laughed. "Artemis had everything in hand once I explained the situation to her."

Oliver stared at her. "Never have I met anyone as strong or courageous as you." He tilted her chin up, meeting her gaze with his intense sea-grey one before leaning down to capture her lips in a tender, lingering kiss that spoke volumes of their love for each other.

Moire's heart raced, but it was a sweet sensation, a far cry from the earlier terror that had gripped her as she soared through the air on the back of a dragon. She allowed herself to be lost in the moment, savouring the taste of him, the feel of his strong hands cradling her face.

As they broke apart, the sound of powerful wings beating the air drew their attention skywards. Artemis descended gracefully. Valiant trumpeted a greeting, and the two dragons bumped muzzles.

"I came to save the woman and wyvern," Valiant grumbled.

"You are too late." Artemis opened her jaws and grinned at her mate.

Moire stepped forward, letting go of Oliver. There was something she had to say to the female dragon. "Artemis, you promised you would give Darius Blackwood a chance to explain his actions."

"I did. His response was inadequate, so I told him to get off me." The dragon narrowed her eyes.

Moire knew better than to argue the criminal's fate. His actions had resulted in his demise, and he had only himself to blame. "Artemis, may I present the real Captain Hartford."

Oliver bowed to her. "I am honoured to meet you, Artemis."

"And I you, Captain Hartford." Artemis walked towards them on three legs; something was cradled against her chest with one of her forelegs.

Oliver stepped to Moire's side. "I thank you for dealing with the criminals who kidnapped Moire and Faustus."

"It was not me alone. You have chosen well in your mate. She is loyal, brave, and intelligent. Like the lunar dragon who has bonded to her line." Artemis extended her limb and uncurled her claws. She held a green egg, its shell laced with silver. "She also made a compelling petition despite her lack of shoes or proper clothing. I gift you my offspring, Captain Hartford, for your line."

Moire stared at Oliver, then at Artemis, then at the egg. "But...we cannot have two dragons."

"Why not?" Artemis huffed. "You are both worthy. Constance chose you, Moire Tobin. Valiant and I chose Captain Hartford. Take our child, keep them safe, and tell no one for now. If the Draco Legion doesn't like it, they are welcome to try to take our offspring away from you when they emerge from their shell." Then, she laughed at whatever scene played out in her mind.

"We will stand with you, Captain, should they try." Valiant joined her with a sniggering chortle. "You could have left me something to do, Artemis. It has been ages since I was allowed to flame anybody."

The dragon continued to grumble about the lack of any wars as he wandered to the edge of the cliff with Artemis.

"Two dragons." Oliver stared at the egg in his arms. He looked at Moire, and he let out a whoop of joy. And she joined him. Soon, humans, dragons, a wyvern, and a piptere were shouting their excitement to the moon.

Moire took Oliver's hand and laced her fingers with his. "I cannot wait to write our story all about our dragon family."

"Do you think you could ride Valiant back to Eadred Manor?" Oliver kissed her knuckles.

"With you at my side, I will soar," Moire answered.

PART III

———

1825

EPILOGUE

Nathair Abbey, Wyldefen, rural England

MOIRE AND OLIVER followed the advice Artemis gave that night. They hid the egg in a place known only to them and their dragon family. After all, much could change in ten years...

MOIRE AND OLIVER were married in a small ceremony expertly arranged by Charlotte and attended by those they loved and who loved them. Katherine excelled as matron of honour, and Samuel gave Moire away. Oliver bought an abandoned estate called Nathair Abbey, and the couple brought it back to life. Faustus's temporary tether to Moire sank into the rich soil at Nathair, and he was soon joined by two young wyverns, so he was never alone.

When Constance became a fledgling at one month old, the family journeyed to London for the Hartford family to be formally admitted to the ranks of the Draco Legion. Much excitement erupted at the sight of a rare lunar dragon on English soil, and Moire promised to correspond with interested parties about the dragon and her particular skills as she grew older. That lunar dragons bonded to a female line was a secret they kept to themselves. Only once they determined how to honour that bond through the generations to come would they inform the Draco Legion that Constance was bonded to Draca Hartford, not Drac Hartford.

In a series of unfortunate events, Samuel's uncle, the viscount, died of a heart attack while over-exerting himself with his much younger wife. As she had not given him an heir, the title settled on Samuel's father. Sadly, the older Mr Radcliffe did not enjoy his new rank for long as he suffered a fatal hunting accident only a year later. The new viscount and his viscountess moved into Gormsby Hall with their young family. Katherine had always embodied the strongest traits of both her parents, and that odd combination of vanity and kindness allowed her to flourish in her new role. While she organised entertainments to amuse herself, they appealed to the upper levels of society. Her invitations were much sought after by all Wyldefen society, and further afield when the viscountess purchased a townhouse in London. The viscount preferred to stay at his country estate, but the couple always looked forward to the months they spent together. As odd as their relationship appeared to others, they loved each other deeply, and in their particular case, absence really did make the heart grow fonder. They also gifted Moire with as many books on dragons in their library as she wanted, and those volumes formed the beginning of the knowledge she would amass over the years.

Captain Forbes and Ruth Radcliffe married in a marvellous ceremony and moved to live at his family estate in Oxford. The families were frequent visitors to each other's homes, made easier by having dragons for faster travel, and they often spent weeks at a time with one another. The handsome couple became renowned for the poignant ballads that the captain wrote and Ruth put to music.

Sir George never changed, apart from waking up one morning to discover wrinkles. He retreated from society rather than show an ageing face in parlours and ballrooms. Or perhaps it was because his clothing was no longer the latest fashion and often repaired as no tailor would extend him credit.

Augusta's grand match to the duke never eventuated. It transpired that he dallied with her to throw the society hounds off the scent as he negotiated his actual match with a much wealthier and *younger* heiress. After the Chellums moved to another property, Augusta retreated to Eadred Manor with Sir George. Without Moire to manage their finances and attempt to rein in their spending, they lived in much-reduced circumstances, hounded by the bailiffs, selling off furniture and paintings to pay their bills and letting staff go who could not be paid. Sadly, bitterness further twisted Augusta's personality. She blamed Moire for her situation, which further widened the split between the sisters.

Henry Tobin married a wealthy, and much older, widow. He spent some years gleefully emptying the coffers of his new wife. Sadly, he miscalculated how long it would take to gain control of his inheritance, and his funds ran dry while his uncle still enjoyed rude good health. Henry met his end in a darkened alley after failing to pay substantial debts owed to a rather unforgiving criminal. An extremely distant, and exceptionally grateful, relative was found as the new heir.

Over the years, Moire added to their family—both human and dragonkind. They were blessed with twins, a boy and a girl. Opal visited them and while the peacock-coloured piptere remained free in the surrounding forests and was often spotted with Lunette, the pipteres preferred to hunker down inside the abbey over winter and during storms.

Although Moire tried, the army refused to allow her to have a pack of drakes to roam the forests around their estate. Her curiosity in that department was stymied. Or it was until her nephew Elijah joined the army the day he turned fifteen and was promptly selected by a drake hatchling. He promised to write long letters to his aunt to tell her all he learned about the wingless dragons and the tight family bonds they formed. Moire nurtured the hope she could convince him and his pack to visit one year when they were all fully grown so she could observe them in person.

Moire wrote books on dragonkind and travelled around England, giving talks and educating people. Over the years,

Moire earned a reputation for the depth of her knowledge and her rare bond with dragons, pipteres, and wyverns. Oxford University was so impressed that, not wanting to lose out to Cambridge, they invited her to be a guest lecturer.

Oliver retired from the Navy but started a shipping business with his friend Captain Forbes, which grew to have six large vessels carrying cargo around the world. He always captained Moire's expeditions around England and further afield. Dragons trusted him, and his reputation among them grew. Over time, he found his calling when away from his beloved ocean, hearing disputes and grievances between dragons and their families. No one wanted to risk a dragon suffering in silence like Caliban had, ever again. Oliver became a respected magistrate and often consulted with Moire before making his judgements.

As TWILIGHT SETTLED over the abbey, the family gathered in the sheltered courtyard between the stables and the house. They laid thick blankets on the cobbles to be more comfortable as they waited. Moire's veins bubbled with excitement and anticipation. Beside her, her husband shared her joy and expectation. Their children fidgeted with restless energy. Constance, the majestic lunar dragon who was an integral part of their family, lay curled beside them, her pearlescent scales gleaming in the fading light. Their three wyverns would join them as soon as night blanketed the land.

"When will it be time, Mama?" young Sebastian asked,

his eyes never leaving the precious egg nestled among soft blankets. He favoured Moire with his dark hair and curious brown eyes and sat at her side.

"Soon. Faustus told us it was about to hatch. That is why we fetched the egg from its hiding place," Moire replied.

"Papa says dragons have an excellent sense of timing," chimed in Lily. She stood behind her father and leaned on his shoulders. She possessed the sun-lightened brown hair and sea-grey eyes of Oliver. Where Sebastian was thoughtful, Lily was bold. It was her that led her twin into trouble while her brother got them out of it.

"Indeed, they do. During battles, I trusted Valiant to know the perfect moment to attack an enemy vessel," Oliver said.

Moire closed her eyes and reached for the quiet strength within her. A strength that had grown and entwined with her love for Oliver. Tomorrow, she would start a new book about the latest addition to their family and their rare, two-dragon status.

"Do you think they will resemble Artemis or Valiant?" Sebastian asked, intelligence brimming in his gaze.

"I think the dragon will look like itself. Just as while you possess some traits of both your parents, you are unique," Moire said.

"Look!" Lily cried and pointed at the egg.

A faint crack had appeared on the silver-swirled surface, and the air around them hummed with energy.

"It has started." Moire knelt and peered at the shell, willing the creature within to break free.

They all watched in wonder as the crack in the egg widened. The anticipation in the courtyard grew palpable.

"When it is bigger, we will be able to have dragon races. Constance will win, of course, because lunar dragons are the fastest," Lily said with the sage wisdom gained in her eight years of life with dragons.

"This dragon will be bigger and stronger than I," Constance said in her melodic voice.

Time stretched, and the moon rose to bathe the courtyard in its silvery glow. The wyverns emerged from their burrow and sat to one side to watch. As the temperature dropped, the family leaned against Constance's body for warmth as she curled protectively around them. Her luminous silver gaze fixed unblinkingly on the rocking egg. More hairline fractures raced around the surface. Then, one began to widen, inch by agonising inch. The sound of it was like the snap of ice breaking beneath the weight of winter's first snowfall.

The children's excitement bubbled up within them. Even serious Sebastian leapt to his feet and bounced on his toes. Lily danced and sang a song to welcome the hatchling. Tears moistened Moire's eyes. Her daughter sang the same lullaby that her mother had to comfort Caliban as he slipped from his life but with a faster and happier tempo.

"Almost here, little one," Moire whispered. Her eyes never left the ever-widening crack that now all but encircled the egg. "Just another push."

"Will the hatchling know who we are?" Sebastian asked.

Oliver ruffled his son's hair. "Of course it will. We have given it our love for ten long years. It will know us as its family. Just as Constance knew your mother because of the time she had spent where she lay hidden while in her shell and the tales Faustus told her while she waited to hatch." Oliver referred to the lunar dragon's incubation inside Caliban's barrow. A place where Moire often sat and read or dreamed during the long years of the egg's internment.

The crack stretched wider, groaning like ancient trees bending beneath the force of a storm. The anticipation in the air was a living thing, wrapping itself around Moire. The final moment arrived with a sharp, crisp snap that echoed through the courtyard like a whip. The egg's halves fell away, revealing the hatchling within. It had spread its wings wide to push aside its prison. Covered in the gooey substance that had sustained it for its long incubation, it took one slimy step forward.

"Ew!" Lily breathed. "It needs a good bath."

Moire laughed. "All newborns do."

She grabbed the soft towel and dampened one corner in a bowl of warm water. Then she shuffled forward to wipe down the dragonet. Oliver did the same from the other side, while their children watched in quiet awe.

As they cleaned, more was revealed. The dragonet was a dark silver but laced with swirls and patterns of blue and green like a stormy ocean. It stretched out limbs that were at once strong and impossibly fragile.

"Look at its eyes, Oliver," murmured Moire, unable to tear her gaze from the creature that now blinked up at them with curiosity. Its orbs were a deep green, flecked with silver and blue around the pupils.

"Aegir. I am male," the hatchling croaked as he butted against Oliver's hand. "And hungry."

They laughed, and Moire wiped tears of happiness from her cheeks. "Aegir. If I recall correctly, he is a Norse god of the ocean. How fitting for my sea-faring love."

"I'll fetch the food!" Lily raced to the kitchen for a bowl of meat.

Sebastian took a soft cloth from the pile and gently dried the dragonet as his parents cleaned off the last of the yellowish goo. Lily returned with a bowl of meat, and Oliver showed the twins how to feed the hungry creature without losing a finger. Not that Aegir would deliberately bite them, but he was very hungry and eager to have a full tummy.

When Moire glanced at Oliver, pride and joy shone in his eyes and she felt the full force of his love for her, and it was as expansive and deep as the ocean. Her heart swelled with such happiness that it threatened to engulf her completely.

"Is it all right to touch Aegir?" Lily asked, her gaze flicking between Moire and the dragon.

"Of course. Just be gentle," Moire said.

"Like this?" Sebastian extended a tentative finger towards the hatchling. He touched the tiny snout, and Aegir sneezed, eliciting a startled giggle from the boy.

"Exactly like that. They like to be petted somewhat like cats," Oliver said.

"He is so soft and warm. I didn't expect that," Lily marvelled, stroking the hatchling's delicate scales. Her face lit up with wonder as the dragon leaned into her touch, his eyes half closed in contentment.

"Neither did I when I first met Constance." Moire glanced at the dragon who had unfurled her body when they all moved to tend to Aegir. The memory of her friend's hatching still made gratitude flow through her. Constance's arrival had been the balm that soothed old wounds.

Once he had eaten his fill and burped, Aegir began to explore his surroundings, testing his newfound limbs with hesitant steps. His wings fluttered awkwardly, nearly tripping the tiny creature before he regained his balance. With his distended belly, he waddled like a rotund old man.

Moire watched her children, their eyes alight with wonder and love as they followed Aegir around the courtyard. He stopped before Constance and gazed up at the substantially larger, adult dragon.

"It is hard to believe he will one day be bigger than her," Oliver said as he took Moire's hand.

Constance gently nuzzled Aegir in welcome, and then she blew a soft snort of warmed air over him.

"I have been preparing our statement to the Draco Legion. While it is unprecedented for one family to have two dragons, they are bonded to two different lines that will split apart with future generations. The old fuddy-duddies will simply have to open their minds to a matriarchal line." Moire leaned against his side. She had taken advantage of the last ten years to write, discard, and start afresh the statements that would need to be made about their unique family arrangement. They also had the full support of both Valiant and Artemis, the parents of Aegir.

It never ceased to amaze Moire that the magical creatures were part of the Hartford clan.

"Here's to a future filled with adventure," Oliver declared, raising an imaginary toast to the newest member of the family.

"To us...all of us, and especially the dragons who have made our lives truly magical," Moire said. Her heart soared as she gazed at the faces of those she loved most.

Together, they would soar to unimaginable heights.

Together, they were unstoppable.

THE END

History. Magic. Found family.

I hope you have enjoyed my fantastical spin on a classic by Jane Austen. PERSUASION has always been my favourite tale, I just thought it needed dragons! If you would like to be the first to hear when I add another stand alone romance to this series, or if you want to dive deeper into my worlds, or learn more about the odd assortment of characters that populate them, then you can join the community by signing up at:

https://www.tillywallace.com/newsletter

ALSO BY TILLY WALLACE

For the most complete and up to date list of books, please visit the website: https://tillywallace.com/books/

Available series:

Tournament of Shadows

Manner and Monsters

Highland Wolves

Grace Designs Mysteries

Magic of Wyldefen

Leaf and Scale

ABOUT THE AUTHOR

Tilly drinks entirely too much coffee and is obsessed with hats. In her spare time she writes whimsical historical fantasy novels, set in a bygone time where magic is real. If you love found family and comfort reads, come and escape reality in her tales.

Email: tilly@tillywallace.com
Web: https://www.tillywallace.com
STORE: https://www.tillywallacebooks.com

If you would like to support Tilly for as little as a coffee a month, her *Caffeination Crew* read early chapters of her current work, vote on story ideas, and read exclusive short stories and novellas. You can find more information at: https://www.patreon.com/TillyWallace

patreon.com/TillyWallace

facebook.com/tillywallaceauthor

instagram.com/tillywallaceauthor

bookbub.com/authors/tilly-wallace

goodreads.com/tillywallace

www.ingramcontent.com/pod-product-compliance
Lightning Source LLC
Chambersburg PA
CBHW050850210726
48290CB00004B/1160